Dear Reader,

Christmas is a special season, and at Silhouette Books, we've created a special tradition to celebrate this time of giving—*Silhouette Christmas Stories*. This year marks the fifth volume of our Christmas collection, and I think you'll find it a treasure from start to finish!

Ann Major has written a heartwarming story of a lost love and the miracle of wishes, Santa and Christmas in "Santa's Special Miracle." Rita Rainville's "Lights Out!" holds all the wit, charm and high-voltage humor we have come to expect from this talented author. Critically acclaimed for her military romances, Lindsay McKenna has created a touching portrayal of the power of love in "Always and Forever." In Kathleen Creighton's "The Mysterious Gift," two lonely people find that the magic of Christmas is really the magic of love when a mysterious gift appears.

From beginning to end, these four gifted authors have created a special gift for you, their readers, with this collection. All of us at Silhouette Books thank you for your support, and wish you the very best this holiday season and in the coming year.

Happy Holidays!

Isabel Swift
Editorial Manager

D0043956

SILHOUETTE Christmas STORIES 1990

ANN MAJOR
RITA RAINVILLE
LINDSAY McKENNA
KATHLEEN CREIGHTON

Silhouette Books®

Published by Silhouette Books New York

America's Publisher of Contemporary Romance

SILHOUETTE BOOKS
300 E. 42nd St., New York, N.Y. 10017

Silhouette Christmas Stories
Copyright © 1990 by Silhouette Books

ISBN: 0-373-48230-2

First Silhouette Books printing November 1990

The publisher acknowledges the copyright holders of the
individual works as follows:

Santa's Special Miracle
Copyright © 1990 by Ann Major

Lights Out!
Copyright © 1990 by Rita Rainville

Always and Forever
Copyright © 1990 by Lindsay McKenna

The Mysterious Gift
Copyright © 1990 by Kathleen Modrovich

SILHOUETTE and colophon are registered trademarks
of the publisher.

America's Publisher of Contemporary Romance

Printed in the U.S.A.

CONTENTS

SANTA'S SPECIAL MIRACLE

Ann Major

A recipe from Ann Major:

CHRISTMAS DATE-NUT FRUIT CAKE

4 whole eggs
2 lbs (8 cups) pecans (whole halves)
1 lb (1½ cups) whole Brazil nuts
2 cups flour
2 cups candied pineapple
2 cups candied cherries, halved
2 cups dates
1 cup sugar
½ cup rum or *½ cup bourbon (I use bourbon)*
2 tbsp vanilla
2 tsp baking powder
½ tsp salt

In a large bowl, beat eggs. Gradually add sugar and vanilla. Cream together. Add flour, baking powder, salt, nuts and fruit, mixing well with large spoon after each addition.

Line 2 bread loaf pans with wax paper, glossy side inward. Divide mixture between pans. Firmly mash into pans, making sure all air pockets are removed and mixture is compact.

Place in *cold* oven. Set oven at 325° F. Bake for 1 hour or until knife inserted in center of cake comes out dry.

Remove pans from oven and pour rum *or* bourbon over cakes while hot.

Serve cake sliced into thin pieces as a snack or dessert, adding ice cream or whipped cream as desired. The nuts and fruit may make the cake appear like stained glass. Any way you serve it, this cake is beautiful in appearance and delicious in taste.

Chapter One

Oh, why had she let Sara and Jim and their children talk her into driving with them into San Antonio to shop?

Lights and red and gold velvet streamers sparkled from the ceiling of San Antonio's River Center Mall. A festive, last-minute mania infected the shoppers and salespeople who hustled and bustled everywhere.

But Noreen Black couldn't get into the Christmas spirit. Instead she felt a quiet desperation, an aching loneliness. Oh, sure, she'd bought half a dozen gifts. Sure, she was being jostled along in the crowd like everybody else during the holiday season. And right now she was struggling to keep a tight grip on Darius's little hand as well as manage her huge shopping sacks. But unlike everyone else who seemed in a joyful mood, Noreen felt only despair.

Suddenly through the crowd Noreen saw a tall man with broad shoulders and darkly handsome good looks threading his way toward her.

It couldn't be! No! Not Grant! Not after all these years. Not when she had Darius clinging tightly to her fingers.

She wanted to run, to cry out. Instead her panic overwhelmed her, and she did the most foolish thing of all. She simply froze.

Then, right before he headed into a luxurious lingerie shop, the man turned and saw her. She felt an instant sensation of doom. For a fleeting second he studied her with one of those quick, assessing, male glances. He saw a beautiful woman in her early thirties who was tall and delicate of feature. A woman who had enormous, dark, frightened eyes. A woman with a shocking mass of jet-black hair bound untidily in a lopsided knot. A woman who wore a bright animal-print scarf and baggy sweater and had a Bohemian air about her. But she was not someone he knew. He smiled briefly and vanished inside the shop.

He was just a stranger. A stranger with gray eyes instead of Grant's vivid, beautiful blue ones. A stranger who probably thought her too dull in her unfashionable clothes, or too skinny. He wasn't Grant. Wasn't even remotely like Grant. Still, it took a second for Noreen's shock to subside.

Just being in San Antonio was enough to make Noreen as nervous as a cat, and today, despite her cheery pretenses, had been no different. San Antonio was part of her past, part of that other life that she had deliberately walked away from five years ago, part of Grant. Even the briefest visit to the city could fill her with an intense sensation of loss and loneliness and leave her depressed for days. A part of her had died here, and she had never recovered.

Of course, living as she did only fifty miles away in a Texas town so small and so poor that it had no doctor or shopping facilities, she had to come into the city from time to time. Never once had she run into Grant or his mother, but the threat of that happening had always been in her mind. She found herself look-

ing around with a strange mixture of excitement and
dread in the pit of her stomach, as if she were unconsciously searching the crowd for Grant's black head,
for his tall, wide-shouldered form.

Darius suddenly yanked free of his mother's grip,
and Noreen felt close to panic again. Then she saw
that he was racing for the line of children waiting to
talk to Santa. Darius loped ahead of her as eagerly and
trustingly as a puppy, his short quick legs spraddling
everywhere, shoestrings snapping in all directions, sure
his mother would follow at her proper adult pace.

Watching him, she smiled fondly. Instead of Velcro
fasteners, he insisted on shoelaces because his best
friend's teenage brother, Raymond Liska, had laces.
It did no good to tell Darius that big brothers could
have laces because they were able to tie them.

There was an empty bench right in front of Santa's
Workshop, and Noreen sank down on it, piling her
bundles beside her. Her feet ached all the way up her
calves to her knees. She loosened her scarf. It wasn't
even noon yet, and she was exhausted from shopping
and from chasing Darius—two jobs she vowed long
ago never to take on simultaneously.

But Christmas was coming soon, and all four-year-
old boys had to talk to Santa at least once. Darius had
talked to five Santas since Thanksgiving. Every time
he had done so, his big blue eyes had grown huge as
he'd leaned into Santa's ear and whispered. When
she'd asked him what he wanted he'd refused to tell
her.

"Santa knows," he would say wisely.

Today Noreen had dragged him to every toy store in
the mall. With huge shining eyes, Darius had handled

the toys, at first with exuberant enthusiasm, until she'd asked him, "What do you want?" Then he had reluctantly set the toys back at cockeyed angles on the shelf. His darling baby-plump face had become still, and his answer had been reverent and enigmatic.

"Santa knows."

"You must tell Mommy."

"Why?"

Little did he know that she had almost nothing for him under the tree. That was the main reason she had let the Liskas persuade her to come into San Antonio.

As Noreen watched Darius jump joyfully into Santa's plump red velvet lap she thought, *At least he'll sit still for a second and I can catch my breath.*

"Silent Night," her favorite Christmas carol, was being piped over the sound system. For the first time since seven that morning when she'd climbed into the Liskas' Suburban, she relaxed. She glanced down at her wristwatch. She and Darius still had an hour to shop before they were to rendezvous with the Liskas and their four children for lunch on the river at Casa Rio.

Noreen groaned inwardly as she watched Darius unwrap the peppermint candy cane that Santa had given him and whisper into Santa's ear at the same time. Santa was going to have sticky ears. Sugar made Darius absolutely hyper. He wouldn't eat lunch, and he probably wouldn't nap on the way home.

"So what special present do you want Santa to bring you this year, young man?" Santa asked.

"Special?" The word was new. Darius licked his candy cane thoughtfully.

"The best present you've ever gotten?" Santa prompted.

Darius whispered again, but Santa couldn't make out the whisper and told him so.

Darius's eager, piping voice rang through the store. "The best present ever? A daddy that's even better than Leo's, that's what!"

Noreen looked up sharply at her son, all the old sorrow upon her. Her brown eyes grew bleak. She had tried to explain so many times to Darius that his father was in Heaven. She'd framed her favorite picture of Larry and kept it in Darius's room.

Noreen scarcely heard Santa's low rumble. But she heard her son's matter-of-fact reply. "Nope. Just a daddy."

"What about a toy truck or a car?"

Darius shook his black head as stubbornly as his father would have. As stubbornly as any Hale.

Santa was setting the child down, helping him get his balance as Noreen came over and gently took Darius's hand.

"You could have told me what you wanted," she said softly to her son, her voice immeasurably sad.

"Do you think Santa can really bring me a daddy?"

"Honey, I told you how your father died. You have his picture on that little table by your bed."

Darius's big blue eyes, so like his father's and his Uncle Grant's, grew solemn at that memory. "But I need a real live daddy, too."

She rumpled Darius's black hair. "A daddy is...well...er...That's a very complicated present."

"That's why I asked Santa, Mom. 'Cause he's magic."

Noreen remained silent. She turned helplessly back to Santa, who had been eavesdropping. But Santa was no help. With a merry jingling of tiny bells, he just tipped his hat and gave her an audacious wink.

For a moment she remembered her marriage, Larry's death, Grant, the bitter loss of it all. And suddenly she was so cold inside that she could feel nothing else.

Noreen was in a hurry now, a hurry to leave the mall and make it to the Casa Rio by one-thirty to meet Sara and Jim and their brood. She had shopped in a frenzy ever since she'd found out what Darius really wanted for Christmas. She couldn't provide the father he wanted, but she could get him other things. Now she was so loaded down with bags that she could no longer hold them all, and Darius was even carrying the two he'd bought for Leo and another friend.

They were on the escalator when the nightmare she had dreaded for five long years became a reality.

There was no time to prepare. No time to run. She and Darius were trapped on that gliding silver stairway.

They were going down.

Her ex brother-in-law was going up.

Fortunately, Grant wasn't looking in her direction when she saw him. She went rigid with shock, turned her head away, and lifted her shaking hand to cover her features. But not before his harsh, set face had etched itself into her brain, and into her heart and soul, as well.

He looked tired. Tired and haggard in a way that wrenched her heart.

But he was as handsome as ever. He was taller than other men, and broader through the shoulders. So tall he dwarfed her in comparison. His face was lean and dark, his hair as thick and black and unruly as her own, his eyes the same dazzling blue she remembered, his mouth still as beautifully shaped.

As if she could have forgotten him.

As if any woman could.

Her heart was beating like a mad thing gone wild. She was almost safe. They were gliding past each other. She would probably never see him again. Why would she? He was a Hale and, no doubt, by now one of the most powerful lawyers in San Antonio. She was a nobody, a small-town librarian.

How many nights had she dreamed of him? He had probably never given her another thought.

A fatal impulse possessed her. Forgetting her fears for Darius, forgetting she was risking her new life in doing so, she couldn't resist glancing over her shoulder for one last glimpse of him.

She did so just when Grant was looking back.

Their eyes met.

And so did their souls. One fleeting instant of mutual longing bound them before other, darker emotions stormed to the surface.

Slowly his black brows drew together—in a smoldering rage or in hate, she did not know which. Terror welled up in her.

Fortunately, the moving escalators were crowded. Fortunately, the railing was high, and Grant couldn't see that she was with a child.

"Norie!"

The husky sound of his voice crying her name cut her like a knife.

Grant shouted a second time as she scrambled to get off the escalator, pulling Darius, juggling packages.

One of her packages fell. She looked back. Her new pair of sparkly red high heels had tumbled out of their box. But she raced on, into the nearest store where she grabbed a wild assortment of jeans and tops and took Darius with her into a tiny dressing room.

There she stayed for an hour, reading to Darius in a whispery voice from one of the storybooks she had bought for the school library.

A long time later, a saleslady called to them. "Does anything fit?"

She heard male voices in the next fitting room, saw a pair of male legs on the other side of the divider of her stall. It was only then that Noreen noticed she'd grabbed men's jeans, and she and Darius were hiding in the men's fitting room.

She began to laugh silently, a little hysterically, and Darius watched her with huge worried eyes.

When Noreen and Darius were a breathless thirty minutes late to the Casa Rio, the Liskas were too dear to criticize.

They were a handsome couple. Jim was tall and dark, gentle and strong. His wife had soft brown hair, brown eyes, and a sweet face. They'd been high school sweethearts and had one of the happiest marriages Noreen had ever seen.

Noreen sank down beside them, offering neither excuses nor explanations, and let Jim order her lunch.

Sara, who'd grown up in a small town and simply adored gossip, studied Noreen's white face with avid curiosity.

Fortunately, before Sara could start quizzing her, the children took over. First Leo knocked over his soda. Then Darius tried to feed a chip dipped in hot sauce to a pigeon, leaned back too far in his chair, and nearly fell into the river.

At last the chaos of lunch was over and the Liskas had bribed Raymond to take his younger siblings and Darius off to ride the paddleboats.

The table was set in a cool and shady spot. Mariachi music was being played softly in the background. Sunlight sparkled on the river and shimmered in the golden leaves overhead. Jim, who worked as a science teacher at the same school Noreen did, was finishing the last of his beer. Sara was holding his hand. Noreen sipped her cup of tea.

"We'd better enjoy this before the kids come back," Sara said. "Noreen, the kids were terrible in the mall. I guess it's just that they're all so excited. Leo wanted everything in sight. Raymond kept teasing him, telling him he'd been so bad Santa was bringing switches this year. How was Darius?"

"He told Santa that he wants a daddy."

Jim put down his beer bottle. His dark eyes lit with humor. "That's certainly going to set the town on its edge. I can just see the headline now: Town's Mystery Librarian Gets Son A Daddy!"

Noreen didn't smile. "Darius is getting older. He wants things that I can't always give him. I'm not quite sure what to do about him anymore."

"No parent ever is," Sara said.

A devilish half smile curved Jim's mouth as he pulled his hand free of Sara's and leaned toward Noreen. "I think Darius has a good point. He does need a daddy. But no more than you need a husband."

"What? If ever I heard a chauvinistic remark—"

"Jim's full of them," Sara said placidly.

"You've practically buried yourself alive these past five years," Jim continued.

"Why, that's not true. I stay very busy with my job and with Darius. You know I'm as involved as anybody in civic projects."

"You're still the town mystery," Jim persisted. "You came to town five years ago—pregnant and single."

"That sounds so deliciously sinful," Sara said, "like a soap opera or something. You know it wasn't like that."

"I was a widow," Noreen replied tautly.

"Who still wears her wedding band, but goes by her maiden name. People know just what you want them to know. They know you're the school librarian."

"And a good one," Sara said, still trying to make peace.

"They know you moved in with Miss Maddie, that you inherited her farmhouse last year after she died. Not that anyone thinks you shouldn't have. Not after the way you took care of her after she went blind. They know that in the summers you hold the best story hour in the county every Wednesday morning at 10:00 sharp. They know you're a woman without pretensions. You're as plain as earth. As simple as water."

"Thanks." Noreen still wasn't smiling.

"I meant it as a compliment."

"Don't be mad, Norie," Sara said, folding her hand over Jim's again. "That's the way he compliments me, too."

"If I'm so ordinary, then why can't people be satisfied that there's nothing to know?"

"Because you don't talk about your past. You're running away from something or someone. And everyone wants to know who or what."

"Why—why, that's nonsense." But Noreen's slim fingers were so tensely clenched around her teacup that every vein stood out.

Jim leaned over and gently unclenched her hand. "Is it? Then why don't you accept a date with Mike Yanta the next time he asks you out?"

"Because..."

She looked at Jim and then looked away. Her dark eyes grew luminous with a pain she could neither share nor explain.

Her two dear friends would never understand. They didn't know she was a Hale by marriage. They knew nothing of her wealthy background. They wouldn't understand if she tried to explain.

People like them would have considered the Hale wealth and power a blessing. They wouldn't know that money could be the cruelest of weapons. It could be used to destroy love, to wield power, to sever the closest bonds that could exist between a man and a woman.

Noreen had learned all about money and its misuse by bitter experience. First she had lost the man she loved. Then she had lost her husband. She was determined not to lose her son.

Unbidden came the memory of Grant Hale on the escalator.... Of his arrogant tanned face... Of his husky voice calling her name...

Chapter Two

Noreen was shivering as she gripped the steering wheel of her truck and strained forward to see through her fogging windshield. The last lights of the town were growing dimmer in her rearview mirror. The sky ahead was black; the narrow, curving road that led to her farmhouse treacherously slick with ice. And it was still sleeting.

Texas weather. Yesterday San Antonio had been sunny and warm, so warm it had been impossible to believe that today could be this dark and wintry with cold.

Because she didn't like driving the lonely road by herself, Mike Yanta had offered to follow her home. But she had known he would have expected an invitation to come in, so she had refused.

It was nearly midnight, and Noreen was tired. She hadn't slept much the night before. Instead she'd lain awake in her icy bedroom, listening to all the eerie creaks her farmhouse made as the norther howled. And she'd been thinking of Grant. Thinking of how his face had seemed leaner and harsher. Remembering how his eyes had pierced through her. Today had been no better. The past had seemed very near, all the old conflicts as deeply troubling as before.

Although she was off for the school holidays, she'd spent the day sewing Darius's cow costume for the school's annual Christmas pageant. Darius had stood by the sewing machine "to help." He had helped by losing pattern pieces and stabbing a stray pin into his bare toe.

She was on her way home from the Liskas where she'd left Darius to spend the weekend with Leo. Sara and Jim had invited her to dinner, and they'd had Mike Yanta over, too.

Darius's cow costume was neatly folded in the passenger side of the cab. Tonight's pageant had been a success, with Leo and Darius both starring as cows in Jesus's manger.

She was nearly to the bridge and the gate that led to the road to her house. Suddenly a blur of red and white lights up ahead and off to the right dazzled her. With a mitten, she wiped at the cloudy windshield.

Taillights jutted out of the ditch beyond the bridge. A pair of headlights shone like twin cones cocked at a crazy angle. A black Cadillac had skidded off the bridge and was stuck in the ditch.

Carefully, she drove across the bridge. When she came alongside the car, her truck slid to a halt with a hush of wet tires. She leaned across her passenger side and rolled down the window. Icy air blasted inside the truck. Dear God. She couldn't see any sign of life. Suddenly she was afraid of the dark and the unknown. Never had the road seemed more abandoned or forlorn. Just for a second, she toyed with the idea of driving on to her house where she could call for help. But the thought of leaving someone seriously injured in this cold stopped her.

The road had no shoulder, but she pulled off anyway, turned on her hazard lights, and set the emergency brake. She fumbled blindly under the seat for her flashlight and a crowbar, found them and jumped out.

Frigid gusts tore at her white woolen poncho and whipped her flimsy skirt. Her white boots sank into mud as she stepped off the road. When she reached the Cadillac, the mud was oozing over her ankles.

Frantically, she banged on the tinted window on the driver's side with her crowbar and shouted. Precious seconds were ticking past.

Then there was a feeble sound from inside. She caught her breath.

She made out a man's voice. "Help me open the door."

She struggled with the handle, tugging upward against the heavy door with every ounce of her strength until it gradually yielded. A man's strong hands were pushing at it from the inside.

"Get your keys and turn off your lights," she yelled.

The man could be dying and she was worrying about his battery.

But he obeyed.

"Can you hold the door by yourself, so I can get out?" a huskily pitched male voice asked from the depths of the Cadillac.

"I—I think so."

It took all her strength, but she managed the door just long enough for him to climb outside. The night was so dark she could only make out the shape of him. Once he was free, the door slipped out of her grasp and slammed with a thud.

"Sorry," she murmured in breathless apology.

"Hey, listen, honey, there's nothing to be sorry about. I was trapped till you came along."

His deep voice was muted and weak, but it was achingly familiar. "Grant?" Just for a second she flashed her light on his face.

"Damn."

He closed his eyes and ducked his head, but not before she recognized the high chest, the carved jaw and strong cheekbones, the jutting chin and the aquiline nose. Dear God. There was blood on his dark brow, in his hair.

"Merry Christmas, Norie," he muttered. "I didn't mean to land my Cadillac in your ditch."

"You're hurt," she whispered, tearing off her mitten, touching his face gently, even the sticky bloody place, smoothing his inky hair before she remembered he was the last man she should ever touch in such a familiar way.

She jerked her hand away. "What are you doing here?"

"I knew the welcome wouldn't last long." His voice was filled with the same bitter, insolent arrogance she remembered. "I was coming to see you. It's colder than hell. Can we get in your truck?"

Noreen stumbled backward, away from him, her white poncho billowing in the crisp, cold air, and when he tried to follow her, he staggered.

She moved toward him, not wanting to touch him, knowing she had to. Wordlessly she gave him her hand and he clasped it tightly. Although his fingers were icy, her flesh burned from his touch. She began to tremble. He put his arm around her and leaned on her heavily as she helped him pull himself out of the ditch.

He was so weak she had to open the truck door for him. Her groping hand found Darius's cow costume and tossed it behind the seat. Grant heaved himself inside and collapsed.

When Noreen climbed behind the wheel, she was instantly aware of how big and male and virile Grant was beside her. As always he was wearing a flawlessly cut three-piece suit. His lawyer uniform, he'd once jokingly told her. The cuffs of the pants were as muddy as the hem of her white skirt.

"Why did you want to see me?" she whispered, her breathing as rapid and uneven as his.

His mouth curled contemptuously. "It was crazy, I know. But then, our relationship always was a little crazy."

The conventional Hales had thought her too uninhibited.

"More than a little."

His fathomless eyes were boring holes into her. "Yeah. More than a little."

"You should have stayed away."

"Maybe you're right," he muttered thickly. "I tried to talk myself out of coming a dozen times." But he reached for her hand, and with the last reserves of his strength, he pulled her hard against him. As his muscular body pressed into hers, she began to tremble all over again.

Anger flared in his eyes. "But then maybe you're wrong."

"Grant, please, let me go," she begged in a small voice. "It's been five years. We're strangers now."

"Whose fault is that? You ran away."

That old familiar undercurrent of electricity was flowing between them, even more strongly than ever before.

"Because I had to," she said desperately.

She felt the heat of his gaze on her mouth, and the emotion in his eyes was as hot as the night was cold. With a light finger he gently touched her red lips, traced the lush, full curve of them.

Her own eyes traveled languorously to his hard handsome face, and she felt the old forbidden hunger for his strength, for his wildness, for the feel of his powerful body on hers.

A long tremulous silence hung between them.

"It's wrong, Grant." She gasped out the first coherent words that came to mind. "So wrong."

"Maybe so, but whatever it is, it's lasted five hellish years."

"You should be out with one of your beautiful women."

"Yeah, I probably should be."

He let go of her, and she jumped free.

He fell weakly back against his seat as she started the truck.

Grant lay woozily with his head against the cold glass. No telling what he'd done to his Cadillac. No telling when he'd get to Houston to check on his apartment projects, but at the moment, he didn't much care. His right knee throbbed, and so did his chest where he'd banged it hard into the steering wheel. Every bump in the road made the pain worse, but he said nothing. He was too aware of this woman, too aware of how she still stirred him.

Tonight when he'd stepped free of his car, she'd seemed like an angel, a Christmas angel, in her white swirling clothes and gypsylike looped earrings. Funny, because he'd never really cared much for Christmas. As a child he'd thought it the loneliest season of the year. His wealthy mother had been too busy socializing to pay much attention to him or Larry, and Grant had never known his real father or even his real father's name.

The truck skidded, and Grant watched Noreen struggle with the wheel to maintain control. She was such a fragile, delicate thing. She was the kind of woman that made a man feel protective. He didn't like the idea of her driving this lonely road at night.

The fragile scent of her perfume enveloped him, tantalized him. She was as sweet as roses. And as prickly, too.

Five years. To remember. To want. To do without. And he wasn't a man used to doing without. At least not where women were concerned.

She'd thrown that up at him once.

You only want me because I belong to your brother.

Well, she'd been wrong. Larry had been dead five years, and here was Grant. He was such a fool for her, he'd come the minute he'd found out where she was.

Why? Norie wasn't the traffic-stopping kind of glamorous beauty Grant usually dated. But she was lovely in her own way. It wasn't her black hair, her red lips, her breasts, not her slim body—none of the things he had wanted from other women. It was her, her personality, something inside her that captivated him. Something that was quiet and powerful and completely honest.

He loved the way she liked to read quietly. The way there was always an aura of contentment around her. The way she was so gentle with children. The way she'd almost tamed Larry. Even the bright, offbeat styles she dressed in appealed to him. Norie didn't try to pretend to be something she wasn't.

Grant had gotten off to a bad start with her. He hadn't met her until Larry had written to their mother that he was seriously interested in her. Georgia had become hysterical. "This girl's different, Grant! Smarter! Larry's going to marry her if you don't drive up and stop him!"

"Maybe she's okay."

"No, she's a gold digger like all the others who've tried to trap him before."

It had never occurred to either Grant or his mother that Larry might be trying to stir her up and get some maternal attention.

Bad start. That was the understatement of the year. That first night in Austin had been a disaster.

Just like tonight, Grant thought coldly, suddenly furious with himself for coming. Why the hell had he bothered? She was as unfriendly as ever. He'd driven all this way, wrecked his car, and she'd hardly had a single kind thought.

"So, how long are you here for?" she asked.

"That depends on you," he replied grimly.

"There's no motel in town, and I don't feel like driving twenty-five miles to get you a room and then back again. It's nearly Christmas, but I—I can't very well put you in the stable."

He knew she didn't want him anywhere near her. But the mere thought of sleeping in the same house with her made him shiver with agonizing need.

"Cold?" she whispered.

"Thanks for the invitation," he muttered, getting a grip on himself.

She started nervously twisting knobs on the dashboard, adjusting the heater. "We'll call the wrecker in the morning."

A gust of hot air rushed across his face. His hand covered hers on the knob, and he felt her pulse quicken. "Hey, there's no reason to be so flustered. Honey, it's just one night."

She pulled her hand away and let him fix the heater.

"Right. It's just one night," she murmured, with an air of false bravado.

"I hope I'm not putting you out," he said softly. Without touching her again, he swept his gaze over her body.

The silence in the cab was breathlessly still.

"Oh, I have a spare bedroom."

"Then you live alone?"

There was another long moment's silence, and he wondered if there was a new man in her life. He thought she blushed.

"Y-yes."

She was lying. He felt it. "What a shame," he murmured, pretending to believe her.

But she didn't hear him. She was leaning on the steering wheel, turning the truck, braking in front of a locked gate.

She got out and unlocked it. The least he could do was slide across the seat and drive the truck through.

So he did. She relocked the gate and climbed back inside.

"So, do you do this often?" he demanded, the mere thought making him angry all over again.

"What?"

"Drive home alone? Get out and struggle with that damned gate in all kinds of weather?"

"As often as I have to."

"You need a man."

"So I've been told."

That rankled.

"But I don't want a man."

His taunt was silky smooth. "Then you've changed."

And that made her good and mad.

She stomped a muddy white boot to the accelerator so hard his head snapped back. A sudden blaze of pain exploded somewhere in the middle of his brain.

"Ouch!"

"Sorry," she said.

But he knew she wasn't.

He rubbed his head. At least she wasn't indifferent. But then, she never had been. Neither had he. That had been the problem.

Chapter Three

So this was where Norie had been for five damn years. This was what she preferred to the kind of life a Hale could have given her, the kind of life *he* could have given her.

As she drove, Grant stared in wonder at the small farm, the falling-down picket fence, the white, two-story, frame house built on a scant rise beneath towering pecan trees. The windmill. Why had she chosen this instead of him? Instead of everything he could give her?

The house was probably eighty or ninety years old. He'd been in old houses like this one before, houses that were built so they would catch the summer breezes and the windmill would be driven. In the winter such shabby structures were too vulnerable to the cold north winds.

A screened-in porch was on either side of the building and there was a veranda across the front. A solitary yellow bulb by the front door was the only source of light. He noted the tumbledown cistern in the backyard and the large flowerbeds where she could grow flowers in spring and summer. A clothesline was strung from the corner of the house to the back gatepost. There was a small enclosed yard.

She parked the truck in front of the house. Everything seemed so bleak and cold to him—so remote. He was used to living in the middle of town, in a beautiful home, surrounded by beautiful things—antiques, carpets, tapestry, crystal.

"It's not the Hale mansion," she whispered.

Was he so obvious? "You ran from all that."

"I never belonged."

"You could have."

"No." The tortured word was torn from her throat.

For a second longer she stayed beside him, so close he could almost feel the heat of her body. Then she threw open her door and ran up to the house. He followed at a much slower pace.

He felt almost sure there was no man in her life. Even though it was dark, he saw that the grass was too high. There wasn't much firewood left. The gate latch needed fixing. He stumbled and nearly fell when the bottom two steps gave beneath his weight because the wood was rotten. A splintering pain centered in his hurt knee, and he had to stop for a second.

"You okay?" she whispered.

"Great."

She was fumbling with the key when he caught up to her.

"The lock keeps sticking."

"That's because your hands are shaking. Let me help you, Norie."

She handed him the key, dropping it into his open palm, careful not to touch him. "A lot of things are broken around here."

His knee throbbed. "I noticed."

He opened the door, and she led him inside, into an icy living room with high ceilings and tall windows. She pulled the chain of an ancient Tiffany lamp. There were wooden rocking chairs and a battered upright piano. The atmosphere was homey, but everything— the furniture, the paint, the curtains—had a faded, much-scrubbed look. There was no central heat. He saw a single gas space heater at one end of the room. It was an old-fashioned house, the type kindly grand- mothers were supposed to live in.

"Like I said, it's not the Hale mansion," Norie apologized again. "But would you mind taking off your shoes?"

She was about to lean down and remove her own muddy boots, but he grabbed her arm. At his touch a sudden tremor shook her. He felt a strange pull from her, and he couldn't let her go.

"Do you really think I give a damn about your house?" His voice was rasping, unsteady. "I came to see you."

For a moment longer he held her. She didn't strug- gle. He almost wished she had, because he probably would have pulled her into his arms. Her expression was blank; her dark glittering eyes were enormous. He could think of nothing except how beautiful she was. Unconsciously she caught her lower lip with her teeth, and that slight nervous movement drew his gaze to her mouth.

They were alone, in the middle of nowhere. It had been five years. Five long years. He wanted to kiss her, to taste her. But he had made that mistake before— twice—the first night he'd met her, and on her wed- ding day.

He swallowed hard. "Thank you . . . for letting me stay."

He saw intense emotion in her eyes.

Although it was the most difficult thing he'd ever done, instead of drawing her closer, he released her. She leaned down and pulled her boots off. As he bent over to do the same, the shock of pain that raced from his knee up his thigh made him gasp.

"You're hurt," she said, kneeling before him. "I'll do it."

Standing, he could see nothing but the gypsy-thick waves of her dark hair glistening in the honey-gold glow of the lamp as they spilled over her delicate shoulders. Her loop earrings glittered brightly. He felt her quick, sure hands on his ankles. He caught the dizzying scent of her sensuous perfume. No other woman had such drowsy dark eyes; no other woman possessed this air of purity and enduring innocence that mingled with something so free, so giving.

He had always wanted her. From the first moment he'd seen her angel-sweet face and known the beauty of her smile.

He'd only meant to stop by and see her on his way from San Antonio to Houston, to inform her that Larry had not left her penniless. Grant had intended to take no more than an hour from his busy life. He had a big case to prepare for next week and his Houston project was a mess.

He hadn't expected all his old feelings for her to be stronger than before. It was only one night, he'd told her. One night alone together. Nothing to get flustered over. But his hands were shaking.

Right, he thought grimly. One night. Alone. Together.

The time stretched before him like an eternity. Every slowly kindling nerve in his body burned for her. He clenched his hands into fists.

"There." She was done.

Smiling up at him, she placed his shoes neatly beside her boots and led him through a series of icy rooms. Since the house had no halls on the lower floor, each room opened into the next. To get to the kitchen and the stairs that led to the upper story, they had to walk through her bedroom. It was large and airy—too airy on a night as cold as this one. As they passed through it, he saw a large four-poster bed, a library table full of books and magazines, and a television set. A large Christmas tree decorated with handmade red and gold ornaments stood in the corner. He caught the crisp aromatic odor of fresh spruce. There was a nativity scene sandwiched in between the books on her table.

"Why is the Christmas tree in your bedroom?" he asked.

"Because we—"

"We?" he demanded. Grant gazed at her for a long moment. "I thought you lived alone."

Norie's breath caught in her throat. "I—I do. What I meant to say is that I spend most of my time there." She flushed under his hard scrutiny. "I don't like to heat up the whole house." She lowered her gaze to avoid his unfaltering one.

He hadn't practiced law for fifteen years without developing an almost uncanny sense about people. She was lying—covering something up. But what? Scanning the room again, he found no trace that a man might share it with her.

He shrugged. The best way to find out was to leave it alone—for now.

The stairs were difficult. His knee hurt so badly he could barely climb the steps, and he felt weak again when he had struggled to the top. He followed her from the dark hallway into a charming bedroom with frilly curtains and yellow flowered paper. The room was as icy as the rest of the house.

She knelt on the faded carpet and lit a fire in the space heater, then rose and went to the bed to find the cord and controls to the electric blanket. He crossed the room to help her.

Together they located the switch, pulled the covers back, and plumped the pillows. It seemed an intimate activity suddenly, unmaking the bed, and he stopped before she was through. For a moment he stood without moving, watching her, enjoying the simple beauty of her doing this simple thing for him.

"There," she said softly, smoothing the blanket. "The bathroom is right next door. I'll put out fresh towels. If you're still the same size you were, there are some boxes of Larry's clothes under the bed." Her eyes darkened. "I—I never got rid of them."

"I haven't put on an ounce."

He felt the heat of her eyes move swiftly over his body, mutely confirming his statement. And then she smiled in her unutterably charming way and blushed rosy pink before she glanced down at the carpet in front of his toes.

"I'll leave you to settle in, but I'll be back . . . with something hot to eat." Her tone was light and a little breathless. "You're probably starving."

"Oh, I am." His own voice when he answered was oddly hoarse. He gave her a look that told her it wasn't only food he was hungry for.

She backed away, stumbled against the doorjamb, blushed again, and was gone.

Damn. She was afraid of him.

The jeans Grant found in the box under the bed fit his muscled body like a snug second skin. The black turtleneck sweater molded every hard muscle in his torso, shoulders, and biceps. Well, maybe he'd put on an ounce. Or maybe as he'd gotten older he'd gotten into the habit of wearing looser-fitting clothes. Comforting thought.

As soon as he finished dressing he climbed into the bed to get warm. He lay beneath the toasty electric blanket, listening to the sounds of Norie bustling about in the kitchen beneath him. Outside, the wind was swishing around the corners of the house and whistling under the eaves. But his pillow was soft, the electric blanket warm. The room was beginning to seem almost cozy. He felt a baffling contentment, to be here, alone with Norie, so far from his own exciting but hectic life.

It was odd, Norie choosing this ice-cold house on a remote farm outside of a dying town, as opposed to the life she could have had.

Why?

He had never understood her.

Not from the first.

Maybe that was why he'd made so many mistakes.

His thoughts drifted back in time. Back to the first night when his mother had sent him to Austin to save his little brother from a scheming older woman.

"Noreen Black is a penniless little nobody. Some sort of Bohemian—an intellectual! An orphan who was raised in north Texas on a dirt farm. She's twenty-seven to Larry's twenty-three. I'm sure she's out to catch him," Georgia Hale had shrieked before Grant left for Austin. "Do you want the same thing to happen to your little brother that happened to you?"

Grant had been making vast monthly payments on a settlement to the beautiful young woman who'd deliberately married him so she could take him to the cleaners. Remembering the bitter consequences of his own mistake, he'd driven off to Austin determined to pay off Noreen Black before she had Larry completely in her clutches.

When Grant had knocked on the door of Miss Black's little apartment a couple of blocks west of the UT campus, a soft welcoming voice had answered. "Larry?"

"Larry's brother."

She'd thrown open the door. "Grant! Larry's told me all about you."

The "scheming older woman" was a slim girl with enormous dark eyes. Her cloud of dark hair was tied back with a green scarf, and huge silver loops danced at her ears. She didn't look twenty, much less twenty-seven. There were books scattered untidily on the dilapidated couch, red plastic dinette chairs and table. She had a pencil tucked behind one ear and had padded barefoot to the door in a pink and black leotard

and tights. Tendrils of damp curls clung to her forehead. Her smile was the sweetest he'd ever seen.

His gaze roved the length of her body, passing
downward over a flawless neck and shoulders, gently
rounded breasts, a narrow waist, and long, shapely
legs.

"Lovely," he said in a low voice.

Unconsciously Norie drew back, crossing her hands
over her breasts.

"I—I was studying, but I stopped to exercise. To get
the oxygen flowing again. I—I wasn't expecting company..." She trailed off uncertainly.

He couldn't tear his gaze away from the curve of her
thighs, and Norie's color deepened.

"Are you looking for Larry?"

"No, I came to see you."

"I don't want to be rude, but I do have a big test
tomorrow."

She was giving him, Grant Hale, the brush-off.
Anger coiled in him as tight as a spring. Of course she
was. She was after Larry. Somehow Grant managed to
keep his voice calm. "Surely you have time for a quick
dinner. I drove all this way just to meet you."

"I—I'm on a very limited budget."

"I'm buying."

That seemed to settle it.

"Well...since you drove all this way..."

She smiled so disarmingly that a shiver of un-
wanted male excitement darted through him. She was
good, really good, at working a man with her charm,
he thought cynically. He could see why Larry had
fallen for her.

"It'll only take me a minute to dress. Make yourself at home. There's soda in the refrigerator."

While he waited for her, he rummaged about in the kitchen. There was, as she'd said, one soda in her tiny refrigerator. He saw milk, eggs, hamburger meat, canned goods, a few plastic dishes. A tight budget, she'd said.

Not for long, not after she caught Larry.

She returned wearing a red embroidered Mexican smock, red painted earrings, and silver jewelry. Grant complimented her on the outfit and drove her to an elegant restaurant on Town Lake.

She ordered the least expensive thing on the menu.

A trick, Grant thought.

To his amazement, he began to enjoy himself. In the candlelight, with her shining eyes and her pretty, sweet smile that seemed to be for him alone, she was beautiful. Larry was forgotten.

Grant began to drink, rather too much. He never got around to offering her money to leave Larry alone. Instead he talked about himself, about his secret dreams. He told her about Susan, their divorce, the hurt of it all. He told her things he'd never told anyone else. How as a child he'd secretly wished to know his own father. How he'd wanted love, how he'd grown up without it, how it was something he no longer believed in.

Then she'd told him about herself, about her loving parents, about their wonderful life together on their small farm until her parents had died in a car accident.

"I want all that again," she whispered. "You see, I do believe in love. More than anything, I want a home, children. I even know what I'll name them."

"What?"

"The boys will be Darius and Homer. The girls Galatea and Electra."

Grant laughed. Her fingers were toying with the tips of her silverware, and his hand brushed against them accidentally. He felt a warm tingle at the touch of her flesh. She drew her hand away and looked at him, her beautiful face still and silent and tender.

"I—I got those names out of books," she said in a rush. "I always loved to read, even as a child. Especially after Mother and Daddy died. I have a master's in English, and I've taught for three years. I'm studying to be a librarian. And now...I really do need to get home. That test..."

She was lovely, lovelier than any woman he had ever known.

She drove. Because she knew Austin better, and because she hadn't drunk any alcohol. On the way back into town, he was grimly silent.

She parked in the dark in front of her apartment building.

"I had a wonderful time," she whispered. Her face lit with a guileless, naive happiness. Her eyes were sparkling in the darkness.

"So did I." Grant ran his hand up the pale smoothness of her bare arm.

"You're not like Larry."

At her mention of his brother, Grant's mood turned grim. "No?"

"Not at all."

"I came because Larry wrote that he was serious about you."

"What?"

"Don't pretend you don't know," Grant murmured in a coaxing, cynical rasp.

"I'm not pretending. He's just a good friend."

The wine and the hard liquor Grant had consumed made his thoughts swim. She was so soft and lovely, this gypsy girl, so totally different, she mesmerized him. His emotions were in turmoil. "You're poor. He's rich."

"I had no idea." Her voice was a tender whisper. "He seemed so young and so mixed-up. I felt sorry for him."

"I told you not to pretend with me."

"Grant . . ." She looked lost.

He swore under his breath. "You're good, girl. Very good. Maybe you can fool Larry with your angel face and your innocent, sweet Bohemian act, but you can't fool me. All night you've tantalized me, smiled at me, beckoned me with your beauty. You don't love my brother."

"No, I don't."

Silver bracelets jingled. She reached for the door handle, but his larger hand closed over hers. The minute he touched her, he was lost.

She was warm satin flesh. Her pulse raced beneath his fingertips. He was on fire. His gaze rested on her soft lush red mouth for one second only. Then his lips covered hers. He circled her with his arms. She tried to cry out, but his hot, ravaging mouth stifled all utterance. She was trembling with fear, and with some other emotion that more than matched the power of his own blind passion.

She was warm and sweet like heated honey. An angel who was erotic as no wanton could ever be. Shock waves of desire surged through every aching nerve in his body. He wanted her, as he had never wanted another. This funny, seemingly innocent woman-child who was poor, who was a gypsy girl.

Her slim body was crushed beneath the power of his weight, and the hands that had been pushing against his chest stopped pushing. He felt them curl weakly around his neck, and she pulled him closer, returning his kisses with guiltless wonder, sighing softly in rapture. So there was fire in her, too. Fire for him as well as for his brother.

At last Grant let her go.

"I want you," he said. "I'll give you everything Larry would have given you and more. Except a wedding ring. Like I told you, I made that mistake once before."

Her lovely face changed subtly, quickly, from the soft glowing expression of a woman newly in love to that of a woman who'd lost everything.

"You really think that I . . ." A sob caught in her throat.

His expression was harsh.

Her luscious, passionate mouth, swollen from his kisses, quivered. Her face was very pale. He saw the sparkle of new tears spill over her long lashes. Her beautiful neck was taut, her head proudly poised and erect.

"I've made mistakes, too," she said softly in a small, brave voice that didn't quite mask her utter despair. "And tonight . . . you, Grant Hale, were one of them."

He tried to stop her when she tried to go.

"I'm not what you think," she whispered. "And you're not what I thought."

He was forcibly struck by the sorrow in her pain-glazed eyes. She got out of the car and ran all the way to her door where she dropped her keys and struggled with the lock for a long time. He knew she was weeping so hard she couldn't see.

Flushed with anger and frustrated desire, he watched her fumble about, thinking he should help her, thinking he should go, thinking he would forget her, and knowing deep down he never could. When she vanished into the gloom of her apartment building, he started the car and burned rubber in his wildness to get away.

But he'd never forgotten her stricken, tear-streaked face. Not even after she'd married his brother on the rebound. Not in the five years since Larry's death.

Chapter Four

There was a whisper from the doorway that had nothing to do with the wind.

Grant opened his eyes and saw Norie standing there, holding a plastic tray with two cups of steaming hot tea, milk, and Christmas cookies. She'd removed her poncho and was wearing a white sweater that clung to her slender body, and a soft woolen skirt. She seemed to hesitate on the threshold, as if she had doubts about the wisdom of joining him in his bedroom.

Her hair fell in dark spirals, framing her lovely face and neck. Her dark eyes were immense and luminous. Just the sight of her looking so gently innocent and vulnerable made his own body feel hard and hot with wild ravening need.

The wind whistled, and the house shuddered from a particularly strong blast.

"Come in," he murmured.

"I was afraid I'd wake you," she replied breathlessly.

He watched her set the tray down on the table by the bed. She handed him a cup of tea and a plate of homemade cookies. Neither spoke for a while, and the silence seemed awkward and heavy to both of them.

"It seems funny...you being here...in this house," she said at last.

"What do you mean?"

"You're used to more glamorous settings—New York, Europe. You've been all over the world."

"I feel at home here . . . with you."

She stared into her teacup. "We're nothing alike."

"In a way that's true. But there's an old cliché. Opposites attract."

"You never liked me." Her voice was low, whispery.

The knowledge that she had run away and hidden from him for five years weighed heavily on his heart. "I liked you too much," he said through gritted teeth.

Her teacup rattled precariously in its saucer, and she looked up. "Can we talk about something else?"

"Fine. What?"

"I—I don't know. What can two people as different as we are find to talk about?"

Hard pellets of ice pinged on a piece of tin nailed to the roof.

"Maybe the weather." His tone was derisive. "Bad night."

"Yes, it is."

That was all either of them could think of for a very long time. He was too aware of her beauty, too conscious of his need to run his hands through her black hair, to kiss her lush red lips. He felt white-hot with need. There was an awful, passionate, unbreakable tension in that silent room that was tearing them both to pieces. What was going on here? Suave, sophisticated Grant Hale never had trouble talking to a woman.

Desperate for distraction, he forced himself to remember the past. Norie had always been different, unconventional. She'd been an enormous amount of trouble to him. First he'd tried to stop her from marrying his brother. The problem was, she hadn't even known Larry was that interested in her until Grant had told her. Larry had written that letter to his mother when he'd been drunk, in the hopes of stirring her up. Hales were like that. Stirring was in their blood. Larry liked to be the center of a family drama.

Norie had been so upset about what happened between herself and Grant that night in Austin that she'd begun to see Larry in a more favorable light. She'd felt sorry for him for having such a materialistic mother and brother; she'd believed that was why he was so wild and unhappy. In the end she'd acted on impulse for the first time in her life and married Larry. But the marriage had never been a happy one. Not with Georgia's continual interference. Not with her threats to disinherit Larry because he'd chosen such an unsuitable bride. Not with Larry's weak, wavering nature.

They were married for two years. A month before he died, Larry had left Norie to please his mother.

It was the most horrible irony to Grant that he'd driven the only woman he'd ever loved straight into the arms of his brother who had never really cared for her.

Then, right after Larry had killed himself on his motorcycle, Norie had run off for no reason at all.

Norie didn't care about success or money. In fact, Grant wouldn't blame her if she was terrified of money and how it could twist people. She didn't care about knowing the right people, or traveling to the right places. She didn't have a single status-seeking cell in her body. She didn't know anything about fashion or fads. There was no way she could ever fit into his life. Their values were nothing alike. He needed a woman who could shine at cocktail parties, a woman who knew how to be an elegant hostess. A woman his mother could brag about to her friends.

He had had all that.

And it was empty as hell.

He wanted *this* woman. And he didn't care if it cost him everything he had, everything he was.

Maybe they could talk about the cookies.

The Christmas cookies really were quite interesting. Some of them were expertly painted. There were green Christmas trees with silver balls and red-and-white Santa Clauses. But some of the cookies were painted with a violent, primitive awkwardness. Grant picked up a particularly brilliant, clumsily painted cookie.

"Who painted this?"

She shut her eyes. Her voice was trembly. "A—a little friend."

He remembered Larry telling him about all the neighborhood children that flocked to their house whenever Norie was home. She'd baked for them. Larry had been bored by children.

Norie's teacup rattled again in its saucer, and she quickly changed the subject. "How did you find me?"

"Yesterday morning, I was reading the paper. There was a mention of a UIL meet in Karnes City. I read through the students' names and the names of the teachers and school personnel accompanying them. I saw Noreen Black. I'd been looking for Noreen Hale. After that all it took was a few phone calls. Imagine my amazement when I found out that you were living only fifty miles away. If you hadn't run from me yesterday, we could have settled everything then."

"Settled what?"

"Larry left you an estate, of course. Did you imagine you were penniless?"

"I don't want Larry's money." Her dark eyes flashed. "I never cared... about his money. Anyway, we were separated when he died."

"It's yours, nevertheless. I've been managing it for you ever since."

"I'm sorry to have put you to so much trouble."

His voice was velvet soft. "I didn't mind. I liked knowing I was helping you, Norie."

"I don't want your help."

His gaze roamed her shapely length as heatedly as if he touched her. She began to tremble. Then she stiffened.

"You're afraid of me," he said gently. "Why?"

"I'm not afraid." But her voice was a slender thread of sound.

"Then why did you run from me in San Antonio?"

"Grant, I..." Her throat constricted.

"I came here to help you, Norie."

"I'm perfectly fine. I—I don't need your help."

"I know that I wasn't always your friend. In the beginning Mother and I—"

"I don't need either of you," Norie pleaded desperately.

He felt just as desperate. "Did it ever occur to you that maybe we, that maybe *I*, need you."

"No. No..." She set the teacup down, her hands fluttering in protest. She got up and was slowly backing away from him.

"Norie..."

"You need to go to sleep now. I'll be back to turn off the heater later."

"Norie!"

But she was gone.

Norie was in her bed in a warm flannel nightgown, removing her heavy earrings. She picked up a book review of a children's story. But the black print blurred when she tried to read. She kept thinking of Grant. She felt a throbbing weakness in the center of her being. He seemed so hard and tough, so masculine. So sexy with every muscle rippling against the soft black cloth of that sweater. She'd always been both fascinated and disturbed by him. She still was—and he knew it.

But he was a Hale, and even if he wasn't the weakling Larry had been, he was still Georgia Hale's son.

Grant was so smooth with women, so experienced. And Norie knew next to nothing about men, especially men like him.

What did he really want with her?

One thing she knew. She had to get him out of her life before Darius returned on Sunday.

Darius! A shiver of apprehension raced coldly over her flesh.

Why hadn't she thought? She remembered the way Georgia had used her money to turn Larry against her. Georgia could be subtle; she could be ingratiating. But she liked to control everything and everybody. Especially Larry, her favorite son. If she found out that Larry had had a child, what might she do to get control of Darius? Would she use her money to destroy

Norie's relationship with her own son as she had used it to destroy her marriage to Larry? What if Georgia found some way to take Darius away?

In a flash Norie threw back her covers and got up. In her bare feet she scampered across the cold floors, removing every trace of Darius—his Christmas stocking laid out in front of the tree, his gifts, his tennis shoes and socks that he'd taken off by her bed. She dashed upstairs, hid these things in his room under his bed, and pulled the door tightly shut.

And to think that after Larry's death Grant had been so grief-stricken she'd almost told him that she was pregnant.

On her way downstairs she saw the pale thread of golden light under Grant's door. The door creaked when she opened it, but Grant didn't stir. For a second longer she studied him. He was beautiful with his long inky lashes, his tanned skin, his dark unruly hair, his powerful body. He had thrown off some of his covers. She watched the steady rise and fall of his powerful shoulders. Hesitantly she tiptoed to the heater and turned the knob at the wall.

The room melted into darkness.

The room would cool down quickly, so she went to Grant's bed to arrange his covers.

She was about to go when suddenly his warm hand closed tightly over hers.

She was caught in a viselike grip.

"I—I thought you were asleep," she murmured breathlessly. "I didn't mean to wake you."

"I'm glad you did." His voice was like a hot caress. "What have you been doing? Your hand is as cold as ice."

His concern made her pulse leap. "A few house-hold chores downstairs."

"It's a shame for a woman as lovely as you to live out here all by yourself. To have to do everything by yourself."

She couldn't answer. She felt all choked-up inside, and she was too aware of his nearness, of his warm callused hand imprisoning hers.

There was a long moment of charged silence. She caught the musky scent of him, felt the warmth of his body heat.

"Why did you run away?" he murmured. She felt his fingertips stirring her hair. "Was it because of the way I felt about you?"

"What are you saying, Grant?"

His fingers were smoothing her hair down around her neck, and she wanted nothing more than to be pulled into his arms.

"I wanted you from the first minute I saw you," he murmured huskily. "I thought you belonged to my brother. Not even that mattered."

"I was a challenge."

"Once I might have agreed with you. Mother sent me to end your relationship with Larry, but the minute I saw you, I had my own reasons for wanting to end it. I wanted you even when you belonged to my brother. That's why I was always so nasty the few times I saw you after your marriage. I couldn't deal with those feelings." Grant's hand kept moving against her scalp in a slow circular motion that was mesmerizingly sensuous. "I've persecuted myself with guilt because I drove you away. I haven't always been the kind of man a woman like you could admire."

No... She remembered the holidays they'd been forced to share when she'd been Larry's wife. Georgia had been coldly polite, but Grant had been unforgiveably rude.

If only he hadn't been touching her and holding her, Norie might have fought him. But she felt his pain and she had to relieve it. "Georgia wanted me out of Larry's life. When he left me, I felt completely rejected by all the Hales. After he died, I thought you wanted me gone, Grant. That's why I left," she admitted softly.

"What?" His hand had stilled in the tangled silk of her hair.

"I overheard your family talking after the funeral. Your mother had worked so hard to break up my marriage. She said Larry never would have died if he hadn't married me, that I'd made him unhappy. You can't imagine how terrible that made me feel. It was clear everyone wanted me gone. Everyone. I thought I heard your voice."

"The Hales can be a crazy bunch. Maybe they did say those things, but I didn't. After the funeral I had to get off by myself. I felt so bad about Larry. He was so spoiled, so young. He died before he ever knew who he was or what he wanted. He couldn't stand up to Mother. I left the house for the rest of the day. When I came back, you were gone."

"It doesn't matter now."

"It does to me." Grant's voice was hard and grim, determined. "I should never have left you alone with them."

He pulled her closer, so close she was quivering from his heated nearness. So close her pulse throbbed unevenly.

"What are you doing?"

His lips touched hers, gently at first. A gasp of heady pleasure caught in her throat.

"Honey, I think it's obvious. For seven years I've wanted you more than I've ever wanted anything. Or any woman. You thought I didn't. I should have done everything in my power to stop you from marrying Larry. After the wedding I couldn't admit to those feelings, not even to myself. We've always been at cross purposes. For five years I've searched for you. Now there is nothing to keep me from claiming you."

Nothing but her own common sense and her will to preserve the placid life she'd made here for herself and Darius. Her heart raced in panic.

"Grant, no—" Norie twisted to evade the plundering fire of his mouth.

He covered her parted lips with his, and with heated kisses teased them to open wider. His hands ran over her body and lifted her gown. She felt dizzy. Uncertain.

"Please, don't do this," she murmured helplessly. "We're all wrong for each other."

"I know." There was the hint of cynicism in his tone of voice, but his eyes were dark with passion.

"But—"

"I don't care. Not anymore. I just want you, Norie. And if I can have you—even if it's only for one night—I will."

"Your family—"

"To hell with my family. If I can have you, I don't want anything else."

"You're a Hale."

His breath drew in sharply. "Not really, gypsy girl. I told you that my real father deserted Mother shortly after I was born. When Mother married Edward Hale, she forced him to adopt me. She wanted both her sons to share the same name so people would think of us as real brothers instead of half brothers."

Norie had heard all that before. To her he was a Hale, and that was that. She tried to pull away, but Grant held her fast, with hard, powerful arms. And he kissed her.

She tasted him. Her tongue quivered wetly against his. A thousand diamonds burst behind her closed eyelids. She drew a breath. It was more like a tiny gasp. Suddenly she was clinging to him with quaking rapture. His male attraction was something she could no longer fight. He ripped back the covers and pulled her down against the solid wall of his chest.

"Norie. Norie..."

Her name was sweet as honey from his lips.

Inexpertly, she caressed his rough, hard jawline with trembling fingertips. Her dark eyes met the smoldering blue fire of his gaze.

"You're mine," he said inexorably. "Mine."

Then he began to kiss her, his mouth following every curve, dipping into every secret female place, lubricating her with the silky wet warmth of his rasping tongue until she was whimpering from his burning hot kisses.

Her dark eyes flamed voluptuously, and she was as breathless as he in a mad swirling world of darkness and passion and wildness that was theirs alone.

She wanted him more than anything in the world.

And yet...

"I—I can't," she pleaded desperately, placing her fingertips between her lips and his. "I want to, but I just can't."

His grip tightened around her.

A sob came from her throat.

On a shudder that was half anger, half desperation, he let her go.

For a long moment she hesitated.

"Go," he commanded, a faintly ragged edge to his breathing. "Go, before I change my mind."

Then she fled, away from Grant's warmth, out into the cold, empty darkness of the house.

Chapter Five

Norie lay in her icy room, in her bed, her nerves and muscles wound so tightly she jumped with every blast of the norther outside. At last she drifted into fitful sleep, only to be plagued by dreams of Grant. She would then awaken with her pulse throbbing unevenly and lie listening to the wind. Yet it wasn't the storm outside that was battering her heart and soul, but the one within her.

Her slim fingers curled and uncurled like nervous talons, twisting and untwisting the sheets. She wanted Grant. More than she ever had.

His presence made her aware of the emptiness of the past five years. She had accomplished nothing by running away. If she didn't send him packing soon, she knew she would be lost. There was only one thing to do—call the wrecker first thing in the morning. The sooner Grant left, the sooner she could start all over again to try to forget him.

But the next morning when she picked up the phone, it was dead.

No sound came from upstairs, so she assumed Grant was still asleep. She dressed quickly in the dark, cold house, ate a bowl of bran with a banana, and went out to her truck.

The road into town was glazed over with ice, and she went only a quarter of a mile before deciding to turn back. Better to spend the day with Grant, than to kill herself trying to get rid of him.

Only when she got back to the house and found him in her kitchen scrambling eggs, she wasn't so sure. There he was, large and male, making himself at home, dominating the room with his virile presence. He was watching her. His blue eyes flamed in a way that told her he was remembering last night. Treacherous, delicious shivers danced over her skin, and she blushed uneasily. That made him smile.

"The phone's dead," he murmured without the faintest note of regret in his voice.

She was toying with her woolen scarf nervously. "That's why I thought I'd try to make it into town to try and get a wrecker, but the road's too icy."

"I'm glad you had the sense to come back." There was a quiet, intimate note in his low-toned remark.

She was pulling off her coat and scarf, and he was watching her again. His intent, hot gaze savored the beauty of her flushed face and the soft curve of her breasts.

"You'd better keep an eye on those eggs." She pivoted sharply and hung her things on a peg by the door.

"Looks like you're stuck with me for another night," he said mockingly. "I've got one more day...and one more night to change your mind." His voice was a honeyed caress.

She gasped uneasily. "That's not going to happen."

His eyes darkened to midnight blue as he stared at her thoughtfully. "Something tells me you're not so sure."

She felt another treacherous blush creep up her neck and saw his quick smirk of male triumph. What was he, a mind reader? "You think you know so much!" she snapped, exasperated. "Those eggs are going to be dry as dust."

He turned off the stove. "I never was much good at talking and cooking at the same time. I get distracted easily." His voice grew huskier. "The eggs didn't have a chance against a distraction as lovely as you." He grinned in an impish, teasing way that made him even more incredibly handsome.

She was horrified by the pleasure she felt at his compliment, horrified at the warm, wonderful confusion that was totally enveloping her, leaving her defenseless.

She stared at him, speechless for at least a minute. She wanted to think of something to say that would be so spiteful he would leave her alone, but words failed her. All she could do was sweep haughtily out of the kitchen into her bedroom. She slammed the door on the low rumble of his male chuckle.

He was seducing her, teasing her, laughing at her for her weakness where he was concerned. As experienced with women as he was, he probably considered her an easy conquest. Somehow she had to summon the strength to fight him. But as she made her bed and picked up her things, she was aware of every sound that came from the kitchen. He sang and he clattered plates. Pots banged on the stove.

She decided her only option was to ignore him, to try to stay as far away from him as she could possibly get. So she went into the living room to dust. But wherever she went, he allowed her no peace. He called her into the kitchen saying he didn't know what plate to use or where the salt and pepper shakers were. And when she was reaching up to get the objects he wanted, he was right behind her, his body so close, so warm, that it was all she could do to resist the fatal impulse to step back into his arms. The rest of the morning and the afternoon he pestered her in the same way.

Later that night, after dinner and the dishes, he went up to bathe, and she thought she was safe. But while she was cleaning the pantry, he called down to her from his bedroom.

At first she ignored him, but he wouldn't stop calling to her. Surely he was the most stubborn man on earth.

When she trudged up the stairs at last, she found him standing in the middle of his bedroom trying to look hurt and helpless. He said his shoulders were so sore from the wreck that it hurt him to lift his arms and button his shirt. It took only a second for her senses to register his physically disturbing state. His unbuttoned blue shirt contrasted with the dark bronze of his damp skin. He smelled clean and male. She caught the sensual scent of his aftershave. His black hair was jet dark, wet and curly.

They were alone. This was their last night together. Her last chance. She should run back downstairs at once.

But she could only stare at him, thinking he was as darkly beautiful as a muscled pagan god. She could only feel dizzy and weak with a sickening longing to touch him and caress him.

His blue gaze was electric. "Come here, Norie," he commanded gently.

She began to tremble, but she lacked the strength to move either toward him or away from him. It was he who closed the gap between them with two swift silent strides.

His shirt swung open further. He stood so close she could feel the heat from his body, see the wetness that glistened on his bare chest.

He had asked her to button his shirt. In that moment it was as if she had no mind of her own. Very slowly she reached toward him, intending to bring the edges of his shirt together. Instead her fingertips slid beneath the soft blue fabric to touch the hard curves of his muscular chest and torso. She felt bone and muscle. His skin was like warm, polished bronze. Her slim fingers tangled in the hair on his chest and then splayed in wonder over the place where his heart pounded with excitement.

He sucked his breath in sharply as her soft hands moved on, wandering in sensuous exploration, lovingly pushing his shirt aside, over his shoulders, then more urgently wrenching it off, and tossing it to the floor. Gently, her lips followed the path of her hands, kissing him first in the spot that concealed his violently thudding heart, then following every curve of his hard muscles.

She would have stopped touching him and kissing him, if only she could. But she was hot, as hot as he was. At last she lifted her head helplessly, and found that his blazing eyes were upon her radiant face. His gaze studied every inch of her face with such tenderness that she almost stopped breathing. Very slowly he leaned down and kissed the black shining curls at her temples. Then her cheek. Then her throat. She felt his breath falling warmly against her skin like heated velvet whispers. Only the tumultuous drumming of his heartbeat betrayed his restraint.

"Don't fight it," he whispered. "You can't." He balled his hands into fists. "I know, because I can't, either." His voice was a ragged, hoarse sound.

Very gently he drew her into his arms and toward the bed. And she let him.

He was right. She couldn't fight him. She was weak. She wanted him too much.

His hand curved along her slender throat. His finger wound a strand of silken black hair into a sausage curl and released it, letting it bounce against her satin throat.

"Open your lips," he instructed huskily.

He brushed a soft, sweet kiss across her mouth, and then he, too, was lost. All of his careful control was disintegrating. He was shaking against her. His breath drew in sharply, loudly, fiercely. He kissed her again, harder and hotter than before. He held her so tightly she felt that her own body was fused into his. His mouth moved against hers, his tongue moist and urgent as it slid between her parted lips to taste the warm, sweet wetness within. She let her tongue touch his.

Norie's knees became weak, but it didn't matter because he was lifting her into his arms and carrying her to the bed.

Her lashes fluttered lazily, hopelessly shut as he stirred her with his lips and hands to erotic, feverish, passionate ecstasy.

Outside, the flat Texas landscape was bleak and barren and frozen. The wind was howling wildly. It was going to be another stormy night.

Inside, the two lovers were lost to the world and conscious only of each other. For them, there was only the wonder of their passionate extravagant present. For Noreen, only the wonder of having Grant at last.

He was still forbidden.

He was still a Hale, no matter how he denied it.

Tomorrow she would probably be sorry.

But tonight, as she lay enfolded in his crushing embrace beneath crisp cotton sheets, he was hers. Recklessly, gloriously, completely hers.

She abandoned herself heedlessly to the night, to the mounting passion of her lover, to her own wildness that had lain dormant until now. At last, she discovered the ecstasy that she had read about in books and always wanted but never known, not even during the brief unhappy years of her marriage.

After it was over—their fierce, molten mating—he buried his lips in her silken hair and breathed in the sweet, clean smell. She ran her hands over his magnificent body that glistened with sweat, and she reveled in the beautiful strength of his hard, muscular physique.

Tears of joy flooded her eyes.

She felt vulnerable, soft.

Gently he brushed her wet cheek. "Forgive me," he murmured quietly.

"For what?"

"For all the wasted years." He clasped her tightly. "For that first night in Austin, all those years ago. For your wedding day when I insulted you with the kind of kiss no brother-in-law should ever give a bride.''

"Don't," she whispered shudderingly. She put a fingertip to his lips.

"I was wrong, Norie. So wrong. I thought... I thought I was protecting Larry."

"I know."

"I always loved you, but I couldn't admit I was wild with jealousy when you married Larry. I couldn't admit that you might love him. I treated you badly. I stood by and watched Larry pit you against Mother. He always loved to be fought over.'' Grant ran a light finger down her belly. "No more. At last you are mine."

Noreen let him stroke her hair, let him kiss her again. She even let him remove the wedding ring she'd continued to wear for Darius's sake. Yes, tonight she belonged to Grant. Tonight was their dream. Tomorrow would be soon enough to awaken to reality.

His black head lowered and his parted lips moved over hers tenderly, nibbling for a time, forcing her mouth open again, slowly, teasingly, while his hands traced over her body and then pulled her closer. She could feel his heat beginning to flame all over again.

"I thought you were hurt."

He laughed softly. "I have miraculous recuperative powers."

Noreen's hand slid down his hair-roughened chest, stroking his flat muscled stomach, hesitating, then moving lower. She touched that hot, warm part of him that told her just how fully aroused he was.

"Indeed you do," she whispered on a wanton giggle.

"And you're one sexy...librarian."

"Oh, Grant," she breathed against his lips and threw her arms about him. "I thought things like this only happened in books."

"So you like this better than reading?"

"Much...much better."

He chuckled huskily.

And that was the last thing either of them said for a very long time.

When Grant awoke the next morning, he was alone. Outside, everything was covered with a layer of frost and the sky was white and wintry. Inside, the room was cozily warm. Norie must have turned on the heater before she'd left him and gone downstairs.

If only she'd stayed in bed, it would have been so much easier to face her. He got up quickly and began to dress. The hall outside was icy as was every other room in the house except his and the kitchen.

Norie was in the kitchen bending over the stove. She looked pretty in her looped earrings and a pale yellow dress that emphasized her slim waist and the curve of her breasts. The sight of her made him remember last night. His heart gave a leap of pure happiness.

He smelled bacon and eggs, freshly brewed coffee and baking biscuits. The wooden table in the middle of the room was set with handmade red place mats and blue china. Everything was so charming, so perfect, and the most perfect thing of all was Norie.

He shut the door, and she turned, and he watched the flush on her cheeks rise in a warm blush of color. Their glances met. He smiled, and she set the spatula down, hesitating, but only briefly, before she stepped joyfully into his open arms.

He kissed her gently, on the brow first, and then her mouth, and she surrendered heedlessly to his lips. He thought, this is how marriage would feel. He would wake up, and she would be there—every day.

"I feel very lazy, very spoiled," he said. "Can I do anything?"

"I wanted to spoil you. Did you sleep all right?"

"Perfectly."

"And your knee?"

"Much better."

"Everything's almost ready. Nothing fancy."

"I don't want fancy." He reached out to touch her cheek.

"The phone's back on," she said quietly.

Her eyes, meeting his, were intense and thoughtful. She turned back to the eggs, and Grant opened the refrigerator out of old habit just to inspect its contents. Inside, he saw a turkey.

"So you're going to cook a turkey for yourself out here, all alone?"

Her face changed. "I—I cook Christmas dinner every year."

"For anybody special?" he demanded, sounding both stiff and disconcerted.

The room grew hushed.

She wouldn't look at him, but he saw the color rise and ebb in her cheeks. She seemed to hesitate. "If you're asking about another man, there isn't one."

His stomach tightened. What was she hiding? In some indefinable way, she had erected a barrier. He felt shut out of her life again and angry about it. But what right did he have to say anything?

"How long till breakfast?" His voice came out harsh and loud from the strain of controlling both his curiosity and his temper.

She had turned away and was stirring something on the stove. The spatula was clanging rather too loudly. "Six or seven minutes."

"I think I'll walk down to my car." His words, his manner, were a careful insult.

"Fine."

At the door he turned. "Norie..."

She drew a sharp breath. "Just go."

He jerked open the screen door and stomped out, his footsteps crunching into ice and shattering the frozen stillness of the morning.

A wan sun shone through the thin white clouds and made the layer of frost on his black Cadillac sparkle. It was going to take a wrecker, all right, to get it out of the ditch. Grant wouldn't know till then if he would be able to drive it or if it would have to be towed. But his mind wasn't really on the car. It was on Norie.

Last night, she'd been sweet and warm and loving. This morning she couldn't wait until he drove himself and his car out of her life.

Why?

Impatiently, he grabbed Norie's rolled-up newspaper and pulled it from her mailbox. Then he headed briskly back to the house.

Six minutes, she had said. He stopped in the middle of the road to think. Okay, so she had managed without him for five years. She was independent and proud. It was stupid to think he could storm into her life and take over in the first forty-eight hours. His gaze wandered over the farm. Not bad. For a woman alone, she had a lot to be proud of.

Sure, the house could stand some paint, but in the sunlight with every window pane glimmering, it wasn't nearly as bad as he'd thought in the darkness the other night. A magnificent spiderweb hung on a low branch. In the frozen sunlight, it seemed to be spun out of crystal gossamer lace. Along a fence a line of bare trees stood out sheer and black. The farm and its isolation appeared peaceful, almost beautiful this morning. He remembered how she liked to grow things. Maybe she was afraid he would want to take her away from all this. Maybe there were people here, friends who mattered as much to her, or more, than he ever could.

Grant felt on edge. He'd never liked going slow, waiting. Hell, they'd already lost seven years.

He started back to the house. He was barging around the back of it when his ankle caught on a handlebar, and he fell against a low shrub. He barely managed to catch himself.

"What the..."

At his feet he saw a tangle of shiny red metal and wire wheels. A tricycle. He pulled the thing out of the hedge and set it upright on all three wheels. For some reason he remembered the clumsily hand-painted cookies. Her little friend must have left it.

He remembered how she'd always loved children, and it seemed a shame that she had to content herself with little friends she had over to paint cookies, a shame that she didn't have any of her own. She would make a wonderful mother; she would be nothing like his own unmaternal, socialite mother. He could give Norie marriage, children.

"Grant!"

He looked up.

She was in the doorway looking soft and lovely and calling him to breakfast.

Over breakfast the barrier between them was still there. But he tried to enjoy himself, anyway. The food was perfect, but he hardly tasted the biscuits and the bacon and the coffee. All that mattered was Norie. He tried to concentrate on her. She was telling him as she had on that first night about her childhood in north Texas, about her parents. Soon she had him talking about himself, telling her how he'd always wanted to know his real father but his mother was ashamed of that early marriage and would never allow it. But all the time Grant was talking, he kept wondering what was wrong.

"So how did you end up here?" he asked at last, switching the conversation back to her.

"The very same day Larry was buried, after I got home to Austin, Mike Yanta, the school superintendent here, called me and offered me a job. It seemed like the perfect solution."

"And was it?"

"In a way. I love the school, the children, the story hours. I know everybody in town, and everybody knows me."

"The perfect life." His voice was unduly grim.

"More or less. For me anyway."

"But are you fulfilled?"

He wanted just one word from her, one word to show that she cared. But even before she answered, he knew she wouldn't give it.

"Are you?" she whispered.

"I used to think so. I was a success. That's all I considered. Until I met you."

"I probably make a tenth of your income, but it's all I need." She was twisting her napkin nervously.

Her *all I need* certainly didn't include him. A little muscle jumped convulsively in his jaw. "I told you part of the reason I came was business. Larry named you as his only beneficiary."

"But I thought . . ."

"Mother controlled most of the money, and she still does. But Larry had a sizable trust all his own. I've managed that trust for you for the last five years and more than tripled the original amount. You are not a poor woman."

Norie was very pale, and she was shredding the napkin into pieces. "I told you I don't want it."

"But it's yours," he said harshly.

"I—I don't feel that it is. Georgia wouldn't want me to have it."

"Mother changed her mind about you a long time ago."

"I don't believe you!"

"When you ran away, when you never came back to claim your inheritance, Mother came to realize that you hadn't married Larry for his money after all. She wanted me to come here. She even told me to tell you that she's sorry. I was wrong about you, too. In the beginning I thought you were after Larry's money. Hell, you weren't even after Larry."

"Not till you came and your coming made Larry so mad he wanted to show you and Georgia he could live his own life. But he failed. We both failed."

"It took me a while to figure out that's how it happened. I was a fool not to see the truth the minute I met you. You're the most honest woman I've ever known, and the most loving."

Her eyes grew enormous and she gripped the table. "Grant... You're just as wrong about me now as you were then. I'm not the saint you seem to think I am."

"To me you are. You shouldn't be living alone. You should be married."

"I've been married."

"You should have children this time. Do you remember telling me that you wanted a big house with four children? You even knew what their names would be."

She turned white. "Homer, Electra, Galatea, and...Darius," she whispered, rising slowly from the table.

He laughed. "So you still remember?"

She seemed uneasy suddenly. "I used to be such a bookworm. Those names appealed to me when I was a child."

"You planned a big family. Aren't you waiting a little long to get started?"

A burning color washed back into her face, and she said quickly, "Life doesn't always work out the way we plan it."

"It's not too late."

She looked at his face for a long time, and then she looked away. "I—I wish I could believe that, but I can't." Methodically she began to stack the dishes. "This is real life. You and I—we're so different. I'm what I am. I like flowers, kids, friends, wide-open places. You're a Hale."

"I'm a man. You're a woman."

"It's not that simple. We can't just erase what happened. I can remember dozens of beautiful women on your arm. How long could you be happy with me?"

"Forever."

"Do you think Georgia would ever allow that?"

His stomach went tight and hard, as if Norie had punched him there. "Do you think I'm like Larry? Do you think I would allow anyone, even my mother, to come between me and the woman I love?"

"If not her, then her money." Norie's voice was a bitter, tormented whisper. She walked to the sink with the dishes and shoved the handle of the faucet. Water splashed loudly. "You've accomplished what you came here to accomplish . . . and more." She flushed. "We've got to get your car pulled out of that ditch. Then you can go."

At the terrible finality in her low voice, Grant felt something inside himself break and die. It was as if his heart was being twisted and wrenched, and the agony was unbearable.

He hardly knew what he was doing as he sprang blindly to his feet. His chair crashed behind him to the floor.

"Grant!"

He moved toward her and jerked her hard against his body. A dish fell and shattered in the sink.

"So you think money, any amount of money, could change what I feel for you?" His hard gaze flicked over her pale face. She seemed small and defenseless against his enormous body. "What did last night mean to you anyway?" he demanded roughly.

"I—I don't know. I don't know. I just know I've got my life and you've got yours."

"Is that really all we've got?" Grant studied her, straining to read her expression. But she seemed a very long way away. "Damn it. I can't let you go."

"You don't have a choice."

"There's always a choice, Norie. Always. That's all life is."

She began to struggle, fighting him silently to escape, but she was like a child in his grasp.

His mouth took hers. He held her against him until she stilled, crushed until she did nothing more to stop his hands as they molded her curves to fit the tough contours of his body.

When she fought him no more, when she became smooth and warm, when he could feel her quickening response, only then did the stubborn will to conquer her with the force of his own passion subside.

Tenderly, he kissed away the salty tears that had spilled down her cheeks. At last he withdrew his mouth, his hands. Norie drew a long breath and opened her eyes. Then she pulled herself free of him and stumbled shakily backward toward the kitchen door, one of her hands clutching her throat. For a numb moment she could only stare at him.

"Norie, please..."

For a second longer those big, scared eyes were upon him.

Then she broke and ran.

Chapter Six

The icy morning air was biting cold as it seeped through her jean jacket and her thin yellow dress. Noreen was pale and shivering, and her unhappy dark gaze was fixed on Jimmy Pargman and his wrecker and the muddy black Cadillac he had just pulled out of the ditch. In his car, Grant was coolly ignoring Norie as he tried to start the engine. His lean face was set and hard. He had not spoken to her once since he'd kissed her and she'd run out of the kitchen. He was now just as anxious to be gone as she was to be rid of him.

Her heart beat jerkily. In another minute Grant would drive away, this time forever, unless she did something to stop him—and that was something she would never do. Because of Darius. Because she was too afraid of the Hale money and of what Georgia might try to do if she found out about Darius.

But as Norie looked at Grant, she felt a terrible stab of longing. More than anything she wanted to cross the road, to fling herself into his arms. To forget how different they were. To hold him, to touch him, to smooth that black tumbling lock out of his face...just one last time. Her eyes swam with unshed tears. And this weakness made her despise herself.

Fragments from last night kept replaying in her mind like newly edited film clippings. She remembered the way his fingers had unbuttoned her gown, the way his hands and mouth had roamed everywhere until she was as thoroughly and wantonly aroused as he.

How could she have let him? How could she have been so totally unlike herself, so shamelessly forward? She was the one who had gone to him when he'd called, to his room, to his bed, knowing what might happen.

She had forgotten Darius, forgotten everything that really mattered to her. Nights like that were probably commonplace to a man like Grant, to a man who could have any beautiful woman he desired.

The Cadillac's engine purred, and Norie felt a hopeless, sinking sensation in the pit of her stomach. She closed her eyes. She had to forget him! To go on as if last night had never happened. To go on as if her feelings for him didn't exist.

When she opened her eyes again, she saw the Liskas' familiar blue Suburban coming toward her.

Sara was bringing Darius home! Dear God!

Grant opened the door of the Cadillac just as Sara braked alongside Norie and rolled down the windows on her side.

"Hey, Mom!" Darius's blue eyes were wide with curiosity as he looked first at her, and then at the Cadillac across the road. "Guess what? Raymond let Leo and me play his Nintendo, and we didn't even break it."

For a paralyzed, horrified moment Noreen couldn't speak. Then she managed a weak, "That's great, hon."

Grant was paying Jimmy, so he didn't notice Darius.

Noreen touched Sara's arm. "Why don't you drive on to the house? I'm almost through here. We'll have tea while the kids play."

"Who's he?" Suddenly Sara saw the tears in her friend's eyes. "Hey..."

"Later, Sara," she whispered chokily. "I'll tell you everything."

"Why do I know you really won't?"

"Please..." The sudden huge knot in Norie's throat made it impossible for her to explain.

Sara's brown eyes softened with compassion. She stepped on the gas just as Jimmy did the same. The Suburban turned off to head toward Norie's house. The wrecker headed back into town.

Noreen and Grant were left alone, standing on opposite sides of that desolate bit of asphalt in that wide-open landscape that seemed to stretch away forever. Noreen stole a glance at him. He was looking at her, too. And they were as mute and awkward with one another as if they were strangers.

Grant opened his trunk and pulled a shoebox and briefcase from it. He opened the shoebox and dangled a pair of sparkly red shoes from the tips of two lean fingers.

Her heart was pounding with fright. She had no choice but to cross the road and retrieve them.

She came so close to him, their steamy breaths mingled. Her hands touched his briefly. Warm skin against warm skin. They both tensed in acute awareness of one another. Then she was snatching her shoes from him and replacing them noisily into their tissue

paper and box. He was briskly unsnapping his briefcase and pulling out a thick sheaf of legal documents.

She raised her eyebrows.

"These papers deal with your inheritance." His
voice was harsh and loud.

"I told you I don't want money, Grant."

"That may be, but getting rid of it is going to be a
little bit more complicated than that." His dark face
was as stern as death, his blue eyes unreadable.

He handed her his card. It was so crisp and sharp it
cut her fingers.

"Call my secretary and make an appointment. I'll
have her help you do whatever you decide to do about
it."

He was so coldly formal Norie's blood seemed to
freeze in her veins. He was killing her. She almost
broke down. Instead she met his chilling blue gaze.

Not a muscle moved in her beautiful face. Nor did
she allow even the glimmer of a tear. She held herself
as rigidly as he.

"All right," she managed, forcing herself to speak,
surprising herself by sounding calmly unconcerned.

For a moment longer he stared at her. His mouth
hardened. "So, it's goodbye? This time for good?"

When she said nothing to break the frozen silence,
he opened the door of his car and hurled his great
body angrily inside. "Have it your way. It's not even
goodbye." He twisted the keys viciously in the ignition. "Merry Christmas, Norie."

As his big car zoomed away from her, the tears she
had held back slipped down her cheeks in a scalding
flow.

She watched his car until it vanished into the big empty landscape, and the knowledge that she was doing the right thing didn't help her at all.

"I'm sorry, Grant." Her voice was low and muffled by her sobs. "So sorry."

But he was too far away to hear her. Too far away to know of the desperate pain in her heart that his leaving caused her.

Norie sat at the same table where she'd shared breakfast with Grant only an hour earlier. On the surface, everything was just as before. Except for the fact that it was Sara who was seated at the table with her.

There was no visible trace of Grant in the kitchen. No visible trace of him anywhere except in her heart.

The farmhouse was cozily warm. Sara had lit several of the space heaters, both upstairs and downstairs. The two women were in the kitchen dipping their tea bags into their cups. Leo and Darius were in Norie's bedroom looking at the ornaments and presents.

"So who was he, Norie?" Sara demanded quietly. Her soft brown eyes were aglow with curiosity and concern.

Norie sipped her tea, too upset to reply. She wondered if her life would ever be the same without him. Instead of answering her friend, she listened to their sons in the next room.

"Yeah, Leo, I made this one."

"I could tell 'cause you forgot to paint the reindeer's hoof."

"And I popped the popcorn and stringed it. Mom made most of the good things though."

"You don't have as many presents as me under your tree."

"That's 'cause I want something special. See, Santa's gotta bring it all the way from the North Pole. And it could smother in his bag."

"What do you want?"

"Santa knows."

"I bet it's a dog."

"It's sorta like a dog. Only better."

The boys began to whisper conspiratorially.

But Norie couldn't hear them. Her own heart was pounding too hard.

"Mom!" Darius yelled from the doorway.

"Darius, that's your outside voice," she murmured softly, correcting him out of maternal habit.

His impatient tone was only a fraction softer. "Where's all my stuff?"

"In your room."

"Everything?" He cocked his four-year-old brows as arrogantly as any Hale.

She nodded.

"Mom, I had things out where I wanted them."

She smiled. "Out is where you want everything." But she was talking to an empty doorway. The boys were racing each other up the stairs like a pair of rough-and-tumble puppies.

"Boys! Leo! No running!" Sara called.

They pretended not to hear. The wild footsteps careened up the stairs and down the hall overhead.

"They sound like a herd of stampeding elephants." Sara giggled.

Norie cringed when doors opened and slammed. "So much for minding."

"They're just excited over Christmas," Sara said.

Norie sipped her tea.

"So who was that very attractive man?" Sara repeated her earlier question.

Norie had dreaded this. "My brother-in-law."

"What happened to his car?" Sara eyed the plump stack of legal papers in their blue folders that Norie had placed on the edge of the table. "Why was he here?"

"Sara, it's something I can't talk about, not even to you."

"Jim's right about you being mysterious."

Galloping footsteps crashed down the stairs, and a breathless Darius flung himself into the kitchen. "Hey, Mom, who slept in the guest bed upstairs?"

Sara arched her brows knowingly, and Noreen turned red.

"Can we play in there, Mom? The fire's on, and it's real warm."

"No!" The single word was too sharp, and Darius, who was not used to such sternness from her, looked hurt. More gently she said, "You bring your things down here where we can watch you."

"But we want to play up there by ourselves."

"No."

"You never let us."

"Darius!"

Mother and son stared at one another across the kitchen. Darius's lower lip swelled mutinously.

"Darius, remember about Santa. He rewards good little boys."

Darius gulped in a big breath.

Then Leo said, "Can we build a house by the tree with blankets and cushions?"

"Of course, but try not to make too big a mess."

Sara laughed. "You don't mind asking the impossible."

Leo was running back up the stairs, and Darius was right behind him.

The showdown was over. At least the one between mother and son. Norie knew that Sara was more determined.

"So your brother-in-law spent the weekend here?" Sara asked softly. "With you? Alone?"

Norie got up to pour more water into the kettle. Then she went to the stove. Her back was to Sara. "He skidded into the ditch. I couldn't very well leave him there."

"Something tells me you didn't want to leave him there."

"Much as I love you, Sara, I'm just not ready to talk about Grant."

"Well, I'll be here when you are."

"I know. You have always been my dear, dear friend."

It was a long time before Norie could turn around and pretend to Sara that everything was normal.

The next few days were the bleakest and loneliest Norie had ever known. They were even worse than when she had come to town pregnant and alone to live with Miss Maddie. No matter what she did or where she went, Norie couldn't quit thinking of Grant.

When she was Christmas shopping, she would see things she wanted to buy for him. She'd even bought one gift—a beautiful blue silk dress shirt that would look wonderful on him because of his blue eyes. It had seemed so stupid and silly, buying a present for a man she would never see again.

When she got home, she hid the gift under her bed. But sometimes she took it out to admire it secretly and dream of really being able to give it to him.

At night she lay awake thinking about him, seeing in her mind his every gesture, his every smile, remembering the exact things he'd said to her. Most of all, she remembered the way he'd gently, tenderly, brought her again and again to shuddering heights of ecstasy.

And every time she looked at Darius, she saw Grant. With his black hair and dazzling blue eyes, Darius was almost a miniature replica of his handsome uncle. Darius did not mention the special gift he had asked Santa for again, but every time Norie looked at him she knew that he was silently longing for a father—as once Grant had longed for his father. She felt Darius's special excitement, his expectancy, and these things only made her sadder.

Somehow she got through the days and the nights.

It was Christmas Eve, the night her church held a beautiful candlelight service. Norie was sitting alone on a wooden pew watching Darius, who was in the children's choir. Her black dress was tied at the waist with a handmade lavender sash. As always, large loops dangled from her ears.

Darius and Leo were wearing white choir robes with huge red satin bows tied beneath their scrubbed chins. They looked like angels, and they sounded like them too, as their voices and those of the other children filled the sanctuary with the lovely familiar melodies of sacred Christmas carols.

The service was an hour long, and it was a time of beauty and peace for Norie. All too soon the lights of the sanctuary were put out. For a moment there was darkness except for a single candle. Then the candles of the congregation were lit one by one. A hush filled the church, and Norie whispered a prayer that made her own candle flutter gently. *Merry Christmas, Grant. Be happy. Wherever you are.*

"Silent Night" was played, and so many candles were lit that the church became more brilliant than she'd ever seen it.

She felt an arm brush her waist possessively, and she turned.

Grant was there beside her.

For a moment he stood without moving, just looking down at her. Then he smiled at her boyishly, charmingly. His eyes were filled with tenderness and warmth, and some powerful emotion she couldn't be sure of.

She could barely see him for the mist of emotion that rushed at her.

"Grant..." A radiant smile broke across her face.

Black hair, blue eyes. He was movie-star handsome in a dark, conventional suit and tie as he towered beside her.

Her pulse stirred with a thrilling joy.

His hand closed over hers, and suddenly she knew how much she loved him. It didn't matter that she could never be as socially correct as his mother or the other women he had dated. Norie was still scared, scared of loving him, but in all her life she had never felt the swell of love that she felt for this man. The past—Larry, the Hales, their money and its misuse, all the grief, the rejection, and the heartbreak—no longer mattered so much.

"Merry Christmas," she whispered, her voice warm and light and happy.

"I had to come, gypsy girl," he said quietly.

His low, raspy voice was the most beautiful sound she had ever heard; more beautiful even than the sound of the angels. Gently he touched one of her gold loop earrings.

Her lashes, strangely heavy, fluttered down, but she felt the warmth of his caring in every cell of her body.

For her the world held promise once again.

Shyly, she squeezed his strong hand.

She was wrapped in happiness as she listened to the haunting loveliness of the last verse of "Silent Night."

For the first time in years Christmas really seemed a time of love and renewal and rebirth. Then she glanced up and beneath the glimmering jewel-bright stained glass windows, she saw two angelic-looking little boys in white robes and red bows. Darius's big blue eyes were wide and curious as he studied Grant. Then he smiled happily, knowingly, and he sang so joyously that Norie imagined she could hear his voice soaring above all the others in the choir and congregation. It was Christmas Eve, and Darius believed very firmly in the magic of Christmas.

Darius!

Grant still didn't know about Darius!

Dear God. She made a quick, silent prayer.

After the hymn was over, and the lights came back on, Norie managed to slip away from Grant and ask Sara to keep Darius for an hour or two, so she could be alone with Grant and explain.

Then she rushed out of the church and found Grant waiting for her by her truck.

Chapter Seven

Norie's eyes kept flicking apprehensively to the bright reflection of Grant's headlights in her rearview mirror. What would he say? What would he do when she told him about Darius? Grant had always believed in her honesty.

Never before had the drive home seemed so long. How in the world would she go about explaining?

There's something I haven't told you...

A little something I have to explain...

I wanted to tell you, Grant, but...

How could she make him understand why she had run away? Why she'd been so afraid of the Hales and what their money might do?

Larry had married her because she was different, and he'd wanted to defy his mother. Norie had been caught in the middle of their troubled relationship. She'd been too naive to pick up on the secret machinations that were weakening her marriage until it was too late. Larry's incessant extravagances had made it all too tempting to him to go to Georgia for the money he needed, and all too easy for Georgia to use this as a weapon to destroy Larry's fragile new loyalty to Norie.

After Larry's death Norie had felt utterly rejected. She'd been afraid that she might still be too naive to prevent Georgia from using her money to divide her from her son. No, Grant would never understand.

The high-ceilinged rooms glowed with rosy, welcoming light and warmth and smelled sweetly of fir and spruce. Norie was in the kitchen nervously making tea. Darius's things were everywhere, but Grant hadn't seemed to notice. He'd been too busy lighting the heaters and laying out his presents for her in front of the Christmas tree.

He had taken off his jacket and was kneeling by the tree. From where she stood, Norie watched him with a longing that was so intense it bordered on pain. She marveled at the play of powerful muscles in his back beneath the fine fabric of his shirt every time he moved, at the way the light shimmered iridescently on his blue-black hair.

Finally he became aware of her and met her gaze with a hungry, flushed look that made her cheeks glow even brighter than his. As she moved toward him, he picked up a small green present wrapped with a golden bow. "I want you to open this one first, gypsy girl," he said in a deep, husky voice.

"Now?"

"Now," he said softly.

She remembered the blue silk shirt hidden beneath her bed. "I bought you something, too."

"Did you?" He grinned at her. "I wasn't sure whether you'd be glad to see me or whether you'd throw me out."

She nuzzled her face against his shoulder. "It's a good thing you didn't call. I would have told you not to come. But now that you're here..." She slid her pale hands upward across the broad expanse of his chest until they found the knot of his tie, but she was so clumsy at loosening it that he had to help her. Unbuttoning the first three buttons, she slid her fingers inside and touched his hot, warm skin. "I'm glad you came," she whispered in a hushed voice. "So very glad." With her lips she began to explore the hollow at the base of his throat.

"I kept thinking about your turkey. It seemed a shame for you to be out here all alone, eating by yourself," he said in a low, hoarse tone, pulling her closer.

"You better not have come back just because of my turkey."

He gave her the small present. "I want you to open this one first. It will explain everything."

Her fingers shook as she tore into the glittering ribbon and then the green paper. Inside was a white cardboard box, and inside it, a smaller black velvet one. She snapped the inner box open instantly.

A solitaire diamond engagement ring winked at her from black velvet.

Her breath caught. She stared at the ring for a long moment, then looked back up at him.

"Well?" he whispered. "Do you like it?"

Gingerly she touched it, tracing the finely cut stone, the gleaming band with her fingertip. Her gaze blurred. "It's beautiful, Grant. The most beautiful ring in all the world."

"For the most beautiful woman."

"But are you sure?"

He smiled down at her. "I love you, Norie. Marry me."

She ought to tell him. About Darius. Now.

But she was too dazzled by Grant's words, by the tenderness shining in his eyes. So she just stood quietly and let him slide the ring onto her finger and twist it so they could both watch it catch the light and shimmer.

"There, it's a perfect fit," he said, pleased.

"Grant, I'm not the right kind of woman . . ."

"Hush." His hands were in her black silky hair. He pressed her face against his chest and smoothed her hair. Softly he said, "You're so beautiful, Norie. The whole time I was gone, every day, every hour, I was thinking of you."

"So was I."

"I nearly picked up the phone to call you a thousand times. But I knew what you'd say. I needed you so much. I felt so hopeless, so lost."

"So did I."

"No more, gypsy girl."

"What about Georgia?"

"She will accept you. I swear to you she will."

Then he lifted Norie's face toward his, and he bent slightly to cover her lips with his. He kissed her ever so gently. She moaned and raised her arms to encircle his neck. Her heart had begun to thump erratically. Waves of desire pulsed through her, and she knew she had to stop him.

Finally she got the words out. "Grant, there's something terribly important I have to tell you."

"What could be that important?" His hand cupped her chin and he lifted her face again so he could resume kissing her. "More important than this?"

Their lips met. His tongue dipped into her mouth again just as the front door flew open with a bang. Norie scarcely heard the eager footsteps as her child ran inside, the door slamming behind him. She was too aware of Grant tensing in surprise.

"Mom! Hey, Mom, I'm home!"

Suddenly Darius stopped and stared in disbelief at the vision of his mother in a man's arms, the two of them framed in the doorway with the lights of the Christmas tree twinkling behind them.

Norie withdrew slowly. Still holding her hand, Grant stepped back a single step to stare at the diminutive replica of himself.

Darius was still in his "church clothes," but just barely. His shirttails were wrinkled and hung loosely out of his slacks, his tie was crooked, and his shoelaces were dragging. Norie was sure that in all his life, Darius had never stood so absolutely still for so long without being told to. His blue eyes were open wide with wonder.

"Santa is awesome!" Darius shouted in his outdoor voice, using his idol, Ray Liska's, favorite word. Then Darius ran happily toward them, never doubting for a moment that he would be a welcome addition in the big man's arms.

Grant knelt slowly to the child's level.

"Santa really did bring me a daddy." Darius let out a big sigh. Then he touched Grant's sapphire tie tack. "You are real! Boy! You even look a little like me."

"What's your name, son?"

"It's Darius."

"Darius?" Grant looked up at Norie. His face was dark, unreadable.

"Hey, can you play football?"

"I played in high school," Grant told him almost absently.

"Awesome."

Darius didn't usually hug people he'd just met. But he made an exception with Grant and laid his cheek against Grant's trustingly just for a second before pulling himself free and dashing eagerly toward the kitchen.

"Hey, come on. I gotta lot of things upstairs I want to show you."

Grant stood up slowly. As Darius dashed up the stairs, Norie's soulful eyes sought Grant's and silently pleaded with him to understand. But he looked past her, his expression closed and hard. Without a word he left the room and followed Darius.

Norie stayed downstairs, her heart filled with an agony of doubt and regret. She could hear their voices—Grant's deep baritone mingling with Darius's overly excited shouts.

Why was her life always like this? Just when she was sure she loved Grant, she'd ruined everything. She wouldn't blame him if he hated her.

An hour passed before Grant came down again. Norie was in the kitchen, sitting silently at the table. The tea she had made for herself had gone cold while she'd waited nervously, hopelessly.

He sank down heavily across from her, his jaw rigid, his eyes dark. "That kid's got energy. He was so excited, I had to bribe him to get him down for the night."

"We have to talk," Noreen said.

"That's the understatement of the year."

"Grant, I was going to tell you."

"When? Did you ever stop to think what the past five years have been like for me? I cared about you. After Larry died, I wanted to help you. I would have done anything in the world to try to make you happy. But what were your feelings for me? My only brother died. Knowing where you were, knowing about Darius would have meant everything to me. Not only to me. But to Mother. Larry was her favorite child. I was very little comfort to her."

"I want to explain."

"It's too late for that. I'm going."

"Grant, no."

He looked up. "Don't you understand? I believed in you. I believed that deep down you cared something for us, for me. You think the Hales rejected you. Honey, by keeping Darius from us, you rejected us. The one thing I never expected from you was dishonesty of this magnitude."

"I wanted to tell you," she said softly, each word carefully enunciated. "I almost did, the day of Larry's funeral. But then I heard all the Hales talking, and I thought you felt the same way."

"Norie, none of it matters anymore. You're free of me and the Hales. If you're so afraid of us, you don't need to be anymore." Slowly he got up. "I'm going. I won't tell Mother. Be happy. You're finally really, truly free of us all."

Norie went to him and put her arms around him. "But you know that's not what I want anymore." She was speaking rapidly, desperately.

At her touch, everything in him went as still as death. He released her gradually, slowly pushing her away, all the time staring into the shadowy depths of her eyes.

"Grant, please—" Her lips barely moved as she whispered.

But he wouldn't let her finish.

"Tell Darius... Tell him, Merry Christmas from me tomorrow, will you? Tell him...maybe next Christmas Santa will do the job right, and he'll get a daddy who'll teach him how to play football. I'm not the right guy."

Then without speaking to her again, Grant turned and strode out of the house, letting the door close behind him on a whisper of icy air.

Tears pooled in Norie's eyes, but she didn't chase after Grant. He had decided to go, and no matter how much she wanted him to stay, she knew that no amount of pleading could persuade him.

The house seemed frigid and empty, as frigid and empty as her own heart.

She heard a slight sound on the stairs, and knew that Darius had not gone to bed after all. He came into the kitchen, his eyes as big and sad as hers. He was dragging his favorite red teddy bear.

"Where's Grant?"

"I don't know."

"Will he come back?"

"I don't know that, either," she admitted.

"But he's my special present from Santa."

She took him into her arms and ruffled his black hair. "Mine, too, darling," she murmured softly.

"Mine, too. But he's your uncle, and you'll see him from time to time."

Darius sat on her lap and sucked his thumb.

"You're a big boy now, Darius. Big boys don't suck their thumbs."

He pulled his thumb out reluctantly. His face was very serious. "I didn't ask for an uncle. I asked for a daddy."

"Well, it isn't Christmas yet. Maybe, just maybe, Santa realized he'd delivered our special present too early. Go back to bed. Santa doesn't come until little boys are asleep."

"Do you really think he'll send Grant back?"

"Maybe, if we both pray very hard."

"Mom, do you really believe in magic?"

Behind them the Christmas tree lights were softly aglow. Grant's ring was still on her finger. His other gifts were still under the tree. Her gaze stole to the manger scene that she and Darius had built together, to the tiny figure of the baby Jesus.

"Yes, in a way," she replied gently. "You see, when it's Christmas, I believe in miracles."

Chapter Eight

Norie sat up in bed, her heart beating expectantly, not knowing what it was that had awakened her.

And then she knew.

It was Christmas Day.

She fell back against her soft cool pillow in a daze of happiness.

Her bedroom was cozily warm. Someone had come in earlier and lit the space heater. From the kitchen wafted the aroma of coffee and bacon and biscuits. A man's deep husky voice was accompanying a radio that was playing "Joy to the World."

Grant had come back to her as she and Darius had prayed he would.

She listened to Grant sing with her eyes closed, his baritone washing over her, caressing her.

At last she got up, pulled on her robe and stumbled barefoot across the cold floors into the kitchen.

"Grant?" His name was a broken cry across her lips.

His dark gaze smoldered with love for her.

"I thought it was you," she managed to utter dreamily. Then she was flying across the kitchen into his arms. "You did come back."

Tenderly, he enfolded her into his strong arms and lowered his black head to the long pale curve of her beautiful neck. She felt his hands smoothing the snarls from her sleep-tangled, silken curls.

"I had no choice. I know from experience that life without you holds nothing but emptiness. I love you, gypsy girl. I always have and I always will."

"Enough to forgive me?"

His dark eyes moved over her face, and his expression grew momentarily soft. "There's nothing to forgive."

"Last night I was afraid you despised me."

"I was angry. But after I calmed down, I understood why you did what you did."

"I should have told you about Darius years ago. Instead I ran away."

"We drove you away," he said gravely.

"After Larry died and I heard your family saying they didn't want me, I felt completely alone. The only thing I had was my unborn child. When Mike Yanta called and offered me this job, I took it. I came here and made a life for myself, but because I never resolved my conflict with you and your family, there was always something incomplete in my life. You see, I wanted to belong to your family, to be a real Hale, for Darius's sake as well as my own. I knew I was keeping your mother's only grandchild from her. But I was afraid of her, afraid that she might try to dominate my child the way she had dominated Larry. I was afraid she might use her money to alienate Darius from me. But I couldn't forget you, Grant. No matter how hard I tried."

"Mother won't use her money like that again. She knows she made a terrible mistake." Grant's tone grew gentler, lower. "But I was as guilty as she. From the first, I was insensitive to you. To the person you really were. I hurt you. I promise I'll be more careful in the future."

"Oh, Grant..." She could scarcely speak. "My values were so wrong. I was so mixed-up about the power of money that I attached more importance to it than I should have. I should have believed in you, in myself." She winced as she thought of all the hurt she had caused everyone. "I'm always going to wonder what would have happened if I'd been stronger and hadn't run away in the first place."

Grant took her anguished face between his hands and tilted it back. "That's something we'll never know. Maybe we needed these years so we'd know how much we nearly lost."

"And how much we really love each other." She had never dreamed that he loved her so much, that money and its powers no longer could seem frightening.

She pulled away a little from him then, smiling up at him, but he drew her back and kissed her. His hand wrapped around the back of her shoulders. His hard mouth slanted over hers in fierce possession.

A long time later they pulled apart, breathless.

"Darling," he murmured. "How do you think Darius would feel about Santa bringing him a grandmother and a grandfather for Christmas as well as a daddy? You can say no..."

She smiled up at him mistily and placed two fingertips over his mouth. "Hush... I don't want to say no. I want you to call them and invite both of them for Christmas dinner. It's a little late, I know. Georgia usually has so many invitations. They'll have to drive fifty miles."

"They'll come."

Grant sought her lips again. Then he rained hot urgent, kisses over her forehead, her brow, her throat, before stopping to cradle her face in his hands and peer into her eyes.

"It looks like Santa brought all of us a lot more than Darius asked for." Grant kept holding her. "If I didn't know better, I'd say today is the next best thing to a miracle."

"Santa's special miracle," she breathed.

"And mine," Grant said. His dark face grew solemn. "Darling, I—I have a confession to make." For the first time his confidence seemed to desert him.

"If it's about other women...don't..."

"It's even worse than that."

Her black brows arched quizzically.

"It was because of me, that the phone went dead that morning. I tampered with it that night, you see. I had to have you by fair means or foul."

For a long moment, she stared at him in stunned surprise. Then her expression grew radiant. "I guess you were just helping Santa work his miracle."

"I love you," he whispered.

She took his hand and squeezed it. "Let's go upstairs and tell Darius."

The kitchen door by the stairway banged against the wall. "I'm right here, Mom!" Darius shouted exuberantly right before he burst into the room dragging his blanket and his teddy.

Norie put her fingers to her lips.

"I know, Mom. My outdoor voice . . ." In a softer, more tentative tone, the child whispered, "Right here . . . Dad."

Grant knelt down and folded the little boy into his arms. "Right here . . . son." Very gently he lifted him from the ground.

"Are you really going to stay?" Darius demanded eagerly.

"Forever."

Norie drew a deep breath of pure happiness.

"Merry Christmas, Norie," Grant whispered, his blue eyes dazzling bright, as he drew her closer into the warm circle of love.

Holding Darius tightly, Grant bent his head and kissed her.

* * * * *

Author's Note

For me, Christmas is a very special time of family, love and renewal. It is truly a season of miracles.

A beautiful pecan tree hangs over my backyard. I know Christmas is coming when the pecans start falling and the squirrels start racing about collecting them. My mother (who loves fresh pecans nearly as much as the squirrels) uses the nuts to make homemade candy—divinity, pralines, fudge and my Aunt Bill's recipe for carmelized fudge. I use them to make pralines and date-nut fruit cake. I've included the recipe in the front. Now my daughter is old enough to bake cookies for her friends.

With three children in our house, there is always great excitement as Christmas approaches. My two younger children, Kim and Tad, insist on putting up the Christmas tree the day after Thanksgiving. I guess just seeing the tree in the living room is a daily reminder that Christmas is really coming soon. My older son, David, decorates the outside of the house.

Usually, before Christmas, we go to our city's local production of *The Nutcracker*. My sons used to object, but now they look forward to it as a pleasant ritual. And then on Christmas Eve there is a beautiful candlelight service in our church. After attending the service we go to my parents' for eggnog.

On Christmas Day, I cook a big turkey dinner for my family and all of our relatives who live in town. At some time during the holidays, we drive to the Texas hill country, where my husband's parents and sisters have homes, and we spend several days visiting them. If we make the trip before Christmas, we always go into the woods to help them cut down their Christmas tree.

I always look forward to Christmas, and I hope that this year's Christmas will be special for each and every one of you.

Ann Major

LIGHTS OUT!

Rita Rainville

A recipe from Rita Rainville:

This recipe should probably be called *Grandma's* Graham Torte, because the only time we ever had it was when we lived in Chicago and went to visit Grandma. When I grew up, she eventually—and grudgingly—gave me the recipe. It's one of my favorites because not only is it delicious, it's easy—and when I bake, *easy* is a priority with me.

GRAHAM TORTE

4 eggs
1 lb (5 ¼ cups) crushed graham crackers
2 cups milk
1 ½ cups sugar
1 cup butter or margarine
4 tsp baking powder

Preheat oven to 350° F.
Combine crushed graham crackers and baking powder. Set aside.

In a large bowl, cream together butter and sugar. Add eggs, milk and graham-cracker mixture. Blend well.

Put mixture in ungreased 9″ × 13″ pan. Bake for 45 to 50 minutes. Cool.

Serve with whipped cream.

See? I said it was easy. And you won't have to worry about leftovers!

Chapter One

One alligator, two alligators...

The instant the radio died, Carroll Stilwell jumped up and mentally began counting. She freely admitted that her groan, uttered as she trotted to the bay window that overlooked both her deep front yard and that of her new neighbor, was loud, self-indulgent and self-pitying. She was entitled.

Three alligators, four alligators, five alligators...

Unconsciously using her eight-year-old daughter's favorite method of tolling the seconds, she twitched the lace curtains apart and stared across the sunlit half acre of pine trees, waiting for the rangy, broad-shouldered man to erupt out of his front door.

Six alligators, seven alligators, eight alligators...

Slade Ryan had moved into the sprawling house next door—a house much too large for a single man, everyone in the small mountain community nosily agreed—just two weeks earlier, and in that time Carroll had already devoured her month's emergency stash of chocolate-covered caramels. The tension was definitely giving her an ulcer, she brooded, morbidly prodding a slim finger at her belly.

Nine alligators, ten alli—

Even though she had kept her expectant gaze riveted on the front of his house, Carroll still winced when the sturdy oak door flew open and the big, dark-haired man exploded out onto the porch and down the stairs, heading straight for her place. He wore his work clothes—faded jeans and a maroon knit shirt. Over the past fourteen days she had learned that his appearance at her door in snug jeans and a colorful shirt meant that he had been sitting in front of the computer—at least, until the power had failed.

One part of her mind noted that he was getting faster; yesterday it had taken him eleven alligators. Another part registered the set of his wide shoulders and the long-legged stride that had all the elements of an angry stalk, despite its fluid grace. He definitely wasn't coming over for a friendly chat.

So what else was new? she asked herself wryly. With the single exception of their first meeting, every time she had talked to Slade, he had been ready to wring somebody's neck. No, not somebody's. Kris's.

Sighing philosophically, Carroll headed for the front of the house, arriving just as a fist pounded on the door. She cracked it open and looked up into furious gray eyes.

"Where is he?" Slade demanded, resting one big hand on the doorjamb.

Carroll's tentative smile widened a bit as she took in his straight, dark hair; it looked as if he had been trying to tear it out at the roots. "Now, Slade, you wouldn't hurt an old man who looks like Santa Claus, would you?"

He exhaled sharply. "Right now I'm ready to throttle an old man who *thinks* he's Santa Claus." He didn't raise his voice. He didn't have to. Carroll had a strong hunch that most people ran for cover when he bit off his words that way. "Where is he?"

It didn't take even a second's thought on her part; she did what she had always done: protected her grandfather. "How would you like to talk about it over a cup of coffee and a piece of Mom's famous graham torte? She made it this morning."

He gave her a harried glance. "I don't want to be fed, I just want to stop him. He's driving me nuts!"

"It's fantastic," she forged on. "You've got to try it. You can yell at him later." She held out her hand and waggled her fingers. "Come on."

As usual with Slade, she got more than she bargained for. He took her hand, lacing his fingers through hers, stopping only when her soft palm rested snugly against his hard one. Startled, she looked up and met his waiting gaze. A definite mistake, she decided belatedly. His silvery eyes had the same expression of masculine hunger that she had spotted several times before. And it bothered her now just as much as it had then. She didn't need a complication like Slade Ryan in her life. No, all in all, with things as they were, it was safer to have him mad.

Besides, Carroll reminded herself as she turned and led him toward the large, cheerful kitchen, he *did* have a legitimate grievance. Her grandfather, Kris K. Ringle, was a man with a mission: an obsessive determination to turn their small town into a winter fairyland of twinkling lights. And he was going to do it before Christmas or bust. *This* Christmas. The townspeople, to a man, woman and child, were crazy about the idea, and they supported his efforts. Just as they had last Christmas, and the one before that, and the ones before that.

This year, they had even volunteered to do without electricity for a couple of hours each afternoon so Kris could test the lights he had strung all around town. And therein lay the problem. He didn't test *every* afternoon between one and three, just when he could no longer do his testing at night. Unfortunately, the closer Christmas came, the more frequently the need arose.

It was a cozy arrangement, the sort of thing that could only happen in a small town. The people who were at home declared a moratorium on cooking and housecleaning, using the two hours for leisure time, doing anything that didn't require the use of electricity. Even the small shops in town had rigged up various emergency alternative methods of recording sales—some of them quite creative—to use when they sold their wares to the tourists.

And in the way things had of happening, the tourists from San Diego and the surrounding cities were charmed by the spirit of small-town cooperation, and intrigued by the ruling passion of one aging, plump, determined man. The fact that he *did* look like Santa Claus merely added a piquant element to a good story. The early tourists had told their friends, who in turn told *their* friends, and now the small town had a steady stream of visitors coming to check on the progress of the lights and, incidentally, contributing to the economic enhancement of Pinetree. Since the stream swelled noticeably during the holiday season, everyone was happy with the arrangement—the chamber of commerce, the business owners, the residents.

Carroll cast an oblique glance at Slade's stubborn expression as she waved him to a chair with her free hand. Well, she amended, *almost* every resident. Slade

Ryan, with his high-tech computer graphics and an imminent deadline, was the one glaring exception. He was definitely not a happy camper.

When Slade slid his hand to Carroll's wrist, he felt a shock jolt through her body and allowed himself the indulgence of a split-second fantasy. It was over before it was fully formed, because if Slade was anything, he was a realist. Carroll Stilwell's pulse wasn't racing because she had an uncontrollable urge to crawl all over him and drag him off to her bedroom. No, much as he would like to think it was, there was another reason.

The wary expression in her deep blue eyes said it all. As far as she was concerned, he was a stick of dynamite about to go off, and she wanted her family to be out of range when he blew.

"I don't bite," he assured her grimly.

"Really?" She raised a skeptical brow, then looked pointedly at the large hand holding her wrist captive. It was strong and tan, dusted with dark hair. When he reluctantly released her, she filled two mugs with coffee and cut a hefty piece of the torte for him. After transferring everything to the table, she slid into the chair across from him. "You could've fooled me," she told him, leaning back and eyeing him with a severe frown. "You're as cranky as a hungry bear."

Slade winced. She had a point. He was. Both bad-tempered and starved. And he'd been that way since the day after he had moved in, the day she had strolled over with a home-cooked meal, a welcome to the neighborhood, and a smile that practically knocked him to his knees. His body had gone on alert, and it hadn't eased since.

Short blond hair just skimmed her jawline. Her deep blue eyes were candid, curious and cautious. He had ticked off the first two items the instant he'd opened the door. The rest hadn't been long in coming. One glance at his expression had apparently triggered her alarm system, and her changing smile had both warned him not to get his hopes up and attempted to reassure him, just on the off chance that he had a knee-jerk masculine reaction to the meal she was offering. It told him clearly that the food was only a neighborly gesture; she wasn't aiming for his heart via his stomach.

He'd opened the door and fallen in behind her when she'd carried the steaming casserole to the kitchen. Her lance-straight back, slim waist and swaying hips had made his palms tingle. She reminded him of one of the long-stemmed mountain wildflowers, bright yellow, with a deceptive air of fragility. When she'd turned, her eyes widening at his speculative expression, the lady hadn't been pleased. With a blink of her lashes, the No Trespassing signs had been posted.

They were still up.

Suddenly, Slade was tired of the whole mess. Tired of the way she leaped protectively between him and her grandfather, tired of being on the other side of the signs. Especially tired of the edgy look she got whenever he came into sight. He swallowed a bite of the rich cake and made an appreciative sound. "How'd Christy's appointment go?" he asked casually.

Carroll blinked, surprised at his mild tone. But not being one to overlook a gift from the gods, however small it might be, she plunged into the new topic with enthusiasm. With any luck, he would forget that he'd come over ready to raise hell with Kris, she thought optimistically.

"Fine. The doctor took another X-ray and made reassuring noises, said again that it wasn't a bad break and that she's healing fast. He wants her to keep the cast on for another few weeks. I think that it's more because he knows that her only speed is fast than because she really needs it. So she'll still be thumping around on crutches for a while, endangering everyone's toes."

Slade savored her smile. It was warm and tender, not the cautious curve of her lips that she usually aimed at him. Of course, neither the warmth nor the tenderness was for him, but he would take whatever she was offering. For now. "Christy's had a rough time."

"The first day or so," Carroll agreed. "But now she's really milking the situation for all it's worth."

Slade placed his fork on the empty plate. "But think of the boon she's been to the community theater group. They have a Tiny Tim on genuine crutches."

"The whole cast is spoiling her rotten. They're also hobbling around with bruised toes." Carroll grinned. "Be warned, she's really getting into the role. In the last couple of days she's perfected a waiflike look that will have you believing she's underfed and neglected." She got up and brought the coffeepot over to the table. Filling the mugs, she said, "I've come to the conclusion that my daughter is a ham at heart."

"Maybe she comes by it naturally."

Carroll sat back down and stared at him thoughtfully. "You mean my mother?"

He nodded. "It's not that much of a leap from an artist to a budding actress. Where did Noel study?"

She laughed softly. "Upstairs." When Slade mutely pointed toward the ceiling, she nodded. "Yep. When I was a kid, Mom and Kris turned our place in San Diego into a boarding house. One of the lodgers took off in the middle of the night, leaving his paints behind in lieu of the rent. Mom decided it was an omen. She sold the house, and we moved up here, where she could be inspired."

Slade shrugged. "Whatever it takes. Apparently it worked. Her landscapes seem to be pretty popular."

"Um-hmm." Carroll didn't try to conceal her pride. "The word's finally getting around."

"Where was your dad while all this was going on?" Slade asked, finally giving in to his rampant curiosity about her. In the past two weeks, in her efforts to keep him away from Kris, she had talked at length about her grandfather, her mother and her daughter. She had said *nada*, zippo, about herself or the men in her life.

Now it took Slade all of three seconds to decide that he'd been patient enough. He would have preferred that she volunteer the information, but since she obviously didn't intend to, he wasn't above taking advantage of the situation. If she wanted to keep him out of the basement, away from Kris, she could damn well talk.

The smile left Carroll's face. "My father took off when I was a baby." Her tone told him that the subject was closed.

"Why?"

She shot him an aggravated glance. After seeming to weigh her options, she sighed. "Good question. He never said."

"He just left?"

"Yep. In the middle of the night, just like the lodger with the paints."

"Must have been rough."

"We managed," she said briefly.

"What happened to *your* husband?" He slid it in fast, before she could offer him another piece of cake or change the subject. She didn't like it, and he really couldn't blame her. Her narrowed eyes told him to go to hell.

"Are you always this rude?" she demanded, temper adding color to her cheeks.

Slade's shrug was a lazy movement of his wide shoulders. "No. Only with people who are as close-mouthed as you. And then only when it's important."

Carroll's brows rose. "Important?"

His steady gaze held hers. "I need to know just how softly I have to walk around you."

"I don't think I understand." Her puzzled frown etched two vertical lines between her brows.

More to the point, she didn't *want* to understand, he reflected, even as he nodded and kept his voice patient. "I want to know what happened to the man in your life. As I see it, there are several possibilities. You could have had Christy without the benefit of a wedding, you could be divorced, or you could be a grieving widow." *Or you could have a lover.* He was wise enough to keep the last option to himself.

Carroll concentrated on lacing her fingers around the mug. "Does it really matter which it is?"

Slade nodded again. "Yeah, it does. I'd walk more softly around a grieving widow."

"How much more?"

His sudden grin startled her and sent her pulse tap-dancing, made her resolve to tether her impetuous tongue. It also answered her question: only as much as he had to. She fussed with the coffeepot. "I don't know how we got on this subject," she said carefully, "but it's not going to get us anywhere, so why don't we just drop it? I don't need a man in my life, how-*ever* he walks."

Slade took a swallow of coffee, watching her over the rim of the cup. He waited until some of the tension went out of her shoulders before he asked, "So what happened to him?"

Carroll closed her eyes, her sigh a gust of irritation. When she finally turned her gaze to Slade, he was placidly drinking his coffee, waiting. And he would keep on waiting, she realized with a sudden flash of insight. Waiting and asking until he finally got an answer. The neighborhood grapevine contended that he was a top-notch design engineer, doing something hush-hush for the military on his state-of-the-art computer. She didn't doubt it for a second; he had the typical engineer's annoying habit of asking questions, then digging with pit-bull persistence to get the answers.

With an impatient wave of her hand, she gave up. "It's an old story, and a dull one. He did exactly what the other two did—walk. Only *I* got the courtesy of an explanation. He was looking for something."

"He had you and Christy, and he went looking for more?" Slade's gray eyes registered disbelief. "He's a fool."

Carroll stared at him. "Where were you years ago when I needed to hear that from someone besides my mother and grandfather?" she finally asked with wry humor.

"Where is he now?"

"Last I heard, he was in some over-the-hill hippie, vegetarian commune."

Her casual shrug told Slade all he needed to know. She wasn't mourning the loss of a husband. She'd had the strength to rebuild her life, and she wasn't wasting any time looking over her shoulder. If her steady gaze was any indication, she was, apparently, happy.

"You're better off without him," Slade said flatly.

She nodded. "I couldn't agree more. Actually, I feel a little sorry for him. I have full custody of Christy, and he'll never see her grow up. He has no idea what he's missing."

Slade raised his mug and sipped thoughtfully, his eyes never leaving her face. He liked what he saw. Life had made her strong, yet she still had compassion for a loser ex-husband. She wasn't bitter, but she knew her own value and wouldn't let the guy within a hundred feet of her or Christy. Which was exactly as it should be.

Carroll wasn't beautiful, he reflected. She didn't have the anorectic, hollowed-cheekbones and exotic glamor found in fashion magazines. She was small-boned and barely came to his chin. Slim, but not excessively so, with a neat little bottom that had kept him awake more nights than he wanted to count. Her steady blue gaze reflected intelligence and a lively sense of humor. Straight blond hair framed her face and usually looked as if she had been running her hands through it. No, she wasn't beautiful, Slade reflected, but the sum total of what she was had a lethal effect on him.

He leaned back and was idly considering the state of his hormones when Santa Claus threw open the door.

Chapter Two

Slade blinked at the sight before him and silently corrected himself. First you'd have to swap the old man's blue sweatsuit and hightop tennies for an outfit of red velvet, fur and boots; *then* he would be Santa Claus. Kris had blue eyes that actually twinkled beneath thick snowy brows, ruddy cheeks, a glistening white beard that fanned out over his chest and a frame that needed no artificial padding. He also had a booming voice and an inextinguishable supply of enthusiasm. Fanaticism might be a better word, Slade decided.

"Slade!" Kris beamed at him, slamming the basement door and pulling up a chair next to Slade's. "The very man I want to see. The word's out that you're a hotshot engineer. Exactly what is it that you do?"

After a slight pause, Slade said briefly, "Right now, I'm designing a type of radar for the military."

"Ah." Kris blinked and returned to his primary concern. "Ever do much with electricity?"

Slade nodded cautiously. "Some."

"Ha!" Rubbing his hands in satisfaction, Kris chortled, "Just what I thought. I need your help."

Eyeing the old man's expectant smile with fascination, Slade demanded, "You want *my* help?"

"Right." Kris nodded, pleased by what he apparently considered an eager volunteer.

"Mine?"

"Sure. Can you come down to the basement? I want to show you something."

"Wait a minute." Slade held up a restraining hand. "I have a slight problem of my own that we need to discuss."

Kris blinked, his blue eyes thoughtful. "You mean the power?"

Slade nodded grimly.

"About it going off, you mean?"

He nodded again.

Kris's face brightened. "I *knew* you were going to fit in around here, boy." He swiveled around to Carroll and demanded, "Didn't I tell you that you were wrong about him?" Turning back to Slade, he said, "I suppose when it went off, you knew I needed help."

"Not exactly."

"And you came right over," he continued, ignoring Slade's terse reply. "What a neighbor!"

"Kris—"

"Ready to pitch right in and help. I didn't even have to ask!" He jumped to his feet. "Well, that's the way things work sometimes. You worry and fret about a problem, and then you turn around and find the answer sitting in your kitchen." He opened the basement door. "Come on down and let me show you what I'm wrestling with."

"Kris, I'm not—"

"Tch, don't be modest," the old man urged, his cheeks rosy with barely suppressed excitement. "It should be a snap for someone like you. I know what I want. I just don't know how to get it. Come on, we've only got four weeks." Taking in Slade's puzzled

expression, he added, "Until Christmas Eve."
Bounding down the stairs, he called back over his
shoulder, "That's when *all* the lights I've strung
around town go on and stay on for a week."

"Well, hell." Slade glared in frustration at the
empty doorway, then swung around to Carroll, his
frown deepening when she grinned. "He doesn't listen."

"I know."

"The only reason I came over here was to tell him
to stop that damned testing during the day."

"I know."

"What does he mean, *all*?"

"He's going to dazzle us in degrees. Some lights go
on in two weeks, more the following week, and
more—"

"I get the idea." He ran a hand through his dark
hair, making it stand on end. "He's hell-bent on getting me involved in this idiotic project."

"You're absolutely right." At that point, she honestly didn't know who needed protecting, her grandfather or Slade. "Why do you think I've been trying
to keep you two apart?"

"To save his neck."

Carroll nodded thoughtfully. "There is that," she
admitted. "But actually, I've been thinking of you,
too. I know how Kris is. He works on the premise that
everyone has the same enthusiasm for his schemes that
he does, and before his unsuspecting victims know
what's happened, he's suckered them in."

Resting his hand on the edge of the open door, Slade
said firmly, "I'm not a victim. I guess I'll just have to
set him straight, won't I?"

"I guess you will." Carroll picked up her mug and made a small toasting gesture. "Good luck." Her smile was rueful. It wasn't easy to pop her ebullient grandfather's balloon, to rain on his parade. Slade would need more than luck.

When he hit the middle of the stairs, Slade caught a glimpse of Kris's workshop that made him stop in midstride. By the time he reached the bottom, he knew he had underestimated the redoubtable old man. So what else was new? he asked himself disgustedly. He had misjudged the entire family.

On the basis of a few short days of observation, he had decided that he'd moved in next to a den of dreamers. Carroll, who seemed free to come and go at will, had been his first mistake. He'd pegged her as a dazzling wildflower who apparently didn't have to worry about basics like paying rent and finding a job. Then he'd learned that she ran a flourishing secretarial service from the house, enabling her to be home with Christy and keep an eye on her flighty mother and loony grandfather.

After Christy's first visit, he'd mentally labeled her as precocious and a bit spoiled. Wrong again. She was bright, talented, articulate and fiercely loyal. She also wanted a father and had apparently set her sights on him.

His first encounter with Noel had been on his front porch. She had been gazing abstractedly through a spray of pine needles at a billowing formation of cumulus clouds, not even turning to acknowledge his greeting. His gut reaction had been that she was playing the part of a vague, eccentric artist. Another mistake. She wasn't playing at anything; she *was* a vague, eccentric artist. A very good one.

And Kris? The score was now four out of four. He'd been convinced that the old man was merely a lunatic with a light-bulb fixation. Now, taking an assessing glance around the well-equipped workshop, Slade realized that neither the man—nor the problem—was that simple.

Kris was bent over a platform that took up the entire center of the basement. He waved Slade over without looking up. "Come take a look at this."

Slade hesitated, first taking in the brightly lit room. Over in one corner was a massive desk strewn with papers. Behind it, covering almost the entire wall, shelves strained under the weight of books. A power saw stood at the end of a long workbench that bristled with tools. They all looked well used. The room smelled pleasantly of wood shavings and lacquer.

Slade finally joined the other man and looked down at the platform. "My God. It's the town."

Kris slanted a look up at him and pushed his round, wire-framed glasses back up his nose. "What do you think of it?" Pride gleamed in the pale blue eyes.

"It's...magnificent." It was more than that. It was mind-boggling. Kris had contoured the hills with mathematical precision and placed each miniature wooden house with the same exactitude. Minuscule pine trees lined the streets and surrounded the homes, while a profusion of greenery represented the tangle of oaks, maples and cottonwoods that grew among the pines. It was a detailed, precise replica of the entire town; every house, every tree—at least as far as he could tell—was represented.

Trouble. He was looking at a platform full of the stuff. He was no longer dealing with something as simple as an old man's hobby, Slade realized. Nor was the operation merely a diversion to keep boredom at bay; Kris's precision work and attention to detail made that quite clear. No, what he had here was commitment and dedication, a problem of epic proportions. One massive headache.

"Kris," he said abruptly, "you've got to do something about these lights."

"Umm." The older man tilted his head and nudged a tree a bit to the left. "I know. That's why I asked you down."

"Every time the power goes out, my computer dies. When it comes back, I've lost whole chunks of my design."

Kris moved the tree back to its original position. "The trouble is, I just don't have enough juice."

"And every time it happens, I get further behind on my deadline."

Kris prodded his glasses back up his nose. "The power company's getting a tad upset, too."

"I've got a lot riding on this design."

"But I think I've figured it out."

"Kris!" Slade scowled at the portly man's backside. "Are you listening to me?"

"Why else would I ask you down here?" Kris turned and beamed at him.

If he says *ho ho ho*, I'm going to throttle him, Slade decided. "Then what are we talking about?" he demanded instead.

"Power, juice, electricity!" Kris clapped him on the shoulder. "You're going to show me where to put some small generators."

"The hell I am!"

"You got a better idea?" Kris's hopeful glance would have melted Scrooge.

"Yeah. Tear all the lights down and forget the whole thing."

"Umm." Kris smiled absently at the joke as he shifted another tree. "I thought maybe a generator here and another one here." He pointed to a couple of houses. "What do you think?"

Slade's exasperated gaze followed the pudgy finger. Kris was obviously an advocate of selective listening; he heard only what he wanted to hear. "It all depends on how much voltage you're using," he said reluctantly. "Do you have any idea how many lights are out there?"

"Of course."

"How many?"

"To the last bulb?"

Slade sighed. "A round figure will do."

"A little over five hundred thousand."

"Five hun—" He stopped, astounded. "I don't believe it."

Kris shrugged apologetically. "We're still pretty small."

"You can't have that many lights out there. It's impossible," Slade said flatly.

Kris spun around and darted over to the desk. After slapping at several piles of paper, he muttered in satisfaction and pulled a thick binder from beneath a stack of catalogs. He thrust it into Slade's hands.

"Here. Take a look. Every house, every tree, every lamppost is accounted for—the number of lights and voltage for each."

He pulled out two chairs and watched with barely concealed satisfaction as Slade dropped into one and turned the pages in disbelief. "What I'm aiming for," Kris confided, "is to build up to a grand finale on Christmas Eve. Two weeks from tonight, I'm turning on the first batch. That's about half the lights and a few of the animated scenes. I've got enough juice for that. The following week I add another twenty-five percent. That's iffy. Then, the last week, on Christmas Eve, the whole kit and caboodle goes on! We'll outdo New York City. At least, we will if the power holds out. So the last two weeks are where I need a little help."

Slade shot him a skeptical look. "A little?"

Kris grinned and measured an inch of space between his thumb and finger. "About that much."

"Do you have a calculator?" Slade waited while Kris unearthed it from beneath another pile of paper, then flipped through the pages again, rapidly plugging in some numbers. He finally looked up, shaking his head. "You can't do it."

"Yes I can," Kris said calmly. "I just have to find the way."

Slade handed him the notebook and calculator. "Good luck."

"I don't need luck. I need you."

"You can't have me," Slade said, holding his voice even with an effort. "I have a job. I work at it every day. If there were more than twenty-four hours in a day, I'd work longer. The reason I'm not working now is because the power went out." He glared at Kris, who was watching him with a placid expression. "Do you know *why* the power went out?"

"Of course!" Kris's smile said *"gotcha."* "Because I don't have enough juice."

Four hours later, Slade climbed the stairs to the cheerful kitchen. Pale yellow walls, oak cabinets and several large windows made the room light and airy. If Carroll had still been sitting at the table it would have been even brighter, he concluded after a quick look around.

Instead, Christy, a miniature edition of her mother, sat there. She was bent over a cup of milk, her face hidden by a fall of silvery hair as she dipped a chocolate-chip cookie in the milk, then popped it in her mouth. When she saw him, she waved, pointed to her bulging cheeks and swallowed, wiping off her milk mustache with the tip of her tongue.

"Hi, Slade." She tilted her head and waited until he closed the basement door. "You helping Kris with the lights? He said you were going to." Pressing the tip of her finger on a crumb, she eyed it thoughtfully before swiping at it with her tongue. "He told Mom that even Santa Claus was gonna have a tough time delivering *this package.*" Unblinking blue eyes that were a genetic gift from Kris and Carroll examined him.

Her matter-of-fact tone didn't reassure Slade. Kids often said things without even a minimal understanding of the subtleties involved. At least, he thought they did. Eyeing her waiting expression, he reflected that he'd give a lot to know her position on the existence of Santa Claus. Did she still believe? And if she did, did she think Kris was on permanent loan from the North Pole?

"He really isn't Santa Claus," Christy said kindly.

Slade blinked. She not only looked like her mother, she sounded like her. "He isn't?"

"Nope." She offered him the plate of cookies and waited until he had selected one before she helped herself. Dipping it in the milk, she asked, "Did he say he was?"

He sat next to her. "Not exactly," he said cautiously.

"Sometimes he does," she confided before sucking the milk from the cookie. She seemed to enjoy the slurping sound. "He gets people all mixed up."

"But not you?" Slade downed his cookie and reached for another.

"Uh-uh." Her hair cascaded around her face in a silvery curtain when she shook her head. "Kris told me all about it a long time ago. The real Santa lives in the North Pole." While she chewed and swallowed, she looked up to make sure Slade was listening. Apparently satisfied by his fascinated gaze, she took up the tale. "Kris is his helper—probably his most important one, don't you think?"

Slade nodded.

"Anyway, wherever we live, that's where Kris works for him."

"What are his, uh, duties?"

Christy finished her milk and shrugged. "Whatever he has to do to make Christmas better. He said when we moved here he knew his job was to light up the town. He spends almost all his time downstairs making scenes for people's yards and for the park."

Slade snagged another cookie. "It'll take a miracle to do it the way he's got it set up."

"Kris says that a lot of times *people* make miracles." When Slade didn't answer, she said cheerfully, "Anyway, once all the lights are on, and the snow comes—"

"Snow?"

She nodded. "Snow."

"I didn't know it did. Snow here, I mean."

"I don't think it ever has." She slid her tongue over the milky froth on her lips. "But this year it will."

"You sure about that?"

She nodded emphatically. "Kris said so. Anyway, when it snows, Kris is going to have a huge sleigh pulled by two horses and deliver presents to everyone in town. The horses' names are Blitzen and Rudolph."

"They would be," Slade muttered. "Where do the presents come from? You're not going to tell me Kris—"

Christy shook her head again, this time impatiently. "The older people know Kris isn't Santa Claus. They're bringing the presents. But the little kids don't," she warned, "so don't tell them."

Slade raised his right hand. "I promise."

"Okay." She slid off the chair and grabbed her crutches. Slade tucked his feet safely beneath the table. When she reached the door, she turned back to look at him. "So are you?"

"Going to help him?"

She nodded, waiting. Her worried blue eyes never left his face.

"I—"

"Don't bug Slade," Carroll said briskly, appearing in the doorway. With gentle fingers, she absently smoothed her daughter's hair away from her face. "He'll do whatever he thinks is best."

"But, Mom—"

"Christy." The single word was a definite warning.

"Okay." The girl sighed and slid a gloomy look at Slade, her expression brightening only when he lowered one eyelid in a slow wink. Planting a hasty kiss on her mother's chin, she said, "I gotta go now. I told Nana I'd come up to see her."

As her daughter thumped down the hallway, Carroll said, "A word of warning. Don't encourage her. She's every bit as persistent as Kris."

Slade grinned. "Too late. She already knows she's got me wrapped around her little finger." He lifted the plate. "Cookie?"

"I'd rather have information." But she came over and took one, nibbling on it absently. "You were down there a long time."

"Yep. I was."

"Well?"

He leaned back, enjoying her impatience. "We struck a compromise."

"This ought to be good," she muttered skeptically.

"Hey, with a man like Kris, I take what I can get. He's promised to let me know when he's going to test, so I'll have time to shut down before he does any more damage. What could be fairer?"

"And in return, what does he get?"

Slade sighed in wry exasperation. "Me."

Chapter Three

The next afternoon Slade leaned back and gazed complacently at the colorful graphics on the monitor. For the first time in two weeks he looked at the image on the screen and knew that it would remain exactly where it was. Serenity, he reflected with a wry grin, was a rare and precious commodity, vastly underrated until it was gone. As if agreeing, the automatic save clicked softly and filed away the work he had done for the past fifteen minutes.

Shrugging his tight shoulders, Slade looked at his watch and realized he'd been working for five hours without a break. He didn't have to do that anymore, he reminded himself, settling deeper in the chair. Marathon sessions to cram in what he could before the aging menace next door zapped the computer were a thing of the past. Kris had promised: no more hijinks with the power. At least, not without a warning. That would do; all he needed was a running start. Even thirty seconds would give him enough time to save what he had done and turn off the machine.

With Pinetree's personal Santa finally under control, Slade reflected, maybe now he had a chance of convincing Carroll that he had more than one mood: rotten. He needed to change his image—at least as far as she was concerned. It probably wouldn't be easy.

But it would be worthwhile. Definitely. Fortunately, her daughter thought he was fine just as he was.

But when courting was a prime concern, a man needed every advantage he could get. Courting? Slade blinked thoughtfully as he mulled over the outdated word. Yes, he decided. Courting. An old-fashioned word for what he suspected was an old-fashioned woman. Home and hearth, family and loved ones, were a priority with her. It was obvious in everything she did. And after one look at her, he'd discovered that he had some very traditional values of his own.

He wanted a wife.

Not just any wife. Carroll. He wanted to be one of her priorities. Carroll. Or to be precise, Christmas Carroll Stilwell. Christy had shared that little known fact on one of her visits, adding that the name had been her grandfather's idea. He hadn't been surprised. He had also assumed that any man who would name his only child after a holiday song would flex a little muscle to carry on the seasonal tradition when his grandchild arrived. But Carroll had presumably decided that enough was enough and dug in her heels when her turn rolled around. As far as he knew, Christy was simply Christy.

Carroll. Carroll Ryan. It had a nice ring, he reflected complacently. He would get to work on it. Use some charm. That was the key. He would charm her right out of her socks. And maybe a few other things. Right. He would definitely work on it. But first... His gaze sharpened, and he leaned closer to the screen, frowning. Nope, the configuration wasn't right. He moved the cursor, his fingers speeding over the keys, modifying, realigning. A few minutes later he leaned back and reached for his calculator.

Slade was vaguely aware that outside a new din had been added to the racket of foraging birds. It began uncertainly, a brass instrument wobbling its way through the first few measures of "Taps," ending in a dissonant squawk somewhere around the ninth note. A kid with a trumpet, he decided. Practicing. He checked the calculator's digital display and groped for a pencil. Go ahead and play, kid. Hang in there. Satchmo didn't make it to the top by quitting when he hit a few sour notes.

Slade double-checked his figures. He had learned to live with noise the same way he lived with other distractions: he ignored them. Actually, he could live with anything as long as— He glanced up from the calculator and swore in a soft, savage monotone. His words were terse and distinctly Anglo-Saxon as he glared at the blank monitor. Damn it, this time the old man had gone too far!

He stalked out of the room, gathering speed as he went. By the time he reached Carroll's front's steps he had forgotten about charm and courting; his thoughts were more homicidal than romantic.

Carroll opened the door. She had something white smeared on her chin. "You thumped?" she inquired, eyeing him in resignation.

"Where is he?"

"Didn't we do this yesterday? I thought you two had agreed to a cease-fire."

"We did. He just violated the conditions," Slade told her grimly. "Where is he?"

Sighing, Carroll stepped back and waved him in. "Where else would he be?" She led the way back to the kitchen and down the basement stairs, pointing to the far end of the room where Kris was absorbed in a mass of wires that reminded her of a hoard of skinny brown snakes at feeding time. "I'm the referee and timekeeper. No hitting below the belt, and stop when someone starts bleeding." She sat on the bottom stair and watched Slade weave his way around the center platform to the end of the workbench.

"Damn it, Kris, you promised!"

Kris separated one wire from the rest and handed it to Slade. "Here, hold this." He placed the others on the workbench and studied them with a puzzled frown. "Promised what?" he finally asked.

Slade dropped the wire on the bench. "To let me know when you were going to test again!"

Preoccupied as he was, Slade's undisguised anger got through to Kris. He looked up, placid blue eyes meeting stormy gray ones. "I did. You must not have been listening."

"I have a telephone right on my desk. It didn't ring. Not once."

"Of course not," the older man agreed equably. "I didn't use the telephone."

Slade sighed sharply and shoved his hands in his pockets to keep them from curling around Kris's neck. "All right, I'll bite. How was I supposed to know?" He scowled at his bright-eyed tormentor. "I'll warn you right now that I'm not into ESP, and I don't believe in mind reading."

Kris smiled. "I couldn't agree with you more." He spun around and trotted to his desk. He turned back to Slade and held something aloft. "Here! This is what I used."

Slade squinted. "What is it?"

"My old cornet." Kris cradled the discolored horn in his arm like a baby. "I found it in the attic yesterday after you left and thought I'd give it a try. Different, huh?"

Slade was speechless.

"Haven't played it in years. Too many years." He shook his head regretfully. "People shouldn't put aside things that give them pleasure. They rush around too much these days—"

Slade took a ragged breath. "Kris—"

"Running here and there, spinning their wheels when they could be—"

"Kris!"

"—doing things like playing their old cornet." He patted the instrument and carefully set it on the workbench.

Slade stared, first at the old man, then at the horn. He had misunderstood. Obviously. Kris couldn't have said . . . "Are you telling me that you found an old horn, played "Taps" on it and expected me to know that you were going to test the lights?" he demanded.

Kris beamed. "Ha, you recognized it! I must not be as rusty as I thought. Of course that's what I'm saying. But—" he held up a pudgy index finger, then pointed at the opposite wall "—first I opened the window facing your house so you could hear me. In fact, I stood right there and blew *out* the window."

Slade glanced over his shoulder at Carroll. When she just shrugged, he turned back to meet Kris's expectant gaze. Yelling at him would be like kicking a cocker spaniel. "Couldn't you have just used the telephone?" he asked with a resigned sigh.

Kris shook his head. "Can't stand the things. All they do is make a lot of noise and interrupt busy people. I never understood what possessed Bell to come up with such a nuisance. With a little more effort, he could have managed something really good."

"I'm not asking you to conduct a lengthy conversation, for God's sake! When I answer, just say you're going to test and hang up. Is that asking too much?"

Kris stared at the ceiling and smoothed his luxuriant beard. "Why don't we compromise?" he finally suggested. "When I get through playing the cornet, you'll have a full minute. From beginning to end, that should give you about two minutes. A little longer when I get to work on 'The Flight of the Bumblebee.'"

A few minutes later, safely upstairs, Slade paced the length of the kitchen. On the return trip he demanded, "Is that what he calls a compromise? I do what he wants?"

Carroll picked up a pastry bag and squeezed gently, leaving a squiggle of frosting on a piece of waxed paper. "Don't fight it," she recommended. "I speak from experience. You're not going to change him. Take your two minutes and be grateful."

He pulled out a chair and straddled it, folding his arms across the back and staring moodily at the table. It was covered with frosted cookies cut in the shapes of bells, wreaths and trees. "Has he always been like that?"

"Like what?" Carroll murmured absently, tracing a ribbon on one of the wreaths, muttering when she smudged it.

"Stubborn as a mule. Uncaring. Unaware of what's going on around him."

Carroll looked up and regarded him thoughtfully. "Stubborn, yes. The rest, no. For years he was a political cartoonist for a large newspaper. He knows better than most what reality is like. But when he retired he decided to concentrate on what *could* be, on the nicer things in life. That's his world now, and *I'm* not going to yank him out of it."

Slade watched her meticulously add ornaments to one of the trees. "You do this for fun?" he asked with genuine curiosity.

"Good question. It might be fun if I had any of Mom's talent." She made a zigzag design on a bell. "If I had my choice, I'd be curled up on the couch with a good mystery."

"Then why—"

"Because last summer Mom donated ten dozen of these little suckers to the church holiday bazaar, and now she's involved in a painting and can't do them. So I—"

"Naturally. You."

Startled by his dry tone, Carroll looked up, her brows lifting. "You sound disapproving."

His steady gaze held hers. "I think I am."

"I hate to point this out," she said reasonably, "but you don't have the right. What I do is my own business." Oh dear, she thought inadequately. Another man who has the solution to my problems.

"Supposing I say that I want the right?"

"I'd tell you that you can't have it," she said promptly.

"Why?"

"Because I like my life just the way it is. I'm independent. I do what I want. I don't need someone around who disapproves of my family and criticizes everything I do."

"Is that what your husband did?" he asked quietly.

"Yes, and for a second you sounded just like him."

"I hate to see you being taken advantage of."

Carroll concentrated on a wreath. "Offering to do something for the people I love is a far cry from having them take advantage of me. It's my choice. *Mine.* And I'll never turn control over to another person," she vowed with sudden heat. "Never again."

"Sounds like you got burned."

"I did." Her swift glance dared him to offer sympathy.

He didn't. "How old were you when you married old what's his face?"

"Jeffrey. Nineteen."

"Just a kid."

"I didn't think so at the time, but you're right."

"And now," he gave her face an assessing glance, "you're what? Thirty? Thirty-one?"

Scowling, she snapped, "Twenty-eight."

"And you figure you haven't learned anything in the last nine years?"

"Of course I have. Plenty."

He gave a satisfied nod. "Then you know that you're a strong woman."

Carroll glared. She really did hate arguing with logical people.

"And that marriage wouldn't mean turning control of your life over to anyone else."

"Marriage?" she asked in a startled voice. "Who's talking about marriage?"

"I am."

Carroll eyed him uneasily. Trouble, that was what he was. A big, broad-shouldered bundle of it. She'd seen it all in his speculative glance that first day, and she'd wanted no part of it—or him. Of course, that had been easy to say, but the blasted man was a walking, talking temptation. He had the kind of rugged dark looks that women fantasized about, and when he wasn't sending murderous glances at Kris, he was dangerously appealing. Why, she didn't know, because she wasn't usually drawn to engineering types. Pragmatic, honest to a fault, logical and blunt, he wasn't a man one would consider especially charming. Except, of course, for his smile. It flashed at unexpected moments, totally disarming her.

Now she eyed him suspiciously, wondering what he was up to. He didn't mean anything personal, she told herself firmly. He couldn't. He was probably going to quote some statistics about second marriages. Or something. Just in case, hoping to divert him, she asked brightly, "Are you planning to get married?"

Slade's gaze didn't waver. "I hope so."

Carroll snatched up another bell and absently frosted it. "Be sure to tell us—"

"You'll be the first to know."

He didn't look like a man who had statistics on his mind, she concluded glumly, her heart skipping a beat.

Now what? Take the bull by the horns? "Slade," she began hesitantly, "I hope you're not—"

"I am. Marriage." He grinned at her stunned expression. "You. Me. Us." He picked up a tree and nibbled on it absently. "I knew the day I met you, but I thought you might need a little more time."

Carroll's fingers tightened around the bell. Her gaze slowly rose from a handful of crumbs to his intent gaze. "More time?" she echoed. "Your idea of more time is two weeks? I think you're stark, raving mad!"

Chapter Four

"'God bless us, every one.'" Christy leaned companionably against Slade's shoulder as he sat at his desk, her arm tucked through his. "What do you think? Do you like it that way? Or is this better? 'God *bless* us, every one'?"

Slade grinned. He couldn't help it. He should have been working, *had* been working, but she was collecting opinions and apparently needed his. She was so earnest. Her straight bangs framed anxious blue eyes, vividly reminding him of another pair of blue eyes that were equally concerned these days—for a far different reason.

"There're only two more," she told him. "'God bless *us*, every one,' and 'God bless us, *every one*.'"

"Why the rush to decide right now?" He ran his hand through her cornsilk hair, ending with a teasing tug. "You still have three weeks until the show, don't you?"

Christy nodded. "But we're rehearsing, and it's the very last line of the play, and since everyone in town is coming, it's gotta be a . . . a smasheroo."

"Smasheroo?"

She nodded again. "That's what Kris said. So which one do you like best?"

"What does your director say?"

Christy wrinkled her nose and heaved a gusty sigh. "She told me to experiment. So I have been, and now I'm collecting votes. Which one do you choose?"

Carroll had been right about one thing, he reflected. Christy *was* as tenacious as Kris. "They're all pretty good," he hedged, "but you missed one. How about, 'God *bless* us, *every one*'? Would that work?"

She repeated the words in a whisper, her face brightening. "Yeah!" Leaning closer, she kissed him noisily on the cheek. "Thanks. You're terrific!"

He gave her a quick, one-armed hug. "Any time. The door's always open."

Sudden doubt clouded her face. "I just remembered, Mom said I shouldn't come over here so much—that I probably bother you."

"It's nice of her to be so concerned," he said slowly, realizing with a shock just how much he would miss her unannounced visits. "You don't bother me, but she doesn't have any way of knowing that, does she? Do you suppose it would help if I told her I enjoy having you drop in?"

"I don't know. I already told her," she added in a burst of honesty, giving the floor an embarrassed poke with the tip of her crutch. "She said that Kris has already messed up your work schedule, and maybe you're too polite to tell me when you're busy."

And maybe she's running just a little scared, he concluded, narrowing his eyes. Or maybe a lot scared. Maybe what she really wanted to do was ease him out of their lives. Totally. He tugged gently at Christy's hair again, bringing her gaze back to his. "Do you think she'll feel better if I promise to tell you when I'm too busy to visit?"

She nodded, then shrugged. "I don't know."

"We'll give it a try and see how it works. If I'm in the middle of something and can't stop, I'll let you know. Agreed?" When she nodded, he held out his hand. "Let's shake on it." Once they had completed the solemn little ceremony, he smiled and said, "Be sure and tell your mother."

"Okay, but I think I'll wait a little while. She's making a gingerbread house for the bazaar, and she always gets nervous when she does that," she confided in a rush. "I'm going to stay out of the kitchen till she's done."

Outside, a cornet burst into a series of staccato squawks. Slade tilted his head, automatically reaching out to punch the save key, wondering if the agitated toots meant that Kris was beginning work on the bumblebee tune. Well, he was entitled. The day before, he had rendered a shaky but recognizable version of "Taps."

Slipping the disk into its protective sleeve, Slade grinned in anticipation. Since he couldn't work, he had an overwhelming urge to see Ms. Christmas Carroll when she was rattled. Turning to Christy, he said, "What do you say we go visit your mom?"

"The gingerbread house," she reminded him.

"Maybe I can help."

She looked doubtful, but grabbed her jacket, tucked her crutches under her arms and hopped along beside him. "I think she's worried about something," she blurted.

He glanced down at her troubled expression and slowed his pace even more. "What makes you say that?"

"Maybe it's money. That's about the only thing she gets upset about."

"Why do you think she's worried?" he repeated patiently.

"Because she's real quiet, and kinda stares at things but she doesn't really see them. She only acts like that when something's bothering her." She slanted a glance up at him. "Do you think maybe if she was married she wouldn't be upset?"

"I don't know. What do you think?" He had a strong hunch that marriage *was* a factor here. With a child's unerring instincts, Christy had zeroed in on the right problem; she just had the wrong angle.

"I think she feels bad because I don't have a daddy," she said with a self-important little jiggle and all the subtlety of a sledgehammer. "I think she'd feel better if she married someone who liked kids, don't you?" She paused thoughtfully, then said, "Especially girls. Someone big, so we could both sit in his lap. And since we all have light hair, maybe someone with dark hair. Real dark," she clarified after taking a long look at Slade's near-black hair.

"Anything else?" he asked blandly, wondering what she would do if he scooped her up and gave her a big hug.

"It would be okay if he worked at home instead of going away every day," she assured him. "Mom does that already, so we're all kinda used to it. And he shouldn't be too old. How old are you?"

"Thirty-four."

"That's a good age." She hopped a few feet on her good leg, then stopped and looked at him with a puzzled frown. "What's so funny? Why are you laughing?"

"I have a weird sense of humor. Watch out. Don't trip over that tangle of weeds."

Once inside the house, Christy opted to visit her grandmother and warned him again about going into the kitchen. He nodded and stayed where he was until she thumped her way up the stairs; then he turned and took a good look around.

The house was decorated for Christmas.

Somehow, he realized, the simple statement didn't adequately cover the situation. Candles, greenery, wall hangings and wreaths were just the beginning. Every flat surface was covered with miniature houses, carolers and snow scenes. The large coffee table had been converted into a crèche, with squads of angels and shepherds. Several snowmen looked on with interest. The floor-to-ceiling tree, almost hidden beneath an avalanche of ornaments, took up one corner of the big living room.

In the dining room he discovered more of the same. Brightly colored ornaments and candles formed a centerpiece for the table, and the walls were covered with garlands of pungent pine boughs tied back with enormous red velvet bows.

Even the kitchen had been decorated. He cast a swift glance around and decided that the brightest ornament was sitting at the table scowling at a wobbly wall on the gingerbread house.

"Who decorated the house?" he asked, pulling out a chair. "Kris?"

Carroll jumped and looked up. "I didn't hear you knock," she said pointedly.

"I came in with an escort. She warned me that you might not be in the mood for company."

"You should have listened." She squeezed a blob of frosting onto the recalcitrant wall and attempted to anchor it. "Are you trying to tell me that the decorations are a bit overdone?"

He shook his head. "Just trying to decide if it's a genetic or an environmental influence."

"Try sentimental. We just can't seem to throw any of it away. Some of the stuff is Kris's, some my mother's, some mine. Now Christy's started stockpiling things."

"Tell me about it. I think I've just been added to her collection."

"That's nice," Carroll murmured, temporarily bracing the wall with a tin canister. "There, that should hold it until it dries." She looked up and blinked thoughtfully at his satisfied grin. "You've been what?"

"You heard me." Amusement gleamed in his eyes. "She proposed."

"One of these days I'm going to have to explain to her about age differences," she muttered, wondering if her bluff would work. When his grin broadened, she knew it hadn't.

"She thinks I'm just the right age. For you."

"Oh, God."

"I didn't accept. Yet. I thought I'd better clear it with you first."

"This isn't funny, Slade. You can't encourage her when she says things like that."

"I don't think I could have stopped her. Besides, all she wants is a father."

"All? *All?*" She glared at him. "Maybe you've missed one of the links here. In order for *her* to have a *father*, *I* have to have a *husband*."

"No, I caught on to that right away."

"Good for you." She jumped up and collected a handful of dishes. Taking them over to the sink, she said, "I'm all for encouraging dreams, everyone's dreams. But not this one. Not for her, and not for me. I'm not about to put our futures on the line again. She was too young to be hurt when her father walked away—"

"You weren't," he said quietly.

Carroll stiffened. Grateful for the small task, she scrubbed the few dishes carefully. It was a reprieve. When she finished, he was still there, still waiting. She turned around, stormy blue eyes meeting understanding gray ones. "No, I wasn't too young. I've already told you that. Later, I got mad, but I was one of the walking wounded for a long time. No one will ever do that to Christy. At least, not while I'm around to stop it."

"Too much protection can turn people into emotional cripples," he commented. When she whirled around, outrage written all over her face, he held up a hand. "Wait a minute. Hear me out. I know you've been both mother and father to her, and it couldn't have been easy. You've done a wonderful job, one to be proud of, but you can't protect her from life. People go away, people die, and we all have to learn to deal with it. We can't refuse to trust and love because we're afraid that somewhere down the road we're going to be hurt. We may avoid some pain that way, but we miss out on a hell of a lot of pleasure."

Carroll slapped the dish towel on the counter, her eyes raking over him angrily. "That all sounds very philosophical, but unless you've gone through it, you don't know what you're talking about. Have you ever been hurt like that? Has anyone ever walked out on you, betrayed your trust? Made you feel like a gullible fool?" She took a deep breath and glared at him.

"Yeah."

Blinking uncertainly, she moved nearer and perched on the corner of the table. "You're kidding, right?"

"Nope. Five years ago." He gave her a level glance. "My partner walked off with our business, and my fiancée walked off with my partner."

"What did you do?"

He shrugged. "Got mad. Got bitter. Blamed them. Didn't trust a soul outside of my family. Cut off my social life and turned into a workaholic while I started over again."

"I'm sorry, Slade." Her voice was subdued. "I was mad, or I wouldn't have said that. I shouldn't have asked."

He shrugged again. "It's over and done with. Past history." He waited several moments, then shot her a swift grin. "You're not going to ask, are you?" He shook his head. "A stubborn woman. I'll tell you anyway. I recovered. Somewhere along the way, I realized that I shared some of the blame. I had been a rotten judge of character. I had known them both for a couple of years, but I didn't *know* them, if that makes any sense."

She nodded.

"I have another partner now." He pushed himself away from the table. "Lecture's over," he said briskly. "Since we can't work, how about walking into town? Maybe I'll tell you how my search for a new fiancée is going."

Chapter Five

Carroll gestured toward the towering trees. "Once the lights go on, hoards of people will be driving in to see them. You can't imagine what it's like. Cars are bumper-to-bumper, snaking up one street and down the next. The traffic gets so bad most of us don't even bother using our cars, so if you have any shopping to do, you'd better hop to it." Her voice was breathless as they followed the winding road into town. "We always stock up ahead of time, as much as we can. All the store owners love the crowds, of course, and the gas station leases a few more tow trucks, because cars overheat and have to be hauled away."

It wasn't the altitude that had her gasping for air, nor was it the exercise. She was accustomed to both. It was just that she had talked, without stopping, for the fifteen minutes it had taken to walk from the house to the center of town. Babbling was more like it, she amended silently. She had covered the weather: brisk and getting cooler every day; Kris's prediction of snow: unlikely; the town: an ideal place to raise children but not big on social life; Christy's belief in the existence of Santa Claus: teetering; and Slade's lack of holiday decorations: she had some she would loan him. Innocuous fare, admittedly, but better than the alternative. She didn't want to hear about his fiancée—past: the idiot; present: nonexistent; or future: chicken!

Carroll took a second to give herself a mental pat on the back. Her effort had been heroic, to say the least. It wasn't easy to be bright and chatty when your body was simmering with tension and—yes, damn it—a betraying sense of anticipation. If they gave medals for performance under racking circumstances, she deserved one. Maybe two.

Because Slade Ryan was nothing but pure temptation.

And she was very susceptible.

His crisp black hair was the kind that made her fingertips tingle. And for a woman who professed to be disinterested in men, she was alarmingly distracted by him. No, having Slade around for the past several weeks had proven one thing: she wasn't immune to that old devil, sex. When he was near, she almost forgot about a father who had walked away with no apparent regrets, followed by a husband who had done the same. *Almost, but not quite.*

It wasn't that she thought he was lying; Slade seemed to be an honorable man, but she hadn't known him long enough to be certain. At any rate, if he made a commitment, he seemed to be the type who would honor it. He talked about marriage, and he probably meant it. Now. But, regardless of his present intentions, he could always change his mind. People did. Not just men, she thought, being fair: *people.*

And on that fragile foundation she was supposed to build a future? Trust her own future—and her daughter's—to something so uncertain? No, thank you. Slade Ryan might be the sexiest man to come down the pike in...all right, admit it, her entire life, but sexy didn't count when the chips were down. It helped, but what really counted was staying power.

Carroll wasn't a gambler. She never hid the fact that risk-taking wasn't high on her list of priorities. She was far too practical. Too level-headed. Not very exciting qualities, she was quick to admit, but *some-body* in her family had to have them. At the age of twelve she had learned that both Kris and Noel were blithely indifferent to financial matters. If things were left to them, they would stuff bills and paychecks in an old box and expect some metaphysical happening to straighten out the ensuing mess. That was when she had studied a book about budgeting and learned to write checks and reconcile a bank account. As she remembered, Noel and Kris had given loud cries of joy, signed checks when requested, and otherwise washed their hands of the entire situation.

Good old steady, Carroll. She wasn't rash or impulsive. Her only legacy from Kris and Noel was her boundless optimism, the belief that things almost always happened for the best. Running her own business had merely emphasized the merits of planning ahead, being organized and adhering to a schedule. Dull, she thought glumly. Deadly dull. Whatever had made a man like Slade even look at her, much less propose marriage? She blinked. Well, he hadn't exactly proposed. What he'd done was casually drop the idea right in the middle of their conversation.

Whatever. The point was, dull or not, she was still tempted. And the sad part was, if she told her family what he wanted, she wouldn't get a bit of sympathy. Kris had taken to him like a long-lost son and would consider her insane for even hesitating. Noel wouldn't care one way or another, as long as Slade didn't interfere with her painting. And Christy? Her daughter considered him prime father material. She had taken one look at Slade and fallen in love.

And her own reaction? Carroll admitted that she was terrified. She had forgotten what it was like to have a man around, especially one who allowed his steamy glances to reveal just how much he wanted her. It had been a long time since her body had hummed with pleasure when a man looked at her. It was scary. It was exhilarating. And very frustrating. And now, if she said no, he would walk out of her life. Of course, if she said yes, he might do the same thing—just a bit further down the road.

Slade cleared his throat. "Hello? Are you in there?"

"Hmm?" She glanced up and flushed when she met his intrigued gaze. "Sorry. What did you say?"

"How hard do you think it will hit Kris when he realizes that all those lights aren't going to work?" he repeated patiently.

She stared at him. "They *can't* not work. He's fussed over these plans for years, ever since Christy was a baby, and he's promised that this is the year they all go on. Look over there." She waved in the direction of the park they were passing. "There are a couple of hundred trees in there, and they all have lights. Animated scenes run all the way through the place. He designed every one of them. He cut them, painted them and hooked up all the mechanical stuff in his workshop. And look at all the decorations on the homes." She shook her head. "No, the question isn't how will he take it, the question is how to make it work."

Slade swore softly. "It's not the houses that I'm concerned about. They're each capable of supporting their own lights. It's all this other stuff—the park, the trees along every road, even the streetlights! This is an old town, Carroll. When they set up shop, they weren't anticipating power demands like this. There is *no* way it can work." He didn't sound happy, but he spoke with flat assurance.

"Can't you do something?" Carroll winced at the outright pleading in her voice.

"I'm not a miracle worker," he told her with an exasperated sigh. "He'll be okay with the first batch of lights, and if he follows my advice and does some rewiring, he'll even make the second. But not the third. His plans for Christmas Eve are nothing but a dream."

Carroll couldn't think of a single thing to say except that she believed in dreams, that without them the world would be a bleak place. Since the thought was optimistic but not very helpful, she kept it to herself, aimlessly kicking her way through a pile of maple leaves while she mulled things over. At first she didn't hear the lingering whistle. It was a typical appreciative male whistle, the kind that women all over the world pretended to ignore.

"Hey, Blondie, how about a few fast games later?"

Carroll's welcoming smile faded when Slade turned his head slowly, his narrowed eyes zeroing in on three grinning young men. He took a deep breath and seemed to grow about a foot. He was angry, she realized, staring at the muscle flexing in his jaw. No, what he was was furious!

"Slade! Wait a minute," she whispered urgently, tugging at the sleeve of his jacket, stunned by his reaction. "They're friends, Slade. *Friends*. They're also just kids—homesick kids, at that. They're from Camp Pendleton." She waved in the direction of the massive U.S. Marine camp less than fifty miles away. "They were part of the gang who helped Kris put up the lights."

"What does he mean, *games*?" He didn't take his narrowed eyes off the three, who were loping toward them with the enthusiasm of half-grown pups.

"Checkers," she said hastily, still alarmed by the tension emanating from his lean frame. "After they finished with the lights, the kids all came to the house for pizza, and I played checkers with the redhead."

"The one with the big mouth?" he said grimly.

"Slade, for heaven's sake! He was only teasing. He's a nice boy. They're *all* nice," she added firmly.

"Hey, Carroll, how's Kris doing? When do we get to see these famous lights?" They drew to a halt, glanced curiously at the silent man beside her, then turned back to her, basking in the warmth of her smile.

"The first batch goes on tomorrow night." She held up her hand to stop them and said, "Slade, I want you to meet Jim, Mac and Red. Kris couldn't have managed the lights without them. Guys, this is Slade Ryan, my new neighbor."

As soon as the four men had made appropriate introductory noises, Red turned back to Carroll. "We've been talking about this—" he gestured toward a bedecked row of trees "—and we figure Kris is going to have a lot of trouble with all this stuff."

The other two chimed in.

"We're ETs at Pendleton," Jim told Slade. "Electronic technicians."

Mac shot Carroll a worried look. "We were talking to one of our instructors and telling him about the setup here. He says it's never going to work."

Noel was in the kitchen, industriously crushing graham crackers with a rolling pin, when they walked in. She was wearing narrow-legged jeans and a large paint-speckled flannel shirt, and looked almost as young as her daughter.

Slade glanced at the pyramidlike mounds of golden crumbs resting on every flat surface in the room. "Starting your own bakery?" he asked pleasantly, deciding to give it one more try. He had yet to have a conversation with Noel that actually resembled a conversation.

She looked up from her task, her unfocused gaze settling on the wall beyond him. "My log looks like a crocodile."

"You've got enough crumbs here to make a dozen tortes," he persevered, slanting a mystified look at Carroll.

"A crocodile with rigor mortis." Noel shook more crackers from the box and added them to the crumbs on the large piece of foil. She attacked them so briskly that her gray bangs bounced on her forehead and her long braid swung over her shoulder and settled between her breasts.

Slade poured himself a cup of coffee and tried again. "Christy showed me your studio the other day."

"It looks like a Florida swamp."

"It didn't look that bad," Slade soothed, pushing his chair away from the spraying crumbs. "Not nearly as bad as my place gets when I'm in the middle of a project."

Carroll made a choking sound behind him.

Noel stopped abusing the crumbs and reached for a large glass bowl. She dropped in two cubes of butter and dumped sugar into a large plastic measuring cup. When she poured it into the bowl, her eyes narrowed as the butter gradually disappeared. "Snow," she murmured thoughtfully. "That could be it." She stared down into the bowl. "Yes, that's definitely it. I'll cover the damned alligator with an avalanche." She tossed the measuring cup aside and trotted out of the room.

"Was it something I said?" Slade asked wryly, watching her disappear through the door.

Carroll gazed at the piles of crumbs and gave a faint sigh. "No, you did just fine. Unless, of course, she eventually realizes that you were comparing her room to a Florida swamp."

Slade eyed her quizzically. "She was talking about a painting?" he hazarded.

Carroll nodded, adding eggs and milk to the bowl. "Right. Every time she gets stuck, she comes down here and mashes crackers. If I'm lucky, she doesn't find a solution until the torte's in the oven."

"*Every* time?" He gave her a doubting glance.

Carroll turned off the hand mixer. "We have a skeptic in our midst," she murmured, walking over to a large cabinet and opening the door. "Come see for yourself."

Slade came to a halt behind her. "Good God." The cabinet was full. The only item in it was graham crackers, boxes of them.

Carroll chuckled. "It's cheaper than a shrink."

Her soft laughter was the sweetest sound in the whole world. He reached for her, his hands cupping her face. When he lowered his head, she tilted hers, meeting him halfway. Her lips were as sweet and eager as he'd dreamed they would be. Her breath was as ragged as his. Her sigh, and the way her body melted against his, told him more than she wanted him to know. When he reluctantly lifted his head, she made a soft, bereft sound.

"This is only the beginning for us, honey," he muttered, running his thumb gently over her full lower lip. Over the pounding of her heart, Carroll heard Christy thump through the dining room, and alarm flared in her eyes.

"Slade!" She attempted to move away and realized that she was pinned between the cupboard and Slade's hard body. "She'll see us!"

"Would that be so bad?" But he stepped back and watched her run a shaky hand through her hair.

"Yes."

"I think you might be surprised," he murmured, smiling down at her. She might straighten her hair, but she couldn't erase the look of dazed pleasure from her dark eyes. "As I said, honey, it's only the beginning."

Christy swung through the door, her intelligent blue eyes darting from her mother's tense expression to Slade's small smile. "God bless us, every one!" she whooped.

Chapter Six

"Ha! Did you hear that? What did I tell you?" Kris gleefully smacked the workbench with an open hand and looked up from the small television, where a weatherman was drawing arrows on a map of the western states. "Cold front up in Canada, and the pressure's dropping here. Know what that means?"

"It means that you're a raving optimist," Slade muttered, turning several pages in the big notebook and frowning at the figures. "Not that it's going to snow."

"We'll see." Kris snapped off the television and turned to face the younger man. "I think you ought to marry the girl."

Slade stilled. "Which girl?"

Kris snorted. "How many are you chasing? If you're looking at any other women the way you're watching my granddaughter, we got a problem." He waited. "If you don't know how to ask her, I've got a couple of foolproof suggestions."

"No thanks." Slade met the old man's expectant gaze. "Somehow you'd manage to turn things into a three-ring circus."

"You don't seem to be getting anywhere," Kris grumbled. "Christy needs some brothers and sisters, and I need some more kids around the house. We could call one Holly, one Ivy and one Harold."

"Harold? Why would anyone name a boy—" He stopped, trying to consider Kris's unique point of view. "As in, 'Hark, the...'?" he asked suspiciously. When Kris nodded, he said emphatically, "No way. No kid of mine is—"

"It's not a name I'd choose myself," Kris agreed, "but it was the only one I could think of for a boy off the top of my head." His face brightened and he snapped his fingers. "There's always Rudolph."

Slade groaned.

"Of course, if you haven't even gotten around to asking her yet, I don't know why you're so concerned. It seems to me that you're jumping the gun just a bit."

Slade sighed resignedly. "I've asked her."

"And?"

"She'll marry me."

"Did she say so?"

"No. But she will. When the time is right."

"Right?" He paced back and forth in front of Slade impatiently. "What's to be right? You ask, she says yes, and you get to work on little Holly and Ivy. And Harold. Or Rudolph. Maybe I should talk to her."

"No."

Kris pursed his lips at the unequivocal word. "No?"

"Butt out, Kris. We'll handle this ourselves." Shooting him a narrow-eyed glance, Slade said, "I mean it. If I hear that you've said one word to her about this, I'll come down here with some snippers and make this the darkest Christmas you've ever had."

Kris ignored the threat. "Speaking of lights, what are we going to do on Christmas Eve? Are you working on it? Time's passing, boy."

Slade slammed the notebook shut and surged to his feet. "I don't know what we're going to do. You don't have a magic wand to wave over the town, and neither do I." He hesitated. "Maybe you're just going to have to settle for the lights you're turning on tomorrow."

Patting him on the shoulder, Kris said, "Don't worry about it, boy. I know you'll do it. And while you're taking care of that, I'm getting the rest organized. When the play is over and everyone comes out of the community building—the one in the park, you know—the rest of the lights will go on, and I'll come riding through the snow in the sleigh." He rubbed his hands in anticipation. "Then we'll deliver the presents and get done in plenty of time for the potluck supper and candlelight service at church. Which reminds me, I'll have to get Carroll to run a notice off on the computer and let everyone know the schedule."

"Why don't you just play 'Taps' and let them guess?" Slade asked, heading for the stairs.

Kris gave a gentle cough. "By the way, I did say *we'll* be delivering the gifts. Do you want to wear an elf costume and help me on the sleigh?"

Carroll tied a red ribbon around the last plastic-wrapped torte, listening to the rumble of the men's voices in the basement. Apparently operating on the theory that it was better to join 'em when you couldn't beat 'em, Slade was no longer trying to work during the two afternoon hours. The decision hadn't come easily, she remembered, grinning faintly. After three more incidents with lost design parts—two where he had been in a distant part of the house and couldn't get back in time, and once when his concentration had been so intense he simply hadn't heard the cornet—he had surrendered, claiming that it was either that or throttle Kris.

Life was getting complicated, she decided, her smile fading as she stared at the lopsided ribbon. Now he spent that time at her house, ostensibly conferring with Kris, but somehow ending up with her. And driving her crazy. He hovered, he stood too close, he sat too close, he smiled at her, his *eyes* smiled at her, for heaven's sake! And he watched her, and waited.

It wasn't as if he were bombarding her with proposals, she reflected, tugging at the bow. No, his approach was more subtle than she had anticipated, like that of a man attempting to tame a wild animal. He touched her, lightly, as he passed, allowing the gesture to be a hair more than fleeting, but not allowing it to threaten. When he *was* too close, he stretched the time just a smidgen beyond her comfort zone, then moved.

Subtle, yes. And it was working.

That and the memory of his kiss. Their kiss. She took a deep breath and let it out slowly. Slade had made certain that she wouldn't mistake it for a platonic, neighborly, holiday greeting. He had also brought back unsettling memories.

She had almost forgotten how it felt to have a man's strong arms wrap around her, pulling her close. Almost forgotten the convulsive movement and hardening of his body. The ache, the languid melting, of her own. The ragged breathlessness. The heat, blood racing through her veins like a runaway train. Without a single word, he had reminded her of what it meant to be a woman. Not just a mother or a daughter. A *woman*.

She didn't welcome the memory. As a matter of fact, she had kept her life relatively uncomplicated and contented because she *had* managed to forget. Almost. The worst part was that he had brought an entirely new element into the situation. A hunger, a need to touch and be touched, that she had never felt before. Not with poor Jeffrey, not with the few innocuous dates she had allowed herself since he had left.

No, she wasn't happy with Slade Ryan. He could sell his house; he could move anywhere in the world. But she had a daughter to raise, one who was becoming far too attached to him. One who would be broken-hearted if he left. *When* he left. One who, since she had only one parent, needed an extra dose of stability in her life.

"Hi."

Carroll jumped. "You ought to borrow Kris's horn and announce yourself," she said crossly.

Slade leaned comfortably against the counter. "What are you going to do with them?" He nodded at the dozen tortes, wrapped and lined up on the table.

"Take them down to Lindy's boutique. She has a standing order for them."

"She must be ecstatic when Noel hits a real snag."

"Umm." She disappeared into the pantry and came out dragging a large cardboard box. "But she does her best to conccal it."

"Here, let me help." Slade swung the box up on the table.

"I'll pack," Carroll said, sliding in several tortes and adjusting some heavy cardboard shelving above them. "You can haul the box out to the station wagon."

"Grab a coat," he suggested a few minutes later, hefting the box. "It's getting cold."

Carroll buttoned her jacket as she walked down the steps behind Slade. He handled the large carton as if it were no larger than a shoebox, she noted enviously. When he slid in on the passenger side, her brows rose. A man who didn't mind being driven by a woman. Nice.

She settled behind the wheel, squinting up at the leaden sky. "Do you think it's just possible that Kris might be right? Could we really get snow?"

Slade groaned. "Don't even think it. He'd be impossible to live with. He's already bad enough."

Sliding a quick glance in his direction, she asked, "What's he up to now?"

"Aside from wanting me to wear an elf costume and help deliver presents?"

She chuckled. "You can wiggle out of that one. Christy and I are already signed up as Santa's helpers. We can get the job done."

Suddenly the idea didn't sound so bad. They could probably use some help with the heavy packages, he mused. He wondered idly what an elf costume looked like.

"We came at a good time," she told him. "The traffic doesn't get bad until the lights go on."

The lights. Always the lights. Slade leaned back in the seat, taking note of all the lights that weren't connected to someone's house. They were on more trees than he could count, running up and down street-lights, wrapped around trash cans and along the backs of park benches. Probably the only reason they weren't strung around mailboxes was due to a federal ordinance prohibiting such shenanigans.

"Here we are, and there's a parking place right in front," Carroll announced with satisfaction. "You get the box and I'll open the door."

Lindy, a slim woman with graying hair and a broad smile, beat her to the door. "Hi. Come in. You're an answer to my prayers." She stepped aside to let Slade in and waved him to the counter. "Thank God it's a big box. However many you have, I can use even more. Believe it or not, I've got a waiting list for these babies."

Carroll closed the door, stepping past a rocking horse, several homemade dolls and a baby carriage. Two of Noel's landscapes hung on the opposite wall, both marked with Sold signs. Lindy not only carried exquisite gifts, she was an outlet for the local artists and craftsmen. "At least your customers aren't standing outside pounding on the window. You've got them well trained."

Lindy opened the box with eager hands. Looking up at Carroll, she laughed softly. "I can't afford to lose any customers, and I was afraid that if they hung around here, Kris would have lights strung on them. I told them I'd call when I had the cakes in my hot little hands."

She turned to Slade and measured him with a frankly assessing gaze. Giving an approving nod, she held out her hand for a businesslike shake. "I'm Lindy Miller. No, you don't have to tell me who you are.

Slade Ryan, right? You're helping Kris with the lights. He tells us you're going to get the lights turned on for Christmas Eve. We've been waiting for this for years.'' She took the rest of the cakes from the box and turned to Carroll. ''I understand the chamber of commerce is trying to get some local TV coverage for the big event.''

''TV?'' Carroll asked faintly, turning to Slade. He looked as stunned as she sounded.

''Are you sure about that?'' he asked.

Lindy's nod was definite. ''Tom, my husband, is the treasurer. He told me that Kris came to their meeting last Tuesday and said everything was arranged. The play will end at five, we'll all go outside in the park, the lights will go on, and all the animated scenes will start up.''

She gave them a droll look. ''Kris has ordered snow, so it *will* be snowing. He'll come out with Anderson's hay wagon decorated like a sleigh—pulled by Blitzen and Rudolph, of course—and hand out the presents. That's the part they thought a news program might be interested in.''

She paused to count the cakes and write a receipt for Carroll. ''By the way, the chamber invited all the marines who helped with the lights up for the festivities. Those who can't get home are coming. Yesterday Tom and I spent some of the chamber's money and bought gifts for them. Naturally they're all invited to the potluck supper.''

''Naturally,'' Carroll echoed, darting a glance at Slade's expressionless face.

''We'll get all their names to you before Christmas Eve,'' Lindy added.

"Fine."

The heavy silence in the car was finally broken by Slade, just as they pulled into the driveway. "TV? Did you know about this?"

Carroll slammed on the brakes and snapped off the ignition. "No, I didn't." Turning to him furiously, she said, "Do you really think I'd let you walk into a situation like that without any warning? What kind of a person do you think I am?"

"Loyal. To your family."

"You're right," she admitted, curling her fingers around the steering wheel. "I am. But I also have a sense of fair play. I would have told you."

"Sorry." He reached across and brushed his thumb over her knuckles. "I should have known."

In silence she turned her palm up, lacing her fingers through his. "What are you going to do?" she finally asked.

In a voice heavy with defeat, he said, "I don't know. I haven't been able to convince Kris that he's asking the impossible any more than I've been able to convince you that I won't desert you the first time you turn your back."

Chapter Seven

I won't desert you.

It was a little after three in the morning when Carroll admitted the obvious: sleep was a lost cause. She tossed back the blankets, shrugged into a warm robe and quietly went down to the kitchen. A few minutes later she carried a cup of tea into the dark living room, curled up in the corner of the sofa and covered herself with a woolly afghan. From where she sat, she could see light streaming out of Slade's office windows.

I won't desert you.

He was still working. An anxious frown drew her brows together. He didn't take care of himself, she fretted. Guilt etched the furrows even deeper between her brows. If it weren't for Kris and the two lost hours each day, Slade probably wouldn't still be at the computer. But for all she knew, Carroll thought hopefully, he was a workaholic who simply preferred toiling twenty hours out of every twenty-four.

Gloom settled again. More than likely he *had* to be there. When he had moved to Pinetree, Slade had undoubtedly expected to be isolated, to produce quantities of work. A mountain cabin had probably seemed an ideal location. Then Kris had appeared and blown not just holes, but craters, in his schedule.

I won't desert you.

Carroll concentrated fiercely on her train of thought. Slade. Work. Schedule. Kris. Slade wasn't given to sulking or complaining. He also didn't talk much about his work. She realized with a mild sense of surprise that she hadn't the foggiest idea what he was doing over there. Oh, he answered direct questions and murmured something about radar; she had even seen the colorful graphics on his monitor, but they meant less than nothing to her. She would ask him after the holidays, she decided, sipping her tea.

So Slade would neither complain nor sulk. What *would* he do? Exactly what he *was* doing. Work every minute that he could. He would make his deadline come hell or high water. Whatever it took, he would do. And in his spare time—such as it was—he would fret about the problem that Kris had created.

I won't desert you.

She tossed aside the afghan and jumped to her feet, admitting that she had stalled as long as she could. *All right!* He wouldn't desert her. So he said. And he undoubtedly meant it. For now. But so had Jeffrey.

Jeffrey.

Okay, admit it, Carroll. At least to yourself. Say it just once. Jeffrey had been no more mature at twenty-two than she had been at nineteen. He'd had no more grasp of the depth of the vows he had taken than she had. They had thought they were in love. And they had been—with love, not each other.

Reality had been living in a tiny apartment that they couldn't afford, having no marketable job skills and learning that she was pregnant the third month of their marriage. Even so, reality had barely dented her optimistic outlook. "Things will work out," she had said. Repeatedly. But reality had presented a different face to Jeff, one that he found frightening. He didn't wait for things to work out. He left when she was seven months into her pregnancy; he had never seen his baby. He had never called or written to ask about her. Carroll divorced him and gave Christy her maiden name, and now there was no remnant of Jeff in her life—except for memories.

But Jeff wasn't the villain of the piece, Carroll reflected. There was no villain. He had been weak, and they had both been very young. But still, something good had come from the situation: Christy.

Carroll stared out the window at the lights slashing into the darkness around Slade's house, remembering. Something else had happened. She had grown up. She had managed to return to school and get a good grounding in secretarial work and business administration. It hadn't been easy, but with the help of Kris and Noel it had been possible. Running her own business had been her goal, and had become her achievement for the past four years.

Her life was predictable, secure, just the way she wanted it to be. She was independent and in control, also just the way she wanted to be. And she was happy. Carroll took one last lingering look out the window and turned away. She *was* happy.

Upstairs, she crawled into bed and pulled the covers up to her ears, trying to ignore the haunting refrain that had made it impossible to sleep.

I won't desert you.

Late the next afternoon, Carroll decided to brave the evening traffic so she could drive Christy into town. They wanted to be in the park when Kris turned on the first bank of lights. It was a long-standing tradition on their part, one that not even a cast and crutches could prevent.

"Will we eat at Barney's?" Christy asked.

"Don't we always?"

"Can I get a hamburger and a malt?"

"Don't you always?"

"Then we'll walk over to the park?"

Carroll nodded. "Yep."

"Then we'll walk all through the park and look at all the scenes?"

"Um-hmm."

"The lights only stayed on a couple of seconds last year," Christy pointed out. "There wasn't much to see."

"True. We're hoping that won't happen this year."

"Then we'll go visit all the stores?"

"Every one of them. Do you have your shopping list and your money?"

Christy patted the front pocket of her jeans. "Right here."

"Good. Now all we have to do is figure out how to keep your toes warm."

"I think I've got that covered." Slade leaned against the doorjamb holding two large socks.

"Slade!" Christy turned around and beamed at him, doing a little jig, one crutch just grazing her mother's toes. "Everything's just like I told you. We're going to eat at Barney's, then go to the park, then go shopping. Aren't you glad you decided to come?"

"Very, squirt." He motioned for her to sit on the large upholstered chair and went down on one knee. Working a thermal sock over her toes and the surrounding cast, he said, "But it's your mother's party, and maybe she'd rather just go with you."

"Oh, no, she wouldn't! Would you, Mom?"

Looking from imploring blue eyes to provoking gray ones, Carroll gave up. She knew a lost cause when she saw one. "The more the merrier," she said dryly.

"Thank you." He nodded in her direction. "Dinner's on me tonight."

Christy bounced in the chair. "Great! Can I have a hot fudge sundae?"

He pulled the sock up as far as it would go, then began working a wool one over it. "You may have whatever your mother allows you to have," he told her.

"I was thinking of ordering you a vegetarian plate," Carroll warned, pulling coats, scarves, hats and gloves from the closet. "All *green* veggies."

Christy grinned. "They don't really have stuff like that at Barney's," she assured Slade.

They used the station wagon, so Christy would have room to stretch out her leg. For once Carroll was grateful for her daughter's nonstop chatter. She identified every house for Slade, telling him the names of the owners and all their children, describing pets when they existed.

It would have been an awkward ride without her, Carroll admitted, because Slade's words still hung heavily between them. At least, as far as she was concerned, they did. She didn't know what to say to him. Obviously something needed to be said, but just as obviously, now was not the time. Not with Christy along.

"We're in luck," Christy said to Slade as her mother pulled into a small lot by the park. "The tourists only get out of their cars to visit the stores. Then they get back in and drive around to look at the lights. They don't know that the best place to be is in the park."

"That's right," Carroll agreed. "And we don't tell them. Come on, we'd better get a move on if we're going to eat before Kris turns on the lights."

Eating at Barney's was a bit like inviting all the neighbors in for dinner, Slade decided. Almost everyone in the place was a local, and almost all of them had something to say about the Christmas display.

Lindy from the boutique stopped at their booth with a tall, slim graying man who pumped Slade's hand. "Hi, I'm Tom Miller. Lindy tells me you're the man who's helping Kris with the lights. Can't tell you how long we've been waiting for this. We all thought they were going to come on last year, and they did— for about five seconds." He shook his head. "Then we had a power failure to end them all, and we lost most of our regular lights for about an hour. Sure hope you two have it figured out this time. Did Lindy tell you about the TV coverage?"

Slade nodded. "I wish I could say that things are going to be—"

"Mr. Ryan?" An elderly woman with blue tinted hair eased in beside the Millers and gently nudged them on their way. "I'm Matilda Gateway, president of the Woman's League, and I want to express my appreciation for your efforts on our behalf. No, don't try to get up, please. It's impossible in a booth. We are all most grateful to you. Kris says your help has been invaluable. We've waited for this Christmas Eve celebration for years, and now, finally, we will have it. Imagine, it's just two weeks away!''

That was only the beginning. Slade's food grew cold as one person after another stopped by the booth with assurances that they were looking forward to the festivities on Christmas Eve.

Carroll touched his hand, wincing as it clenched into a fist. ''Slade, I'm so sorry,'' she whispered miserably while Christy was waving to a friend. ''I had no idea it would be like this.''

His eyes narrowed. ''Kris hasn't told a soul that there's a problem with the rest of the lights, has he? Are you finished?'' he asked abruptly, looking at his watch. ''We should probably start walking. At least we know *these* lights are coming on.''

Anticipation was in the air. People streamed into the park, calling greetings and stamping their feet to keep warm. Most of them were hopeful, but as one man pointed out, they had felt the same way the past year and the ones before that. As the hour approached, silence fell.

There was a collective gasp as the lights went on, spontaneous applause as the animated scenes began to bob, teeter and whirl. It was spectacular, Slade admitted. He was impressed. So was the crowd.

There was no doubt about it; Kris had done an impressive job. Everyone in the park said so. They told Slade and Carroll and Kris himself, when he strolled grandly down the avenue. Kris beamed and promised a grand finale on Christmas Eve.

Slade stared at him impassively and muttered to Carroll, "I can't take any more of this. Let's get out of here." They wound their way through the park, Christy tucked protectively between them, heading for the stores.

"Mom, look over there!" Christy pointed. "There's Mac and Red and all the other guys. I bet they came up just to see the lights tonight. Hey, Mac!" She waved and picked up speed.

The marines, eleven of them, turned at her call, then swept forward, surrounding them. Mac grinned down at Christy. "After all our work, we had to come and see what it looked like."

"Are you coming up for Christmas Eve?" Carroll asked.

He nodded. "None of us have enough time to get home, so we'll all be here."

"We'll look forward to seeing you," Carroll told him as they all turned in the direction of the shops. "Remember, you're invited for dinner."

As they strolled down the illuminated walk, Mac dropped behind with Slade. In a troubled voice, he said, "I don't see how the old man can add another fifty per cent to all this." He gestured at the brilliant display.

"He can't."

The two men exchanged glances.

"He's really setting himself up for a fall."

"A big one," Slade agreed. "And to make matters worse, they're talking about getting TV coverage for the big event."

Mac stared at him. "You're kidding."

"I wish I was."

"Can't you stop it?"

Slade shrugged. "Not me. I'm new around here. This thing is like a snowball rolling downhill, getting bigger and faster with every turn. Kris wants more lights." He gestured to the people around them. "They want more lights. The whole town wants more lights. So in two weeks they're going to have TV cameras on hand to record the biggest fizzle in history."

"So what are you going to do?"

Slade swore. "What am *I* going to do? Nothing. Kris asked me for advice, and I gave it. I told him it was impossible."

"Then what happened?" Mac finally asked.

"He didn't believe me. He said we'd just have to find a way to *make* it work. *I* would have to find a way to make it work."

"Oh, jeez."

"Exactly."

Carroll looked at the sleeping girl in Slade's arms. "Thanks for carrying her up. I never would have made it."

"My pleasure." And it was. His arms tightened reflexively around Christy before he bent down and placed her on the bed. "Want me to make some coffee while you tuck her in?"

Downstairs, as he measured the coffee, he thought of Carroll's wary glance and resigned nod. She looked about as thrilled as someone leaning against a stone wall, waiting for the firing squad to appear. Watching the thin stream of coffee trickle into the glass pot, Slade wondered how it would feel to have her face light up when he walked into a room, to share with the rest of her family the soft look of joy that deepened the blue of her eyes.

He leaned against the counter and forced himself to relax. He would know. Sooner or later, he would know.

Chapter Eight

"Why so grim?" Carroll stood in the doorway, an inquiring expression on her face. "Something happen to the coffeepot?"

He moved aside and gestured. "It's fine. I was just thinking."

"About Kris and the lights? I'm sorry he got you involved in all this." She took two mugs out of the cupboard, and reached for the powdered cream.

"Forget the lights. Forget Kris."

Carroll's hands stilled, and he could see tension in the set of her slim shoulders. "Then what—"

"Us. You and me. Slade and Carroll."

Apprehension and relief mingled somewhere deep within her. Finally. No more waiting for the other shoe to fall. No more pretending. Now they could talk it out and put it behind them.

She chose her words carefully, the ones she had rehearsed in the dark of the night. She kept her voice firm. Friendly. Kind. "Us? You make it sound as if we're a couple. We're not. There's a Slade Ryan who lives over there—" she pointed in the direction of his house "—and a Carroll Stilwell who lives here with her family. Two separate people, Slade. Neighbors, but that's all. Please don't read any more into it than there is."

"That's all?" He flashed a smile that was a distinct challenge. "Friends? Maybe not even that, if what you say is true. Acquaintances?"

She sighed, eyeing his smile warily. It made her think of a cat about to pounce. She didn't trust him. Not at all. She might have known he wouldn't make this easy. "Friends," she murmured. "Definitely friends."

He shook his head. "No."

"No?" Her breath caught somewhere deep in her lungs.

"Uh-uh." He lounged against the counter and extended his hand. "Come here and I'll prove it."

Carroll watched the strong hand as if it were a snake. She might have known he would have something up his sleeve! In his own quiet way, Slade was just as devious as Kris. "No. I don't need proof." She snatched up the mugs, filled them and handed him one.

Calmly, he put it on the counter and held out his hand again. "All you have to do is take my hand."

"That's all?"

He grinned at her skeptical tone. "No."

"Then what?" It was like pulling teeth to get anything out of him.

"Kiss me. And then tell me we're only neighbors."

Carroll tried to add cream to her coffee and realized that her hand was shaking. Kiss him? She might as well rent a billboard advertising the fact that he was driving her crazy. She shook her head and cleared her throat. "I don't see what that would prove."

"I think you do. I think that's why you're so nervous."

"I'm not nervous!" she said stoically, then dropped the spoon and sprayed coffee all over the sink. Closing her eyes for a moment, she took a calming breath. "No." Her voice was definite. "I don't believe in playing games to solve problems."

He kept his hand where it was, waiting for hers. "It's no game, honey. This is real life. If you can kiss me and tell me it means nothing to you, I'll go away and leave you alone."

He wasn't going to move, she realized, knowing it with sudden certainty. He would stay right there, in his own stubborn way, holding out his hand until she proved that he was wrong. Once she did, he would go. Ignoring the feeling of loss that washed over her, she told herself briskly that it would be for the best.

And what would it take? Three seconds? Five? Ten or fifteen, at the most. Fifteen seconds compared to hours of silent pressure? To a life turned upside down? As far as she was concerned, there was no contest. She could do anything for fifteen seconds—hold her breath, stand on her head, anything. Even kiss Slade and convince him that she didn't feel a thing.

Slade knew from the tilt of her chin that he had won. The first round, at least. She would come to him and try to make her body lie, but it wouldn't. Because it couldn't. He knew that from their first kiss.

"All right." Carroll turned to face him, looking like a martyr being led to the lions. She stepped forward, clearly intending to give him a swift peck on the lips, faltering only when his hand reached out to grasp hers.

He stayed where he was, leaning against the counter, and brought her to him slowly, letting her feel his hunger. He slid his hands into the back pockets of her jeans and urged her closer. She was soft and warm and smelled of summer flowers.

The instant he touched her, Carroll knew she had made a mistake. She was tucked in the cradle of his parted legs, her body off balance and lying along his. He was hard and hot, and obviously not in a hurry. Her head rested in the hollow of his shoulder, and his big hands smoothed down her back and settled on her buttocks, pressing her closer.

"Slade—"

"Shh."

"This isn't—"

"Yes, it is."

His voice was deep, rumbling against her ear. The tip of her nose touched his neck, and he smelled of something spicy and clean and very male.

Her arms slid around him and she arched closer when his lips touched her earlobe. Shivering, she uttered a soft, throaty whimper. "No."

He chuckled. "Umm."

"I don't want this."

"You've got it."

"It's too complicated."

"We'll make it simple."

When he lowered his head, her mouth met his, willing and oh so sweet, tasting like honey. And her body didn't lie. It melted into his like sunshine, gifting him with her own special brand of warmth.

When his fingertips skimmed her hair, she sighed. He was a big man who knew how to be gentle. Quiet and intense, Slade was a man who touched emotions in her she hadn't even known she had, made her blood roar like a freight train and sparkle like wine. Slade was a man who—

Startled, she dropped her hands to his chest and pushed. He lifted his head and slowly, reluctantly, let her go. She stepped back and took a deep breath, finishing her last thought. Slade was a man who would be big trouble in her life.

Gray eyes gleamed down at her. "Well, what's the verdict? Friend, acquaintance, significant other—or husband material?"

"Don't be cute," she said coolly.

He waited.

"All right! So I was wrong."

"Ah."

"In a way."

"What way?"

"We're more than neighbors."

He smiled.

"But that's as far as it goes."

He waited again.

"I told you before. I like my life just the way it is. Peaceful, uncomplicated—"

"Dull?"

"Maybe." She stared at him. "But that's the way I like it. Darn it, Slade, we're no good for each other."

"Translated, that means I'm no good for you." He folded his arms across his chest, his level gaze a challenge.

She didn't flinch. "Exactly."

"How do you know?"

"I don't," she admitted. "Not for sure. But I'm not going to take the risk. Go back to your work, Slade. Help Kris, if that's what you want to do, but leave me alone."

He reached out and brushed her cheek with the back of his hand. "I'm going to be around for a long time. You might as well get used to me."

Chapter Nine

Slade left Carroll standing in the middle of the kitchen and walked across the pine-studded ground to his house. He looked up at the black sky and counted the few stars visible between the scudding clouds, then buttoned his shearling jacket. After opening the door and walking straight through to the office, he dropped into his chair and stared at the blank computer screen.

He didn't know if forcing a confrontation had been the worst idea he'd ever had, or the best. And if Carroll's stunned expression was any indication, he might not find out for quite some time. She hadn't looked like she was in the mood to make any rash decisions. Which was precisely as it should be, he reflected grimly. This was something she had to decide for herself. Because as much as he loved her, ached for her, there was one thing he couldn't do for her.

He couldn't give her trust.

And nothing would work for them without it. Especially not marriage. They both knew that. She believed that most men were as faithless as her father and that blockhead Jeffrey, and there wasn't a thing he could do to change her mind. He couldn't force her to believe in him. He didn't want her to marry him, then wake up each morning and look at him with eyes that wondered if he would be gone before nightfall. He shuddered. No, he could handle a lot, but not that.

Determination narrowed his eyes. Carroll didn't know it, but she needed him as much as he needed her. She needed to know that a man could love her the way he did, that he would still be around when the time came to celebrate their fiftieth anniversary. Somehow, he would convince her. He would give her a little more time if that was what she needed. Or if she needed prodding, he would prod.

Absently, he turned on the computer and reached for the disk. Once he finished the design and delivered it to his partner to begin the bidding process, then figured out what to do about Kris, he would have all the time in the world.

Kris. The old man was as much trouble as his granddaughter. More. Now he even had the U.S. Marines worrying about him. Slade leaned back and stared blankly at the toes of his shoes. The U.S. Marines. Interesting.

The screen suddenly came alive with colorful graphics. Slade ignored them, following the tenuous trail of what had to be the craziest idea he'd ever had.

The U.S. Marines?

Early the next morning, long before the rest of the family was stirring, Carroll took her cup of tea into the living room and stared out the window. That she happened to be looking in the direction of Slade's house was sheer coincidence, she told herself. It had nothing at all to do with the man himself. She always watched the sun spread its golden blanket over the hills beyond his place. The fact that there was no sun this morning, that the sky was a sullen gray, also had nothing to do with anything.

Habit. That was all it was. She certainly wasn't camped here by the window to catch a glimpse of one of the world's most aggravating men. Anyway, he was probably already at work. That was where he spent most of his time—in front of his computer. Well, after last night's little trick, that was fine with her. He could sit there until he turned green from radiation.

She took another sip of tea, frowning. No, that wasn't fair. He didn't spend every waking hour at the computer—her daughter and her father had seen to that. Each of them had infringed on large chunks of his time. And, she admitted grudgingly, he had given them more than they had asked for. Especially Kris.

Her gaze sharpened, and she leaned closer to the window. Slade's pickup truck was gone. He kept his precious Mercedes in the garage, but his pickup was always in the carport. Except for now.

Telling herself that she wasn't a bit curious, that she was only going out to get the morning paper, she set aside her cup and went to the front door. Before she opened it, she saw the note.

It was taped to one of the small glass panes in the door. Black ink, written in an aggressive scrawl, her name on the front.

Carroll, I have to go to town. Be back as soon as possible. I love you. Don't worry.

Her heart gave a little leap, which she tried to ignore. Instead, she concentrated on the last two words. Worry? Why should she worry? Men always claimed the right to come and go. Mostly go. That was fine with her. If he came back, he came back. If he didn't, what else was new?

Eight days later, Christy poked her head through Carroll's office door. "Mom?"

"Hmm?"

"Have you heard from Slade?"

Carroll shook her head. "Not yet."

"Where do you suppose he is?" Christy leaned against Carroll and gave a forlorn sigh.

"Honey, he has a job, remember? He'll be back." *Maybe.*

"When?"

"I don't know."

"The play's in six days."

Carroll gave her a swift hug. "He knows that."

Four days later, Kris sat perched on the corner of her desk. "What have you heard from Slade?"

"Nothing. Why?"

He gave an elaborate shrug. "No reason."

"Come on, Kris."

He shrugged again. "The day after tomorrow is Christmas Eve, and he's going to take care of the lights."

Carroll's sigh was slightly ragged. "I don't know what to say."

Kris patted her shoulder and bounced to his feet. "Too bad he missed the second batch, but he'll be back in plenty of time," he assured her.

"Sure." *If we're lucky.*

"Mom!" Christy bounced into the office, her face flushed with excitement. "Look what they just brought from Patty's flower shop!" She held a white box in either hand. "This one's yours." Her blue eyes snapped with excitement. "And this one's for me."

Carroll held her box with fingers that shook. "You first," she said, smiling as Christy tore open the lid.

"Oh, look! Isn't it gorgeous?" She lifted a small corsage with a crimson tulip decorated as a bell. "There's a card, too." She lifted a glowing face. "It's from Slade, 'for the star of the show tomorrow night.'"

Carroll opened her box and stared down at a delicate white orchid. The card said simply *Save me a seat*.

That was all it said, but it meant so much more. And she knew—no, she believed—that he meant every word.

She handed the box to Christy and said urgently, "Honey, put these in the fridge. I have to run into town for a minute."

Christy's eyes grew even brighter. "For more presents?"

Carroll nodded, grinning. "This one's for Slade."

The morning of Christmas Eve, Carroll held her cup of tea and looked out at the empty carport. Robe-clad and yawning, Kris and Christy shuffled in, heading straight for the window. They both turned at the same time, alarm widening their eyes.

"He isn't here," they said in unison.

This time there was no hesitation, no qualification.

"He will be," she said in a serene voice.

Later that morning, Kris received a telephone call. It was a measure of his concern that he answered without complaint. Two minutes later he charged out of the house, calling that he would see them at the play.

Later still, when Carroll drove Christy into town and parked by the playhouse, they saw that the marines had landed. Mac, Red and the rest of them, under Kris's supervision, were doing something with the lights.

Carroll hugged Christy. "Good luck, darling."

"Mother! You're supposed to tell me to break a leg."

"I'm afraid to." She tapped the cast with a grin. "You'll be wonderful." She hurried away to join the audience.

The show was just beginning when Slade eased into the seat beside her and reached for her hand. She felt the tension emanating from him and asked, "Is everything all right?"

"Keep your fingers crossed," he whispered, then settled back with a satisfied grin. He did ask one question during intermission. "What is Christy's legal name?"

A peculiar expression crossed Carroll's face. "Why?"

"Just wondering. A point of reference, you might say."

"She made me promise not to tell anyone."

"I'll take a vow of silence if I have to. Just tell me."

She swallowed. "Christmas Stilwell."

Slade's eyes closed briefly, and he muttered, "I might have known."

Thirty minutes later, with the sound of Christy's, *"God bless us, everyone!"* still ringing in the room,

Slade jumped to his feet and led the enthusiastic applause.

As the audience straggled outside, they went backstage to collect Christy. Beside herself with excitement, she hugged Slade and announced, "I'm going to be an actress."

"You already are." He rumpled her hair. "A good one, at that." Glancing swiftly at his watch, he said, "Come on, we've got to get outside."

"Slade?" She looked at him anxiously. "Are the lights going to go on for Kris?"

He squeezed her hand. "I don't know," he said honestly. "But you know Kris. He believes in miracles. Anything can happen."

"He believes in *people*," Christy said firmly, clutching his hand.

When they joined the crowd outside, Carroll winced. "Oh no. Look over there."

Slade's gaze followed hers, settling on a man wielding a minicam and a woman with a microphone talking to Tom Miller. "So they got their TV coverage. Let's hope it's worth their trip up here." He swung Christy up in his arms so she could get a better view.

The crowd looked at the digital clock on the bank across the street and began a soft countdown. *"Ten, nine, eight..."*

"Slade," Carroll began, then stopped when he draped his arm around her shoulders and tugged her closer. "Thank you for the flowers."

"Five, four, three..."

He looked down and smiled.

"Two, one!"

Tears stung Carroll's eyes as a glorious profusion of color flowered to life around them. Lights glistened and glowed, illuminating the entire town. They came on, and they stayed on.

Christy turned an awed face to Slade. "I bet we could light up the whole world."

He groaned and tightened his arm around her. "Don't mention that to Kris. Please."

Carroll nudged him. "How did you do it?"

Shaking his head, he said simply, "I didn't. We can thank the U.S. Marines."

Her brows rose. "Oh?"

"I told them the problem, and they decided they could use a little positive PR. They donated the use of a diesel generator, and the boys volunteered to do some rewiring." He smiled complacently and nodded toward the minicam. "Tom should be telling the world about it right now."

The church choir softly sang "Joy to the World," and soon everyone joined in. Carroll wiped a bit of moisture from her cheek, then dabbed at the tip of her nose. She blinked and looked around her. It was. It really *was*!

She looked up, her eyes meeting Slade's. He grinned ruefully and shook his head.

It was *snowing*.

Right on schedule, Kris drove down the street, booming greetings to one and all. The hay wagon did indeed look like a sleigh. Rudolph and Blitzen, mercifully, did not look like reindeer. Eleven grinning marines sat among the pile of presents.

When Santa parked his sleigh, Slade handed Christy up to one of the marines, then found a quiet spot for himself and Carroll to watch.

"I didn't put my gift on the sleigh," he told her quietly.

"I didn't, either."

They reached into their coat pockets, and each of them brought out a small box. When they exchanged them, Slade said, "You first."

It was a ring, a solitaire diamond, sparkling and darting, reflecting the dazzling lights all around them.

"Will you marry me, Carroll? Will you trust me to love you the way you should be loved? Will you—"

She stopped his words with her fingers. "First, open your present."

He lifted the lid. Taking out a small enamel pin, he said, "A dove?"

She shook her head, smiling uncertainly. "It was as close as I could come to a homing pigeon. It's silly, I guess, but I wanted to tell you that I know you'll always come back."

He slid the ring on her finger, and they both looked up to see Christy watching, doing an awkward jig in the crowded sleigh. Carroll threw her arms around his neck and tugged, bringing his mouth down to hers. Hunger and trust and love blended in the brief kiss.

Behind them, her voice shrill with excitement, Christy called, "God bless us, every one!"

Holding Carroll tight against him, Slade asked, "How do you feel about Harold if the first one's a boy?"

"I hate it," she said promptly, her voice muffled against his jacket.

He smiled. There was hope. "Merry Christmas, darling."

"Merry Christmas."

* * * * *

Author's Note

One morning, lying in bed, half-awake and half-asleep, the idea for this story came to me. I thought of Kris and his lights, Noel and her painting, a girl who wanted a father, a woman afraid to love and a man who had enough love for all of them. I liked the idea and planned to do something with it. Someday. Several days later, my editor called and asked if I would like to do a Christmas story. Timing is rarely that perfect.

I love everything about Christmas.

I still look at tinsel, trees, lights, TV specials, poinsettias, garlands and wrapped presents with wide-eyed wonder. I love shopping, crowds, carols and cards with family news and special messages of love. Most of all, I enjoy family get-togethers and seeing old friends.

It's a season for dreaming and believing.

It's a season that suits me quite well because I have a lot of Kris in me—I'm big on dreaming impossible dreams and reaching for stars. And, like Kris, I believe that dreams do come true—you just have to be willing to work at them.

From me and mine to you and yours, a shower of blessings. May you have health, joy, prosperity and love. May you dream big, and may all your dreams come true.

Happy Holidays,

Rita Rainville

ALWAYS AND FOREVER

Lindsay McKenna

To L/Cpl. Jim Flint and
Cpl. John Connelly, USMC—Vietnam veterans
and dear friends who served with me
at Moffett Field, USNAS, California, 1965.
You served with pride and patriotism.
I salute you.

A recipe from Lindsay McKenna:

My mom took a fruitcake recipe and changed it around to please us—by adding black walnuts, which we gathered every fall.

RUTH'S CHRISTMAS FRUITCAKE

9 eggs (or enough to measure 2¼ cups)
1 lb raisins
1 lb candied cherries, cut up
1 lb walnuts (or black walnuts, if you can find them!)
¼ lb candied citron
¼ lb candied orange peel
¼ lb coconut
3 cups unbleached flour
1½ cups shortening, softened
1½ cups sugar
⅔ cup orange juice
1½ tsp baking powder
¾ tsp salt

Preheat oven to 300° F. Line and grease two 9″ × 5″ × 3″ loaf pans or one 10″ × 4″ tube pan. Set aside.

Cream together shortening and sugar until fluffy. Beat in eggs. Set aside.

Sift together flour, baking powder and salt. Alternately stir flour mixture and orange juice into shortening mixture. Blend in fruits and nuts.

Fill pan(s) to almost full. Bake loaf cakes for 2½ to 3 hours. Bake tube cake for 3½ to 4 hours. Cover with foil during last hour of baking. Cakes are done when toothpick or knife inserted in center comes out clean.

Chapter One

Captain Kyle Anderson jogged up the sidewalk toward Captain Mike Taylor's base home. Was he too late? Kyle was supposed to go with his best friend, who was getting married tomorrow, to pick up their Air Force dress uniforms from the base cleaners, but he'd overslept. Damn!

Rubbing his smarting, bloodshot eyes, Kyle rapped his knuckles sharply against the door. Tomorrow, Mike was marrying Gale Remington, an Air Force officer he'd met a year ago. On Christmas Day, of all things. It was like Mike to do something romantic like that.

Kyle's breath was coming out in white wisps as he stood restlessly, hunched down into his dark blue wool coat, waiting to see if Mike was home.

"Mike?" His voice carried impatiently as he waited at the door, knocking even more loudly. Looking around, Kyle realized he was probably attracting the attention of every Air Force wife in base housing. They'd probably be looking out their windows to see who was shouting at 0800.

He'd overslept because of jet lag. Four days ago, Kyle had flown to Castle A.F.B. from Udorn, Thailand, where his fighter squadron was based, to be best man at Mike's wedding. But because of time-zone changes and the need to unplug physically and emotionally from the duties of a fighter pilot in Vietnam, Kyle was exhausted.

The door opened. Kyle grinned, expecting to see his friend from boyhood. Instead, he saw Gale, Mike's beautiful fiancée. His smile slipped considerably in surprise, his eyes widening as she opened the screen door.

"Hi, Kyle. If you're looking for Mike, he took off about fifteen minutes ago for the cleaners."

Pulse skyrocketing, Kyle drew in a shaky breath. He stood there, tongue-tied. Ever since he'd been introduced to Gale three days ago, his world had been out of control like a jet in a flat spin. The moment he'd looked into her incredible forest-green eyes, something wonderful, something terrible had happened to him. Once, twenty-five-year-old Kyle would have scoffed at the idea of falling head over heels for any woman on first sight. But he wasn't laughing now.

Placing his hands on his hips in a typical arrogant jet-jockey gesture, he covered his reaction to her. "Hi, Gale." God, did she realize what she did to him? It was agony to be around her because he wanted to simply absorb her, lose himself in her sunny smile, and stare into those dancing eyes that held such sparkling life in their depths.

Gale smiled shyly. "Mike said you might be late. He'll pick up your uniform." She forced herself to look away from Kyle's hawklike blue eyes that were large with intelligence. If there was such a thing as brazen self-confidence, Kyle possessed it. His stance was cocky and unapologetic. He was a proud eagle standing before her, knowing he was the cream of the Air Force pilot crop because he was an Academy graduate. Her pulse was doing funny things and she tried to ignore it. Since meeting Kyle, an exhilarating force swept through her whenever she thought of him or saw him. When Kyle looked at her with that burning intensity, she felt shaky, her carefully mapped out world falling apart.

"I overslept," he said with a laugh. He wasn't going to admit to her he couldn't shake the jet lag. Gale looked vulnerable and pretty in a pink long-sleeved blouse. The red apron tied around her waist and the dark brown slacks showed off her slim figure. She didn't look like a captain or a meteorologist, but she was both. Her hair, a pageboy of shifting brown color interlaced with gold and a few delicate strands of burnished copper, barely touched the collar of her blouse. He had to get away. It wasn't good to be here alone with her. God knew he'd taken great pains *not* to be alone with Gale—because he hadn't known what he'd do if he was. She affected him deeply.

It wasn't Gale's fault. She was hopelessly in love with Mike. Kyle rationalized his attraction to Gale by telling himself that because she was Mike's fiancée, he naturally liked her. "Look, I'll come back later," he said, his mouth growing dry.

"Nonsense, come on in. Mike's due back in less than half an hour and he wants you to stay for breakfast. Why go all the way back to the B.O.Q. just to come back later?"

Hesitating, Kyle glanced at the watch on his wrist. A half hour. It would look stupid to leave if Mike was going to be back that soon. "Well..."

Gale stepped aside, looking up at him. A large part of her wanted him to leave because in his presence, her emotions vibrated with a strange yearning she'd never experienced. But etiquette dictated differently. "You look tired. Come in. I've got a pot of fresh coffee." She knew Kyle had flown from Thailand to attend the wedding. The strain of what the war had done to him showed on his lean face, around his eyes and in the set of his mobile mouth. Heat fled through her, sweet and unexpected, as she stared at him.

She knew that, like every other arrogant, self-assured military pilot, he wasn't going to let on he was tired, much less exhausted by the war or the flight home. No, Kyle was like his fellow pilots: his callous, cocky exterior hid a vulnerable interior that was rarely shared with anyone. From the moment she'd met Kyle, she'd sensed a warmth and gentleness beneath that facade, and for some reason, Kyle's ebullient, joking presence had been able to lift the fear from her heart. Thirty days after the wedding, Mike, too, would leave for Thailand and become a part of the war. Gale feared losing her young husband.

Taking off his garrison cap, Kyle gave a nod. "Tired?" he teased. "You know us handsome, unabashed jocks aren't fazed by such things." He stepped into the warmth of the small living room. He could smell fresh coffee in the air and inhaled the scent deeply. And bacon was frying. His stomach growled, but he was also hungry in a different way. After he shed his coat, Gale hung it in the hall closet and beckoned him to follow her to the kitchen. He spotted a small Christmas tree, all decorated, in the corner of the living room. The lights blinked merrily, reminding him of the joyous holiday season.

"I promised Mike I'd have breakfast waiting for him when he got back." She smiled and pointed to the table. "Sit down. I'll get the coffee."

A bright red cloth covered the round table, and a Christmas decoration sat in the middle of it. Gale's thoughtful touch, Kyle was sure. "Thanks," he said. Tensely, he sat down and watched Gale move to the stove to pour his coffee. Mike had lived alone here for a year, and from the letters Kyle had gotten from him, he'd thought the house would be cold and barren. It wasn't with Gale present. The place had a light feeling with the winter sunshine filtering in through the kitchen window, embracing Gale's slight form and making her look radiant. Like a starving man, Kyle watched each small movement she performed. There was a sureness and grace to Gale he'd never seen in another woman.

Rubbing his eyes, Kyle tried to figure it out for the thousandth time. What was it about Gale that had thrown him for a loop? He couldn't want her, couldn't be fantasizing about kissing her or having her for himself when Mike was going to marry her. What the hell was wrong with him? It wasn't as if he didn't have his choice of women. Maybe it was the war. He hadn't been the same emotionally since he'd started flying the dangerous missions, although he never discussed that with anyone. Not even his fellow pilots.

"Here you go. You like it black, don't you?"

Kyle took his hands away from his eyes, and nodded, gazing at her long, slender fingers around the white mug. "Black—yes."

She smiled understandingly. "You look like you could use about seventy-two hours more sleep."

"Nah. You know us fighter jocks are as tough as they come." He kept his eyes on her as she walked back to the stove to turn the bacon in the skillet. "It comes with the territory," he said, sipping the scalding hot coffee. The heat burning through him was raging out of control. Didn't he have any command over his feelings toward Gale? How could this have happened? Why?

Glancing over her shoulder, she said, "What? The war?"

"Yeah. Flying missions every other day over Hanoi and back is—" He hesitated, not wanting to use the word *killer* because he saw the worry in Gale's eyes. In a month, Mike would be joining his squadron. They'd be flying together—a boyhood dream come true. He and Mike had grown up in Sedona, Arizona, spending hours dreaming of careers as military pilots. Trying to disarm the anxiety he saw in Gale's eyes, he forced a smile. "It's a piece of cake." That was a bald-faced lie, but there was no sense in further upsetting her.

She raised an eyebrow. "It's dangerous."

With a shrug, Kyle muttered, "Not to us. Jet jocks are trained to take the heat."

"Oh, please." She laughed. "You guys are all alike. It would kill you to admit you're scared, have doubts or any other human frailty."

He grinned broadly and sipped the coffee. It was good and strong, just the way he liked it. "The only human frailties we possess are eyes to scope out good-lookin' women like yourself. Mike sure got lucky."

Gale blushed hotly. There was nothing displeasing about Kyle Anderson, either, but she kept that thought to herself. More than anything, she was drawn to the raw confidence that emanated from him like a beacon.

"How did you get so cocky?"

"You mean confident?"

She grinned. "I don't think the two words have anything in common, Kyle."

"Sure they do. You can't sit with an F-14 strapped to your rear carrying a ton of weapons if you aren't a little cocky *and* confident."

The imagery frightened Gale, although she knew it shouldn't.

Kyle tilted his head as he saw her expressive eyes darken. He'd never seen a woman who was so transparent with her emotions and feelings. It was a delightful and touching discovery. No wonder Mike had fallen in love with her. "Sorry," he muttered with a forced smile. "I'll try and keep the war talk to a minimum. I can see it's scaring you."

"It does, Kyle." She studied him in the silence. "Doesn't it you?"

"What?"

"Scare you, flying with a load of weapons?"

He shrugged. "I don't know...I never really analyzed it that way before."

It was her turn to smile. "If you did, you probably wouldn't be a fighter pilot."

His grin broadened. "You're probably right. Some things, I learned a long time ago, don't merit being looked at too closely."

"Is that anything like looking a gift horse in the mouth?"

"Exactly." Kyle laughed, his spirits lifting like a fierce wind. He couldn't recall having felt this happy before. He tried to analyze why Gale affected him like a heady wine. Five minutes ago, he'd felt like hell warmed over. Now, all that tiredness and depression had miraculously gone away. Was it because of the kindness he saw in her face? Those dancing green eyes that looked beyond his bravado and saw the real him? Or was it Gale's full, soft lips, which reminded him that there was something left in the world that wasn't hard, harsh or ugly?

"I think Mike's the luckiest guy in the world. Imagine him snagging you."

She turned to the kitchen counter to busy herself. It was too easy to stare into those dark blue eyes that made her go weak and shaky inside. "You're making it out as if he captured the most beautiful woman in the world," she teased. "And I'm not. I'm just an Air Force captain."

"No one said women in the service aren't beautiful."

"Please."

Kyle laughed softly as she turned and gave him a dark look over her shoulder. "Now, that's the *truth,* Gale."

"Sure. Fighter jocks have more lines per square inch than any other male I've ever run into."

"Sounds like an indictment."

"More like a chronic disease with you guys."

He sat back, immensely enjoying her sense of humor. "That's another thing I like about ladies in the military—they have a fine sense of humor."

"And probably the last thing you look at or consider when you meet one."

"Now, Gale . . ."

"Now, Kyle . . ." And again, she laughed. The merriment in his eyes stole her breath away. There was more happiness there than she'd ever seen before. "You're just like Mike," she accused gently, "all strut and stuff, but underneath, a very nice guy."

"God, don't let *that* get out! The guys over at Udorn think I'm one mean fighter behind the stick."

Rolling her eyes, Gale got eggs from the fridge, then returned to the stove to cook them. "Here we go again. Make sure no one knows the real guy who wears those pilot's wings. Really, Kyle, did they make all of you out of the same mold?"

"Well, we went through flight school together."

"Instead of teaching you how to fly, I swear they put all of you through the same personality training."

"That's not so bad. I mean, look at us—we're confident, good at what we do and besides that, we're good-looking."

"I give up. If I didn't know any better, I'd say Mike was here and not you."

Sipping his coffee, Kyle smiled recklessly. "Well, Mike and I are like brothers, but there are a few differences. I'm four months older than he is."

Gale knew there were other, more profound differences. Mike was laid back; Kyle was far more aggressive. She wondered if Mike would turn out the same way after being in combat.

Forcing herself to return to the task at hand, Gale busied herself with scrambling the eggs while the bacon finished frying. Her hands trembled. Trying to laugh at the absurd notion that Kyle's presence was responsible, Gale focused on Mike. She had met him a year ago over at Operations, where the meteorology department was located. He'd come in early one morning, angry over the fact his weather plan hadn't been ready in time for his flight. On his return to base two days later, Mike had taken her out to an expensive restaurant in Sacramento to apologize for his less-than-gentlemanly behavior. Over the next six months, they'd fallen in love. Their happiness was complete until Mike abruptly received orders to Thailand. They had decided to get married before he left.

Frowning, Gale stirred the eggs briskly in the hot skillet. Vietnam. War. Death. She felt her heart contract powerfully with fear. It wasn't fair that Mike was going to be torn away from her a month after they became husband and wife. What in life was fair? Not much. Kyle's face haunted her. Shutting her eyes, Gale took a deep breath. What kind of crazy joke was being played on her? She loved *Mike!* So what were all these new and startling feelings she'd had since she had been introduced to Kyle?

Forcing herself to concentrate, Gale removed the skillet from the burner and put a lid over it to keep the eggs warm. At twenty-three, she thought she knew herself. It was true Mike was the first man she'd fallen in love with, but she'd had a lot of dates throughout college before joining the Air Force. Now, the nights she'd tossed and turned, dreaming of both Mike and Kyle, had left her nerves raw and taut. How could she be attracted to Kyle? Perhaps because he was Mike's best friend and they were similar in some ways.

Reaching blindly for the skillet that held the bacon, Gale bumped the pan containing the hot grease off the electric burner. Unthinkingly, Gale reached out, trying to catch it. Hot grease splattered across her right hand. Pain reared up her arm, and she cried out, leaping back as the skillet crashed to the floor, the grease flung in all directions.

"Gale!" Her scream galvanized Kyle into action. In an instant, he was at her side, his arm going around her shoulders, holding the reddened hand that had been burned.

"Oh, damn..." she sobbed, gripping her wrist, trying not to let the pain overwhelm her. Sinking against his strong, supporting body, Gale felt safe. Kyle's breathing was punctuated, harsh near her ear, his breath moist against her cheek.

"So stupid," she whispered, a catch in her voice. "I—I'm sorry...."

"It's all right. Come on, get over to the sink. Cold water will help," he whispered, guiding her in that direction. The burn on her hand didn't look nasty but still his heart was pounding in his chest and he felt shaky. After fumbling with the handle on the cold-water spigot, Kyle turned it on and forced her hand beneath the stream.

The water hit her flesh and Gale sucked in a breath, then bit her lower lip.

"Lean on me," Kyle ordered huskily as he felt her tremble. She obeyed him. Her perfume, light and delicate, struck his flaring nostrils. It was the way she fitted against him that nearly unstrung him. Her hair, slightly wavy, felt like silk against the hard line of his jaw. Kyle ached to lean down and kiss her. "Take it easy, easy..." he coaxed, his voice low and unsteady.

For several minutes Gale was unable to do anything except feel. Feel the lessening of the pain, feel Kyle's strong, powerful body against hers. His breath was choppy, and she was aware of his heart beating frantically in his chest where she lay against him. His touch was excruciatingly gentle as he placed a cloth over her hand after turning off the faucet.

"Come on, sit down. You're shaky."

Wasn't that the truth, Gale thought, allowing Kyle to guide her to a chair at the table. Her watery knees had nothing to do with the burn, but with him holding her as if she were some fragile, priceless treasure.

Worriedly, Kyle studied her, his hand firm on her shoulder. Gale was waxen, and when she raised those dark, long lashes to look up at him, he felt as if someone had gut punched him. Dizziness assailed him, and his grip tightened on her shoulder momentarily. Large eyes, huge black pupils surrounded by a vibrant green, stared back at him. Gale's cry had torn him apart, ripping away all his pretenses, his good sense.

Kyle went to the sink and dampened a wash cloth. Gale sat with her head bowed. She looked so hauntingly vulnerable her shoulders slumped forward. Fighting all his rising, chaotic feelings, Kyle crouched in front of her.

"Here, this ought to help," he said. He removed one cloth and laid the new one across the injury. Kyle heard Gale breathe in raggedly, but she didn't cry out.

He kept a grip on her arm. His heart refused to stop thudding in his chest, his pulse pounding until every beat was like that beat of a kettle drum being played within him.

When Kyle looked up and saw tears form and then fall down Gale's cheeks, he lost what little control he had left. "Don't cry," he pleaded thickly, cupping her cheek with his hand. He stared deeply into her eyes.

"Oh, Kyle . . ." she choked out.

Her lips parted, lush and inviting, and Kyle started to lean forward.

"Hey, where's everybody at?" Mike called from the living room.

Kyle froze, his hand slipping from Gale's face. He stood, dizzied and shocked by what had almost happened. "In here, buddy."

Mike appeared at the doorway. Dressed in his blue winter uniform, he took off his garrison cap. Immediately, he went to Gale's side and knelt on one knee next to her.

"Honey?" He gently cradled her hand. "What happened?"

Gale made a frustrated sound. "I made a dumb move at the stove and splashed grease over my hand, Mike. It's nothing. I'll be okay."

Kyle backed away in a daze. What the hell had just happened? He had been ready to kiss Gale! Shocked, he left the kitchen and went to the living room. Hands shoved into his pants pockets, Kyle was angry and upset with himself.

Gale was barely able to think. If Mike hadn't arrived when he had, she knew Kyle would have kissed her. His eyes had been hooded, stormy with unrequited need. She trembled, but it wasn't out of fear. It was out of anticipation of the unexpected. When Kyle had held her, he'd made the pain go away. She shook her head, forcing her attention to Mike, who had retrieved some salve to put on the minor burn.

It was all craziness! It was the stress of the wedding, the war and the fact that Mike was going to leave in a month. The pressures on all of them were great. Kyle was Mike's best friend, Gale rationalized, and he had simply reacted out of loyalty.

Kyle slowly paced the perimeter of the living room, head down in thought. Mike would never know what had transpired. The wedding would go on as planned. Kyle would be Mike's best man, and he would be happy for both of them....

Savagely rubbing his face, he knew it had to be the jet lag, the shock of stepping out of the war in Southeast Asia and returning to the States. It had to be.

Chapter Two

Gale sat in the living room of her base home, several letters and a magazine in her lap. The house was quiet. Deadly quiet. She had just gotten off duty at the meteorology department and the holiday stretched out unendingly before her. This year there was no tree in the corner, no decorations in evidence, not even Christmas music to take the edge off the silence that surrounded her. The coolness in her home seeped through her uniform, making her feel chilled more than she should be.

Six months after marrying Mike, he'd been lost over Hanoi during a bombing raid. Was he a prisoner of war—or dead? No one knew. She slowly looked at the first letter, wishing it was from Mike, but it wasn't.

Instead, it was a neatly addressed envelope from Captain Kyle Anderson. Gently, she ran her fingers across the crisp envelope. Kyle... Her grieving, shattered heart filled with warmth and a thread of hope. Kyle had signed up for a second tour so he could be with Mike during his first. When Mike had been shot down by a SAM missile, Kyle had been there. He'd seen the whole thing.

Mike had often said Kyle was like the brother he'd never had. Since the time Mike had been listed as missing in action, Kyle had written to her at least once a week, fulfilling his duties as a friend who wasn't there to help her over the terrible days and nights of loneliness. In his first letter, Kyle had told her that Mike had made him promise to care for her if he was ever shot down and became a POW or M.I.A. Like the Marines, the Air Force took care of its own, Kyle had informed her. And because of his promise to Mike, he would do his best to take care of her, even though they were half a world apart.

With a sigh, Gale saw that the other two letters were bills. Her parents were dead, so there was nothing from family. Her sister, who lived in Haight Ashbury, was opposed to the war and to Gale being in the service. Gale expected nothing from Sandy as a result. They were on opposite sides of an ideology that had divided them for the past four years.

This would be her Christmas present: Kyle's letter was a precious, life-giving gift. Inevitably, Gale's spirits lifted, as they always did whenever she received a letter from him. Opening this one slowly, savoring the fact that it was several pages thick, she settled back to find a tiny shelter from a storm that hovered around her twenty-fours hours every day.

* * *

December 16, 1974

Dear Gale,
This is your hot-rock jet jock writing to you from a place where a Christmas tree would *never* grow! I'm

sitting here at a bar in Udorn trying to write to you under some pretty severe conditions: beautiful Thai bar girls dressed in decidedly tight dresses, loud (and lousy) music, cigarette smoke so thick you could cut it with a knife, and a lot of pilots making eyes at all the bar girls.

Of course, yours truly is the only one doing something praiseworthy—writing to you! How are you? In your last letter, you sounded down. Don't give up. I *know* Mike will be back. Somehow, some way. And me? Brazen (to use your word) as ever. Yes, I still fly a mission over Hanoi just about every other day. And no, I haven't had any close calls. Are you kidding me? The ace at Udorn? Come on! This jock has one and a half tours under his belt. I'm considered the Old Man around here. All the younger jocks always gather around me when I sidle up to the bar, wanting stories. So I oblige them.

Thanks for the tin of cookies! My God, they were a hit around here! You know how our post office works don't you? Those enlisted guys have noses on them like bloodhounds. They smell each package. The ones that have cookies in them are somehow detoured or "lost." When the package finally finds its way to the officer, the food that was in it has mysteriously gone. All the guys who work over at the post office are overweight. I wonder why?

However, because you told me ahead of time that you were going to make six dozen chocolate-chip cookies and send them to me for Christmas, I went over and warned all those guys to keep their hands off—or else. Your cookies got through unscathed. How did you know my favorite was chocolate chip?

I'd die for those. Between the box my mom sent and yours, I was the cookie king here at Udorn. And don't you think the other jocks weren't wandering over to my hooch to bum a few. Yes, I shared them, like you requested. Would I hoard them? Don't answer that. I carried out your wishes to the letter. You made a lot of jocks happy. I gave some to the enlisted guys on the flight line, too. Those guys bust themselves twenty-four hours a day, and it was a good feeling to make them smile. They thank you, too.

Hey! Gotta zoom off. One of those beautiful Thai ladies is giving me a look I can't resist. Look, you take care of yourself, hear? Your letters are like life to me here at Udorn. I really enjoy getting them. Don't stop! I won't, either. I promised Mike that I'd take care of you, so expect a letter once a week.

Merry Christmas, Gale.

Your Friend, Kyle.

*   *   *

December 24, 1974

Dear Kyle,

I want you to know that your lively letter—which sounded like a buccaneer swashbuckling—was my Christmas gift. I sat here with two bills, a magazine and your letter in my hand. Your letter, by far, was the one I wanted to open and read.

I had to giggle about the Great Cookie Heist! Just to brighten your day, I'm sending another box (air mail, of course, so it doesn't take three months via ship to reach you) of chocolate-chip cookies. Keeping busy is my only way to keep my sanity, and it's nice to be able to cook for someone who loves my cooking so much. So, in your own way, you're helping me, even if it's something as simple as appreciating my cookies. Baking them keeps my mind off so many terrible thoughts I shouldn't be thinking.

Enough of my maudlin musings. I hope the bloodhounds of the Udorn post office can't smell these. I've triple wrapped them in foil, plus wrapped each cookie individually to make sure no odor escapes to get their attention. And I've disguised them in a plain cardboard box instead of sending them in a suspicious round tin, which I'm sure tips them off that it might be cookies or other goodies inside.

Hi, I'm back. I started this letter an hour after getting yours. When I'm lonely, I write letters to my friends here Stateside. Yours is the only one going overseas. It's Christmas Day now, and I got lonely. I'm learning to turn on the radio or television set just so I can hear the sound of another human voice. What hurts is when the nightly news comes on and they show at least fifteen minutes of footage on the Vietnam War. I forget that it's going to come on, and then, some part of me focuses in on it, no matter what I'm doing. I'll hurry to the living room to shut it off, but it's like I'm mesmerized by some power and I just stand there watching and listening to it. What's wrong with me? Why do I have to watch the shooting, the killing they photograph?

It's worse on the radio because I never know when some news flash is going to come over it. At least with the television on—and if I can remember to turn it off—I only have to avoid hearing it at 6:00 p.m. and

11:00 p.m. I'm learning all these little tricks to avoid pain. Amazing what a human being will do, isn't it?

Thanks for listening to me. Just talking to someone, another military person, helps. I don't say anything to anyone around here because they all have a husband, brother, sister, son or daughter over in Vietnam and I don't want to depress them or make them worry any more than they already do. Thanks for being a compassionate ear. Please, fly safe. You're in my prayers every night along with Mike.

Warmly, Gale

* * *

December 23, 1975

Dear Gale,

Merry Christmas! I tried calling you yesterday, but the airman over at Ops said you'd just gone home after twelve hours of duty. I was going to call you and tease you unmercifully because I hadn't yet received those chocolate-chip cookies you promised to send this year. Now that I'm Stateside and stationed at Homestead AFB in Florida, I wonder if the cookies really got lost in the mail or if the same guys in the post office over in Udorn are now stationed at Homestead with me. I'll fill out a form at the post office, but it won't do any good.

You sounded better in your last letter. I know it's tough to go on without knowing about Mike, but you're a fighter and I admire your courage under the circumstances. Just hang tough. It's all you can do.

So, you're going to be stationed at Travis AFB, eh? Busy place. You'll be there for three years and get plenty of opportunity to visit San Francisco—lucky lady! Have a bowl of clam chowder down on Fisherman's Wharf for me, will you? It's one of my favorite places. I like the smells, the color, the people and activity. Quite a place. Take a cable-car ride for me, too. I like that bell they ring. Makes you want to get up and dance up and down the aisle while they're ringing it, ha, ha.

I can't believe you want me to tell the story of my life! Me, of all people! All I do is give you a hard time, lady. So I make you laugh a little. Nothing wrong with that. I figured it out: fifty-two installments, one letter a week to you, three or four pages at a time, and I ought to have my autobiography finished in the forthcoming year. Brother, are you a glutton for punishment, but, if that's what you want as your Christmas present, I'll indulge your whim. Next letter, I'll start. Can you see it now?

"I was born in Sedona, Arizona, to a grocer and his wife. I was red, wrinkled and too long. My mother, upon seeing me for the first time, broke out in tears because I looked so ugly. Of course, she reassures me that as I grew and filled out, I was the cutest kid in Red Rock county."

Whew, that was close! I'm such a handsome devil now that I couldn't let that info slip out to my flying buddies. I'd never hear the end of it.

Is this the kind of thing you're wanting to hear about in my letters? The down-and-dirty life of Kyle Anderson? Ha, ha. I think you're a real masochist, Gale—a new and provocative side to you I never realized existed. Okay, okay, I can hear you nagging me in the next letter to quit quibbling and get on with it.

So—Merry Christmas! You get fifty-two installments over the next year about me and the story behind this fantastic jet jock. It ought to hit the *New York Times* bestseller list, don't you think? Nah, don't tell me now. Tell me next Christmas, okay?

I know you don't have anyone to go home to for Christmas, and you've already said you'll spend it there at base. I really think you need to get away for a while and get some down time. You've worked yourself to a bone this year, Gale. Even I take time off and go see my folks in Sedona once a year. Why not take the thirty days leave you've got coming and get some R and R? I worry about you, sometimes. You're a strong lady with a warm heart, but stop and smell the flowers, huh?

Merry Christmas, Gale. As I hitch my foot up on the brass rail of the O Club bar, I'll lift a toast to you.

Your special friend, Kyle

* * *

December 30, 1975

Dear Kyle,

I can't believe you didn't get the cookies I sent! Are you *sure* they're missing? Or do you just want two huge batches to hoard? Knowing your love of desserts in general—and cookies specifically—I wouldn't be a bit surprised if you fibbed to get a few extra dozen.

I'm so happy you've decided to send me your autobiography. I'm going to do the same thing. Not that I have had a terribly exciting life, but I think that's only fair. As you get writer's cramp and the next letter is hounding you to be written, you can fondly think of me having to write to you, too. Only, I won't see it as a royal pain as perhaps you might as the weeks roll by. Letters have been a life-sustaining source for me, giving me hope and often lifting me out of the depression I allow myself to get into.

Actually this year, I'm doing better. But I want to get on with writing my life story to you, too! I hope you won't be bored to death. I can see you sitting at your desk, feet up on it, letter in hand, snoozing away. Ha, ha.

Okay, here goes nothing. Promise me if you do get bored, tell me. I'll stop my autobiography. As I said before, my life's pretty nonedescript (my opinion).

I was born in Medford, Oregon. Unlike you, I was a pretty baby (according to Mom). She said everyone in the hospital oohed and ahed over me. I don't really remember. However, my star status quickly sank because my older sister, Sandy, really hated me. Sibling rivalry and all that, I suppose. Mom said Sandy (who was four years old when I was born) started having temper tantrums every time Mom picked me up to breast-feed me.

My father, who wasn't long on patience or very tolerant of such childish things, stood about two evenings of Sandy's shrieking and did something about it. He warned her that if she started screaming again, he was going to pick her up by her feet and dip her head in a bucket of water. I guess Sandy believed him because she never ever again had a temper tantrum. I'm not condoning what he did, but I wonder what psychologists would say about it. Sandy is the one who became a hippie in Haight Ashbury. She went to San

Francisco when she was eighteen and got into the drugs and flower-children culture. I forget how many times she's been arrested.

I often wonder why she turned out the way she did. Mom said I was the favorite of the family because I was a sweet, quiet baby. Later, I was the "good girl" who did what was expected of her, while Sandy started to rebel. I know this letter is supposed to be about me, but I think every person is somehow fashioned and shaped by those around them. I ache inside because Sandy hates the military and, therefore, hates me.

I just wish she could overlook my job, Kyle, and see me, her sister. We got along well as kids. It's just that in our teenage years, Sandy got wild and had awful fights with Dad. When our parents died in that car crash when Sandy was eighteeen, I think it drove her off the deep end. That's when she took off for San Francisco.

Me? Well, I got shuttled between my father's two brothers and their families for the next four years until I turned eighteen. To this day, Sandy and I have never gotten together to talk about the loss of our parents. It would have been nice if she could have stayed around for the funeral. I really needed to be held. Looking back on it, I'm sure she did, too, but there was no one else who could hold us like our parents. I remember standing in front of the two coffins with my aunt and uncle on either side of me.

I never again felt so alone. Well, I should amend that. I felt that alone when I got the telegram telling me that Mike was shot down. The same kind of awful gutting feeling. Looking back on my short life, I wonder if I'm always destined to lose the people I love.

I don't mean that to sound maudlin. It's just that I see people live their lives in cycles where things get repeated. I hope the cycle changes. I want Mike home, safe and alive.

Your friend, Gale

* * *

December 20, 1976

Dearest Gale,
This letter ought to reach you in Medford, Oregon, hopefully *before* Christmas, not after it.

I was TDY (temporary duty) to Anchorage, Alaska, (where Santa Claus lives) until four days ago. The temperature extreme between Anchorage and Florida is alarming. I'm coming down with a cold. (I can see it now—the next letter I receive from you will tell me to drink lemon juice in hot water, put myself under a lot of blankets, and sweat the cold out of my body. Better yet, I'll probably receive a bottle of vitamin C, along with a finger-shaking letter demanding "why didn't you dress properly so you wouldn't catch a cold?")

This isn't a normal Christmas for me. Usually, I'd be over at the O Club with the rest of the single guys, playing dead bug or something to make the time pass. Getting stuck with duty around here stopped me from going home to Sedona like I wanted to. This year is different. Can't put my finger on it . . . maybe I'm getting older? Ha, ha. Perish the thought. Older but better-looking. How's that?

I can hear you laughing right now. Did I ever tell you how pretty your laughter is? I like the sound of it.

I intend to call you on New Year's Eve, as always. I really look forward to our talks. I don't know if the post office or the phone company makes more money off us.

When I got back to Homestead, your Christmas present was waiting for me. What a great surprise! You knitted this sweater for me by yourself? Dark blue, for the Air Force, of course. Seriously, Gale, it's beautiful. I just sort of stood over the package after opening it, running my hand across it. It felt soft and yet strong—like you. I never expected such a beautiful or thoughtful gift, Gale. Florida weather isn't very cool for very long, but I'll wear it every chance I get. Thanks.

This is the last installment to the story of my life. Letter #52. Here goes.

Presently, I'm stationed at Homestead AFB, in Florida, doing what I do best: flying. Sometimes, though, I get tired of the military machine and some of its stupider management decisions (and God knows, they abound in great proliferation). If I didn't like flying so much, I'd quit. But what else is there except flying?

I live on base, and the sound of jet engines lull me to sleep. I like that. The house is pretty empty to come home to sometimes. Just depends on what kind of mood I'm in, I guess. The television keeps me company—another human voice, to use your turn of phrase. There's no special lady in my life at the present. Maybe I'm looking for the impossible and I've set my sights too high. I like the fact women are coming into their own sense of identity. That's why I've always admired you so much, Gale. You were a strong, independent woman long before it was popular.

My life revolves around my squadron and the duties therein. I'm lucky: I get paid to do something I love, which is to fly. Still, there's a hollowness in me I can't describe, can't seem to fill, no matter what I do. Maybe it's age or I'm mellowing. Possibly, even changing. Gadzooks! Did I say something personal? I *must* be getting old! Or maybe it's you. You're easy to talk to and share with.

There! That's it! So now, you've got the inside scoop on this jet jock. Now that it's all over, I don't feel as vulnerable as I did when I started writing my life story last Christmas. You're right: jet jocks are a flippant, arrogant lot who would *never* reveal their real feelings, their fears, hopes or dreams to anyone else. But I did to you and it felt kinda good. (Don't let that get around, or I'll never be able to live it down here with my squadron.)

On the other hand, I liked getting your letters about your growing-up years, going through ROTC in college and then into the Air Force. Unlike me, you never did have a tough outer image in front of the real you. I always knew you were a softy with a heart as large as this base. You do so much for others, Gale. I know Mike's parents really appreciate the fact you visited them last year. Mom told me it made them happy. I can't know what it cost you in terms of emotions, but I'm sure it was a hell of a lot. They're lost without word on Mike. You've managed to pick yourself up by your boot straps and continue on. God, I admire you for that. Is there a clone of you somewhere? I'd like to meet her.

Take care, sweet lady. I'll call you on New Year's Eve. A special gift for both of us. You're always in my thoughts.

Kyle

* * *

December 24, 1976

Dearest Kyle,

I'm going to miss getting your weekly letters. To be honest, your letters and phone calls have helped me stay centered during this awful period. You don't see that, though, do you? That's one of the reasons why I could face Mike's parents and stay with them. It was a cathartic experience, but I think, in some ways, healing for all of us.

Well, here's my Letter #52! Last one. I'm surprised you haven't fallen asleep over them yet! What a masochist you are at heart!

Right now, I'm living on base at Travis. The base housing here is like it is everywhere: you can hear your neighbors through the walls. I'm surrounded by families on both sides of me and I really like that. Often, when I don't have duty at night, I'll baby-sit for Susan, who has three small children ranging in age from one through four, or Jackie, who has two, ages seven and ten.

I really enjoy the children. They give me so much hope. When I hear them laugh, I remember back to the good times when I laughed like that as a kid—or even as a grown-up. I especially remember laughing at something you had in every one of your letters. You have been wonderful in giving humor as a gift to me on days when I felt lower than a snake's belly, to use Susan's words. (She's from Texas, can you tell??)

This fall, I planted daffodils out front. The soil here is really bad, but I've tried to prepare it properly so I'll have at least three dozen plants poking their heads up in early March. It's nice to have something of home that you can bring along with you, isn't it? That's why I knitted you the sweater. To tell you the truth, that sweater was knitted during baby-sitting time. I'm surprised you didn't find a dab of jelly, a gob of sticky caramel or some other unidentifiable stain on it! The younger children especially loved to sit with me while I was knitting. And they love to touch things at their age. I ended up using a lot more yarn than it should have taken because they loved playing with it so much! Rather than them handling your burgeoning sweater, I let them play with the extra skeins I kept in my basket.

The kids have been good for me in a lot of ways. Nights are usually filled with helping Susan or Jackie (because both their husbands are SAC pilots who fly B-52s and are away more than they're home—sound familiar???). I've become Auntie Gale to the children, and I rather enjoy my status. There's something about a child's smile when it's given to you, or the touch of a child's hand that just can't be duplicated anywhere else in life. Do you like children, Kyle? I know you were an only child and never had the pleasure of sibling company. Let me know. I'm curious.

Take care. And you're right: enclosed is a huge bottle of vitamin C! You'd better be over your sniffles by the time the New Year call rolls around or you're in deep you-know-what. As always, you're in my heart and thoughts.

Your friend, Gale

* * *

December 20, 1977

Dearest Gale,

Another Christmas. Life goes on, doesn't it, whether we want it to or not? This letter will reach you down in Sedona. I'm sure Mike's folks are delighted you're there again for them. I don't see how you do it. You've got a hell of a lot more courage and internal fortitude than I would under your circumstances. Just your being there has got to lift their spirits. If you were here at Griffiss AFB, which is near Buffalo, New York, I'd give you a big hug and kiss for what you've done for them. You're one hell of a lady in my book.

Well, I'm finally settled into my new base—I have more responsibility, less flying time. I don't like that. If I wanted to fly a desk, I wouldn't have joined the Air Force.

Buffalo is—well, let's put it this way: it's not the most exciting place for a bachelor. We've already got a ton of snow. Hell of a change from my Florida base. I guess I live a life of extremes. I wear the sweater you knitted for me a lot nowadays when I'm off duty.

Until you told me, I often wondered what your favorite flower was. A daffodil. I pictured you like spring flowers, so I was close. Fall is my favorite time of year. I like the riot of color. Makes me think of some invisible painter who's gone wild with a palette of colors, slap dashing them here and there. I like the smells, too. Funny, since I've known you, you've put me more in touch with my senses. I never used to notice subtle shadings or pay attention to smells in general.

You're right: pilots are put in a little box, certain skills they possess brought out and honed to a fine degree, but everything else just sort of sits there, ignored and untended. You're a hell of a gardener, lady. I like being cultivated by you. I like seeing life through your eyes. It's made me see my world differently. Better.

Because of my transfer to Griffiss, I can't be home for Christmas with my parents. Too bad, I'd promised them I'd make it this year. I know you'll drop by and see them for me, you're that kind of lady. Don't tell my mother that I'm unhappy here. Lie. She tends to worry too much. I think she got all her gray hair while I was over at Udorn flying missions over Hanoi. I don't want to be responsible for any more gray hairs on her head. Worst of all, I can't be there while you're there. If nothing else, I could have offered you fortitude with Mike's parents and been there in case you needed a shoulder to cry on.

Hi...this is a supplement. A KC-135 tanker just slid off the end of the runway during an ice storm and I had to go help. Not much for me to do, but as one of the few officers left on base during Christmas, everyone becomes more important or integral than usual. Luckily, the crew is fine. The 135 is going to need some major structural work, but it could have been worse. Much worse.

God, it's freezing cold here compared to Florida. I think my blood's thinned too much. It's dark and gloomy here in the office. I really didn't want any lights on, I guess. It's 1600 and the dusk is coming up rapidly. I was sitting here in my new office, leaning back in my chair, my feet propped up on the desk, a warm cup of coffee in hand, and I got to thinking about you. It was a good, warm feeling, Gale.

You've taken the last few years with so much grace. You haven't faltered at work, and you've gone on without Mike. Hanging in limbo must be a special hell for you. It's got to be. And yet, you survive. The last year's worth of letters from you has explained so much to me about you, how you work, think and feel. Reading about your world has affected how I see mine. I've got the best end of the deal, I think.

Maybe I'm feeling guilty...feeling something, that's for sure...hell, I don't know *what* it is. Maybe it's the holiday blues that strike the military people who can't be with the people they love at special times like this. I think I'm feeling sorry for myself because you're home with people I love and I'm not there to share it with you. So, don't get alarmed at my wallowing. I'm just sharing my wallowing with you for the first time.

We've shared a lot of ground with one another, haven't we? That's the good thing about our friendship. I've never had a woman as a friend. (Don't comment on *that!*) I guess I want to say while I'm in this philosophical mood, that these past few years have been the best of my life. I never had a relationship with a woman that ever got to this depth or that I allowed to get past my jock facade. It's not so bad. In fact, it's damn good. Just thinking of you, of what we've shared these years, makes my heart feel like it's exploding in my chest. If you feel one-tenth as lucky as I do, I'll be happy.

Give my folks and Mike's folks a big hug for me, will you? Tell them I'll make it next Christmas or else, okay? And give yourself a big hug from me.

Warmly, Kyle

* * *

December 26, 1977

Dearest Kyle,

I'm here in the guest room at Mike's parent's home. Your last letter touched me so deeply, that I cried. Oh, I know, you didn't intend on making me do that, but I couldn't help it. Loneliness is something I know well, and so do you, in another kind of way.

More than anything, I wanted to meet you here so we could have celebrated a Christmas together. Wouldn't that have been nice? We both could have drunk a toast to Mike and been here to help support his parents. They still are suffering so badly, I just don't know what to say or do. I talk a lot with Mom about this, and I think it helps to alleviate some of her fears. This year, she really unloaded and revealed a lot more to me than last year. I think she's really beginning to trust me. After all, I was a stranger who walked in, married her son and then left town. I really like her, but she's gotten so many gray hairs worrying.

Mike's dad has internalized the whole thing. His ulcer (which he got after Mike was M.I.A.) tends to act up at this time of year, according to Mom. I spend time with him down at Oak Creek. You know how he loves to fish. I just sit there on one of those smooth red sandstone rocks and let him do the talking, if he feels like it. For the first time, he spoke about Mike. About the possibility that he was dead, not alive. It hurt to hear him feel that way.

I guess men are more pessimistic than women by nature. I hold out hope he's alive. Dad has not. But Mom has. I really wished you had been here. It got pretty emotional for me with each one of them unloading on me. They didn't mean to, but who else could they talk to? I went for a hike on Christmas Day and wished you were here. I know that I could have cried in your arms and it would have been okay. I didn't dare cry in front of Mom and Dad. They were feeling miserable enough.

Oh, Kyle, I just hope this is over soon. What's wearing me down isn't myself as much as those I love, like Mike's parents. It hurts me to see the pain they carry with them daily. With your help, I've been able to put my pain into a perspective of sorts. I don't know what I'd have done without your care and help through all these years. I'm thankful for your support. And, like you, I love where our friendship is going. It's a privilege to know the *real* Kyle Anderson, 'cause he's a far better guy than that jock facade he wears.

I'd better go. I hear Mom downstairs. I woke up early and wanted to get this letter off to you today. I can hardly wait to hear from you on New Year's Eve! Your parents and Mike's can hardly wait, either. How

I wish you could come home for Christmas. Any Christmas! You're dear to my heart, my best friend....

Gale

Chapter Three

December 24, 1978
Travis Air Force Base, California

Any minute now, Major Kyle Anderson was going to walk through the doors of Operations. Gale fidgeted nervously behind the meteorology desk, the only meteorologist on duty Christmas Eve. Her heart speeded up, as it always did whenever she got a letter or received a call from Kyle. How long had it been since she'd last seen him? Five years. Five of the most hellish years of her life. But his letters and later, his frequent phone calls had helped ease her suffering.

Licking her lower lip, Gale moved to the forecaster's desk and sat down. In the other room, twelve Teletype machines noisily clattered away, printing out weather information from around the world. Her mind and heart focused on the fact that within seventy-two hours she would know one way or another whether Mike was alive or dead.

Rubbing her aching brow, Gale closed her eyes, the tears coming. She fought them back, refusing to cry.

Sniffing, she took a tissue, dabbed her eyes and tried to focus on the wall of weather maps. Operations was ghostly quiet. Across the way, one airman was on duty at the air-control desk. Everyone else was with family on this Christmas Eve. Everyone had someone to spend the holidays with.

Two days ago, the Pentagon had informed her that Mike's dog tags had been supplied by Hanoi as belonging to a POW. The North Vietnamese were releasing some POWs and the remains of other servicemen as a goodwill gesture. As to Mike's fate, sometime between December 25 and 28, the Pentagon would know and Gale would be contacted. Unable to stand the suspense alone, she had called Kyle.

More tears came and she wiped them away. He was supposed to go home for Christmas this year. She'd hesitated calling him. She knew how badly his folks wanted to see him and how much he needed to be home. But the pain of waiting alone had driven her to the phone to ask him to come and wait with her instead.

Kyle hadn't sounded as if he wanted to be anywhere but at her side when the news came from the Pentagon. She felt guilty about taking him from his folks and hoped that they would forgive her moment of weakness.

Gale got up and went to the Teleype room where there was a modicum of privacy. She didn't want the airman across the way to see her like this. Even now, Mike's parents waited, having also been notified. They had looked to her for solace over the past few years, especially since they had both come to fear Mike was dead. But they'd never openly admitted that to her.

Kyle was coming to be with her. He'd always kept up her hope, her belief that Mike was still alive.

"How am I going to handle this?" she muttered, burying her face in her hands. *"How?"*

Right now, her emotions were little more than taut butterfly's wings ready to shatter at the slightest movement. Kyle, flying in from Griffiss AFB, was supposed to land momentarily. A part of her was so weak after the years of terrible waiting and wondering, of being in limbo about Mike, that she ached to simply be held by Kyle. Gale knew she'd feel safe and protected from a world gone mad. The peace she'd felt in his arms five years ago when she'd burned her hand would be there, too. Her emotions were playing tricks on her. Gale thought she had heard longing in Kyle's voice when she'd made that phone call, but that was impossible.

She began to absently tear off and collect the Tele-type paper, gathering it from each machine and then clipping it to posting boards. Some of the sheets would be used in plotting the midnight weather map an hour from now. Walking out into the main office, Gale put the weather information on the desk where a clean sheet of map paper lay. Working kept her from thinking. Working kept her from feeling.

Halting, Gale lifted her chin and looked out the windows into the gloomy darkness. The landing apron in front of the building had very few jets parked on it. No one flew during the holidays unless they were on alert duty. It was raining. The gusting wind sent sheets of water across the tarmac. Gale prayed Kyle would be strong enough for both of them. The waiting...the wondering had taken their toll. She was too emotionally drained to be strong any longer.

She moved to the front desk and stood watching the double doors, and she wondered when Kyle would arrive. His letters had been filled with anecdotes about his military life, funny stories about things that had happened to him, stories meant to make her laugh, to pull her out of her depression. During the past year, there had been a wonderful shift in his letters—they were more personal, more about the man, Kyle Anderson, and not the pilot. Those letters were special to her.

Kyle's phone calls weren't frequent. He called on her birthday, Thanksgiving and Christmas, just to check in on her. Kyle knew what it was like to be in the service and alone on holidays. She ached to hear his voice, to listen to him laugh and tell his jokes. There was nothing but good in Kyle Anderson. His loyalty to Mike was unswerving.

The doors opened.

Kyle stepped into the dimly lit Ops area and shook water off his olive-drab flight suit. In one hand he had his helmet bag, in the other, a small traveling bag with two sets of clean civilian clothes inside, including the sweater Gale had made for him. His F-4 Phantom was parked at the hangar, the crew chief having given him a ride over to Ops.

Sensing Gale's presence, he looked up. He hadn't seen her in five years; he hadn't dared. Her heart-shaped face was the same, and so were those haunting green eyes, that full mouth and slender build. Her hair was longer, and he was pleased about that for no discernible reason. The strands were pulled into a French twist behind her head, with feathery bangs barely touching her eyebrows.

It was the look of utter devastation on Gale's pale features that forced him to remain strong, because he

could see that she wasn't. This wasn't the Gale he'd
met five years ago, the woman who had courage under incredible duress. Five years without Mike had
ravaged her in many ways. And still, she was the most
beautiful woman Kyle had ever seen. The years hadn't
dimmed his memory of her. Like a miser, Kyle had
hoarded that precious, sweet memory, pulling it out
from time to time to savor it, knowing that it could
never be anything more.

Putting a smile of welcome on his face, he strode
toward the counter where she stood. He noticed the
airman sitting at the control desk, reading a magazine, not even bothering to look up.

"Hi, stranger," Kyle said, setting his helmet bag on
the counter and the traveling bag on the floor. An ache
seized him, and he wanted to walk around that desk,
pull Gale into his arms and simply hold her. The urge
was overwhelming. Kyle didn't let his smile slip, being
very careful to keep the look of devilry he was famous for in his eyes—and to hide a look of yearning.

Gale stared up at Kyle not believing he was really
with her. She moved without realizing what she was
doing, coming around the end of the counter. The
smile on Kyle's face changed, became nakedly vulnerable, and she saw him open his arms to her. Tears
blinded her, and she couldn't stop herself. In moments, his arms closed around her. He dragged her
against him and held her tightly.

"Oh, Kyle," she said, her voice muffled by his flight
suit, her arms going around his waist. She needed to
lean against someone for just a little while, to seek
protection against the final seventy-two hours of a
five-year marathon that she'd run alone. Then the

words she had refused to say to herself started pouring out of her. "I'm so afraid...so afraid...."

"It's going to be okay, Gale," Kyle whispered, shutting his eyes and absorbing the feeling of her against him. "Mike's coming home. I can feel it. Everything's going to be okay." Every muscle in his body screamed out for further contact with her warm, pliant body, but he kept his embrace that of a friend. "Just hang in there," he told her, pressing a chaste kiss to her hair. The clean, faintly fragrant scent of her body sent a painful surge through him. Kyle dragged in a deep breath, rocked her gently in his arms and fought his personal need of her as a woman.

Now beyond words, Gale collapsed into Kyle's arms. The moment his hand stroked her hair, a small sob caught in her throat. She felt his arms tighten around her momentarily. It was as if Kyle knew exactly what she needed, and beyond exhaustion, she capitulated to him. Each stroke of his hand on her hair took away a little more anxiety, a little more pain and suffering. Finally, after a full five minutes, she was able to ease out of his arms and step away.

Wiping her cheeks dry, Gale managed a shy, broken smile. "Thanks for coming, for being here...."

Kyle shrugged self-consciously. "I'm glad you called. I wouldn't have wanted it any other way, Gale."

"Your parents—"

"They understand," he whispered, reaching out, barely caressing her hair. "I *want* to be here."

"It's been so long since I last saw you."

Too long. The words begged to be said, but Kyle held on to them. He managed a strained smile meant to buoy her flagging spirits. "I know."

Gale sniffed and found a tissue in the pocket of her dark blue slacks. "I'm just glad you're here."

"Hell of a thing," he muttered, forcing himself not to reach out to smooth back several strands of hair clinging to her reddened cheek.

"What is?" She stuffed the tissue back into her pocket, then raised her head and met his blue eyes smoldering with dark intensity.

"The Pentagon springing this on you at Christmastime. I wish they'd waited . . . or something."

With a shake of her head, Gale whispered, "At least I'll know."

The haunted look in her eyes tore at him. Kyle had to stand there, not touching her, trying not to comfort her beyond the province of an old friend. "Buck up," he coaxed huskily, trying to sound positive. "It'll be good news. Mike will be back in no time."

Rubbing her arm because she was suddenly chilled, Gale forced a slight smile. "I hope you're right, Kyle. So many prayers, so many hopes dashed so many times and ways."

"The kind of suffering the wives and families of the men who went over there is a special kind of hell. I can't really know what it's like for you, except that I know it's agony." How could he tell her he hurt for Mike almost as much as she did? Kyle didn't want to dwell on negatives with Gale.

"Despite everything, you look pretty as ever," he said, meaning it.

Gale touched her cheek, feeling the heat of a blush sweeping onto her face. "Thank you."

"Going to say the same for me?" he asked, beginning to grin.

"You look more mature." The war had carved and etched deeper lines into his face. She saw the pain he carried in those lines.

"Have I changed *that* much?"

Managing a wobbly smile, Gale shook her head. *You look wonderful.* She longed to reach out and touch the hand that rested on the counter. A long, spare hand like the rest of him. Kyle was built whipcord lean, with a deep, broad chest and shoulders. His face was narrow, his smile warm with welcome, his eyes hooded by some undefinable emotion.

"Whew, that was close."

"You're such a clown, Anderson," she joked weakly, trying to get a handle on her escaping emotions and to pick up on his effort to lighten the mood of their vigil. Tears had come, but just the way Kyle was behaving helped her to stabilize. The tears went away and in their place, Gale felt an overwhelming lightness sweep through her. "You haven't changed a bit."

His boyish grin broadened. "The same? Usually, at my age, people say I look a bit more suave or some such thing."

She laughed, a terrible burden sliding off her shoulders. "All pilots know they're handsome devils. You don't need me to add to that confident ego you already own." If anything, Kyle had grown more handsome with age. The crow's feet at the corners of his eyes were deeply embedded, and the laugh lines around his mouth were pronounced. A few errant strands of black hair dipped over his wrinkled brow and Gale yearned to push them back into place.

"Touché, Major Taylor." He forced himself to look around because if he didn't, he was going to stare deeply into her eyes, bare his soul and then destroy the fragile truce between them. "Got a cup of coffee for this tired old jet jock?"

"I'm forgetting my manners. You bet I do. Come on around the end of the counter."

"I'm allowed to tread on sacred meteorology territory?"

"Of course. While I get you coffee, why don't you call the B.O.Q. and tell them you've arrived. I made reservations and they've got a room ready. They'll send over a driver to pick you up whenever you want to hit the rack. The number is 920."

With a nod, Kyle rounded the counter. "Thanks, I'll do that." His eyes narrowed when she turned away and went to the Teletype room, where the coffee pot was kept. Gale was terribly thin. Damn! The uniform hung on her. A deep, startling anger coursed through him. War did terrible things to all people, not just the people who fought it, but the wives and family left at home were equally injured by it. No one was left untouched or unscarred. But surely Gale had suffered more than most.

Gale tried not to let her hand tremble when she placed the mug in front of Kyle, but it did. Tucking her lip between her teeth, she looked away, aware of his sharpened gaze. She leaned against the counter, opposite him, listening to the rich timbre of his voice, a healing balm across her taut, screaming nerves. He automatically allowed her to relax, to feel as if everything would be fine.

Kyle hung up the phone. "Thanks for making the reservations," he said, picking up the mug.

"At Christmastime, the B.O.Q. is empty."

"All the bases are deserted. Only the poor schmuck stuck with the duty is around." Kyle glanced at her critically. "Which reminds me, why are you on duty at a time like this?"

Gale shrugged, crossing her arms against her chest. "Why shouldn't I be? If I wasn't, I'd be going stir crazy over at the house. I couldn't just wait, Kyle. I have to be doing something—anything—to keep my mind off the what ifs."

The coffee was hot and strong. Kyle nodded, understanding. "When do you get off duty?"

"Christmas morning at 0700. Then, I come back at 1900 tomorrow evening for twelve hours and then get the next seventy-two hours off."

He glanced around. "So you're here holding down the fort by yourself?"

"Do you see a crowd of pilots standing around needing weather?"

"Not a one."

Gale smiled. "In about half an hour, I've got to plot a weather map, is all."

"And you have to take a weather observation from the roof of Ops once an hour?" Kyle guessed. He watch her nod, thinking how the lights gave her hair a golden cast, like a halo around her head. "How long is your hair?" *Damn!* He hadn't meant to get so personal.

"Believe it or not, almost halfway down my back. Isn't that something?"

Swallowing hard, Kyle agreed. The very thought of sifting his fingers through that thick brown mass was too much. He forced himself to think of Mike and his ordeal.

Mustering a smile, Kyle said, "In three days or less, we'll know Mike's fine and coming home to you."

"I wish I had your optimism."

"My stock and trade."

It felt good to laugh—freely and with happiness. Gale shook her head. "You're good medicine, Kyle. You take away my pain and make me laugh when I never thought I would again. Thanks."

You take away my pain. Kyle looked away from her green eyes which were sparkling with life once again. When he'd arrived, Gale's eyes had been flat with pain, dull with fear. Her words tormented him. Well, maybe he could take some of her worry and anxiety away—if only for the next few days. Sitting up, he took a good look around the office.

"What, no Christmas tree? What kind of place do you run here, Major?"

Gale grimaced. "Want to know the worst of it?"

"What?"

"I don't have a Christmas tree at home, either."

He studied her, hearing the underlying strain in her voice. "Probably haven't had one in years, right?"

"How did you know? Never mind, don't answer that." Gale gave him an exasperated look. "Do you know how disconcerting it is to have someone know me that well?"

Kyle grinned and stood up, stretching fully. Flying in a cramped combat jet from New York to California wasn't his idea of pleasure. "I promise, your secrets are safe with me."

With a smile, Gale reached for his emptied mug. "I don't know how you've put up with me through the years, Major Anderson. I've been a royal pain at times." Some of the depressing letters she'd written to him, in which she'd let her fear for Mike and the real possibility he was dead surface, weren't her idea of chatty letters to a friend. Kyle had fielded her tough, hard questions and issues addressing her trepidation for Mike. He'd counseled her on how to stay sane and try to lead a normal life while she remained in a painful limbo of not knowing.

"Never a pain," Kyle told her, working at keeping his tone light and teasing when it was the last thing he wanted to be with her.

"More coffee?"

"Yeah, please. Hey, you got an old cardboard box sitting around here somewhere?"

She gave him a strange look. "Yes. Why?"

With a shrug, Kyle pointed to the main desk. "I think we ought to put a Christmas tree up, don't you?"

Kyle's enthusiasm was contagious and just what Gale needed. "I think you're right. But cardboard...?"

"Sure." He followed her back to the Teletype room. "When Mike and I were kids in Arizona, we had this tree house in this huge old sycamore in his backyard. A couple of days before Christmas, we'd go up there and make a Christmas tree and leave it in the tree house. You must have seen it when you stayed with the Taylors."

"Mmm. Mike's mother told me how you two used to spend hours playing in that old tree. The view from their home is breathtaking." The surrounding country—the wide, flowing creek and pine forest—was a salve to her spirit when she visited there. Smiling wistfully, Gale straightened, handing him the mug. "That sycamore is still standing out back, you know."

"It must be at least a hundred and fifty years old." Thoughts of the tree brought back a wealth of good memories.

"What did you two do out there with that sycamore?"

Brightening, Kyle spotted an empty Teletype-paper box in the corner. "As I said, Mike and I would make a cardboard Christmas tree for our tree house every year. We'd sit up there with crayons, paper, glue and string for hours putting it together." With a grin, he walked over and picked up the box. "And we're going to do that tonight. A good-luck charm to get Mike back home alive. Ready?"

Gale didn't have time to protest. With a small laugh, she nodded, walking back to the forecaster's desk with him. She watched as Kyle searched through several drawers until he found some colored felt-tip markers.

"Perfect," he muttered, pulling up another swivel chair and motioning for her to sit beside him. "Come on, we've got a lot to do. Normally, this takes a whole day to do up right, and we only have seven hours left before your watch ends."

Sitting down, Gale watched as he placed the markers and white paper in front of her. "You mean, you're planning on staying up all night with me?" Kyle had to be tired from the flight. She saw dark shadows beginning to form beneath his eyes.

"You've got to stay up all night," he pointed out blandly.

"Well...that's different, I have the duty. Kyle, you've got to be dead on your feet. Don't you think you ought to go over to the B.O.Q. and get some rest?"

He shook his head. "No way. I want to be here when you get that phone call telling you Mike's alive. I wouldn't miss that for the world, lady."

Fighting the urge to throw her arms around his shoulders and hug him for his thoughtfulness, Gale didn't do anything. Instead, she muttered, "You're such a glutton for punishment."

Kyle grinned lopsidedly. "Yeah, I know. Now, come on, you've got to help me here."

"Do what?"

"Well," Kyle murmured, picking up the box, "we used to make Christmas decorations of things we liked. You know, planes, cars and stuff like that. Whatever we made had to mean something important to us. Usually we made decorations of toys we *wanted* to get for Christmas."

Laughing, Gale drowned in his amused look. "So, if I wanted Mike, I draw him—"

"And cut him out and put a string at the top of him and then hang him on the cardboard tree I'm going to make for us. Yeah, you've got the idea."

Touched, Gale felt the intensity of Kyle's happiness. Suddenly, they were like two children rediscovering the joy of simple things like playing. "Okay," she whispered, "that's my first decoration, Mike coming home safely to me. To us."

Giving her a wink, Kyle said, "I've never given up on him being alive."

"I—I haven't been as positive as you," Gale hesitantly admitted. She began to make an outline of a man, her husband, on the white paper. As much as she wanted Mike to be alive, she just couldn't shake the awful feeling she was a widow. Still, for the Taylors' and Kyle's sakes, she fought her pessimism.

"No one is going to go through five years without having a few bad days," Kyle said gently. Whistling softly, he tussled with the box and cut off the top and bottom of it. Next, he opened it out and laid it flat on the desk. Glancing down at Gale, he saw her completely immersed in her first decoration.

"Hey, you ought to have been an artist. That really does look like Mike."

Blushing, she managed a quirked smile. "Thank you."

Taking a black pen, Kyle drew the main trunk of their "tree," and then four smaller cardboard branches. "I can remember Mike and I laying on our bellies for hours up there in that tree house, making these decorations. Our moms used to call us down for dinner, but we never came, so they ended up bringing it up the ladder to us."

"Mike mentioned that you two spent a lot of time up there."

"Yeah, we used to talk for hours about what we were going to be and do."

Gale sat back, examining her handiwork. She had drawn Mike in his blue officer's uniform.

She sat back, watching Kyle fashion their tree. He took some tape and fastened the four branches to the trunk. With some extra cardboard, he shored up the bottom so the tree would stand—at a bit of an angle.

"There," Kyle said proudly, studying his creation. "It looks a little naked right now, but when we start hanging the stuff on it, it'll look great."

Stifling a giggle, Gale looked at the tree and then at Kyle. "Doesn't it look a little...scrawny?" As a matter of fact, it looked like a multiarmed scarecrow.

"Nah." Kyle sat down, grabbing some paper and a red marker. "Come on, Major, quit laughing at my artistic efforts and get to work."

Giggling, Gale carefully cut out the drawing. "Now what?"

"You got any string around this place?"

Rummaging around in one of the lower desk drawers, she drew out a small ball of it. "Here you go."

Taking the string, Kyle cut off a small piece. "Just take a bit of tape and put it on the back of Mike, and then hang him."

"Hang him? Do you think Mike would like your choice of words?" She burst out laughing.

"He was always hanging around," Kyle muttered good naturedly as he showed Gale how to make a loop that could be slipped onto the branch of the tree.

"Mike said you were always on his heels," Gale parried.

"It was the other way around."

"You two were inseparable."

"Yeah, we were shadows to one another, that's for sure."

She surveyed Kyle's handiwork. "Nice. Now what?"

"Well," Kyle said with great seriousness, "we always put what we wanted the *most* on the top limb, and then we'd put other decorations in descending order of importance. The lowest branch represented what we wanted least."

Getting up, Gale gently put Mike on the uppermost limb on the right. "There," she whispered, staring at it.

"Looks good," Kyle said, giving her a game smile. He saw the tears in her eyes. "Come on, what's your second wish for Christmas? A fur coat? A new car?"

She smiled and sat down. "I'm not telling. I'm going to watch you for a minute. What's your first choice?"

Kyle saw flecks of gold in the depths of her green eyes. Swallowing hard, he tore himself away from his own need of her. These next few days were for Mike and for her, not for himself.

"Kyle?"

Damn, he was staring at her, something he hadn't meant to do. "Uh...oh, I was going to draw Bell Rock, a red sandstone butte that sits out in the village of Oak Creek, near Sedona." He got to work, carefully making an outline of the butte.

"You need to go home for a while."

He shrugged. "Well, sometime."

Gale read between the lines. "Sooner rather than later. Right?" She saw his mouth quirk. "Kyle Anderson...?"

"Sometime," he hedged. If Mike was dead, he wanted to remain here with Gale, to help her adjust.

She would need someone, since she had no close family. "I'll get there soon enough. Maybe in the spring. It's no big deal, Gale." He looked at her serious features. "And quit looking like you're the Grinch that stole my Christmas. You didn't. I don't want to be anywhere else but here right now. Understand?"

She sat there for several minutes without saying anything and watched him painstakingly draw the red-orange butte. He'd cancelled his own holiday leave to be with her. There was so much sentimentality to Kyle, and so much he was sensitive about. Compressing her lips, Gale still refrained from saying anything, not wanting to spoil the liveliness of the mood he'd created for them. But someday, after Mike returned home, she was going to sit down and have a long, searching talk with Kyle, telling him how much she appreciated his care, his love, as a friend.

"Mike and I used to climb all over Bell Rock," Kyle said quietly. "It's got skirts around it, kind of like a layer cake, smooth and easy to climb over."

Gale relaxed in the chair, watching him begin to color the formation. "So, you were rock climbers, too."

"Well now, Red Rock County is really hiking country. Bell is a hiking butte, not a true rock-climbing experience."

Gale pulled another sheet of paper to her. "I did a little hiking when I was out there last year. I really liked it."

Kyle picked up the scissors and cut out the butte. "So, what's your next decoration?"

"I'm going to draw my home in Medford, Oregon. I'll use a pear tree to symbolize it, though, because it's a huge valley with nothing but fruit orchards throughout it.''

His grin broadened. ''Want me to draw the partridge for it?''

She laughed long and deeply, wiping the tears from her eyes. ''You have a great sense of humor.''

''Thanks. I like the fact you have the good taste to appreciate it.'' Kyle pointed to the tree she was drawing. ''Is that what you want to do? Go back home?'' He knew her parents were dead, but that the house was still there, empty and in her name.

Hesitating, Gale looked at the tree with white blossoms. ''My enlistment's up in four months. I—I've given a lot of thought to it, Kyle. I'm going to leave the service.''

He frowned. ''But you've go a lot of time built up toward a twenty-year retirement pension. Why blow it now?''

She shrugged. ''I guess I want to have a home . . . a family.''

''Oh.''

She met his dark blue eyes. ''I'm tired, Kyle. Tired in a way I can't even begin to describe. I need time to get back to basics, back to things that give to me, not take.''

''A home and children?'' In his opinion, Gale would make a wonderful mother, a spectacular wife.

''Yes. What about you?''

''Me?''

''Sure. Haven't you thought about having a family and kids someday?''

He nodded, trying to contain the pain that mushroomed unexpectedly in his chest. His dreams had been of Gale, of what might have been but would never be. "Yeah...I suppose." And then he made light of it. "You know me, career-oriented all the way. I'll wait until I get my mandatory twenty in, and then hog-tie some good-looking woman who's willing put up with me and my eccentricities."

Gale looked at the clock. It was time to plot the weather map. Rising, she gave him a serious look. "You're far better marriage material than you think you are, Anderson."

Laughing, Kyle sat there, watching her move to the plotting desk. Pulling another piece of paper to him, he glanced at his watch. Time was moving slowly. Didn't it always when something important was about to take place?

December 26, 1978

"How much longer?" Gale asked in a whisper, the question breaking the strained silence. She stood at the window of her base-housing home and stared out at the rainy morning. It was nearly 1000, and still no word from the Pentagon. In the distance, she could hear a bomber taking off, the jet engines creating man-made thunder that reverberated through the overcast sky. Her fingers tightened against the kitchen sink.

"We'll hear soon," Kyle said, sitting at the table. There was a deathly waiting stillness in her home since he'd arrived from the B.O.Q. two hours ago. The tension in Gale's body was apparent.

Slowly, she turned around. Kyle was dressed in a long-sleeved blue-plaid shirt that made his eyes look even darker. Although he was sprawled out on the chair, nursing his third cup of coffee, his long legs stretched out beneath the cherry table, he didn't look relaxed. Searching his composed features, she asked, "Do you think it means bad news if it's taking this long, Kyle?"

He sighed. "They were bringing fifteen bodies back along with twelve POWs. I'm sure they're not releasing any word to the families of the survivors or the dead until they're absolutely sure of identification of everyone," he muttered. "That can take time. They don't want any mistakes."

Gale bowed her head and wrapped her arms around herself because she was cold and shaking inside. "That makes sense." Gale forced a smile, fighting valiantly to look less worried. "They said if Mike was alive, they'd be calling me...."

Gale and Kyle both knew that if Mike was dead, two Air Force officers would come to her house and give her the news in person. It was lousy duty telling the wife and children of a serviceman that he was dead.

The urge to get up, to go over and hold Gale was excruciating, but Kyle fought it. So far, she'd rallied and held her own—until now. "We've got the tree in your front room," he said quietly. He tried hard to keep his tone light, but found it nearly impossible.

She lifted her head. "Does that guarantee a phone call instead of those guys coming to my door?"

"That's a roger."

Turning to the sink, Gale began washing breakfast dishes. Kyle had eaten enough for two men; she hadn't been able to eat at all. The warm, soapy water took away some of the coldness that had been with her since she'd awakened that morning. There was such fear and anxiety pressing in on her, she couldn't shake it—not even with Kyle's caring presence.

Needing something—anything—to do, Kyle got up, collecting the garbage and putting it into a sack. Why the hell were those bastards waiting so long to call her? Why couldn't they let her know the instant the plane had landed if Mike was alive? Was he ill, badly injured? In the hopsital? Dammit, they ought to be telling Gale instead of letting her twist in the wind like this!

Needing to calm his rage over the military officials' insensitive handling of the situation, Kyle took the garbage out to the cans that sat alongside the garage. Then he swept the walk, even though it was still raining. The rain was cooling to his anger and frustration.

Reentering the kitchen fifteen minutes later, he found Gale had finished with the dishes. The place was quiet. Maybe some music would help to dissolve the stillness. Shutting the door, he wiped his feet on the rug and put the broom to one side.

"KYLE!"

Tensing at Gale's tortured cry, he quickly strode across the kitchen to the living room. Gale was standing at the picture window, staring out, her hands pressed against her mouth.

"What?" Kyle said in a hoarse voice as he moved toward her, not understanding until he glimpsed two officers coming up the wet sidewalk toward the front door. "No..." he whispered, reaching out, gripping Gale's arm because she was weaving.

The doorbell rang. Once. Twice. Three times.

Kyle cursed beneath his breath, feeling Gale tremble badly. He looked down and winced. Her eyes were dark and narrowed with pain, with denial. "I'll answer it," he said unsteadily.

Gale stood there, her knees watery, watching as Kyle opened the door. Her world exploded as the two men, both somber faced, told her what she already knew: Mike was dead.

She barely heard their apology and their heartfelt condolences. All she could do was stare at Kyle's ravaged features. There were tears in his eyes, and his mouth was pulled into a terrible line of anguish.

Gale was looking faint. Kyle turned to the senior officer.

"I'll get in touch with you on funeral details in about an hour, Captain."

"Yes, sir, Major. I'm sorry, sir. . . ."

His attention on Gale, Kyle cleared his throat and said, "We all are. Thanks."

"Yes, sir. Goodbye, sir." The officers turned and left.

Shutting the door quietly, Kyle turned to Gale. She looked small and broken standing there in the middle of the large room, her shoulders slumped, eyes filled with terrible reality.

"Gale?" His voice shook as he took the final steps to where she stood. Tears blurred his vision; her face danced before him.

"Mike's dead. . . ."

Standing uncertainly, Kyle gave a jerky nod. "Yeah . . . I'm sorry, so damn sorry, Gale—" He couldn't go on. Reaching out, he pulled her into his arms, holding her tightly, holding her hard, as if to take away her pain, her loss.

The gray morning light filtered through the windows bracketed by beige drapes. Kyle felt the first genuine sob rip though Gale, her entire body convulsing. All he could do was hold her, rock her, murmur words, useless words, of apology, of comfort. But nothing was going to help her. His own pain at the loss of his best friend, someone he'd grown up with, shared his life with, was no less cutting.

They cried together, clinging to each other because nothing else made sense, nothing else existed except the huge walls of pain that battered their hearts.

Eventually, Kyle moved past his first wave of grief enough to think clearly. As he stood there, holding Gale, absorbing her soft, choking anguish, he looked ahead to the next few days. He knew Mike's body would have to be flown to Sedona. Mike's parents would want him buried there, Kyle was sure of that. He'd request emergency leave from his office and make sure Gale had someone to help her with all the details, the endless paperwork that he knew would come.

Sighing, he rested his jaw against her hair, and closed his eyes. Her pain was his pain. So much had been taken from Gale over the years. So much.

Opening his eyes, Kyle stared at the scraggly, leaning cardboard Christmas tree sitting on the coffee table in front of the couch. His gaze moved from the image of Mike to the Bell Rock decoration. Mike was going home. And they'd be going home with him.

His eyes filled with tears, momentarily blurring his vision. Blinking, Kyle shifted his gaze to the second branch, where Gale's pear tree hung. Next to it was the partridge he'd drawn. His arms tightened around her. He knew she'd leave the Air Force and go home to Medford. She would try to pick up the pieces of a life that had been stretched and tortured for five years.

Time . . . they both needed time to grieve for Mike, to remember him, to cherish all that was good about him and the ways he'd affected their lives.

Taking a deep, ragged breath, Kyle simply held Gale, listening to her sobs lessen with the passing minutes, the first storm of grief, of shock, now passing. There would be many other cycles of tears to come, he was sure.

His gaze remained on the tree. Gale had fashioned a pot of daffodils. They were her favorite flower. She said she was going to plant them along the edge of the house in Medford, a sign of spring, of a new beginning.

Yes, there was a beginning for both of them. Kyle didn't look at his own needs right now. Being there for Gale and for Mike's parents was what was important right now. But he would never forget that pot of daffodils. Never.

Chapter Four

December 24, 1979
Blytheville Air Force Base, Arkansas

Kyle frowned, staring at the mass of paperwork on his desk. It was 0800, and he had all day to plow through it. What did it matter? He didn't have anything else to do over the Christmas holiday, so why not use the time to catch up on paperwork when the office was empty and quiet? December was a lousy month for him, he'd decided that a long time ago. The Air Force had ordered him from Griffiss to Blytheville two weeks ago, and he was still unpacking and trying to get situated at his new command. He'd called his folks, apologizing for not being able to come home as he'd planned. There was simply too much work to do here and the holidays were the only time he'd be able to get things in order before the responsibilities of squadron command rested squarely on his shoulders.

"Major?"

Scowling, Kyle looked up toward his sergeant, who stood at the entrance to his office. "What is it, Dickson?"

"A telegram just arrived for you, sir." He brought it forward and placed it in Kyle's hand.

A telegram? Kyle nodded. "Thanks, Dickson."

"Yes, sir." The door shut quietly.

The yellow envelope stared back at him. Who would send him a telegram? He turned it over and ripped it open, a sense of dread filling him. The only time someone got a telegram was when it was bad news. His heart started an uneven beat as he read the short message.

Kyle. Come Home. Gale.

His hand trembled as he looked at the address. Gale was in Sedona, staying with the Taylors. In the past year, they'd exchanged many letters and phone calls, staying in touch, helping to heal each other in so many ways since Mike's death. She had left the service as she'd planned, moved into her parents' home, and was trying to make a new life for herself.

A deep ache centered in his heart as he mulled over her request. The need to see her was excruciating. Looking around his new office, he grimaced. Stay and catch up on his new workload, or go home? There wasn't any question what he wanted to do. Gently tucking the telegram into the pocket of his light blue shirt, Kyle got up. As he reached for the phone to find out when the next flight left for Arizona, his throat constricted. Why was Gale there?

When the reservations operator answered, it took several seconds before Kyle could speak. He recalled the cardboard tree they'd fashioned together last year. A make-believe Christmas tree filled with dreams and prayers. Some had been answered, others hadn't. He cleared his throat, his voice off-key. "Yes, I need a flight out to Flagstaff, Arizona, as soon as possible."

His need for Gale, the new feelings tumbling through him, made him shaky and unsure. For so long he'd suppressed his feelings for her because they hadn't been right under the circumstances. Now she was a widow. Was she asking him home because he was her friend? Or because she felt similarly? Terribly unsure, Kyle closed his eyes and waited to learn the time of the earliest flight to Flagstaff.

Gale shifted from one booted foot to the other, waiting impatiently at the Flagstaff airport. The small jet from Phoenix had landed, and she knew Kyle was on board. Suddenly she felt an incredible deluge of joy as she saw him emerge from the plane parked out on the tarmac. He walked quickly toward the building, an overnight bag in one hand, a wardrobe bag in the other. Her heart beat shifted into triple time as her gaze swiftly moved to his face. The past year had deepened the lines, especially around his mouth. There were still remnants of pain there, if she was reading him accurately.

She scanned his tall, lean form. The well-worn leather bomber jacket he wore proclaimed he was a pilot in the Air Force. His light blue shirt was open at the collar, revealing a white T-shirt and a few strands of dark chest hair. He wore a pair of comfortable jeans and, to her delight, a pair of scuffed cowboy boots. Where had he gotten those? Knowing Kyle, he'd probably always had them, a tie to his Arizona roots and heritage. With his tan, he looked more like a Westerner than an Air Force major.

Kyle smiled, the exhaustion torn from him as he saw Gale waiting restlessly at the rear of the crowd gathered at the doors. Christmas music was playing as he entered the small airport lounge decorated with a tree, tinsel and a cardboard Santa Claus waving his hand merrily to all arriving visitors.

It was Gale that Kyle hungrily homed in on. She was wearing a dark green wool dress, the full skirt brushing her knees. The red scarf around her neck emphasized the blush on her cheeks. The festive Christmas colors enhanced the natural radiance of her features.

He hadn't seen her since last year, since Mike's funeral. A part of him breathed a sigh of relief: Gale had regained her previous weight; her cheeks were no longer gaunt. As Kyle slowly made his way through the wall of waiting people, he saw her in an entirely different light. She looked like a rose in full bloom, her parted lips red and filled with promise, her cheeks deepening with a blush that did nothing but make her sparkling green eyes that much more beautiful.

Shyness suddenly seized Kyle. He stopped in front of her, managing a lame smile of welcome. It was impossible to hug her because his hands were filled with luggage. "Hi, stranger," he greeted her, his voice hoarse.

Gale was equally shy. "Hi, yourself," she whispered.

Awkwardly, Kyle looked around. "Where's my folks?"

Gale laughed softly, tying the belt around her camel-hair coat. "They'll see you at home." Gale motioned to the window. "You know they don't like driving in snow, and Flag has had a record amount this year. I told them I'd brave it and come to pick you up."

"Sounds good. Lead the way, I've got my baggage on me."

Gale turned and walked down the crowded hall. She saw how reticent Kyle was and understood. So was she. They were on an entirely different footing with each other for the first time. Was he here as her friend, or as something more? She didn't know, but she had to find out. "I'm so glad you came."

"Your cryptic telegram made me come." He studied her intently, sensing her nervousness and shyness. He felt just as off balance. Trying to make her more at ease, he said teasingly, "What am I going to do around here for ten days?"

A small gasp escaped Gale and she lifted her chin. "You got ten days?"

Kyle didn't know how to read her reaction. "Yeah. Is that too long?"

"Uh, no...no, that's wonderful! I didn't think you'd stay that long."

"Cryptic telegrams make me nervous. I didn't realize you were down here for Christmas and I thought something was wrong that might demand more than a couple of days of my time."

"Nothing's wrong...I changed my mind at the last minute about spending Christmas in Medford—alone. I—well, Sedona just seemed the right place for me to be, Kyle."

He understood. Five years of her life had revolved around the Taylors. She needed their support as she was still easing through the loss of Mike. Yet another part of Kyle was severely disappointed. "Sedona's always a good place to come," he agreed hoarsely.

She smiled. "The best, Major Anderson."

"Why do I have the feeling I'm the fly and you're the spider, Ms. Taylor?" He met her smile, a sharp ache awakening in him. Gale was wearing her hair long and loose, a golden-brown cloak around her shoulders. It gleamed beneath the lights of the terminal. He wanted desperately to sift those strands through his fingers. He gently shut the lid on his heart's urgent request.

Taking a huge risk, Gale curled her hand around his arm and led Kyle out of the terminal and into the chilly evening air. It was beginning to snow again. "As always, you're perceptive," Gale said with a laugh.

Suddenly, Kyle realized that he'd never felt happier and he laughed with her. Large white snowflakes wafted down slowly from the darkening sky. Taking a deep breath of the cold, frosty air, he shortened his stride to match Gale's. He was home.

"So, what have you got on the agenda for me?" Kyle wanted to say *us*, but decided against it.

Glancing at her watch, Gale said, "Your mom has fixed the two families' Christmas Eve dinner. They're waiting for us. Afterward, we'll decorate both families' trees."

Kyle looked for some hint of unhappiness, of grief, in Gale's eyes, but he found none. Instead, he found excitement and sparkling joy. "That's a nice thing to do," he said, meaning it.

"It's about time we all had something good happen to us," Gale murmured. She squeezed his arm, feeling his muscles tense and then relax beneath her hand. "And for the next ten days, we're going to laugh and have fun, Kyle." Gale held his gaze. "No crying, no tears," she whispered.

"You've got a deal, lady," he returned thickly. Christmas had never looked so good or so hopeful to Kyle. He sensed that Gale had released Mike and put her love for him in a chamber of her heart that held memories. Good, warm memories. Her green eyes were clear, and he saw renewed life within them. Her small hand on his arm felt good—felt great.

"Right after the meal, we'll start with your parents' Christmas tree," Gale said, halting at her bright red sports car. "And then we'll all go to the Taylors'. Mom Taylor has made dessert and egg nog for us." Gale opened the door and smiled. "I have your gift, too. Wait until you see it."

He grinned, hearing the excitement in her voice. Kyle placed his luggage in the trunk of the car. "I already sent you your Christmas present."

"It's tucked under the tree," she said, "and I haven't opened it yet."

"Better not have," he teased. Kyle wanted to lean down and brush her smiling mouth with a kiss. The need to do it was nearly overwhelming. For so long, he'd hurt for Gale, for her loss. The wind swirled, moving her hair restlessly across her shoulders. Snowflakes nestled in the golden-brown strands, and Kyle found himself reaching out, gently removing them one at a time.

Gale stood very still, drowning in Kyle's nearness. When his mouth softened as he lightly touched her hair, she closed her eyes and remembered his gentleness, his ability to give to her. As she opened them, she took a chance and caught his hand in her own, squeezing it because she wanted his closeness.

"Come on, let's go home...."

"Together," he agreed, returning the pressure.

It was nearly 1:00 a.m. before the Anderson household finally quieted down for the night. Kyle led Gale into the den. In front of them was a cheerful fire in the fireplace. Christmas music softly moved through the blue-carpeted room. The laughter, the sharing between the two families, had been nonstop. The Taylors had recovered from Mike's death, obviously happy that both Kyle and Gale were home for Christmas.

It was as if a miracle had occurred in the past year. Kyle remembered how devastated Mike's parents had been. Now, the Taylors were the way he'd always known them—jovial and sharing. His own parents reminded him of joyous puppies, covering him with kisses, hugs and tears of gladness upon arrival. The decorating of both Christmas trees had been bonding, healing.

He sat on the couch facing the fire. Glancing up, he saw Gale studying him, a pensive look on her face. If nothing else, he was aware of how much he loved her. Did she love him? Or did she still see him as simply a friend? He patted the space next to him.

"Come on, sit with me." How would she interpret his gesture? Probably as one of friendship. The fear he felt at trying to communicate that he loved her, had always loved her, scared him. If he put his arm around her shoulders, what would she do? If he tried to kiss her, what would be her reaction? Kyle was scared to death that Gale would turn away from his advances. The thought was shattering and one he couldn't overcome right now.

She smiled and sat next to him, her hand touching his shoulder. The uncertainty in his eyes kept her on edge. The last few hours of sharing and laughter with both families had been incredibly healing. Incredibly wonderful. Whenever she caught Kyle looking at her, an ache of longing had swept through her like a tidal wave. Gale could barely hang on to the words, *I Love you*. Did he still see her only as a responsibility? Someone to be loyal to because of Mike, because of a promise to always take care of her?

Her hand felt good on him, and Kyle tried to stop the need to return the gesture. Her eyes were filled with caring.

"There are so many good memories here," she said quietly.

He laid his head back and stared at the fire. "Yeah."

She wrapped her arms around her drawn-up legs, the full green skirt like a cloak. "You ate enough for three people, Anderson. It's a wonder you don't look like a stuffed turkey."

He grinned, wanting to reach across those few inches between them and put his arm around her. "Tart, aren't we?"

"No more than usual. You just haven't been around enough to see this side of me."

Kyle sobered, lost in the vision of her upturned face glowing with happiness. "We really haven't spent much time together," he agreed, feeling the need to remedy the situation, but not knowing quite how to proceed.

"No, we haven't," Gale said softly. Taking a deep breath, she whispered, "I just want you to know how much all those letters you wrote over the years helped me to keep my hope alive, to keep me laughing instead of crying. You shared so much of yourself with me, Kyle—all the silly, human things that were going on in your life while we both waited to hear about Mike.'' Her fingers tightened on her legs. She wanted so badly to reach out and cover his hands. ''Each letter was like life to me, Kyle. I lived to get them from you. Your words, how you saw life, helped me grapple with Mike possibly being gone.''

''But . . . all they were were things about my career and some stuff happening with my squadron. They weren't intimate or—''

''You don't understand, do you?'' Gale gave him a gentle smile, realizing her words were having a powerful effect on him. ''Your letters were honest, Kyle.''

''What?''

''You were vulnerable with me. Do you know how rare that is between two people? We're all so afraid of getting hurt, of getting wounded, that we protect ourselves. Your letters over the years bared your soul, how you thought, how you felt on such a wide range of topics that I got the pleasure of knowing the man behind that macho jet jock image. Do you understand now?''

Kyle turned and faced her. ''I think I do.'' Or did he? Had she asked him to Sedona just to thank him in person for his years of loyalty to her? That thought was like a knife cutting him.

Gale saw the pain, the devastation apparent on his features. Did he love her? Or had the flame that burned fiercely between them dimmed and died over time? She was unsure of what she meant to Kyle, if anything, beyond a strong, enduring friendship. She wanted to gather Kyle into her arms, to tell him of her love for him, but the time wasn't right. Perhaps it would never be. Getting to her feet, she laid her hand on his shoulder.

"Listen, I think you need some time to think about what I said. Good night, Kyle." She leaned down and brushed a kiss on his cheek. Would he interpret her action as merely friendly, or would he see that she was trying to show him that she wanted much more from him?

Gale saw the surprise flare in his eyes as she kissed him. Why was she being so hesitant when it was the last thing she wanted to be? Why didn't she have the courage to simply blurt out how she really felt?

Deep down inside, Gale knew she was afraid of Kyle's answer. Sometimes the fear of rejection made her less than courageous. Perhaps giving him little hints would help him come to realize what she was really trying to say to him. Perhaps.

Kyle couldn't speak, only feel and feel some more. Gale's hand on his shoulder was focusing his disjointed emotions. Finding his voice, he whispered, "I'll see you in the morning." He wanted to grab her hand, drag her into his arms and kiss her hard and long. The question and hesitation in her darkened eyes made him hesitate. Gale had kissed him. Okay, so it was a chaste kiss. But still, she'd kissed him! Hope flared strongly in his chest. He managed a slight smile, wanting to reach out and at least hold her hand, but he was too afraid. "Good night."

Gale barely lifted her hand. "Good night...."

Kyle watched her leave, the den suddenly feeling empty without her warm presence. The house was dark and quiet. He walked through the living room to the large plate-glass window and looked out over the backyard toward the Taylors' house a mere three hundred yards away. The sky was clear and the stars were large and close, twinkling and dancing.

Thrusting his hands into the pockets of his jeans, he stared at the old sycamore tree standing proud and silent in the darkness. Gale's face lingered before him. Yes, he loved her. The past year had brought that fact squarely to him. He had to make a decision. He realized he'd been waiting, giving Gale time to recover from the news of Mike's death. Now it was clear that she was over her bereavement.

Fresh fear gripped him. Did she love him? Where did friendship like theirs end and a new, different kind of love begin?

Taking a deep breath, he moved away from the window and headed down the hall to his bedroom. The Taylors would be coming over at 10:00 a.m. to open Christmas gifts. And Gale would be with them. Suddenly, the need to see her, talk with her, was overwhelming. It didn't matter how fearful he was of her reaction to his admitting his love for her. He couldn't stand the excruciating wait, not knowing what her answer would be. There was so much to say. The morning couldn't come soon enough....

"Good morning," Gale said, smiling up into Kyle's freshly shaved face. He'd cut himself, and she wanted to reach up and gently press a kiss to his jaw.

Hungrily, Kyle stared into her lovely forest-colored eyes dancing with incredible life. "Merry Christmas," he whispered. She wore a pale peach blouse and cream-colored slacks. Her hair was a shining cloak across her shoulders. Kyle inhaled the flowery scent of her perfume. A tension, a delicious throbbing sensation, ensnared him.

He saw Gale's eyes widen and interpreted that as her also being aware of the sensual pulsation that had now sprung between them—just as it had the first time they'd met so many years ago. Hope swept through him, making him giddy, nervous.

Gale moved to one side as the two families trooped toward the den where the tree stood laden with gifts. She looked up, drowning in his gaze. Did she dare hope? Did she dare read what lingered in his eyes as love for her?

For the next half hour, gifts were opened amid laughter and joking. Kyle brought a gift from beneath the tree and sat down, handing it to Gale. Would she like it? Or would it make her unhappy. He couldn't be sure.

Gale shook the red-wrapped box. "It rattles!" she cried out to everyone, and then laughed with them.

Kyle managed a nervous smile and watched as she tore into the wrapping like a child. His heart beat harder as she opened the box.

Digging through a mass of crinkly red-and-green tissue paper, Gale found a small, oblong bulb. After finding two dozen more, she tilted her head, giving Kyle a questioning look. "Daffodil bulbs." Tears filled her eyes. She held the bulbs reverently. Memory of their cardboard Christmas tree at Travis slammed through her. And so did the memory of a conversation they'd had about her daffodils and the fact they meant a new beginning for her. Sniffling, she gently placed the bulbs back in the box.

"Here," Kyle mumbled, putting his linen handkerchief in her hands. Embarrassed, he looked at his parents and the Taylors. There was understanding and sympathy in their expressions. Gale was beginning to cry in earnest and Kyle felt the need to get her alone.

"Uh, excuse us for a moment . . ." he said, rising, pulling Gale to her feet.

"Take her into the living room, honey," his mother said.

Gently, Kyle put his arm around Gale's shoulders and led her to the other room where they'd have a modicum of privacy. Once there, he drew her to a halt, folding her against him. A groan escaped Kyle as she put her arms around his neck, nestling her cheek against his chest.

"I'm sorry," he muttered, absently rubbing her shoulders. "I didn't mean to make you cry, Gale. Not now . . . God, not after everything you've gone through."

She drew away just enough to see the anguish in his azure eyes. "I'm not sad," she choked out.

"No?" His eyebrows moved upward. "I don't understand."

Managing a small laugh, Gale shook her head. "Oh, Kyle, you're so sweet and good to me. You do things so unconsciously, not even realizing what you're doing."

She was smiling through her tears and he framed her face, feeling the dampness beneath his hands. The urge to kiss those beads of moisture off her thick lashes haunted him. The need to kiss her was more painful than any physical agony he could recall. "Tell me what I did," he said thickly, allowing himself to drown in gold-flecked eyes lustrous with invitation. The thread of hope he clung to grew stronger, and he dared to believe he saw love there.

"My Christmas gift to you is also a set of daffodil bulbs, Kyle." She dropped her eyelids and her voice grew strained. "After I got over grieving for Mike, I went back and reread all your letters. It was then that I realized I care very deeply for you . . . that we've always shared something special." She licked her lips, tasting the salt on them, forcing herself to look up at him again. Kyle deserved her courage now, not her cowardice.

"You're honorable, Kyle. More than any man I've ever known. In the past year, I've realized that although I loved Mike, there was something you and I shared, too. There was a lot of caring in your letters to me. How many men would have written at all, much less as much as you did? Not many, Kyle."

Gently, he removed the last of her tears with his thumbs. "I didn't want to interfere, Gale." He dragged in a deep breath. "I knew you loved Mike. What I felt . . . how I felt about you wasn't important."

She took a huge risk, sliding her hand across his cheek. "You did the next best thing, you took care of me in his absence." Her voice grew tender. "I gave you daffodil bulbs to tell you in a silent sort of way that I want you back in my life, I want to share it with you in a new, better way. That is . . . if you want to. . . ."

He stood there thunderstruck, not believing what he was hearing. Gale stood unsurely in his arms, her eyes giving away her anxiety, her fear that he would reject her brave honesty. A tremble passed through him and he closed his eyes. "My God."

"Kyle?"

He opened his eyes and met her gaze. She had called his name so softly, a plea to him to answer her admission. Her lips were wet with tears, but they parted, begging him to kiss her. How long had he wanted to? The ache intensified within him, and it felt as if his heart were going to be torn apart. Kyle cradled her face with his hands.

Gale stood there, waiting in the silence. Just to touch his mouth, to feel the power and tenderness of Kyle as a man was nearly too much. A fine trembling flowed through her as the world slowed to a halt. She saw hunger in every line of his face, in the stormy blue of his hooded eyes.

He leaned forward, staring at her lovely mouth, and hesitated. It was a dream, a beautiful dream come true.

Tentatively grazing her lips, he felt her breath catch. The second time, he molded his mouth possessively to hers, feeling her fire, feeling her as the young, vital woman she was in his arms. Drowning in the warmth of her lips, Kyle explored her with aching slowness, tasting her sweet, liquid depths. Gale was yielding and hungry, matching his needs, telling him of her desires. There was a lushness to her, a fertileness that made him feel powerful and protective of her. She conveyed so much to him. Kyle felt her love, her commitment to him, unbridled, wild and filled with rich promise. He drowned in a rainbow of emotion.

Kyle gently disengaged from her ripe lips, her half-closed eyes telling him everything. The words, held in abeyance for so long, were torn form him. "I love you...."

Kyle's admission, the emotion behind it, rocked through her. Gale closed her eyes, a whisper of air escaping her lips. He loved her! The words flowed through her heart, and she moaned as she felt his mouth find hers once again.

Surrendering to him in every way, because they each had been denied so much for so long, Gale drowned in the wonderful celebration of his declaration. Gradually, the kiss ended. Looking into his eyes, she whispered, "I love you, darling ... so much...."

Words were useless for what Kyle felt for Gale; only holding her, pressing small, heated kisses against her cheek, eyes and lips could convey his joy. His senses were acute, registering each soft breath she took. He could taste Gale on his lips and savor all the sweetness of her, loving her.

"If this is a dream," Gale uttered with a sigh, her head resting on his shoulder, "I don't ever want to wake up."

Kyle leaned over, caressing her flushed cheek. "It's not a dream. It's real ... we're real."

How long they stood there in each other's arms, Gale didn't know. Finally, Kyle led her to the dark green couch. They sat down, never leaving each other's arms. She closed her eyes, content to be held, to feel the beat of his heart beneath her fingertips. The silence was like a warm blanket surrounding them.

"I'm glad you had the courage to tell me you wanted me for more than just a friend," Kyle whispered against her hair. "I don't know when I fell in love with you, sweetheart, but it doesn't matter."

"It was the letters," Gale replied, content to be held tightly within his embrace. "This past year, I wondered how we couldn't have fallen in love with one another."

Kyle leaned down, watching as her lashes lifted to reveal her joyous green eyes. "I think the first time I was introduced to you, I fell in love with you. I just didn't admit it to myself. I couldn't."

"Something happened that morning I burned my hand," Gale agreed quietly, "but we both denied it. I loved Mike, I was worried for him...."

"A lot was going down."

"Too much."

He absently stroked her long, silky hair. "This past year, I've been fighting a hell of a battle with myself," he told her, his voice gruff with feeling. "My love for you was growing out of control, and I knew I had to wait. I wasn't even sure if you loved me, Gale. I was afraid to say anything."

She sat up, caressing his strong, lean jaw. "I felt the same way. I took a chance and came here, hoping that you would come home when I sent that telegram."

He caught her hand and pressed a warm kiss to it. "You had a lot more courage than I did." He gave her a smile filled with love. "Was I ever glad to get that telegram."

"You had the courage to come. That's all that mattered."

Her eyes were luminous with tears. Gently, Kyle framed her face and kissed them away. "Tears of happiness," he rasped.

"Yes...."

"Marry me, Gale. Now. Today."

She blinked and held his intense cobalt gaze. "Today?"

Caressing her lips, he whispered, "I don't want to spend another night without you. I want to wake up with you in my arms tomorrow morning...for the rest of the mornings of my life. I'll retire from the Air Force so we could be together always and forever."

She looked up at him. "You will?"

He grinned. "Yeah. I'm getting tired of flying a desk when I've got a lot of good years left behind the stick. What would you think of me starting a feeder airline out of Sedona? Me and two other guys have enough money to buy a small commercial-sized plane to start out with."

"It sounds exciting."

Kyle tightened his hands around her. He ached to make love to her, but he stilled his hunger, anxious to see her reaction to his plans. "Exciting, scary and a real adventure."

"So we'd live in Sedona?"

"Yeah. What do you think of that?"

"I like it."

"You could be the meteorologist for the airline. We want to call it Red Rock Airlines. What do you think?"

Gale snuggled closer to him. "I like the whole concept, Kyle."

"It's a hell of a leap of faith," he muttered. "And it's chancy. I've got my life savings, including my stock holdings, tied up in the deal." He slanted a glance down at her. "The bank is going to own me for a long time once we get this feeder airline off the ground, sweetheart."

"So we'll be struggling but happy. It's a wonderful idea and I'd love to live here."

"You really mean that?" Her happiness was paramount to anything he wanted.

Leaning forward, Gale kissed him gently. "With my life, Kyle Anderson. So, I'm married to an airline executive instead of an Air Force major. I don't care what you do as long as you're happy doing it. Okay? I just want to share my life with you. That's all I want."

Closing his eyes, he whispered, "I love you so much. As long as I have you at my side, I can do anything, Gale. Anything."

Her smile was soft. "Darling, the best thing is, we'll do this together. We never have to be apart again, and I'm looking forward to living life with you."

"Through all the ups and downs?"

"Through everything. I love you, Kyle. We're going to be happy. I just know it."

Crushing Gale against him, Kyle knew he would never want anything more out of life—ever.

* * * * *

Author's Note

Serving in the U.S. Navy from 1964 to 1967 during the Vietnam conflict brought new meaning to the holidays for me. Until I joined the military, Christmas was a very special day filled with family members, excitement, warmth and opening gifts. I remember as a six-year-old being unable to sleep on Christmas Eve, then getting up with my siblings, Nancy and Gary, to see what was under the Christmas tree. Another year, Gary got so excited that he threw up on Christmas Eve! My mother, Ruth, decided that from then on, all gifts would be opened on Christmas Eve because she didn't want any of us getting sick with excitement over them.

Those kinds of memories mean so much more when you're stuck in a military base very far away from home. Christmas for servicemen and servicewomen is the loneliest time of year, a time of great vulnerability, since there is no way to go home to be with family. Instead, the military becomes your family. I can remember standing duty over the holidays and looking at the empty Ops building and the quiet revetment area devoid of jets and personnel.

For "Always and Forever," I drew upon my own experience as a Navy meteorologist who stood Christmas duty. My Marine Corps husband, Dave, was stationed in Vietnam for sixteen months. Every day I wrestled with fear and anxiety, wondering if he was alive or dead, because he was in I Corps area out in the bush. The chance of his coming home was very slim. I waited in agony, as every military wife did, hoping I never saw two officers come up to the house to announce he was dead.

The holidays for those in the service can be brightened by letters. They were our lifeline, a godsend, a reminder of a saner, gentler, more loving world than the one we worked and lived in. Besides letters, phone calls were wonderful. And moms sending our favorite cookies and cakes, which we'd all divide among our friends in the barracks. Believe me, you have no idea how much letters mean. If you have a daughter or son in the service, keep those cards and letters going to them.

When Dave was in Vietnam, I wrote a letter to him *every day*. That's close to five hundred letters. They were my outlet for expressing my love—and my fears—for him and to tell him about my job and what was going on at the base. Dave later told me that he used to read and re-read those letters. His buddies did, too, because not everyone got as many letters as Dave did. He admitted that they helped him keep his sanity, his hope that he'd survive.

So, dear readers, know that a lot of me, my experiences and feelings about service life are woven through the strands of "Always and Forever." Being part of the military teaches you so many valuable lessons that civilian life doesn't. I'm proud I served my country for three years. And I'm glad that Dave made it back home to me!

Merry Christmas.

Lindsay McKenna

THE MYSTERIOUS GIFT

Kathleen Creighton

A recipe from Kathleen Creighton:

THE PRETTIEST CHRISTMAS COOKIES IN THE WORLD
(and the best tasting, too!)

2 eggs
2½ cups flour
1 cup sugar
¾ cup butter
1 tsp baking powder
1 tsp salt
½ tsp flavoring (vanilla or lemon, or a combination of the two)

In a large bowl cream together butter and sugar. Add eggs and flavoring and mix thoroughly. Set aside.

Sift together flour, baking powder and salt. Add to the butter mixture and stir in until well blended.

Cover and chill for 1 hour.

Preheat oven to 375° F.

Roll out dough to ⅛″ thickness. Cut into shapes with cookie cutters. *(Note: The trick to rolling and cutting these cookies is to use plenty of flour. Don't be too kind to the dough—it's not important anyway.)* Place on ungreased cookie sheet. Bake 6 to 8 minutes, until delicately brown. *Do not overcook.*

Remove from pan and let cool on racks.

What makes these cookies special is what comes next: DECORATING!

To decorate the cookies you'll need:

Frosting—Sorry, I don't have an exact recipe. I just dump a box of powdered sugar into a bowl, add a couple of big spoonfuls of soft butter, a capful of whatever flavoring appeals to me (rum is nice!) and enough milk to make the right spreading consistency, and mix until creamy and smooth.

Colored Sugar—Blue, green, red. If you can't find it at the store in handy little bottles, make your own! Just put a couple drops of food coloring into a couple of teaspoons of sugar and mix with your fingers until evenly distributed and the shade you desire.

flaked coconut
chocolate sprinkles
colored sprinkles
cinnamon imperials (red hots)
tubes of decoration icing (optional)
cocoa (for chocolate frosting for snowmen's hats and Santa's eyes)

Frost cooled cookies generously with white frosting. Immediately sprinkle with decorations of choice. Work quickly before frosting dries out or the decorations won't stick!

What makes these cookies the Prettiest Christmas Cookies in the World (and the best tasting) is *generous* use of *white frosting*. How you decorate is, of course, entirely up to you, but here are a few suggestions: Christmas trees with colored sprinkle ornaments and green sugar leaves, and a red-hot star on top; reindeer with chocolate sprinkles and a red-hot Rudolph nose; snowmen with flaked coconut snow, chocolate hats and red-hot buttons; blue sugar stars and colored sprinkle sparkles. The simple designs are the prettiest.

That's all you need. Put on some Christmas music (Elvis's "Blue Christmas" is great!) and invite friends and neighbors to help. (Eggnog adds a lot to the spirit of the thing.) Oh—one more thing—the secret ingredient: lots of laughter!

Prologue

He first saw the train in the window of Duffy's Pawnshop on the Monday after Thanksgiving. He hadn't noticed it there the week before; Duffy had probably hauled it out and dusted it off in honor of the official opening of the Christmas shopping season.

It looked strange there, out of place among the cameras and gold watches and Swiss army knives—a rusty, worn-out child's toy sitting slightly askew on a section of bent track.

He wondered who in the world would hock a beat-up old electric train.

In any case, from the price on it he figured Duffy was looking to unload it in a hurry, or else he didn't have a clue what collectors were paying for vintage trains these days. Even in the condition this one was in, somebody was bound to snap it up pretty quickly. It would probably be gone by tomorrow.

But that night, for some reason, he thought about the train. He thought about what it must have looked like when it was new—the gleaming black locomotive, with a shiny silver bell and a headlamp that really worked; the yellow cattle car with a loading ramp that folded down, and the green boxcar with doors that slid open and shut; the bright, shiny red caboose. Somebody must have had a lot of fun with that train. A boy, maybe...and his dad, of course. And maybe his mom, too.

Suddenly he could almost see that train chugging 'round and 'round, engine huffing away, wheels whispering smoothly over the track, whistle sounding clear and shrill. He could see a boy—a particular boy—bending over the controls, face intent, breaking now and then into smiles of pure delight. And the boy's mother, watching, with Christmas lights reflecting in her eyes, and in her hair....

Yes, he thought with a secret smile, it would take some work, but with a little bit of help a boy could still have fun with that train.

The next day, although it was out of his way, he went by Duffy's Pawnshop again. He was surprised to see that the train was still there in the window. Surprised, too, to find it looking so battered and forlorn after the vividness of his daydreams.

For just a moment he paused there, with his hand on the glass, seeing in its murky reflection the boy's face once more, alight with joy and wonder. And his mother's, softer but no less radiant.

Then he turned and went into the pawnshop, smiling his secret smile.

Chapter One

"Andrew," Karen Todd said to her son over breakfast, "I have some bad news." She took a fortifying breath and broke it to him. "The mouse is back."

Andrew's eyes shifted from the cereal box he'd been reading and focused on his mother's face over the top of his glasses. "How do you know?"

How like him, she thought, smiling to herself in spite of the multitude of worries that had kept her awake half the night. The Little Professor, she and Bob had called him when presented with that solemn, analytical stare.

"Did you see him?" the boy persisted, looking both fearful and eager.

"Well, no," Karen admitted. "But I found another mess. I had to throw away a whole box of Crispy Oats, a brand-new box I just bought yesterday."

Andrew tilted his head and chewed thoughtfully, staring into space. After a moment, unable to find a loophole on which to base a rebuttal, he shrugged and said, "I really thought scaring him would work. Mice don't like loud noises, you know. Maybe next time, if we—"

"Andrew," Karen interrupted, and took another breath. "I'm sorry, sweetheart." She flinched and braced herself against the stricken look in her son's eyes. "I'm going to have to set a trap."

With false brightness, like someone clutching at straws, he said, "Couldn't you just put everything in the refrigerator, so the mice couldn't get it? Or . . . or, hey, how's this? We put all the food in jars—you know, glass? And that way—"

"Andrew. . . ."

He gave up then; his lashes fell across his eyes, taking all expression out of his unformed, eight-year-old face. Neatly and methodically he stacked his orange juice glass in his cereal bowl, pushed back his chair and carried both his dishes and the cereal box to the sink— but not before Karen caught the slight but unmistakable quiver in the vicinity of his chin. Love, frustration and helplessness rose in her throat as she watched the little boy rinse his dishes with adult thoroughness and place them in the drainer. The back of his neck looked so slender . . . so vulnerable.

She went to him and put a hand on his shoulder. "Honey, I don't like killing them any more than you do. But I just can't have mice in the house, you know that. I explained—"

He shook off her hand and gave an oddly grownup-sounding sigh. "I know, I *know*. They'll get into the drawers and chew up the clothes to make their nests, and gnaw on the furniture, and it doesn't even belong to us, it belongs to Mrs. Goldrich. And besides that, they go to the bathroom on everything, and they *stink*." He turned to her suddenly, his eyes bright and hopeful behind his glasses. "Do we have to kill them? Maybe we could get one of those traps, you know, like Cinderella? Sort of like this little cage, where the mouse just goes in and can't get back out. And then we could take it out someplace and turn it loose. Or, *hey*— I could keep it for a pet! How would that be, Mom? Don't you think that's a good idea?''

Karen pressed a distraught hand to her forehead. "Honey, I don't think they even make mousetraps like that anymore. I wouldn't know where to look." She'd certainly never seen one at the supermarket or the hardware store. Maybe she could ask at the feed store out on Route 7.... Oh, how she dreaded disappointing Andrew *again*, even more than she dreaded the prospect of sitting alone in the long winter evenings after he'd gone to bed, listening for that horrible, lethal SNAP!

In a tone that bordered on desperation, she said, "I'll see what I can find, okay? *No promises.* Now, you go brush your teeth and get your backpack. Hurry up—it's time to go."

"No, it isn't," Andrew countered matter-of-factly. "It's not even quarter till." He paused, doing the calculations in his head. "We still have...twenty minutes."

"We have to leave early," Karen explained, "so I can drop the car off at Angel's Garage."

Andrew's face lit up. "Cool. Can I go with you? You could walk me to school after."

"Then we'd both be late. Run along now. Scoot." She aimed a gentle swat at the seat of his blue jeans, which he eluded without difficulty.

"Then can I go after school? You could pick me up when you get the car."

"What in the world," Karen inquired with exasperation in her voice, "would you find to do there for two hours?" The subject of her car, and the increasing frequency of its visits to Angel's Garage, was as sore a subject to her as the unwelcome visitor in her kitchen. More so, at the moment.

"Help Tony," said Andrew. He turned in the bathroom doorway to add proudly, "He lets me."

"Well..." Karen said. She coughed and muttered something vague about asking permission, though for the life of her she couldn't understand what her son found so fascinating about that garage and its surly proprietor, Tony D'Angelo. In her opinion, the mouse was more appealing.

Not that the man was repulsive, or anything. Far from it, in fact, which Karen was willing to admit might be at least part of her problem. She had always had trouble dealing in a cool and businesslike manner with men she found physically attractive, and without a doubt, Tony D'Angelo did have more than his share of animal magnetism. He had typically Italian good looks—thick, wavy brown hair and a cleft in his chin, a nose like the ones on old Roman coins, and dark, arresting eyes—looks that were usually described in pulp fiction as "smoldering." But somehow, whenever those beautiful eyes were aimed at her, particularly after surveying the steaming innards of her car for the third time in a month, Karen felt obscurely defensive, as if she were being accused of some particularly unpardonable form of child abuse. The man was often brusque, sometimes to the point of rudeness, and she had to be on guard constantly to keep from being intimidated by his superior attitude—not an easy task, considering she knew absolutely nothing about cars.

She told herself she only went to Angel's Garage because it was the most convenient one, located within walking distance of both her work and Andrew's school, but the truth was that for all his brusqueness, Tony D'Angelo was simply the best mechanic in town. Karen depended on him for her very livelihood. And, what was more, she trusted him.

"Go see Tony D'Angelo—he's as honest as the day is long." She wished she had a day's salary for every time someone had said that to her, beginning with that memorable, baking-hot day last August when she'd arrived in town with her car overheating and wisps of steam beginning to seep ominously from under the hood. "Oh yeah," everyone she'd asked had told her without hesitation, "what you want is Angel's Garage. Tony'll fix you right up, and he won't steer you wrong, either. He's as good-hearted and trustworthy as they come, and a darn good mechanic to boot."

In the three months since, Karen had come to believe in and appreciate the last two attributes of the garage owner's character; of the first she had yet to see any convincing evidence. Why her son seemed to enjoy his company so much, when all he ever did was bark orders at the child, was beyond her.

"What's wrong with the car this time?" Andrew now inquired, shrugging into his backpack and baring his freshly scrubbed teeth for Karen's inspection.

"Nothing, I'm just having it serviced," she said, mentally knocking wood as she brushed traces of toothpaste from her son's chin and tried without noticeable success to flatten his cowlick. "I just want to be sure everything's all set for winter. Everyone's saying it's going to snow next week."

"Cool!" said Andrew with the enthusiasm of a child born and reared in the Southern California sunshine.

Karen just sighed. The thought of something going wrong with her car at any time was a source of nightmares. In the wintertime it was unthinkable.

The car had been a long way from new when she and Bob had bought it, but it had been all they could afford then, as newlyweds. With Bob in the army, it had been primarily Karen's car from the start, and she had always driven it with great pride and proper respect for its venerable age. In another few years, she thought, it might even be considered a classic, although it came from an era not known for distinguished automotive design, and people had been known to break into impolite gales of laughter when she suggested such a possibility.

Still, she was rather fond of the old heap, and in any case, she couldn't afford to replace it even if she'd wanted to. The move had wiped out a good portion of her savings, and the rest had been taken care of by the discovery, during the school's routine vision screening in September, that Andrew had developed nearsightedness and would definitely need glasses. As far as Karen was concerned, Tony D'Angelo's mechanical expertise was all that stood between her and economic disaster. She would forgive him his surliness and put up with his arrogance if he would just—please, God—keep her car running!

"Hey, Mom, what's this?" Andrew asked suddenly as they were leaving their apartment.

Karen, who was struggling with the old-fashioned key and lock, answered absently without turning around, "What's what?"

"Look at this. Somebody must have sent us a present."

"Probably for Mr. Clausen," Karen said, glancing over her shoulder at the large brown box that was sitting on the landing's threadbare carpet, just to one side of the door to their apartment. "The delivery person probably didn't feel like carrying it up those narrow stairs. Just leave it there. Mr. Clausen will see it when he comes back from his morning walk."

"Mom..." Andrew's tone was hushed. "I think it's for me."

"What?"

"Come and look. It has my name on it."

Karen bent over the box, her fingers brushing the letters neatly printed on the top with a black indelible marker. TO: MASTER ANDREW TODD. And that was all. No address, no labels, no return address, no stamps or postage of any kind. "How odd," she murmured.

"Oh boy, somebody sent me a present!" Andrew was already on his knees beside the box, measuring it with his hands. "I wonder what it is. Can I open it? Who do you think it's from?"

"I don't know," Karen said, frowning. "It doesn't say."

"Maybe it's from Santa Claus. Can I open it? Please, Mom, *please*?"

"Of course you can't open it, not right now." Once again, exasperation was creeping into her voice. Karen didn't like mysteries, and the box disturbed her in ways she didn't understand. "You're going to be late for school, and I'm going to be late for work, if we don't leave right now, this minute."

"Aw, Mom..."

"No arguments! We'll just have to wait until tonight to open it." She was already unlocking the door. "Come on, I'll help you push it inside."

The box was both heavy and bulky; it took both of them to get it through the door and into the apartment. Karen wondered, as she locked up for the second time, how on earth anyone had managed to carry it up the stairs and deposit it at the door without making any noise. And who would send her son a package? It had to be someone local, someone she knew, since there was no address or postage. *Who?* She knew so few people in town. . . .

"Oh boy!" Andrew was hopping with excitement. "I wonder what it is! Who do you think it's from, huh, Mom?"

"We'll both find out," Karen said firmly, taking him by the hand and starting down the stairs. "Tonight." There would be a card inside, she told herself, determinedly squelching her own curiosity. All would be explained soon enough.

"Maybe it's from Santa!" Andrew was tugging at her hand like an exuberant puppy. "I bet that's why there's no stamps."

"It's a little early for Santa Claus, isn't it?" Karen said mildly, wondering whether an eight-year-old boy who still believed in Santa might be cause for parental concern.

Andrew paused, looking inspired. "Well . . ." Karen sighed inwardly and braced herself; she knew that tone of voice. ". . . Everybody else starts Christmas this early, so why shouldn't Santa?"

There was more to the argument, of course, a great deal more, but Karen didn't even try to refute it; her mind was already tuning him out returning to her own more pressing problems and questions.

At the foot of the stairs she hesitated, looking toward the closed door at tne end of the hall, wondering ·f Mrs. Goldrich knew anything about the package ᴾerhaps she had even seen who had delivered it.

But she decided against disturbing her landlady at that nour. ⌐hey were late already, and besides, she told herself, there would certainly be a card inside the box.

As they were going down the front steps they met Mɪ Clausen, the elderly gentleman who lived upstairs in the attic of the small, wood frame Victorian, coming back from his morning walk. The cold air had reddened his cheeks and the tip of his nose, and his vapored breath wafted about his head like smoke. A breeze parted his long white beard and lifted a few stray wisps of his hair from his rosy scalp as he swept off his Tyrolean hat in response to their greeting.

"And a good morning to you, Mrs. Todd, young Andrew!" the old man's voice boomed out, as mellow and rich as church bells on a winter morning. His eyes twinkled, as if they beheld delicious secrets. "A beautiful morning! Snow in the air!" He drew a deep breath, expanding his considerable girth as he clapped both hands to his chest. "Yes indeed, snow before the week is out." A large gloved hand intercepted Andrew. "What do you think of that, young man? Do you like snow?"

"Yeah," said Andrew enthusiastically.

The old man laughed and winked sympathetically at Karen, then, with a wave of his cane, proceeded on up the walk.

"I'll bet he sent it," Andrew said in a hoarse whisper as he scrambled across the front seat of the car.

"Why do you think that?" Karen asked, laughing a little, forgetting to scold him for the dusty footprints he was leaving on the driver's seat. Encounters with Mr. Clausen had a strangely revitalizing effect on her, like a brisk breeze.

"I told you," Andrew said, still whispering even though Mr. Clausen had disappeared inside the house and they were now safely enclosed in the car. "I think he's—"

"Andrew!" The car responded to her first attempt to start it in predictable fashion: a cough and then nothing. "That's ridiculous."

"Mom, he looks just like him, and he's even got the same name."

"Andrew..." Karen shook her head and pumped the gas pedal several times before trying the ignition key again.

"Well, he does," Andrew said stubbornly in the ensuing silence.

Karen set her lips firmly and sent up a prayer. This time the engine coughed and sputtered grudgingly to life. She nursed it carefully until it had settled down to a surly growl; then, with a sigh of relief, she backed out of the driveway.

A glance at her son caused her to sigh again, this time with exasperation. What in the world was she going to do about him? He really was too old for these fantasies. Believing in Santa Claus was one thing, but...*Mr. Clausen?*

Andrew spent entirely too much time reading, she told herself. That was the problem. Reading and watching television. He needed to get outside more. He should be spending more time with other children, playing ball, climbing trees. Karen had originally decided to rent the apartment in the little Victorian because it had such a nice big backyard, with grass to run on and trees to climb. She'd thought it would be a good place for Andrew to play. Now she almost wished she'd taken a place in a crowded, noisy apartment building, one teeming with children, children Andrew's age who could teach him how to roughhouse and get his clothes dirty. Her son really needed to be around boys more, she knew that. He needed someone to teach him the things she couldn't, like how to throw a football, and slide into second base. He needed—

But Karen knew very well what Andrew needed. And she shied away from that truth now just as she had for the last five years, ever since a helicopter crash during a routine training operation had killed her husband and robbed her son of his father.

It had been easy, at first; no one expected her to think about it. It was too soon. It takes time, everyone said; just give it some time. But then Andrew had started school, and the questions had begun. All the other kids had dads, why didn't he? Where was his daddy? What had happened to him, and when was he coming back? Karen had answered the questions as simply and truthfully as she knew how, but Andrew was an uncommonly observant and intelligent child, and it hadn't taken him long to find a loophole. *Some* kids, he pointed out to his mother, had more than one dad. Since his own was gone and not going to come back, and since there seemed to be extras around, couldn't she simply find him another one?

Eventually, though, the questions had stopped. Andrew, being both observant and intelligent, saw that his questions made his mother unhappy, and although for a while he still made subtle references to the subject in his bedtime prayers and birthday candle wishes, he finally stopped asking. But Karen *knew*. And sometimes when she looked at her son—a certain way he had of smiling, the tilt of his head, the wistful softness of his jaw and chin—her emotions swamped her, and she had to pretend that it was just her hay fever acting up again.

Emotions—such a painful, confusing stew of them! Anger and guilt, fear and longing, all mixed up together. It wasn't, Karen told herself time and time again, that she expected never to marry again. But such things couldn't be forced; they had to just *happen*, the way miracles do. The way it had happened for her and Bob. They had truly had something special, the two of them. And then, of course, the three of them. The chances of that kind of miracle happening again for her seemed remote . . . impossible.

Every day Karen told herself that she was doing the right thing, insisting on the miracle rather than settling for something less just for the sake of providing her son with a father. But every day she faced the anguish of a mother's guilt, knowing that the one thing her child needed most, she couldn't give him.

"What do you think is in the box?" Andrew asked as the car pulled up in front of the school building with its usual clatter and bang.

Karen leaned over to kiss him. "I don't know. You can have fun thinking about it today. We'll find out tonight, won't we?"

"Maybe," said Andrew casually, grunting a little as he hopped from the car to the sidewalk, "it's what I wished for."

"Oh?" Karen probed with tender amusement, hoping for a Christmas hint. "And what's that?"

"It's a secret," he said, turning to look at her over the hump of his backpack. Then he went on up the walk to the school, smiling his secret smile.

Tony heard the car coming from two blocks down the street. Even flat on his back on a dolly looking at the underside of Mrs. Kazanian's Lincoln, he knew who it was. Inner disturbances caused by the sound of that particular engine made him give the wrench he was wielding an unnecessarily vigorous turn.

"Ouch!" He resisted the natural impulse to stick the injured knuckle into his mouth and swore inventively instead. "Damn bucket of bolts."

Although it would have been difficult for a stranger to tell the difference, and though Tony certainly wasn't about to admit it, his tone was more affectionate than bitter. He had always been a sucker for old junkers and strays. He wasn't sure whether that was because he liked to feel needed, as a girl he'd once dated—a psych major at Fresno State—had suggested, or whether he just liked a challenge. One thing was sure—keeping that old Plymouth of Mrs. Todd's running did present a challenge.

So, for that matter, did Mrs. Todd.

Mrs. Todd. Tony grimaced as the unholy racket died in midcough, a car door slammed, and the lady's voice called with a note of uncertainty, "Hello? Mr. D'Angelo? Is anyone here?"

Mr. D'Angelo. "Yeah!" Tony grunted. "Be right with you."

She was a challenge, all right. In the three months since she'd pulled into town with a broken thermostat and a radiator about ready to blow, he hadn't been able to figure out a way to get beyond that "Mrs. Todd" and "Mr. D'Angelo" nonsense. And he wanted to; he'd known that much from the first moment. He wanted to get to Karen and Tony, and maybe beyond that all the way to the things people called each other in the velvet darkness that had no meaning to anyone but themselves.

He had to admit it was partly her looks, at least at first. Not that she was so spectacular, or that he hadn't known prettier women, but sun-streaked, long-legged blondes just weren't as common in this part of the state as they were where she was from. Apart from that, though, there'd been something about her even then that had intrigued him, challenged him. A certain aloofness—not arrogance; her voice had been polite and her manner genuine, her eyes direct and respectful, and worried—which was natural enough, given the circumstances. Even in shabby, crumpled clothes, tired, sweaty, with wisps of hair sticking to the dampness on her neck and temples, she'd had a natural, unconscious elegance. Blond, aloof, elegant—the classic iceprincess. And yet Tony was certain there was nothing cold about her. There had been warmth in her eyes when she looked at that little boy of hers, and tenderness in her hands when she touched him. He'd seen both vulnerability and courage in the way her lips first trembled, then tightened, when he told her what it was going to cost to fix her car. No, he knew she wasn't cold. The emotions were there, just held in reserve.

Reserved. That sure was the word for Mrs. Todd. Tony understood that; he was reserved himself. He never would have said *shy*. And that was really the problem—he was used to being someone else's challenge, to having other people banging on *his* doors, trying to knock down the walls of *his* reserve. He'd never had to be the one to reach out before, and he wasn't sure how to go about it. How the hell did a reserved man make contact with a woman who was even more reserved than he was?

He already knew quite a bit about her, of course; it was a small town, and not too many out-of-towners came to take up permanent residence. For instance, he knew she'd come from someplace in L.A., that she'd rented an apartment in one of those Victorians over on Sierra Street, that she was single—whether divorced or widowed he wasn't certain, but for some reason he couldn't put his finger on, he would bet on the latter—and that she had a nice little kid. A bit too polite and quiet, maybe. Too reserved, like his mother.

Tony listened to the tap, tap, tap of Karen Todd's shoes coming toward him across the concrete floor of the shop. High-heeled shoes—black pumps, he saw, as they came to a stop beside the Lincoln, a few feet from his head. Nice slender ankles, encased in nylons...sweetly curving calves disappearing under the hem of a brown wool coat...

He wondered if she would still wear those high-heeled shoes when there was a foot of snow on the ground and a windchill factor of twelve below. She worked right around the corner, he knew, at Frank James Insurance, which had made him wonder at first, given old Frank's penchant for fooling around. By this time, though, Tony figured that if old Frank had entertained any ideas along those lines when he hired Karen Todd, he'd been in for a big disappointment.

Taking his time about it, Tony tightened down the last of the bolts and wheeled himself out from under the Lincoln. "Yeah," he grunted as he got to his feet, "what can I do for you?" He gave the woman in the brown coat only the briefest of glances before he turned away, looking for a clean rag on which to wipe his hands—and staunch the flow of blood from his wounded knuckle.

She followed him, stepping gingerly between the front end of the Lincoln and a pile of new tires. She had her hands in her coat pockets and her shoulders hunched up as if she were cold—or nervous. Must be cold, Tony thought; he couldn't imagine why she would be nervous. She'd definitely have to get herself some warmer clothes if she was going to survive a winter here on the steppes of the Sierra Nevadas.

"You said— You told me to bring my car in this morning. I spoke to you about it yesterday. On the phone..."

"Right," Tony said, frowning at his hand. "Tune up, winter safety-check."

"Well, yes, I guess that's...I just want to be sure it's going to be okay in the cold weather. I suppose anti-freeze..." Her voice faltered. "You've hurt yourself."

He glanced up. Her eyes—very light, clear blue eyes, the only startling thing about her—were riveted on his hand. "Nah," he said, "it's nothing. Just a scrape."

Frown lines appeared between her eyes. "You're bleeding."

He'd already noticed that; he was going to have to put a bandage on the damn thing, and probably some iodine, too. Because that wasn't a pleasant prospect, he growled impatiently, "Don't worry about it—happens all the time." Wrapping the rag around his hand, he jammed it into the pocket of his coveralls, where, he hoped, it would be out of sight and out of mind. He couldn't for the life of him understand why, but her unexpected concern unnerved him; he felt as jittery as a kid.

"Okay," he said in the most businesslike manner he could muster, "let's write you up a ticket." He turned away from her, heading for his office. "You want to give me some idea how much you want done on this thing? You just want antifreeze and wiper blades, or do you want a tune-up?"

"Well..." She came tap-tapping after him, slightly out of breath. "I was sort of hoping you could tell me what I should do. I don't have any idea how much everything costs. If you could look at it—"

"Look, I can tell you what you *should* do." Tony sat down on the corner of his desk and faced her, steeling himself against the worried look in her eyes. Push the damn thing over a cliff! he wanted to say, but he didn't. Instead he gave her the bad news, making it blunt, because it was so hard to do. "I can almost guarantee you're going to need points, plugs, condenser— How long's it been since you had all your hoses checked? Battery? I don't suppose you have tire chains?"

She shook her head, squared her shoulders and looked him bravely in the eye. "How much is it going to cost?"

He told her, then watched all the color go out of her face. But after a moment she nodded and said in a quiet, firm voice, "All right, if that's what it needs, do it."

Tony exhaled audibly and reached for a service order form. Avoiding her eyes, he said gruffly, "Look, that's just a worst-case scenario. I'm not going to know what's what until I take a look. Could be all you need's antifreeze and wiper blades. I'll just put down 'Check,' and I'll give you a call if—" He broke off, swearing, as a drop of blood made a neat, scarlet polka dot on the multilayered form.

Chapter Two

Karen stiffened and looked wary, like a bird poised for flight. "What is it?"

"Agh," said Tony disgustedly, and stood up, jerking his head toward the only chair in the cramped office, the swivel chair behind the desk. "Have a seat. I'm going to have to get a bandage on this damn thing—"

"Can I help?" Her voice sounded breathless. Tony paused in the act of unwrapping his hand to look at her and saw that the color was back in her face, perhaps even a little more than had been there before. It made her seem younger, softer. The pads of his fingertips tingled with a disconcerting urge to touch her.

There was a pause while he wrestled with the impulse, and then he said, "Yeah, okay, sure. There's a first-aid kit in that filing cabinet over there behind you—bottom drawer."

The old chair creaked as she swiveled toward the cabinet, groaned when she leaned over to open the drawer, squeaked as she turned back to the desk. Tony watched her, liking the way she moved.

She placed the first-aid kit on the desk, then unbuttoned her coat and shrugged out of it, letting it fall over the back of the chair. The dress she was wearing had a high round neck and long sleeves, and was made of some sort of soft knit material in a dark, somber color—maroon, he supposed. On her, it looked good. The slightly curled ends of her tawny hair just brushed her shoulders and swung across her cheeks when she leaned forward. It looked soft and clean. He imagined that it would smell good, too.

"Just a bandage," he said as she hesitated over the array of medical supplies. "And some of that iodine there—nothing fancy."

She glanced doubtfully at his hand. "Don't you think you should wash it first?"

"Nah, then the bandage won't stick. Look, just cover it up so it won't get in my way. The iodine'll kill everything, anyway." Tony thrust his hand at her, impatient with himself for the disquieting images her presence was fomenting in his mind. "Come on, get it over with. If you want that car of yours by tonight— OW!" That was followed with a sharp, sibilant oath as he tried to jerk his hand away from the stinging brown liquid she'd just poured into the gash on his knuckle.

But before he could, before he knew what she was going to do, perhaps even before she knew herself, Karen Todd had caught his oil-stained hand in both of her soft, smooth, clean ones. The next thing he knew she was bending over it, blowing frantically on the cut and casting him quick, angry glances between puffs. "Why in the world...don't you use the kind that...doesn't sting?"

"Because this way, at least I know it's working," Tony managed to grate between his tightly clenched teeth, then went on swearing.

Karen made a derisive sound and gave him another bright blue glare. "Then you could at least try to be brave," she said as she went on blowing.

After a moment or two of tense silence, he surprised both her and himself by chuckling.

"What's funny?"

Tony muttered, "Nothing." Then he shrugged and smiled. "My mother used to do that."

"Ohh...." The angry glint faded from her eyes. He watched them grow round, luminous, as if she'd just seen something unexpected and wondrous. He couldn't imagine what he'd said or done to put that look on her face, but it had a profound effect on him. Pretty much as if someone had sat down heavily on his midsection.

While he was trying to remember how to breathe, it apparently occurred to Karen that she was still holding his hand. She dropped it like a hot rock and began to rummage in the first-aid kit for a bandage, acting as if his life depended on her finding it. When she did finally locate it, she seemed to have trouble getting the paper wrapping off, and when she went to put it on his finger, Tony noticed that her hands were shaking a little.

He let her struggle with it, not offering to help, just keeping his mouth shut and holding himself very still, watching the way her teeth pressed into the soft pillow of her lower lip, and the way her lashes made crescent shadows on her flushed cheeks. It wasn't until she was finished and they both let go of a breath at the same time that he realized he'd been holding his all the time.

"There—is that all right?" She looked up at him, and the light betrayed a fine film of moisture across the bridge of her nose.

"Yeah, thanks," Tony said absently. "I think that should do it." But for some reason he just went on sitting there, studying her, flexing his hand.

After a moment or two, Karen suddenly pushed the first-aid kit away from her and stood up, groping for her coat. "I, um . . . I have to go— I'm late for work. Is it all right if I stop in after work to pick up the car? Oh—" She paused; he could see her steel herself before she turned back to him. "I forgot— I know it's an imposition, but I promised I'd ask you. Is it all right if Andrew—if my son comes over here after school? He usually comes to my office and reads, or does his homework until I'm ready to go home, but he wanted—he said—"

"Yeah, sure," Tony said. "No problem."

"Are you sure? I don't want him to be in the way. If you'd rather not—"

"He's not going to get in my way," Tony interrupted her, more sharply than he intended. And then, because he didn't want her to think he was annoyed with her, he tried to soften it as best he could with a lopsided smile. "Hell, I'm shorthanded today—one of my mechanics called in sick— I might just put the kid to work."

There was a little silence while she looked at him, face thoughtful, hands in her coat pockets. Then she said softly, "Thank you. That's very nice of you."

Tony made an ambiguous sound—a grunt, or a snort. He couldn't have explained his feelings right then, or why it bothered him that she thought she had to apologize for her kid, and that she was treating Tony like some kind of saint for having him around. He was just a *kid*, for Pete's sake. A nice kid. "Here," he growled, putting an end to the matter, "you want to sign this work order?"

He handed her a pen, but instead of giving the clipboard to her, he left it on the desk and just angled it toward her a little bit, so she'd have to step over close to him in order to sign it. He did it quite deliberately, to test her responses to him, just in case he'd been mistaken before and it was only the sight of blood that had made her so nervous.

What he didn't expect was that it would also be a test of his own self-control.

He drew a long, slow breath. Her hair did smell good—like nothing he could put a name to. It made him think of sunshine and fresh spring mornings, and clean clothes flapping on the line. If he closed his eyes he could feel it on his skin, cool and soft as a whisper....

"There," she said as she put the pen down, breathless again. "Is it all right if I come by right after work? It's apt to be a few minutes past five."

Tony tore off her copy and handed it to her. The tension in him made his movements abrupt and his voice hard. "I'll try to have it done by then, but I can't guarantee anything. I'm short one mechanic, and I've got to finish with that Lincoln out there before I can start yours."

Her face registered dismay, alarm and, at last, pure panic. "But you told me—on the phone—you told me if I brought it in first thing this morning I could have it by tonight. I *have* to have my car. I don't have any other way to get home—or back to work in the morning. And Andrew has to go to school—"

She broke off as Tony abruptly stood up, fished his keys out of the pocket of his coveralls and held them out to her. When she just stared at him, he gave the keys a little shake, making them jingle. "Here, you can take mine. It's the white Chevy out back."

From the look she gave the keys, Tony thought, someone would have supposed he'd handed her a tarantula. She transferred the same look to him and began to shake her head. "Oh, no—no, I couldn't." She took a step backward, away from him. When it looked as if she was likely to keep going in that direction, Tony caught her hand, turned it palm up, placed the keys in the middle of it and folded the fingers over them.

"Lady," he said, holding her closed fist in both of his hands, "didn't you ever hear of a loaner?"

Her eyes locked with his across their clasped hands. He saw something flicker in the translucent blue, darken, and then catch fire. He felt the tension in her muscles as she fought him...and the relaxing when she surrendered. A new emotion swelled inside him: excitement...a strange, fierce thrill of joy.

"All right," she murmured at last. "Thank you." She straightened her shoulders and lifted her head, an unconscious assertion of pride and dignity that touched Tony unexpectedly. Her face was expressionless as she pulled her hand from his grasp, dropped his keys into her coat pocket and placed hers on the clipboard beside the pen. "You'll need these," she said stiffly. "I'll stop by for Andrew at five o'clock."

"No need," Tony said. "I'll bring him home when I bring you your car."

"But you said—"

"I said I didn't know if I could have it done by five, and I don't. Might take me an hour or so longer. Look—" he said when it appeared as if she was going to interrupt him, then had to interrupt himself to take a breath. His voice was gruff; he couldn't believe the tension in him. "Look, I'll get your car done—don't worry about it. I'll have both the car and the kid home by suppertime. Okay?"

She drew a long breath and nodded. "Okay. Thank you. Thank you very much. Um . . . you know where I live?"

"Yeah," Tony said wryly, "I know where you live."

When his office door had closed behind her he said, "Damn!" and let his breath out in a rush. He listened to the sound of Karen Todd's high-heeled shoes tap-tapping across the shop floor and finally fading into silence before he picked up her car keys, tossed them up and snatched them one-handed from the air. Warmth burst through him, and he began to smile.

The mysterious box greeted Karen when she ar-rived home from work, giving her a momentary jolt. With everything that had happened since, she'd all but forgotten it. For the rest of the evening, while she rushed to clean up the apartment, it sat there in the middle of her living room like an unexpected and slightly embarrassing guest—like the pastor on a duty call, she thought, or a wealthy but not-too-pleasant uncle—someone you would really rather not have in the house but couldn't risk offending. She'd straight-ened up around it and moved it in order to vacuum under it, all the while fidgeting with curiosity and vague feelings of resentment.

Who would send her son a package—such a *large* package!—and put no name or return address on it? There was no one in the world who had the right to do such a thing—no one! Andrew's father was dead. He had only one surviving grandparent, his father's mother, who lived in a mobile-home park outside Fort Lauderdale on a fixed and very inadequate income. Every year she sent her only grandson a Christmas card and a five dollar bill, which had arrived right on schedule two days ago. Beyond that there was no one—no uncles, aunts or cousins. Who could have done such a thing? What in the world could it be? And when in the world was that boy going to come home so she could find out?

Any minute, she thought for the twentieth time, looking at her watch. Any minute now.

She looked around, smoothing the front of her dress. The apartment looked reasonably tidy; thank goodness she'd had time to vacuum. Should she have changed out of her dress? She usually put on jeans and a sweatshirt when she got home from work. Maybe she should change right now: she wouldn't want Tony to think she was wearing a dress to impress him.

Oh, but she was! *She was.* And she'd vacuumed and tidied up the place for the same reason. *For Tony D'Angelo?* No, she told herself, she would have done the same thing no matter who it was. She didn't have many visitors. In fact, except for the landlady, Mrs. Goldrich, and that time Mr. James had stopped by on a Saturday to pick up some papers she'd taken home to work on over the weekend—an incident Karen preferred to forget— Tony would be the first. So it was no wonder she was nervous. Oh God, were her hands shaking? She held them up in front of her. No, steady as a rock. Good. She only *felt* shaky. Inside.

The front door slammed; voices drifted up the stairs. Andrew's voice, excited and young, and another, a low, baritone murmur. Karen's stomach knotted. She took a deep breath and one last quick look around. What should she do? Go out to the landing and meet them, or wait for the knock on the door? No, Andrew wouldn't knock, she reminded herself. He would just open the door and walk in, and here she'd be, standing around as if she'd been waiting for them. It would be better to go and meet them.

Just as she got to the door, it opened and Andrew burst in, cheeks red with cold, eyes shining with an excitement even his glasses couldn't hide. Behind him, filling up the doorway, was Tony.

"Hi, Mom!" Disdaining his usual hello kiss, Andrew brushed by her, dumped his backpack on the couch and made a beeline for the box. "See, Tony? Here it is—it's got my name on it! And I get to open it now, right, Mom?"

Suddenly left to face her guest alone, Karen mustered a smile. "Hi. Please—come in." And then, with a little shrug of apology, "I'm sorry, he's been so excited about this...."

"That's okay." Tony's lips curved in a smile—the same slow, sweet, unanticipated smile that had taken Karen so completely by surprise when she'd encountered it that morning in his office. He smiled in stages, she decided—mouth first, then the creases at the corners of the eyes, and finally the eyes themselves. It was the last part that got to her...a warm brown glow as wicked and rich and irresistible as melted chocolate....

"I don't blame him," he drawled as he stepped into her living room. "There's something about a brown cardboard box, especially one with your name on it."

"Can I open it now, Mom? Can I? Please?"

"All right," Karen said in a weak voice, forgiving her son both his rudeness and his grammatical lapse for giving her something to do, for throwing her a lifeline she could use to pull herself away from the magnetism of that smile. She frowned at the box, gathering her wits. "It looks very sturdy. I think we'll need scissors, or a knife. I'll get one—"

Tony was already pulling one out of his pocket. He paused in the process of unfolding the blade, looked at Karen and said, "May I?" She hesitated, then nodded. He dropped to one knee beside the box.

It's because he looks so different, Karen thought, watching as he split the box's taped seams with a few deft strokes of the pocketknife. It was the first time she'd ever seen him in anything but coveralls. He seemed bigger, somehow, in the teal-blue turtlenecked sweater, brown leather jacket and well-worn jeans. Bigger and...sexier.

Sexier? Where had *that* come from? It was a word she hadn't even admitted to her thoughts for a very, very long time; doing so now caused her stomach to perform a curious and rather frightening flip-flop.

"There you go, kid," Tony grunted, folding the knife with a snap and tucking it back in his pocket. "Have at it."

It wasn't Andrew's way to go ripping into something helter-skelter; even as a very small child he'd opened his Christmas presents carefully, drawing out the suspense and maddening those with less methodical habits. Now, though his eyes were shining with anticipation, he folded back the box flaps almost reverently. His hands hovered over the layers of crumpled newspaper underneath, then slowly, slowly lifted them out of the box and laid them aside.

"Look for a card," Karen reminded him. The suspense was getting to her; she felt a strange, shivery excitement. "There must be something that says who it's from."

Tony picked up the discarded newspaper and shook it. "Doesn't seem to be one."

Andrew didn't appear to have heard them. He had taken a newspaper-wrapped object from the box and was holding it in his hands, and the look on his face was rapt, almost fearful.

Though she knew it would do no good to try to rush him, Karen couldn't keep from asking, "Well, what is it?"

"I don't know," Andrew answered, his voice hushed. "It's heavy."

"Well, come on, open it up." Even Tony was showing signs of impatience.

Andrew caught his breath and held his lower lip between his teeth. Then he slowly peeled away the paper and let it fall. For a heartbeat or two he was silent—dumbstruck, it seemed—cradling the small, heavy object in his hands as if it were made of glass, or high explosives.

"What on earth . . . ?" Karen murmured.

"It's a train," Andrew said at last, beginning in an awed whisper and picking up speed and volume as the wonder of it sank in. "This is the engine—it's a locomotive. It's an electric train, a real one. It's a whole, real electric train!"

"Here," Tony said, "let me see that." Andrew handed over the engine and picked up another paper-wrapped package. Karen sat down on the arm of the couch.

"I don't understand this," she muttered, shaking her head. The whole thing made her feel edgy, even angry. She didn't like mysteries, especially those that involved her child. "Who would do this? Who would do such a thing? Where did this come from?"

"It's an old one," Tony said, squinting thoughtfully at the underside of the locomotive. "I wonder if it runs."

"An old electric train?" Karen said on a rising note of disbelief. And then, because it seemed so crazy, so implausible, so unbelievable, she threw up her hands and began to laugh.

"Oh, *cool*!" Andrew exclaimed. "Hey, look at this."

In a moment he had the whole train unpacked and lined up on the living-room rug, the engine and five cars: a coal tender, a flatcar, a boxcar, a cattle car, and, of course, a caboose. The paint was faded and completely gone in spots, with patches of rust showing through, but Andrew didn't seem to notice. He was busy examining each car, exclaiming with delight and enthusiasm over each and every detail—doors that opened, wheels that turned, removable side racks, and on the front of the locomotive, a tiny silver bell.

"Look, Tony..."

"Hmm?" Tony glanced up from the control box he'd been examining, then leaned over to see what wonders Andrew had discovered now.

The two heads came together, bending low over the train...two heads with dark, wavy hair, a little too long at the back of the neck, brushing collars and the tops of ears. And for a moment, just a moment, the picture froze in Karen's mind, as if someone had snapped a photograph. She heard—felt?—a *click*, felt things shift inside her; emotion caught at her breath and rushed stinging to her eyes and nose.

Hay fever, she thought in sudden panic, and rose from the arm of the couch to declare brightly, "Andrew, it's way past your dinnertime. You must be starving."

"Yeah..." Andrew said absently, frowning with the concentration required to fit two slightly bent pieces of track together. Then he looked up, his face alight with the infusion of a new idea. "Hey, can Tony stay for dinner, Mom?"

"Oh—" said Karen and Tony at the same time, and then stopped.

"You can stay," said Andrew, both assuring and imploring. "My mom's a good cook. Do you like grilled cheese?"

"Yeah, sure—with ketchup." Shining with amusement, Tony's eyes met Karen's over the top of her son's head.

"Of course," she heard herself say. "You're welcome to stay."

There was a pause, a moment of silence that seemed much longer than it was. Then Tony cleared his throat and said, "All right, sure. Thanks very much."

"Well," Karen said, "all right, then."

As she made her way to the kitchen on legs that weren't quite steady, she heard Andrew say, "*Ketchup?* On grilled cheese? That's gross!"

Chapter Three

When Karen came back, Tony was on his hands and knees on the carpet, helping Andrew lay track. There was enough of it to make a figure eight that stretched half the width of the living room, from the bay window that looked out over the street all the way to the front of the couch. They'd even had to move the furniture a little to make room for it.

The boy turned as his mother approached, looking like someone who'd just discovered birthday presents. "Hey, Mom—look, we can put our Christmas tree right there, in the middle of that loop over there by the window, so everybody can see the lights. And then the train can go around the tree—won't that be neat? We're getting a big tree this year," he confided to Tony. "A real big one, tall as the ceiling. Right, Mom?"

Karen glanced upward. Tony could see her calculating the height of the Victorian ceiling, the probable cost of a twelve-foot tree, and the logistics involved in getting such a tree up the stairs and into the apartment. Then she uttered the age-old maternal cop-out, "We'll see," as she placed a tray on the floor beside the train track.

On the tray, Tony observed, there were two plates made out of plastic decorated with cartoon characters, two plastic glasses in bright primary colors, two neatly folded paper napkins and two small plastic spoons. On each of the plates was a grilled cheese sandwich nicely browned, a little pile of carrot sticks, and a tiny plastic cup of applesauce. The glasses were filled with milk.

"There," she said, plunking down a bottle of ketchup like an exclamation point. She had her lashes lowered, trying to shield the laughter in her eyes from him, but parted lips and a rosy blush betrayed her. "Now, is there anything else I can get for you?"

Though he was shaking inside with his own laughter, Tony managed to keep his face and voice absolutely deadpan. "No thanks, this is great." Karen's eyes flew open, then widened at the unmistakable challenge in his when he added softly, "If I think of anything, I'll let you know."

Oblivious to any adult undercurrents, Andrew was already tucking into his sandwich, taking bites out of the middle, the way Tony himself had done when he was a kid. The boy did stop chewing, though, to watch Tony pour ketchup on his plate, dip a corner of his sandwich into it and take a bite.

"Is that good?" he inquired, looking skeptical.

Tony offered the ketchup bottle. "Why don't you try it?"

Andrew shrugged. Tony poured him a small dollop. Andrew dipped, took a wary and tentative bite, chewed judiciously and finally conceded, "Not bad." Tony just grinned.

Karen had moved away from them, following the train track. Though he wasn't looking at her, Tony could tell she was nervous again. It had seemed as if she'd gotten over it while she was in the kitchen, but it was back now, once more confirming his suspicions that he was the cause of it. He decided he liked the fact that he made her nervous. Eventually, of course, he'd want her to feel comfortable with him, but right now that fidgety self-consciousness was telling him what he wanted to know, which was that she was aware of him in all the right ways.

"Does it work?" she asked, bending down to give the locomotive an experimental push, rolling it a little way along the track.

She caught Tony with his mouth full, so all he could do was shrug. Andrew, whose mouth was also full, said, "It's going to. Tony says he can fix it—right, Tony?"

For some reason, instead of answering with the confidence he felt, Tony glanced over at Karen. He found her studying him in a way that made him feel uncomfortable; all the nervousness was gone now, her eyes quiet and watchful, full of appeal and an unspoken warning. So he found himself hedging his bet. "Well, I don't know, kid. I said I'd try."

There was a little silence, and then Karen said meaningfully, "Andrew, do you have homework this evening?" It was a tone even Tony recognized.

Andrew groaned. "Spelling. Mom—"

"Better finish eating and get started on it," his mother gently but firmly interrupted. "The train will still be here tomorrow."

Tony, who knew a hint when he heard one, polished off the last of his applesauce and stood up, taking his plate with him. "I gotta go anyway, kid. We'll work on this some other time."

"Tomorrow? Can you come over tomorrow night? Please? Mom, can he?"

They both looked at Tony. He shrugged in what he hoped was an offhand way and muttered, "It's all right with me."

"Mom? If I promise to do my homework first?"

"Well..." Tony could see the ominous "We'll see" hovering on the tip of her tongue, but when she opened her mouth, the words that came out instead were, "All right. *If* you do your homework first. Now, scoot—and take your dishes to the kitchen!"

Obviously satisfied with the terms, Andrew "scooted."

As soon as her son was out of earshot, Karen lifted her head and drilled Tony with a look that reminded him of the one she'd given him that morning when she'd finally accepted the loan of his car.

"Is it true?" she demanded without beating around the bush. "Can you fix that train?"

Tony shrugged. "I think so, yeah."

Her eyes clung to his, searching, searching.... It gave him a strange feeling, as if he needed to take a deep breath but couldn't.

Finally, in a voice tight with controlled emotion, she said, "Please, don't tell him that unless you're sure. Don't promise something you can't deliver. I don't want him—"

"Lady," Tony said softly, "I don't make promises I don't mean to keep."

He saw a flicker of something in those transparent eyes of hers, something he couldn't quite name. And once again, although he wasn't touching her this time, he felt the struggle as she fought him and the easing when she let go.

"So," he said, "do you want me to give it a shot or not? It's your call."

She closed her eyes, let out a breath and nodded. "Yes...thank you. It's very nice of you. Andrew will be so—"

Nice. That damn gratitude again. Impatiently shaking it off, Tony said, "Tomorrow, then? About the same time?"

"Yes. Yes, that will be fine."

"Fine, I'll see you then." He was so distracted that he was out the door before he remembered he still had her car keys. And vice versa. He turned back with a smile that felt trampled. "Oops," he muttered as he handed them to her, "almost forgot."

"Oh—wait a minute, I have your keys right here...." Just like that, she was nervous again, like a bird in the presence of a cat. She flitted away for a minute, came back with her purse, fumbled in it for the keys and gave them to him. "Thank you so much—it was really nice of you to do that. And, uh..." She took a deep breath. "Do you have my bill?"

Tony took it out of his back pocket and handed it over. He watched her unfold it, holding his own emotions carefully in check while he watched hers play like shadow pictures across her face. He thought he recognized dread, all mixed up with pride...blank, uncomprehending shock...and finally, confusion.

"I don't understand," she said, throwing him that fierce blue glare that demanded nothing less than truth. "This is so much lower than the estimate. What about the battery and...all those other things you told me I needed? This is only—" she gave the paper in her hands another glance "—a routine service!"

"Plus wiper blades and antifreeze," Tony pointed out. Then he shrugged and tried to wave the subject off, wanting to get away before she nailed him to the wall; outright lying didn't sit well with his Italian-Catholic upbringing. "Listen, I'd rather tell you the worst up front and have the surprise be pleasant, that's all. Turned out you were in better shape than I thought. It happens. Hey, I'll see you tomorrow night. You can pay me then, okay?"

She hesitated while suspicion struggled with relief, then finally nodded and whispered, "Okay."

Relieved himself, Tony fled. He was two steps down the stairs when he heard her call his name. Feeling as guilty as only an honest man can, he paused and looked back.

She was still standing in the doorway, holding the bill in her hands, and for a moment Tony's heart stopped beating. Then he realized that she looked different somehow. More relaxed, as if a load had been lifted off her shoulders. And he realized then that she had called him by his first name. *Tony* ...

"How's your hand?" she asked softly, a smile in her voice and eyes. Even from where he stood, Tony felt the gentle warmth of it, like candle flames.

He glanced down at his bandaged hand, then looked up at her, slowly flexing it, remembering her touch. "Oh, it's okay," he said gruffly. "You did a good job." *Karen* ...

"Good...I'm glad. Well— I'll see you tomorrow, then."

"Yeah, tomorrow. I'll be here."

"Bye."

"Bye . . ."

Their voices were low and husky, the words uttered absentmindedly, as if, Tony thought, they both knew that what was being said was far less important than things that weren't spoken of at all.

About midway through the next day, it occurred to Karen that she was looking at the people around her in a new light. *Which one?* Which of these people— friends, acquaintances and co-workers—could have sent Andrew that train? Even relative strangers were suspects. Maybe she had a secret benefactor—a fairy godmother, a guardian angel, someone who admired her from afar. Ridiculous as that seemed, it almost made more sense than the alternative, which was that one of the people she knew had sent that box. She'd been over the list in her mind a dozen times. They all seemed unlikely, if not impossible.

Her first thought, before the box was opened, had been of her boss, Mr. James. As unpleasant as that suspicion was, it wouldn't have been the first time the lecherous old so-and-so had tried to get to Karen through her child. But she'd crossed Frank James off the list the minute she saw that broken-down old engine. It just wasn't his style. In the first place, he would never give Andrew something secondhand and in need of repair; he would buy the newest and most expensive thing available—and probably leave the price tag on it "by accident." And, of course, he wouldn't do it anonymously; he would want to be sure he got full credit for his generosity.

Then there was Louise, the other girl in the office with whom Karen sometimes shared lunch and minor confidences, and the closest thing she had to a friend in this town. But she had a husband who worked in the fruit-packing houses, when he could get work at all, and four school-age kids of her own. Why would she spend money and effort on Andrew?

After that, the list got very short indeed. Mrs. Goldrich, the landlady? Ridiculous. She tolerated Andrew, but had never given any indication of possessing a warm or generous bone in her entire body. Mr. Clausen? Well...as a matter of fact, the old gentleman who lived in the attic apartment above Karen did seem a less unlikely candidate than some of the others. Andrew was certainly convinced he was the culprit, anyway. That morning, when they'd met on the front walk as usual, Andrew had told the old man all about his mysterious gift. Mr. Clausen had laughed, clapped him on the shoulder and said, "So, young Andrew, Santa's come early this year, has he?" Afterward, Andrew had given his mother a superior look, one that clearly said, "See? I know I'm right."

Andrew's fantasies aside, the old man did seem jovial and kind, and he appeared to have a genuine fondness for the little boy. But how would an elderly and overweight gentleman who walked with a cane get such a large, cumbersome box up those stairs? And there was the question of expense. Mr. Clausen didn't appear to have much money; he lived in a tiny, one-room apartment, didn't own a car, and always wore the same suit, a vaguely dated three-piece pinstripe with an old-fashioned watch fob looped across the front of his vest. Karen had an idea that electric trains might be expensive. Even old ones in need of repair.

And that, of course, was the biggest question of all: why would *anyone*, friend or stranger, give a child an old, worn-out, broken-down toy? It didn't make sense.

She was still stewing about it, and having a hard time concentrating on work as a result, when Andrew arrived from school. Fortunately, while he was shrugging out of his backpack, she remembered the small package she'd purchased at the hardware store on her lunch break, scooped it up from her desktop and, in the nick of time, dropped it into her purse. Thanks to the train, Andrew seemed to have forgotten all about the mouse; with any luck, the problem would be resolved by the time he thought about it again.

"Hello, sweetheart," she said, remembering just in time that he considered himself too grown up to need help with his jacket. "How was your day?"

"Fine." He held out the construction paper object he'd been carefully juggling. "Here— I made it," he said in the offhand way he always adopted when he was feeling especially proud of himself. "It's a...a polyhedron. It's a Christmas ornament. You can hang it on the tree, if you want to."

"It's beautiful," Karen said, giving it a place of honor on her desk. "Of course we'll hang it on our tree. Now, do you have any homework?"

"Nah, it's the Friday before vacation. No more homework 'til next year. Can we get our tree tonight? After you get off work?"

"Have you forgotten?" Karen reminded him. "Tony's coming over to work on the train."

''Well, he could come with us.''

For a moment she couldn't answer him. She sat there looking at her son's face, at the hopeful light that lurked behind the caution in his eyes, and felt an odd little knot form somewhere in the middle of her chest. *Tony?* She laughed softly and shook her head. ''Sweetheart, I think you'd have to ask him first. And by the time he gets here—''

''I could ask him now. I could go over there—''

''Not today,'' Karen said firmly. ''You were over there all afternoon yesterday. I won't have you getting in Tony's way.''

''But I'm *not*. He lets me help him. He said—''

''Andrew, I said *no*. Not today.''

Andrew retired momentarily to think over his options. ''Can we go tomorrow, then? I could ask Tony tonight when he comes over.''

''Well...'' She took a deep breath and murmured, ''We'll see.''

''If we get a great big tree we're gonna need help, Mom,'' Andrew pointed out, trying to give an impression of innocence by widening his eyes and looking solemn. ''Tony could help carry it.''

''Andrew, about the tree...'' Karen closed her eyes for a moment, then rested her forehead on her hand and looked down at the scratch pad on her desk so she wouldn't have to see the disappointment on her son's face when she told him the bad news. The numbers on the pad were bad enough. Even with yesterday's good news about the car repairs, money was still going to be tight this month. The heating bill, which was *not* included in her rent, was bound to be higher, and she and Andrew were both going to need some warmer clothes. Even if she could manage the cost of the tree, there was still the matter of decorations.

"I'll make decorations," Andrew said when she'd explained it to him. His voice was tight, his face set and stubborn. Karen's heart sank; she knew that look. "I can make some more poly...polyhedrons. And—and those paper chains, like I made in kindergarten."

She drew another deep breath, this one to ease the ache in her chest. "All right," she whispered, caving in. "If you really want to, sweetheart, we'll get a big one. We'll make do, somehow. Now, scoot—go on and let me get some work done!"

Andrew's small hand patted her shoulder. "It'll be all right, Mom, you'll see," he said with a knowing smile, and went off to make some more polyhedrons.

Karen sat with her head in her hands, rubbing at the tightness in her temples. Though it made her feel guilty to admit it, the burden of single-parenthood seemed very heavy sometimes. There was never any respite from it; that was the trouble, no chance *ever* to lay it down, even for a moment....

Tony could help carry it.

Andrew's innocent words popped into her head from out of nowhere, sharp and clear and as impossible to ignore as a silver bell on a holiday street corner. The thought shocked her so much that she sat bolt upright, headache forgotten, heart racing. *Tony?*

It was like opening the door to an overful closet; thoughts and revelations tumbled into her consciousness like an avalanche. Tony! Could *Tony* have sent the train? Yes! Yes, he could have. He seemed genuinely fond of Andrew; he knew where they lived; he was certainly strong enough to have carried that box up the stairs. It made sense—except for one thing. Why would he do such a thing? *Why?*

Andrew answered the door that evening with a breathless and eager, "Hi." Then, instantly curious, he blurted, "What's that?"

Tony growled, "It's pizza, what's it look like?"

"I didn't mean that one," Andrew persisted unperturbed, evading the large flat box Tony had thrust at him. "I meant *that* one—the bag. Is it stuff for the train?"

"You didn't have to do this," Karen murmured, coming up behind her son.

There was something different about her tonight, Tony thought. He couldn't put his finger on anything specific, but she had a kind of radiance, an aura of suppressed excitement, as if she knew a wonderful secret and was dying to share it. Whatever it was, the excitement was contagious; he could feel his own heartbeat quicken as he handed over the pizza box.

"Here, kid, see for yourself," he muttered, relinquishing the brown paper bag from Hoolighan's Hardware and Paint to Andrew, who promptly dropped to his knees on the floor with it in that boneless way kids have. Tony stepped over him and went after Karen, who was heading for the kitchen with the pizza. "Look," he said as he held the kitchen door open for her, "I came over here to fix a train, not invite myself to dinner."

She turned to smile at him over her shoulder. "Are you sure it isn't that you just don't like my cooking?"

"Hey—" Tony held up his hands "—grilled cheese and ketchup happens to be a personal favorite of mine. Last night you fed me, tonight it's my turn. Fair's fair."

Something in his tone warned her. She got a wary look in her eyes and said, "Uh-oh—what kind of pizza is this, anyway?"

"The works," Tony confirmed with wicked relish. "Including olives, onions and anchovies. Hey, I'm Italian. What do you expect?"

She groaned, but mixed it with laughter. Oh yeah, he thought, there was definitely something different about her tonight; if it had been anybody but her, he would have been pretty sure she was flirting with him. Whatever the difference was, the effect it had on his vital signs was both predictable and devastating.

A second or two later, though, she got that closed, careful look on her face again and, like a little girl remembering her manners, said, "Well, thank you anyway. You really didn't have to do this. It's awfully nice of you."

Tony snorted. "I wish you'd quit saying that." When Karen cast him a questioning glance he shifted his shoulders and growled, "Look, let's get something straight. I don't do anything just to be 'nice.' I only do things because I want to, you understand? That makes me selfish, not 'nice.'"

"Bah, humbug," said Karen, as a smile flickered at the corners of her mouth.

"What?"

"Nothing. So—you brought pizza because..."

"Because that's the only way I can be sure I get what I want on it." That smile of hers was so bright and contagious, it was all he could do to repress the urge to smile back.

"And," she persisted, stifling laughter, "you're helping Andrew because you just happen to like playing with trains?"

"Right!" Tony shot back, still scowling gamely. "All men are kids when it comes to trains—don't you know that?"

"Really?" She said it on a quick, indrawn breath, her eyes shining with that strange excitement. While Tony's pulse surged in automatic response, she seemed to teeter for a moment on the brink of saying something else, something of profound important. Then she turned abruptly and opened a cupboard, and he heard the sigh of her exhalation.

I can't do it, Karen thought, as she reached for the plates. I can't ask him. He would only deny it, and she would feel foolish. She'd probably embarrass him, and he'd wish he'd never done it. Maybe, she thought, it was better not to know.

But she couldn't resist saying brightly, as she placed a stack of three plates on the table, "Did you have a train like that when you were a little boy?"

"Me?" Tony coughed and said in his old, gruff way, "Are you kidding? I'm the second youngest of seven kids. My folks raise almonds and peaches, down in the valley. We weren't poor, but we sure as hell didn't have money for things like electric trains."

Frowning and fidgeting, obviously looking for a change of subject, he picked up the empty paper bag that was lying on the counter. "Looks like we were both in Hoolighan's Hardware today," he commented, peering into the bag and then putting it back down.

"Oh, yes." Karen closed her eyes while her stomach rolled over, something it did automatically whenever she thought of the deadly little contraption in the cereal cupboard. "I had to buy a—" she glanced over her shoulder at the kitchen door and lowered her voice to a whisper "—a mousetrap. Andrew doesn't know. I hated to do it, but I've had this problem for a while, and I don't know what else to do."

She looked at Tony, and her breath caught. Audibly. A soft, telltale gasp. He was leaning against the counter with his arms folded across his chest, impossibly handsome, thrillingly masculine, annoyingly superior.

"So," he said, "you've set a trap for your mouse?"

Since she couldn't, for some reason, trust her voice, Karen nodded.

With his chocolate eyes glowing and a smile that was almost tender, Tony said softly, "Have you thought about what you're going to do if you catch him?"

Chapter Four

Tony wasn't sure how long she might have stood there looking at him, her blue eyes swimming with mute appeal, or how long he could have gone on resisting his natural impulse to respond. There was something about those eyes of hers. They made him want to put his arms around her, gather her close and promise her the moon if she would only promise never to let those tears loose. He'd grown up with four sisters and was used to feminine waterworks, but he didn't think he could stand to see this woman cry.

Finally, just when she was opening her mouth to say something, there came a bellow from the living room.

''Mom! Come see what Tony brought!''

Karen replied, ''Coming!'' She cast one last beseeching look at Tony as she hurriedly divided the pizza among the three plates, then picked up two of them and marched out, head high. Tony picked up the third one and followed her.

Andrew was sitting cross-legged on the floor in the middle of the train track, with the engine and cars all lined up in front of him, looking pleased with himself. He had a way of peering out over the top of his glasses, Tony noticed, that made him look like a fledgling owl.

''Hey, look, Mom—paint! It's a special kind of paint, too. It's for metal—to keep it from getting rusty. And there's all the colors, see?'' He'd matched them all up, black for the engine and coal tender, green for the flatcar and cattle car, yellow for the boxcar, and red for the caboose. ''And look, there's white paint for the writing, and even paint thinner, and these little brushes. Do I get to do it, too, Tony? Huh? Can I help?''

''Help? No way. I'm going to have my hands full just getting the thing to run. That's your job.''

''Mine? You mean, I get to do it all by myself?''

''What's the matter? Don't you think you can handle it?''

''Well,'' Andrew said slowly, ''I'm not too sure about the writing.''

''Writing?''

''Yeah, you know—like the name of the railroads and stuff.'' His face was wistful. ''I want it to look just like a real train, with the different names on the cars. I don't know if I can do it right.''

Tony coughed, but it didn't do much to clear the gravel from his throat. He looked at Karen, and when she met his eyes, the look in hers nearly stopped his heart. Without breaking that contact, he said gruffly, ''Well, maybe your mom'll help you. If you ask her.''

''Mom? Please?''

''Of course—'' Karen began in a whisper, then paused and went on briskly, ''of course I'll help. What we need is a book about trains, don't you think? I'll bet the library has some. Tomorrow we'll go and see. Now, have some pizza before it gets cold. Who wants something to drink? Milk or apple juice?''

''Milk, please,'' said Andrew dutifully.

Tony muttered under his breath, "I don't suppose you'd have a beer?"

He meant it half as a joke, expecting the look of maternal disapproval, that old "please-not-in-front-of-the-children" look his mother used to lay on his father. But when Karen murmured, "Sorry," there was a gleam in her eyes to suggest that she, too, might be thinking how well a glass of cold beer would taste with pizza.

He wondered, suddenly, how long it had been since she'd done something for herself, just for fun. How long since she'd tasted a cold beer, taken in an R-rated movie, gone out on a date. How long since she'd thought of herself as a woman—just a woman, young, beautiful, sexy—instead of Andrew's mother. The thought stirred strong emotions in him, some of which he couldn't quite name, but one of which was definitely anger. Not that he had anything against kids in general—he meant to have a couple of his own, someday—or Karen's in particular. He'd gotten pretty fond of the kid, as a matter of fact. But, damn it, she *was* a woman, plus all those other things, in spades. And he knew that, more than he'd wanted anything in a long time, he wanted to be the one to make her remember it.

"I just remembered something," said Andrew, eyeing a suspicious black spec on his slice of pizza. Without impolite comments he'd proceeded to remove everything he considered to be inedible from each piece of his pizza and deposit it carefully on his plate. "We can't go to the library tomorrow, because we're going to go get our Christmas tree." Finally satisfied with the condition of the pizza, he transferred his cloudless blue stare to his mother. "You promised."

"Yes," said Karen, knowing what was coming, "I know I did." The bite of pizza she'd just swallowed lodged in her chest, making the sudden pounding of her heart that much more painful.

"And," continued Andrew with bland innocence, "you said we could get a big one. A really, really big one. You promised."

"Yes," Karen sighed, "so I did."

Tony chewed and swallowed, took a long drink of milk and said thoughtfully, "A really, really big one, huh? You think you and your mother can get a big tree up those stairs all by yourselves?"

"Well," said Andrew, elaborately casual, "you could come with us, if you wanted to. Then you could help us."

Oh boy, Karen thought. Subtle as a truck. She drew a quick breath. "Listen, you don't—"

"Sure, I guess I could do that," Tony interrupted, imitating Andrew's carefully offhand manner. "I'll give you guys a hand. What time you planning to go?"

"I hadn't really thought," Karen said. "Whenever's convenient for you...." Inexplicably, she felt a desire to cry.

"Well," Tony said, "why don't we go early, then? That storm's supposed to get here tomorrow night. Why don't I pick you up around noon? We can go get some hamburgers or something, pick up the tree and get back before it hits. How's that?"

"Yeah!" said Andrew.

"That's...fine." Karen stood, hurriedly gathered up plates and pizza crusts. "Thank you—that's really... very nice of you," she said, and fled to the kitchen.

Alone, she steadied her hands on the edge of the sink and stared at her reflection in the dark window. What's happening to me? she thought, trying to quiet the panic that was rampaging through her insides. Something's happening, and I don't know what to do about it!

It's too soon.

But that wasn't true, not anymore. It had been five years. And it seemed that Andrew had grown tired of waiting for her miracle to happen and had simply taken matters into his own hands.

But what about the miracle? The miracle of love, real love, the kind that lasts forever, the kind that she had known with Andrew's father and that had been so cruelly taken away from her. The kind she had believed she would never know again.

Right now, for the first time in five years, she wasn't sure of that. She wasn't sure of anything. Something was happening to her, and she was frightened.

For the rest of the evening Karen tried her best to avoid the living room. She carried in two more glasses of milk, carried out the last remains of the pizza, and spent more time than was really necessary tidying up the dishes and scouring the sink, running water to drown out the unfamiliar sound of a masculine voice. When she ran out of chores, she sat down to write a Christmas card/thank-you letter to Bob's mother. But after "Dear Elaine..." and ten minutes of listening for the sound of the mousetrap, she abandoned the effort.

After all that, when she finally did gather her courage and return to the living room, both Tony and her son were so engrossed in what they were doing that they didn't seem to notice she was there. She spent several moments gazing at the two dark heads—how uncannily alike they were!—and bathing in the warm, syrupy feelings that vision evoked within her, then retired to her bedroom, where she spent the next hour or so ironing.

And trying not to think. Which was, of course, like reading a sign that implores you to ignore it. The more she told herself not to think about Tony, the more his name seemed to fill her mind, flashing like neon, first one color then another: Tony. *Tony!*

It seemed so unlikely. Almost impossible. It had come out of nowhere, so suddenly, so surprisingly. But . . . when she did allow herself to think about him, really *think* about him, remembering the way he looked at her sometimes, the feel of his hands enfolding hers, the contrast between the gruffness of his voice and the kindness of his actions . . . her stomach felt hollow and her skin too hot. *Tony. . . .*

No! It's too soon, she told herself, pressing her cold fingers to her burning cheeks. Too soon to know whether or not to believe in second miracles.

Andrew knocked on the door to say good-night promptly at eight-thirty, which surprised Karen a little. She'd expected him to put up a fight and beg to stay up later, especially since it was Friday and there wasn't any school tomorrow. She didn't want to ask about it and maybe embarrass him in front of Tony, so she just kissed him, reminded him as usual to brush his teeth and told him that she would be in later to tuck him in.

Tony was in the living room, putting the lid back on the last can of paint. He stood up when she came in and made a gesture with his hand that took in the newspapers spread out on the carpet, the paint-spattered paper towels, the brushes soaking in a jam jar on the coffee table, the towels and engine parts neatly arranged on a flannel cloth.

"Sorry about the mess," he said in the gruff way that was already becoming familiar to her. "Is it okay if we leave it there? I guess I could have moved everything over there by the window, out of the way, but I figured that's where you'd want to put your tree. If you'd rather—"

"No, no, it's all right," Karen hastily assured him. "I don't mind."

There was a curiously awkward little silence, and then Karen said, "Well, did you—" just as Tony said, "Well, I guess I'd better—" They both laughed, and Tony reached for his jacket while Karen tried again. "Did you get a lot accomplished?"

He shrugged his jacket on, making it an answer to her question at the same time. "Hard to say," he said with a little half smile. "I've never worked on an engine that small before."

"But," Karen persisted as she followed him to the door, "you do still think you can get it to run?"

He paused and looked at her. "I sure as hell mean to try."

"I know. I didn't—"

"Hey, it's okay." The smile was lurking again, teasing the corners of his mouth. "So I'll see you tomorrow, I guess. I'll pick you up about noon, and we'll go get that tree.''

"All right," Karen murmured. "Thank you. It really is . . . so very ni—"

"Shh." His finger touched her lips, tingling as if it carried its own electrical current. "Don't say it."

She stared at him, her heart hammering so hard it rocked her, until it seemed as if the silence might go on forever, as if the dryness in her throat was permanent, and she would never speak again.

But the silence wasn't permanent; it lasted for only a second, perhaps two. The sound that broke it wasn't loud, but as shocking in that stillness as cannon fire.

SNAP.

With one small, anguished cry, Karen lurched forward and buried her face in the nylon softness of Tony's jacket.

"Bingo," he said, with sympathy but no apparent surprise.

The instant she felt his arms come around her, she pulled away from him, but it was already too late; his warmth was in her bones, his masculine smell under her skin, awakening dormant instincts and responses. She whispered, "I'm sorry . . ." and brushed at the front of his jacket as if trying to set it to rights. But, of course, it wasn't the clothes that wanted tidying—just her own chaotic emotions.

Tony wasn't saying anything. His hands were still on her shoulders, palms flat against her back, thumbs lightly stroking. His eyes were warm chocolate, perhaps a little amused.

"I'm sorry," she said again, forcing herself to quiet her hands. Her nerves were fluttering like moths in syrup. "It was an accident. That awful thing startled me—"

"Accident, huh?" His voice was a soft growl. "Well, this isn't...."

It was the same little struggle they'd had before. He felt the resistance in her tense shoulders, in the fists pressed against his chest, in that one quick gasp just before he kissed her. Surrender came gradually, by degrees. He felt it first in her mouth, the trembling, the softening, the slight parting of her lips, followed almost instantly by the faintest of sighs. Her hands stopped pushing against him; the fists slowly uncurled; her fingers opened and spread across his chest in a widening pool of warmth. The temptation was strong to pull her closer, to let himself feel her body all along his and explore the warmth beyond those sweetly parted lips. But there was still that tightness in her muscles, the last bastions of her resistance, so he kept it light, a tentative kind of kiss, and left the options to her.

She ended it finally, twisting her mouth away from the gentle contact as if it were a struggle, tilting her face down so that his lips brushed her forehead instead. A tremor rippled through her; she muttered something he couldn't hear.

"Hmm?" he said, massaging her shoulders, monitoring the tension in them.

"Nothing," she whispered, and shook her head. "I didn't say anything."

She couldn't tell him, because she didn't know herself. It could have been any one of the panicky phrases that were ricocheting around in her head: It's too soon! It's been too long! It's not supposed to feel like this! It feels too good . . . too good!

It's not fair, she thought. She wasn't prepared for this. No one had told her that beginning to feel again would be so painful and confusing. Or so frightening.

"You're shaking," Tony murmured. "Does it upset you that much?"

"Upset me?" She hedged, thinking wildly, Oh God, can he see inside me? Do I betray so much?

"I'll take care of it for you, if you want me to." His voice was soft and warm, like his eyes.

The mouse. Karen closed her eyes. Of course, he was talking about the mouse. "Yes," she whispered. "Thank you."

"Stay here." His lips brushed her forehead, and then he was gone.

Karen let her breath out slowly and sank down on the arm of the couch. Her legs were shaking and her heart was beating like—she glanced at the clutter on the floor at her feet and gave a shaken laugh—like a runaway freight train, what else! She sat still, counting her heart's frantic cadence, until Tony came through the kitchen door.

She rose and said bravely, "Well?"

He lifted his shoulders and held out his hands. "Nothing. No mouse."

"What?"

"*Nada.* Looks like the crafty little devil took your bait and got clean away."

"He got *away*?" Karen said incredulously, giving him a long, narrow look. Her heart was slowly filling with suspicion—a wonderful, shimmering, golden suspicion.

Tony gave another eloquent shrug. He looked, Karen thought, exactly like an altar boy with a frog under his surplice. "Must have. The trap's empty. Guess you'll just have to try again."

She said with a shaky laugh, "Well...maybe I'll just wait until after Christmas."

He laughed, too. "Good idea. A holiday reprieve. Well...if everything's okay, I guess I'll see you tomorrow." He touched her chin with a knuckle, nudged it upward and brushed her mouth with his. And before she could do more than catch a quick, surprised breath he murmured, "Good night," and went out the door.

Karen stood where he'd left her, absolutely transfixed. *He'd lied.* Joy and warmth and wonder filled her. He'd lied about the mouse; she was certain of it. He'd disposed of the mouse and then lied about it to spare her pain. What a sweet, beautiful, wonderful thing to do!

In a daze, she wandered into the kitchen. The mousetrap lay on the countertop, disarmed and empty, with not a trace of the peanut butter-smeared cracker she'd used for bait—or anything more grisly—in evidence. She picked it up by one corner and dropped it into a drawer, then leaned her hands on the edge of the sink and stared at her reflection in the dark window. Her face stared back at her, pale and somber and frightened.

Yes! she thought, gripping the cold porcelain while shivers of excitement cascaded through her body. I'm scared—and why not? Falling in love is always scary. And so are miracles.

The next day was dark and cold, with lowering clouds and the promise of snow. December twenty-first, the first day of winter, the shortest day of the year.

After breakfast, while Andrew went to work painting the caboose, Karen mixed up a batch of cookie dough and put it in the refrigerator. While she waited for it to harden, she finished the letter to her former mother-in-law and wrote brief notes in several Christmas cards, some of them to couples who had been friends of hers and Bob's. As always, there was a certain poignancy in the ritual, but this year, for the first time, she was conscious of a growing sense of distance. As if, she thought, she were on a fast-moving train that was carrying her steadily farther and farther away from the times and places of her life with Bob, until now they seemed to her no more real than dots on a distant horizon.

When the dough was hard, she cleared away the Christmas cards and took out the rolling pin and cookie cutters. Andrew heard the preparations and came in begging to help, as he always did. But Karen took one look at his paint-stained hands and sent him outside to play, promising that he could help with the frosting and decorating, which was his favorite part, anyway.

The time passed quickly, while Karen rolled dough and cut out Christmas shapes the way her grandmother had taught her when she was no older than Andrew. "It's the lemon flavoring that makes the difference," she could almost hear her grandmother say. "Put more flour on your rolling pin, Kary, dear...."

Christmas trees and bells and wreaths, stars and angels, Santas and snowmen. "Not too thick, now...

and take them out of the oven when the first tinge of brown shows on the edges!''

Karen was just taking the last pan full of cookies out of the oven when she heard Tony's knock. She carefully slid the cookies onto a dish towel, dropped both the pan and pot holder into the sink, and wiped her hands on her jeans while she took one last look around. Then she went to answer the door.

"Hi," Tony said, breaking into a grin when he saw her. He sounded out of breath, whether from the cold or because he'd sprinted up the stairs Karen couldn't guess. It didn't matter; she was too winded herself to answer his greeting, or to even gasp when he suddenly reached out and brushed at something on her cheek. "Flour," he explained, the smile warming his eyes. "Been baking something?"

"Just some cookies," Karen said, sheepishly rubbing her cheeks. "Oh dear, do I have it all over me? That always happens, I don't know why."

"It's okay. It looks cute on you." As casual and easy as if last night had never happened, as if he'd never even thought of kissing her, as if he'd been walking in and out of her house all his life, Tony moved past her and headed for the kitchen, sniffing the air like a hunting dog hot on the scent. "Hmm...smells good. Can I have one?"

Karen hurried after him, dithering like an overprotective mother. "Well, they're not finished yet. I don't know...."

"Christmas cookies!" Tony's hand hovered over the cookies cooling on the dish towel. He selected a reindeer and gave Karen a look that would have melted a Scrooge's heart. "Please?"

Karen managed a laugh and a grudging, "Oh, all right, if you must. But just wait until you see them all decorated. We make the prettiest Christmas cookies in the world. And the best tasting, too."

"Hmm," Tony muttered with his eyes twinkling and his mouth full. "And she's modest, too."

"Oh, it's true," Karen said simply. "Everyone always says so. My grandmother and I always made them when I was a child." She smiled, remembering. "All my cousins would come to help with the decorating—nobody wanted to be left out—but I was her special helper, because I lived with her."

"How come?"

She glanced at him and shrugged, keeping it light and offhand, because she didn't want him to think she considered herself unfortunate to have been raised by warm, loving grandparents. "My mother died when I was a baby, and...I never knew my father."

Tony's eyes were dark and intent. "No brothers and sisters?"

"No," Karen said, "just me." She smiled and added softly, "Now it's just Andrew and me."

"Hmm." Frowning, Tony popped the last of the cookie into his mouth and brushed crumbs from his fingers. "Speaking of the kid, where is he?"

"I sent him outside for some fresh air. He should be..." Karen leaned over the sink to look out the window. "Yes, there he is.... Oh, look, there's Mr. Clausen. I wonder what they're doing?"

"Mr. Clausen?"

"My neighbor," Karen said, and caught her breath as Tony brushed against her, reaching past her to twitch the curtain out of the way. "He lives upstairs."

Tony's laugh gusted warmly past her ear and teased the wisps of hair on her temple. "Looks just like Santa Claus, doesn't he?"

Karen snorted. "That's what Andrew says." But when she turned to give Tony an exasperated look, she found that his face was closer to hers than she'd expected. And suddenly it was hard to be exasperated about anything...or even to think clearly. She frowned in concentration and whispered, "I'm...a little concerned about him."

"Why?" It was a soft, warm sound that barely altered the shape of his mouth.

"Because..." His mouth...so close to hers. "He still believes in Santa Claus."

A smile hovered, just a breath away. "Don't you?"

"Don't I...believe in Santa—" She blinked, straightened and turned blindly back to the window, her heart beating in a crazy, uneven rhythm. "He doesn't get outside enough, that's the problem. He reads too much. He needs to play with other children more. I wish—"

"Careful..." His hands turned her; his finger touched her lips, lightly, as it had the night before. "Don't forget, it's the season for wishes." The smile on his lips faltered, then tilted wryly. "Hey, don't wish for something unless you know what you're getting into. Believe me, having a bunch of kids around all the time isn't all it's cracked up to be."

Karen whispered, "You sound as if you know." His hands were on her shoulders; she could feel the energy in them, like a force field that shut out the rest of the world and pulled her into his orbit.

"I know," he said harshly. "I'm one of seven kids, remember? Four sisters, two brothers. Hey, if your son likes to read, maybe it's because he was born that way. Maybe he's glad he's got space to call his own, and peace and quiet when he wants it, and privacy. Some kids need those things, you know?''

His eyes were dark, intent...and filled with a certain wistfulness. Karen's heart filled up and turned right over; understanding and insight made a lovely star burst inside her. "Some kids," she said softly, touching his face with her fingertips. "Like...you?"

Of course... A shy, private child in a noisy, gregarious household—was that why he'd taken to Andrew? Did he see himself in her quiet, reserved, bookish little boy?

All through her, in every part of her, emotions were burgeoning. She held very still, feeling the smooth, hard edge of Tony's jaw in her hand, the moist warmth of his breath on her thumb...and smiled as she listened to the chaos inside herself, the tinkling, shimmering sound of a miracle-in-progress.

Tony's lips formed a kiss on the sensitive pad of her thumb; his hands moved inward to the base of her neck, his thumbs describing tender circles on her throat, stroking upward toward the soft underside of her chin. She held her breath and watched his eyes come closer....

"Mom!" The front door crashed back on its hinges. "Mom," Andrew shouted, "guess what—it's snowing!"

Chapter Five

Tony's hands shifted back to her shoulders, then lifted. She let her hand drop away from his face, touched the center of his chest briefly, then took a step away from him, and in a carefully neutral voice called, "In here, sweetheart." She felt shaky, as if she'd been too abruptly awakened from a deep sleep. She felt cold and isolated, as if she were a lost traveler and Tony's arms were a safe warm haven, just beyond reach.

Though he didn't say anything, the look Tony gave her as he widened the space between them must have mirrored her own—one brief glance, searing as a whiplash, full of irony and longing.

Andrew burst into the kitchen, as excited as Karen had ever seen him. "Mom! Hi, Tony! Hey, look out the window. It's starting to snow!"

"Sure is," Tony confirmed, and turned to Andrew with a grin of masculine communion. "Looks like it's coming in early. Well, kid, we'd better get that tree while we still can. You ready to go?"

"Andrew," Karen interjected, "what in the world have you got there?"

Andrew said, "Yeah...just a minute," to Tony and went on with what he was doing, which was taking small, fuzzy brown balls out of his pockets and placing them on the kitchen table. When he'd emptied every pocket, he unzipped his jacket and let an avalanche of the things tumble out onto the table, a chair and the floor. He was beaming, bright-eyed and rosy with pride and cold.

"Look—sycamore balls! Mr. Clausen said I could paint them, to make decorations for our tree. We have the paint, right, Tony? Isn't that cool, Mom? And there's *hundreds* of them out there—except some of them are already coming apart, and they're really *itchy*. Mr. Clausen says not to get 'em on your skin, or they'll give you a rash. What do you think, Mom? See, we don't have to buy any more decorations, we can just make a whole bunch of these!"

"Sycamore balls," Karen said faintly. "Where on earth do you suppose Mr. Clausen got such an idea?"

"Mr. Clausen—" Andrew began, then paused and, with a curiously wary and secretive look, shrugged and said neutrally, "Mr. Clausen knows a lot of things. Maybe because he's old."

"Huh, we used to do these when I was a kid." Tony picked up a ball by its stem, and dangled it between his thumb and forefinger. "Must have been just about every year from kindergarten to third grade. There was a great big old sycamore in the schoolyard, and every fall we'd gather these things and paint 'em for Christmas. We used to dip them in glitter, too."

"Cool! Can we get some glitter, Mom?"

"If we don't get a tree, there won't be anything to hang 'em on," Tony pointed out, dropping the sycamore ball and dusting his hands. "Come on, Andy, let's get this show on the road!"

Karen stifled a gulp of protest as he picked up a star-shaped cookie on the way out the door. Andrew looked at her, grinned, selected a Christmas tree for himself and followed.

"The old guy's right about the itching," she heard Tony confide to her son as they crossed the living room together. "I used to chase the girls with 'em and put 'em down their necks. Especially my sisters—boy, did they hate that."

"Cool," said Andrew, with his mouth full of cookie.

Tony couldn't remember when he'd had more fun in a snowstorm. To accommodate the tree, and because he'd been expecting snow, he'd brought his little four-wheel-drive pickup truck instead of his car, even though it didn't have a very good heater and was going to be a tight squeeze for three. They all piled into the front, Andrew in the middle, laughing, puffing out vapor with every breath and shaking snowflakes all over everything. Tony didn't think he'd ever seen anything prettier than Karen's blond hair with snow melting in it, like tiny glittering stars.

When "Jingle Bell Rock" came on the radio, Karen surprised the heck out of him by starting to sing along. Andrew pretended to be embarrassed at first, but after a while, when Tony started to sing "Grandma Got Run Over By A Reindeer," he laughed so hard he almost fell off the seat. And by the time they got to the tree lot they were all singing along with Elvis's "Blue Christmas" at the top of their lungs.

The biggest tree they could find was a ten-footer, which disappointed Andrew a little bit, until Tony pointed out that once they got it on a stand and put a star on top of it, it was going to be another foot taller,

at least. As it was, it took all three of them to get it into
the truck and lashed down, and it hung out the back
so far they had to tie a red ribbon to the tip of it.

Tony had promised hamburgers, so they went into
the Hamburger Chalet, which was a new, touristy kind
of place that had just opened up in the shopping center next door to the tree lot. Andrew insisted on sitting where they could keep an eye on the truck, in case
anybody tried to steal the tree, which Tony figured was
what came of living too long in a place like L.A. They
all agreed that the Chalet had pretty good hamburgers, though Tony didn't think they were as good as the
ones at Dan's Drive-In out on the highway, where the
crowd used to hang out back in his high school days.

For some reason he got to thinking about all the
girls he'd dated then and in the years since, all the girls
who'd sat across the table from him as Karen was right
now, dipping French fries in ketchup and throwing
him tentative smiles. He wondered how it was that he
hadn't wound up married to one or another of them,
all settled down by this time, as most of his friends
were—and his brothers and sisters, too—with a couple of kids apiece. Not for want of effort on the part
of his family, that was for sure! Especially his sisters,
who never let a month go by without trying to set him
up with somebody, and his mother, who was always
lamenting that he was over thirty now, and time was
passing him by. Why, he wondered, had he resisted the
invitation in those smiles, and all of his sisters'
schemings and his mother's pleadings?

Then he looked at the woman sitting across from
him, blond hair falling across her cheek and dipping
into the collar of her threadbare coat...blue eyes

seeking his from time to time, sometimes shy and puzzled, and other times shining with a strange and contagious excitement. And he thought he knew why. Somehow, when he looked at this woman, things happened inside him. He felt things he'd never felt before...thought about things he'd never thought about before. When he looked at Karen, he thought about going to bed with her, which wasn't unusual. But he also thought about sleeping all night long with her cuddled up beside him, and having her there when he woke up in the morning. And he found himself thinking about babies and private jokes, and the way his mother and father still looked at each other, and held hands in church.

"What?" Karen asked suddenly, smiling but uncertain. "Why are you looking at me like that?"

"Nothing," he said, grinning at her. "Just...looking, I guess."

"Oh God—don't tell me, do I have ketchup on my face?"

"No," he assured her tenderly, "you don't have ketchup on your face. Maybe just a little flour on your nose, though."

"Andrew, tell me the truth. Do I have ketchup on my face?"

"No, Mom. Honest."

"All right." Pink and flustered, she turned that fierce blue glare back to Tony and demanded, "Then what were you thinking?"

"Nothing," he insisted, laughing as his chest expanded with all the things he couldn't say to her yet. "I was just...thinking. Nothing important."

Nothing important. For the first time in his life, Tony was thinking about forever.

By the time they started home with the tree, the snow was coming down in big, fat flakes and beginning to stick to the sidewalks and rooftops. The main streets glistened black and wet, reflecting headlights and Christmas lights in the midafternoon dusk, but on the quiet residential streets, car tracks left meandering ribbons on blankets of pristine white. It wasn't bad yet, but getting thick enough to make Tony glad he'd brought the four-wheel-drive.

He and Karen left Andrew making snowballs on the front walk while they carried the tree up the stairs. They made so much noise laughing and falling down and trying to shush each other that Mrs. Goldrich came out to see what was going on.

Karen immediately straightened her face and said solemnly, "Merry Christmas, Mrs. Goldrich."

With all the dignity he could muster, Tony echoed it. "Yeah, Merry Christmas, Mrs. Goldrich."

The landlady grunted and went back into her apartment, muttering something about paying for any damage to the woodwork. The instant the door closed after her, Karen and Tony collapsed, snorting and giggling, into each other's arms.

Eventually, pulling and tugging, swearing and laughing and getting in each other's way, they did manage to get the tree up the stairs, through the door and into Karen's living room. Tony stood it upright in front of the bay window, right in the center of the loop of train track, and they both stood back to admire it. Then they looked at each other—sweaty, dusty, covered with pitch and pine needles—and the last fitful chuckles sighed away into silence.

A second later she was in his arms, and he was kissing her with a hunger he hadn't even known about until that moment, plundering her mouth as if he were a parched and weary wanderer and she the life-giving spring. Searching her mouth, holding her as if he knew that everything he'd ever needed, wanted, or dared hope for, was right there, in her.

When she pulled her mouth away from his, she was shaking like a leaf. He folded her close and held her while their hearts knocked in crazy, mixed rhythms, and finally said in a ragged whisper, "I've been wanting to do that all day."

"Really?" Her voice was weak and faint; he could feel her arms holding tightly to him, and her face pressing into the curve of his neck.

"Longer than that, actually. A lot longer." He separated himself from her just far enough so he could slip his fingers under her chin. He wanted to see her face, her mouth still swollen and moist from his kiss, her eyes dazed and sultry. Even in the semidarkness of premature twilight he could see his own hunger reflected in her eyes. "Yeah," he said softly, "and I think I'm going to have to do it again...."

But he didn't, not right away. Because this time he wanted to take his time about it, think about it, imagine her lips coming to rest against his, opening under his, the warm, sweet taste of her on his tongue. He wanted to watch her eyes while he slipped his hand inside her coat and discovered the palm-fitting curve of her breast, and under it the trip-hammer beat of her heart.

She gave a sharp gasp when he touched her there, and closed her eyes, not wanting him to see the longing in them. It had been so long, and she'd almost forgotten the feeling. But had it ever felt so wonderful, or so terrible, this pleasure that was almost pain? Oh, how she wanted—but in the next moment, instead of leaning into his hand and inviting further explorations as she wanted to do so badly, she was wrenching herself away from him, trembling.

He called her name in a voice she hardly recognized. "Karen..." And then he said it once again on a soft exhalation as he registered the sound she'd heard already: Andrew's footsteps, clomping up the stairs.

"Hey," Andrew said as he burst into the room, an avalanche of melting snow and childish enthusiasm, "it looks great, doesn't it? And you can see it from down there in the yard, just like I thought. Let's put the decorations on it right now. Can we, Mom?"

"Of course," Karen said faintly. "I'll get them...."

Tony, who'd been standing with his back to them, finally turned and said with gravel in his voice, "What we need to do is anchor this monster to the ceiling so it won't fall over. You wouldn't happen to have a stepladder, would you?"

Karen shook her head. Andrew said, "Mrs. Goldrich has one. Out in the backyard, by the porch where the washing machine is."

"All right." Tony snapped his fingers at Andrew and growled, "Hey, let's go get it. What are we waiting for? Lead the way."

As he followed Andrew out the door, he threw Karen a look that made her insides react in strange, exciting ways. A look of frustration and promise.

By the time they came back with the ladder, she had her meager supply of decorations spread out on the couch, the ones she and Bob had bought for their tiny coffee table tree their first Christmas together, the year Andrew was born. A box of unbreakable red balls, some white plastic snowflakes, a few feet of silver tinsel garland, a single string of lights, and a crumpled gold foil star. She touched the star, remembering how dismayed they'd been when Bob had stepped on it accidentally while backing up to admire the tree, and how they'd comforted each other, and finally laughed about it and decided to keep it anyway, to always remember that first Christmas....

"It's not much for such a big tree, is it?" she said, clearing her throat as Tony came up behind her. "One string of lights isn't going to go very far."

"It's a start." He had that particular gruffness in his voice that meant he was going to say or do something nice. "And... I've probably got a couple of strings lying around my place we can add to it. Um—" he coughed and shifted uncomfortably "—if you want me to, I can bring 'em tomorrow."

"That would be—" she paused, then, with a soft, inward smile, substituted for that forbidden word, *nice* "—great! But are you sure you don't need them?"

"Nah, I don't need 'em. I hadn't planned to put up a tree this year, actually. Too much trouble. I'm going to my folks for Christmas, anyway."

"Oh," Karen said. "I see. Well, then..."

"I always go to my parents' place Christmas Day," Tony said. "For dinner, and... you know. Traditional family get-together."

"That's... nice."

"Yeah."

They stood side by side in silence, watching Andrew maneuver the ladder into place astride the train track. Then Karen said, "What about Christmas Eve?"

"Christmas Eve?" Tony coughed and rubbed his nose. "I hadn't actually made any plans."

"Well," Karen said, and took a deep breath, "would you like to come over here? It will just be Andrew and me. Nothing special, but . . . we'd like to have you, if you don't have anything else planned. I know Andrew—"

"Okay," Tony said, "I'll come." He sort of squinted up at the top of the tree, then looked down at her. "If . . . you come with me to my folks' house on Christmas Day."

"Come . . . with you?" Warmth and wonder flooded her. She turned to him slowly. "Are you sure?"

"Sure, I'm sure."

"They won't . . . your family won't mind?"

She was a little puzzled when Tony burst out laughing. "You have no idea," he said, still chuckling, "how happy they're going to be to meet you!"

The early winter night was upon them by the time they'd finished hanging the decorations—including Andrew's polyhedron—on the tree. The single string of lights winked bravely from the topmost branches and was multiplied by its reflection in the dark window. Outside, the snow fell silently, drifting on the windowsills like painted-on holiday trimmings.

While Andrew and Tony returned the ladder to its proper place, Karen opened two cans of soup— chicken noodle for herself and Andrew, and minestrone for Tony. They ate in the kitchen. While the snowflakes sifted past the windows, Tony told Andrew stories of boyhood adventures and mishaps in the snow.

Watching them, listening to the sounds of their voices, laughing with them, Karen felt warm and contented and happy. Happier than she'd thought she could ever be again. So happy it scared her. Because she knew how fragile such happiness was, and how suddenly it could all be taken away. The fear blew through her like a blizzard wind, shaking her so that she had to get up and leave the table, for fear they would see it and ask her what was wrong.

How could she explain such fear? How could she tell anyone that, standing at the sink looking out at the swirling snow, she felt the same cold inside herself, even though the room behind her was filled with the warmth of laughter and much-loved voices? I'm afraid of happiness, she thought, her heart trembling with both those emotions. I'm afraid of loving again. I'm falling in love with Tony, but— Oh God, how would I stand it if I ever lost him? How could I survive that again?

Watching her, Tony felt the struggle in her as surely as he'd felt it that morning in his office when he'd held her unwilling hands closed around the keys to his car. He could see it in her rigid shoulders, in the white-knuckled hand on the edge of the sink. It was a battle of wills, only this time she was fighting herself, and he wasn't sure which side was winning.

Damn it, he thought, frustration lancing through him, why is she fighting it? Something this good—and it *was* good, he was sure of it—why didn't she just let it happen? It took all of his willpower to keep from throwing himself into the middle of her battle, to keep from going to her right then and there, putting his arms around her and telling her it would all work out fine if only she'd just stop fighting it.

The evening seemed long to Karen, full of tensions and undercurrents to which Andrew, happily, seemed totally oblivious. He worked diligently on the train, painting with his usual deliberation and painstaking care, while Tony reduced the switchbox to an indistinguishable litter of parts and pieces. It didn't look to Karen like anything that could possibly be in working order by Christmas, but Andrew seemed to have no doubts. He chattered away to Tony about how "cool" it was going to be to have the train chugging around the tree on Christmas morning, and how neat it would be to build tunnels and a village for it to run through. Karen just hoped he wasn't setting himself up for a big disappointment.

She spent the evening sitting cross-legged on the carpet, dipping sycamore balls in acrylic paint and spreading them out on waxed paper to dry. And nervously watching the clock. She didn't know whether she was looking forward to being alone with Tony or dreading it, but the closer it got to eight-thirty, the more butterflies there were rampaging around in her stomach.

In any case, inevitably, eight-thirty did arrive, and once again Karen was surprised to receive no arguments from Andrew in response to the gentle reminder that it was his bedtime. He seemed, in fact, to have anticipated the moment, because the paint he'd been using was already put away, and when Tony sternly asked him if he'd cleaned his brush, he held it up and said proudly, "Yep—see?"

That alone woke Karen's suspicions. They grew by leaps and bounds when her son took off his glasses, gave a huge, stagey yawn and, blinking like a sleepy owl, announced, "I'm pretty tired. Guess I'll turn in.... 'Night, Tony. 'Night, Mom."

Turn in? He'd never said that before in his life.

In the doorway, Andrew half turned. "You don't have to tuck me in," he said earnestly. "Just go right on with what you're doing."

That was Andrew, subtle as a truck! Karen was so bemused she even forgot to tell him to brush his teeth.

"What's funny?" Tony asked. She was trying her best to stifle her laughter by burying her face in her hands.

"Oh...nothing." But she made the mistake of looking at him, and just like that the laughter died. Her heart began to hammer painfully; she made a tiny, throat-clearing sound and looked away again. "Well," she said, nodding at the dismantled switchbox and the array of tools spread out on the coffee table, "how's it coming? Do you think you can get it to work?"

"Hey," Tony growled, ignoring her question, "come on up here." Shifting a little to make room, he leaned over, caught her hand and pulled her up beside him. "Forget the damn train. I think you and I have some unfinished business...."

Chapter Six

"'Unfinished business...'" Karen whispered, looking toward the doorway to the hall. She could still hear the sounds of water running, and the indeterminate bumps and thumps Andrew made getting ready for bed.

"Does it bother you?" Tony asked softly, following her glance. He didn't have to say any more.

She smiled and shook her head. "No...in fact..." Her gaze shifted to her hand, which was still clasped in his. His thumb had begun to stroke lightly back and forth along the tendons in the back of her hand, and to explore the sensitive places between the fingers. She caught her breath. "I think he knows."

"You mean this 'Guess I'll turn in' business?"

She nodded, laughing. "He's never been this cooperative about bedtime in his whole life."

Their chuckles merged, stirring eddies of warm air across each other's faces. Tony's fingers touched her chin, rubbed along her jaw, gently persuading. When she lifted her eyes to his, he smiled into them and murmured, "Well, since we seem to have his blessing...where were we?"

"That's about the place," Karen whispered, sick and dizzy with wanting.

When his lips touched hers, she made a sound, something between a whimper and a gasp; her chest tightened, and all her emotions surged joyously. His fingers fanned along her cheekbone and pushed into her hair, holding her head in a warm embrace while his mouth covered hers, sank into hers...slowly, deeply. She sighed and felt that tender merging all through her body, in every part of her, in the tingling, shivering places and the hot, throbbing places, and, most of all, in the empty aching places deep within her heart. Tears sprang to her eyes. She gave a single shuddering sob and pulled away.

But Tony's fingers held her, spreading through her hair, refusing to let her go, gently guiding her face upward, compelling her to look at him. "What is it?" he asked softly. "I don't want to rush you. If it's too soon...?"

She shook her head and said in a distraught and rapid whisper, "No, it's not that. It's been so long— I don't have any control. I'm afraid I can't...I can't trust my judgment!"

His laughter caressed her lips. His tongue teased and cajoled them, inviting them to join his smile. "Sweetheart, I think this is the time for letting go of control. It's not a matter of judgment, it's just...instinct. Don't try to think too much."

"But I have to think! It's happening too fast. I don't know you!"

Oh, but she did...she did. She knew all that was important to know. She knew that he was honest and compassionate, patient and generous. She knew that he was shy and reserved, which only made the intimate things he shared with her the more miraculous and wonderful. She knew that he smiled with his eyes.

Only, his eyes weren't smiling now. Dark, grave and compassionate, they gazed steadily into hers. "Baby," he said softly, "how long has it been?"

She closed her eyes. "Five years."

"And in all that time, you mean to tell me there hasn't been anyone else?"

"No," she whispered. "No one."

"Why not?"

"I don't know, I guess . . . I just wasn't ready."

"And now?"

And now . . . She opened her eyes and looked at him—at his beautiful face, its dark-fringed eyes, chiseled features and warm, sensitive mouth. For some reason it didn't seem so paralyzingly handsome to her anymore, just . . . very, very dear. Oh God, she thought, reaching with trembling fingers to touch him. How did this happen? In such a short time, how did this face come to be so dear to me? How did this man come to mean so much to me? All of a sudden she felt naked . . . exposed . . . frightened. Tears welled up and overflowed. She put up her hands in a futile attempt to stem the tide and sobbed, "I don't know!"

There was a long silence, broken only by a muffled sniff. Then Tony lowered his head and kissed her, gently licking the salty tears from her lips. "You were right," he said in the gruff and tender voice she loved. "It's moving too fast for you. You're not ready. You'll know when you are. Let me know, okay?"

No! she wanted to cry. I am ready! I don't know what's the matter with me. . . . But, overcome with emotion, she could only grip his wrists tightly and nod.

"Hey, it's okay. I'll see you tomorrow." He kissed her once more, lightly, and stood up. Karen stood up, too, brushing at her wet cheeks. He hesitated, reached out as if to touch her, then let his hand drop. "Don't cry," he said in a hoarse whisper, and then he left her.

Karen was glad the next day was Sunday and that she didn't have to fight her way to work, since she had no experience whatsoever driving in snow and would probably have ended up in a ditch somewhere—or worse. Andrew, of course, couldn't wait to bundle up and go outside to play, though his winter clothes were woefully inadequate. His Christmas presents were going to have to be on the practical side this year, Karen thought with a pang as she watched him from the bay window, trying to roll snowballs in a pair of her old driving gloves. Boots, mittens and a warm winter coat—not the sort of things to make a little boy's eyes light up on Christmas morning.

But at least there was the train. It would make up for a lot, if only Tony could get it running in time. *If only...*

Tony came over a little after noon to work on the train, stopping off in the front yard first for a snowy roughhouse with Andrew. They came in together, noisy and laughing, stomping and melting in dirty puddles all over the floor, thereby overriding any awkwardness that might have remained after last night.

After adding the two strings of Christmas lights he'd brought with him to the one already on the tree, Tony settled down to the painstaking task of reassembling the switchbox. Andrew put a second coat of paint on the caboose, and then, bored with that job, spent the rest of the afternoon hanging sycamore balls on the tree and pestering Tony with questions. K ren stayed in the kitchen and decorated cookies by herself.

Just before dinnertime Tony went home, saying he had some things he needed to do and an early work-day the next morning, and promising to come back the next night. Andrew didn't argue or try to persuade him to stay, but Karen caught him looking from her to Tony and back again with worry and uncertainty in his eyes. Oh, how her heart ached for him, for his fear and vulnerability! All her instincts yearned to shield and protect him, but she knew she couldn't, not from this. She didn't know any way to protect her child from the pain and risk of loving someone.

After supper, Karen and Andrew tried to do some more work on the train, but without Tony the apart-ment seemed very quiet and empty, and after a while they gave up and went to bed early.

By the next day the streets were clear, though wet in streaks and patches from melting snow. Karen had intended to take Andrew to work with her, but when they met Mr. Clausen on the front walk, the old man asked if Andrew would like to stay with him instead. Karen had reservations, but Andrew was so enthusi-astic about the idea that she gave in, with the stipula-tion that he was to call her immediately if he had any problems. They both promised readily and earnestly that they would, and went off together hand in hand, beaming at each other with the special glow of Christmas co-conspirators.

Relieved of the responsibility of entertaining An-drew, Karen used her lunch hour to shop for his Christmas presents. With the money she'd saved on car repairs she bought him a warm coat with a hood, rubber boots, and a ski cap and mittens. She also bought an inexpensive calculator, a book of magic tricks and another of silly riddles, a three-dimensional puzzle and some candy canes to put in his Christmas stocking. As for the other people on her list, she'd already brought a big plate of Christmas cookies for Louise and her family, and a smaller one for her boss, Mr. James. She meant to do the same for Mrs. Goldrich and Mr. Clausen. That left Tony.

There was nothing like trying to think of the right gift, she reflected, to make you realize how little you know about someone. She realized that she didn't even know Tony's size, or what he liked or what he needed. Everything she saw was either too expensive or just seemed wrong, somehow. She supposed she could always give him cookies, too, and she would. She knew he would love them. But she wanted to give him something else, something...more. Something that would tell him how she felt about him. Something that was special to her, as he was. Something that was a part of her. As he was, now.

When she got home, she barely had time to hide her purchases in her bedroom before Andrew came crashing through the front door, looking furtive with his glasses precariously balanced on the end of his nose and a big bulge under his coat. He scuttled sideways through the living room and slammed his bedroom door, emerging a short while later looking calmer, but with an air of suppressed excitement. He made Karen take a solemn oath not to go into his room until after Christmas. She made him do the same.

That night, Tony brought pizza again, and two wrapped presents to put under the tree. While they were eating, a cold wind sprang up, rattling the shutters and whistling under the eaves. Inside, the old house seemed to shiver with delicious Christmas secrets....

On the day before Christmas, the insurance office was due to close at noon, and since it was only for half a day, Karen took Andrew with her to work. On the way home, they stopped at the grocery store to pick up some wrapping paper and ribbon, and a few last-minute things for Christmas Eve dinner. Back at the apartment, Karen put Andrew to work in the kitchen arranging cookies on plates for Mrs. Goldrich and Mr. Clausen, as well as a nice big boxful to take to Tony's family on Christmas Day.

"Leave some for us to eat tonight," she reminded him.

Andrew looked at her over the top of his glasses. "And some for Tony."

Karen smiled a secret smile, thinking of the gift she'd found for Tony. The perfect gift, a part of herself. "It's all right, I've already got his put away."

"Oh," said Andrew casually. "That's all right, then."

"Andrew," Karen said, "I've been thinking. How would you like to invite Mr. Clausen to join us tonight?"

"You could," Andrew said, licking colored sugar off his fingers, "but I don't think he can come."

"Why not?"

He gave her a patient look, lifted one shoulder and said simply, "It's Christmas Eve."

"Oh, *Andrew*," Karen said, laughing and shaking her head. It was impossible to be exasperated with a child on Christmas Eve for believing in Santa Claus....

While Andrew was busy with the cookies, Karen wrapped all her presents, including Tony's, and put them under the tree. Then she and Andrew went to deliver the cookies to Mrs. Goldrich and Mr. Clausen.

A man answered Mrs. Goldrich's door and introduced himself as her son, Howard. Through the open door Karen could hear voices and laughter and Christmas music being played on the radio. It made her feel glad to know that Mrs. Goldrich would be happy on Christmas Eve, at least. And somewhat relieved. She'd been feeling guilty about not inviting her landlady to join them, since she was going to invite Mr. Clausen.

But no one was home at Mr. Clausen's. After the second knock, Andrew shrugged and said, "I told you."

"Well," Karen said, "we'll just leave them here, in case he comes back." She ran downstairs and wrote a little note, telling him that he was welcome to join them if he got home in time, then tucked it under the plastic wrapping on the plate of cookies and left everything on the floor in front of his door.

By six o'clock the apartment smelled wonderfully of evergreen and chowder and corn muffins and cranberry tarts, the tree looked festive, dressed in red and white painted sycamore balls and wrapping paper ribbons, the three strings of lights twinkling in the window for all the world to see. The presents were all wrapped and under the tree—except for Andrew's, which were still mysteriously locked away in his room.

Bright with multiple coats of fresh paint, the train waited patiently on its track for the power to send it chugging triumphantly 'round and 'round the Christmas tree....

"Well," Karen said, taking a deep breath and a last look around, "I think we're ready." Good heavens, were there butterflies in her stomach?

"'Twas the night before Christmas,'" Andrew quoted, grinning at her as she tried in vain to flatten his cowlick. "'And all through the house, not a creature was stirring, not even a mouse.'"

Not even a mouse! Karen's heart gave a guilty little bump. Then she laughed out loud and caught her son in a breathless hug. Of course, she thought, it's the night before Christmas! The whole world has butterflies tonight. Wasn't that the magic of Christmas Eve? The suspense, the anticipation, the waiting...the feeling that something wondrous was about to happen.

Tony had butterflies in his stomach when he knocked on Karen's door. The electric train's switchbox was under his arm. He felt like he was seventeen again, standing on Alison Delovitch's front porch with a florist's corsage box under his arm and cold sweat running down his armpits—his junior year, the prom, his first formal date. He'd thought he might die of nervousness that night, but it hadn't been anything compared to this.

He knew how much Karen was counting on his getting that train working in time for Christmas. He'd already taken the engine apart and cleaned and oiled everything, and straightened all the sections of track and checked all the connections. Yesterday he'd taken the box home to work on it where he could concentrate without the distraction of her presence, and he was pretty sure he'd done everything that could be done with it. But until he had a chance to hook it up, he wouldn't know how successful he'd been, and the suspense was just about killing him. He didn't want to disappoint her. He didn't think he could stand it if he let her down.

The door opened, and she was standing there, looking as pretty as he figured it was possible for a woman to look, and suddenly there didn't seem to be enough room inside him for air. So he let it out in a rush and said, "Hi. Merry Christmas."

She smiled and said, "Hi. Come in." She was wearing a long skirt with red in it, and a silky white blouse. There were soft lights shining in her eyes and in her hair. "Let me take your coat."

"Here you go, kid." He handed the switchbox to Andrew. Funny, he thought as he struggled awkwardly out of his coat, in the last week he'd probably spent more of his waking time in this house than he had in his own, and now he felt like a stranger. It was Christmas; that was it. There were too many expectations at Christmastime. Everything was supposed to work out right, nobody was supposed to be disappointed....

"Hey, cool," Andrew said. "Did you get it fixed? Can we hook it up and see if it runs?"

Karen threw him a beseeching look. Tony growled, "Nope, not yet. Not until Christmas Day."

Andrew looked a little let down, but he didn't argue. Karen clasped her hands in front of her like an old-fashioned school teacher and said, "Well, dinner's ready. Is anyone hungry?"

They ate in the kitchen, with the lights out and candles on the table, which was something Tony couldn't remember ever having done before. Everything tasted great, he supposed, although he probably wouldn't have noticed if it had been sawdust and wallpaper paste. Afterward, Karen made him a cup of instant coffee, and she and Andrew took their mugs of hot apple cider, and they all went back to the living room to open presents.

They didn't seem to know quite where to start, so Tony got the big box he'd brought for Karen from under the tree and gave it to her. He had another box for her, a much smaller one, in his pocket. He meant to give it to her later, in private, if things worked out the way he hoped they would. He would just have to wait and see....

"Oh," Karen said, "it's beautiful!" It was an angel, made of stiffened fabric and lace. She looked up and found Tony smiling at her.

"My sister made it," he said, clearing his throat with an endearingly awkward little cough. "It goes on top of the tree."

"Well," she said softly, "let's put it up right now."

Instead of going outside in the cold to get the ladder, Tony lifted Andrew onto his shoulders and held him steady while he took the crumpled star down and put the angel in its place. Then they all stood back to admire it. The angel seemed to smile down on them, her arms spread wide in blessing and protection. It seemed so symbolic, Karen thought as she laid the star in the nest of tissue in the angel's box, put the lid on it and set it aside. She wouldn't throw the star away any more than she would throw away her memories of Bob. She would pack it away along with the other precious things from her past—things like Andrew's baby clothes and her first prom dress. Things she'd outgrown and left behind her long ago....

Andrew was opening his presents with his usual precision and nail-biting suspense, professing delight with everything, especially the mittens. "Hey, cool—now I can make really good snowballs!"

"Uh-oh," Tony said, "I'm in trouble now."

Tony's gift to Andrew was a big, glossy book about trains. "Oh, *cool*!" Andrew said when he saw it and was instantly engrossed.

"Ours is in here," Tony said, reaching over his shoulder to turn pages. "Look—right there. Isn't that it?"

"Hey, yeah," Andrew said excitedly. "Look, Mom, we can copy this picture when we do the writing!"

Karen agreed, hiding a smile. *Our* train? She wondered if Tony knew how much he'd given away with that tiny little slip of the tongue. Tenderness swelled her chest and tightened her throat as she took his present from under the tree and placed it on his lap. She sat down beside him to watch him open it, holding her hands clasped tightly together, vibrating inside with tension.

"It's a humidor," she explained as he lifted the mahogany box out of the tissue paper wrappings. "It belonged to my grandfather. My grandmother gave it to me when I was a little girl, to keep my doll clothes in. I know you don't smoke cigars, but you can keep other things in it, like—"

"It's beautiful," Tony said in a muffled voice, stroking the glossy wood with his fingertips.

"Open it," Karen whispered.

He did, and there were the cookies, wrapped and padded with plastic—green sugar Christmas trees and holly wreaths, blue sugar stars and angels, chocolate-sprinkled bells and reindeer, cinnamon imperial candy canes and funny smiling Santas.

"I told you," she said, husky and breathless with tension. "The prettiest Christmas cookies in the world."

Tony just looked at her. She could see the soft Christmas lights reflected in his eyes, along with all the things that were in her own heart that she couldn't say. The warmth in his eyes drew her; their silence enfolded them both like a web....

"My turn!" Andrew said, and they jumped a little, guiltily, hearts bumping.

He went running off to his room and was back in a moment, hiding something behind his back and commanding, "Close your eyes...okay, now you can open them."

Karen did. A small, wondering "Oh..." escaped her as Andrew placed his gift in her hands.

"I made it," he said, self-conscious and proud. "Mr. Clausen showed me how. But I could only make one, so it's for both of you."

It was Santa's sleigh and nine reindeer, on a base of rough pine bark covered with cotton snow. The sleigh was made from a matchbox, with pipe-cleaner runners, and was filled to overflowing with old-fashioned hard Christmas candy. The reindeer were made of clothespins, with pipe-cleaner antlers. The lead reindeer had a tiny red nose.

"Oh, Andrew," Karen said tearfully, "it's the best present I ever got."

"Hey," Tony said, "where's Santa?"

Andrew laughed and rolled his eyes toward the ceiling, and he and Tony grinned at each other as if they shared a secret.

After that, there was the cleaning up to do, and then it was time for Andrew to go to bed. Once again he went without protest, but he came back in his pajamas to lay his Christmas stocking at the foot of the tree, right beside the train.

Tony wished him a gruff "Merry Christmas, kid." Karen went off to tuck him in and kiss him goodnight. When she came back, Tony was on his knees beside the train track, the electrical plug in one hand.

"Well," he said, looking up at her, "shall we see if it works?"

She knelt down beside him, trying to quell the nervousness inside her. "I guess we'd better...."

Tony put the plug in the socket and turned on the switch. The engine made a churring sound and lurched forward an inch or two. Karen's breath caught; she put her hand over her mouth to hold back a cry of joy.

And then the engine stopped.

Tony swore softly, tinkered with the connections, the track, the engine, and tried again. Again the engine churred, moved a little way along the track and then stopped. While Karen waited in agonized suspense, heart thumping, he tried it again and again. And finally sat back on his heels, shaking his head.

"I guess that's it," he said, his voice husky and muffled. "I've done everything I know how to do. It's just...not going to work." His head was bowed, his broad shoulders slumped with dejection and defeat.

Seeing him like that, her own disappointment, and Andrew's, seemed unimportant. Oh, but *his* pain...his pain was more than she could bear. It filled her up and overflowed. She touched his shoulder and said brokenly, "Oh, Tony."

He turned in a rush and caught her in his arms. They held on tightly to each other, both whispering, "I'm sorry, I'm sorry...."

"I'm sorry." Karen felt the tremors deep inside him as he spoke. "I know how much you wanted—"

"Shh," she said fiercely, "it's all right."

"I'll get it running, if it takes all night. I'll start from scratch. I must have missed a connection somewhere."

"Hush." She took his face between her hands and looked into his eyes. "It's all right. Andrew will understand. You didn't make any promises. He knows you tried." He gripped her wrists and looked away, but she pulled him back. "Oh, Tony," she whispered, while tears ran unchecked down her cheeks, "it doesn't matter. Don't you know that? It doesn't matter. I know it's happened quickly, but I don't care. I love you...."

For a long moment he looked at her, his eyes so dark and intent he seemed angry. Then he closed them and pulled her into his arms. "You love me?" he said wonderingly. She nodded. After a moment she felt him take a deep breath. "I have something for you. I was afraid to give it to you. I figured you weren't ready for it yet. I know it's too soon, but..." He let go of her and leaned back so he could reach into his pocket.

"What's this?" Karen said with a watery sniff as he placed the small velvet box into her hands and opened it for her.

"Just what it looks like." His voice was gruff, more so than she'd ever heard it.

"Oh, Tony..." She touched the shining stone with a wondering finger and began to cry again.

"If it's too soon, just say so. I'll wait until you're ready."

"It's not—oh, Tony, I know I love you, but... I'm scared. I'm afraid."

"What?" he said gently, brushing the tears from her cheek. "What are you afraid of?"

"I'm afraid—" she took a deep breath "—of losing you."

"Hey," he said with a shrug and a lopsided smile, "I'm not going anywhere."

"But you don't know that! You can't tell me nothing's ever going to happen to you! Don't make promises you can't keep!"

Now it was Tony who held her face in his hands, refusing to let her go. He felt the tension in her as she fought him, fought herself, her own fears and feelings. "I can't promise you I'm never going to die," he said slowly, roughly, the words hurting inside him. "But I *can* promise you that I'm going to love you, and Andy, too, until the day I die. That's all I can do. That's all any of us can do, isn't it? Love each other as much as we can, for as long as we have?"

For a long time she looked at him, her blue eyes shimmering with love and tears. "Yes," she whispered at last, "I guess it is."

This time, when he kissed her, she didn't fight it. He felt the leap of joy inside her, and then the melting surrender... and finally the growing and merging... the *oneness* that he knew would last a lifetime.

When he carried her to bed, neither of them thought of Andrew, or the train, or Christmas. But later, deep in the night, Karen stirred and whispered against his shoulder, "What was that?"

"Hmm," Tony murmured, "what was what?"

"Didn't you hear that? I heard . . . bells."

He chuckled. "Not me. I was too busy feeling the earth move."

Her arms tightened around him, and for a minute or two they didn't say anything more. But presently she murmured, "I'm sure I heard something. Don't laugh, but it sounded just like sleigh bells."

"Well," Tony said, laughing, "it is Christmas." And then, seriously, "Do you think it could be Andy? Maybe I'd better go."

"No!" Her arms tightened again. "Please, stay a little longer. Just a little longer . . ."

"As long as you want me to," he said, and kissed her again.

"What's that?"

"Oh no," Tony groaned, "not again."

"No—listen," Karen insisted. "There it goes again. It sounds like—but it can't be!"

"It is," Tony said, sitting up in Karen's bed and dragging a hand through his hair. They looked at each other and said it together, joyously, incredulously. "The train!"

"It can't be," Karen was muttering as she scrambled out of bed and began opening dresser drawers.

"It's morning, Christmas morning. I don't believe this." Tony was pulling on his clothes, looking for his shoes. "I didn't mean to stay. God, Karen, I'm sorry. What's he going to think? Is that really the *train*?"

It was. They stumbled out of the bedroom, tousled but fully dressed, to find Andrew kneeling in front of the Christmas tree with his stocking across his lap. The train was chugging merrily around the Christmas tree, around Andrew, its whistle shrill and joyful in the coolness of the morning.

"Look!" Andrew said when he saw them. "It works, just like you said it would. I knew you could do it, Tony— I *knew* it!" He looked about as happy as it was possible for a kid to look and still stay anchored to the ground. Reserved, Tony thought, his heart just about full to bursting with his own emotions. Just like his mother.

"Merry Christmas," Karen whispered, slipping her hand into Tony's. "I guess...miracles do happen sometimes, don't they?"

All Tony could do was shake his head.

Andrew glanced at them, at their clasped hands, and asked in his direct, matter-of-fact way, "Are you going to get married?"

Tony opened his mouth and closed it again. Karen burst out laughing. "Yeah," Tony said gruffly, "I guess we are. Is that okay with you?"

Andrew shrugged. "Sure." He was suddenly very busy with the train, so his voice was muffled when he asked, "So...are you going to be my dad?"

The little boy's head was bowed; his neck looked slender and vulnerable. Tony put his hand on it and gave it a gentle squeeze. "Yeah," he said, "I am."

"Cool," said Andrew. He suddenly gave the locomotive a push and turned in a rush. Tony caught him in a quick, hard hug. Over the boy's head he sought Karen's eyes and found them resting on him, shimmering with love, reflecting the soft Christmas lights.

Epilogue

"Guess what," Andrew said as he sat down to breakfast on the day after Christmas. "Mr. Clausen's gone."

"Gone?" Karen picked up the box of Crispy Oats, looked at the new mouse-nibble on the corner, sighed and set it down. "Has he gone somewhere for the holidays? Do you know when he's coming back?"

Andrew shook his head. "I think he's moved away."

"Strange," Karen murmured. "How do you know? Did Mrs. Goldrich tell you?"

Again Andrew shook his head; his mouth was full of cereal. "Nope. This morning I went to see him. I knocked, and the door opened. So I peeked in."

"Andrew!"

"Well, he was gone, anyway. All his stuff's gone, too." He shrugged. "I'm pretty sure he's moved away."

Karen gave him a long, searching look, thinking it odd that he didn't seem upset, or even very surprised. She was sure Andrew had been genuinely fond of the old man.

"Maybe I ought to go and see," she said, worried now. All sorts of possibilities presented themselves. Mr. Clausen was old—what if he'd had a heart attack, or a fall? What if he were lying helpless and ill—or worse? I'll go check," she said decisively. "Just to be sure. You stay here."

Andrew just looked at her over the tops of his glasses. "I told you—he's *gone*."

Andrew was right; the tiny garret apartment was cold and empty. From where Karen stood in the middle of it, she could look out the dormer window at the back-yard, where patches of snow still clung to the shady places under the sycamores and along the north sides of fences. No longer lovely, pristine white, it now seemed gray and lifeless—abandoned, like the apartment.

"I wonder why," she said aloud, rubbing at the goose bumps on her arms. "Why would he leave like that, without a word to anybody?"

"Maybe," Andrew said, coming quietly behind her, "he left because it was time."

"Andrew, I told you—" She stopped herself. "What do you mean, 'it was time'?"

"Christmas is over," he said with a shrug. "Maybe it was time to go home."

"Oh…Andrew." Karen sighed and put her hands on her son's small shoulders. "Darling, you don't really believe that Mr. Clausen is Santa Claus, do you?"

"Tony believes in Santa Claus." Andrew's chin was up; his face had that set, stubborn look Karen knew so well. "He told me."

"Honey, listen—"

"And anyway, if he's *not* Santa Claus, then how come he gave me exactly what I wanted? It *has* to be him, Mom, he's the only one I told. It *must* be him." He looked so earnest, so grave, so young….

"You mean you told Mr. Clausen what you wanted for Christmas?" Karen said carefully. Understanding was dawning, revelation coming like a sunrise.

Andrew nodded.

Karen took a deep breath; it seemed that the train mystery was solved at last. And she'd been wrong. "But, darling," she said gently, "why didn't you tell *me*?"

"Because," he said with heart-wrenching simplicity, "I knew you couldn't get it for me."

"But, sweetheart, if I'd had any idea how much you wanted a train, I would have found *some* way—"

"Train?" Andrew's voice was puzzled.

"Well...yes," Karen said, taken aback by the bewilderment in her son's face. "Isn't that what you asked Santa— I mean Mr. Clausen—for? The train?"

Andrew shrugged. There was an enigmatic smile—a secret smile—on his lips, and an unreadable look in his eyes. "Of course not," he said. "I asked him for a new dad."

* * * * *

Author's Note

The Christmases of my childhood and young adulthood were always spent at my grandparents' house. A few days before Christmas, we'd pile into my grandfather's old pickup—Mom and my Aunt Mary and Uncle Russell and any cousins and friends who wanted to come along—and drive up the canyon to cut a tree. We'd find a nice, hardy little piñon and Papa would chop it down, and we'd take turns dragging it back to the pickup. The tree would be installed in the living room on a base made from an old tire. It was Mary's job to decorate it, because she was the only one who could put the tinsel on right. In the later years, we had electric lights, but when I was very small, I remember, we still used candles. They were only lit once, on Christmas Night.

On Christmas Day, the family would gather for dinner. If the weather was nice—and it usually was at that time of the year in that lovely little valley tucked between the arid Tehachapi Mountains and the southernmost tip of the Sierra Nevada—the children would sit out on the porch. The grown-ups sat at the big dining room table, expanded for the occasion so that it stuck out into the living room, with Papa in his overalls presiding at the head and Grandmother flitting back and forth between the table and the kitchen, ignoring everyone's pleas to "Sit *down*, Mama, *please!*"

In the evening, after the livestock had been fed and the cows milked, everyone gathered again around the Christmas tree. The old farmhouse wasn't large, but somehow it always seemed to hold everyone, sons and daughters and in-laws, all the children and babies—especially the babies! There were always a few "extras," too, because anyone who didn't have a place to go on Christmas was welcome at my grandparents' house. And Grandmother saw to it that every person there had a package under the tree. We'd sing carols for a while, until the kids got restless. Then we'd light the candles on the tree and sit in their glow and sing "Silent Night."

Once the candles had been blown out, it was pandemonium, with kids yelling and paper and ribbons flying. Papa's special gift was always a five-pound box of See's candy, which, for the rest of the evening, he took great pleasure in passing around. Finally, stuffed with pumpkin pie and chocolate, loaded down with packages and sleepy children, everyone would drift away. But never very far away. Because to each and every one of us, that old farmhouse was home. And every day my grandparents lived in it was Christmas.

When I was *very* small, we lived for a time with my grandparents. On one of those long-ago Christmases, a box arrived from far away—no one seemed to know where. In the box was a beautiful, brand-new Lionel electric train.

Everyone thought Papa must have bought it, though he steadfastly denied it, and to be sure, it wasn't his way to be modest about his gifts. I think he would have been proud as punch to be the bestower of that wonderful train, as he was with his annual Christmas box of chocolates. So we never knew where it came from, and if Papa knew, he took the secret with him when he left us.

In any event, on this and every Christmas, I wish for you the gifts my grandparents gave to me and to everyone—kin or stranger—who came into their home. Simple gifts: warmth and welcome and unconditional love.

Kathleen Creighton

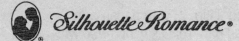

DIAMOND JUBILEE CELEBRATION!

It's the Silhouette Books tenth anniversary, and what better way to celebrate than to toast *you*, our readers, for making it all possible. Each month in 1990 we presented you with a DIAMOND JUBILEE Silhouette Romance written by an all-time favorite author! Saying thanks has never been so romantic....

You'll flip . . . your pages won't!
Read paperbacks *hands-free* with

Book Mate • I

The perfect "mate" for all your romance paperbacks
Traveling • Vacationing • At Work • In Bed • Studying
• Cooking • Eating

Perfect size for all standard paperbacks, this wonderful invention makes reading a pure pleasure! Ingenious design holds paperback books OPEN and FLAT so even wind can't ruffle pages – leaves your hands free to do other things. Reinforced, wipe-clean vinyl-covered holder flexes to let you turn pages without undoing the strap...supports paperbacks so well, they have the strength of hardcovers!

Pages turn WITHOUT opening the strap.

SEE-THROUGH STRAP

Reinforced back stays flat.

Built in bookmark

BOOK MARK

BACK COVER HOLDING STRIP

10˝ x 7¼˝, opened.
Snaps closed for easy carrying, too.

WRITTEN IN THE STARS

**Star-crossed lovers?
Or a match made in heaven?**

Why are some heroes strong and silent . . . and others charming and cheerful? The answer is WRITTEN IN THE STARS!

Coming each month in 1991, Silhouette Romance presents you with a special love story written by one of your favorite authors—highlighting the hero's astrological sign! From January's sensible Capricorn to December's disarming Sagittarius, you'll meet a dozen dazzling and distinct heroes.

Twelve heavenly heroes . . . twelve wonderful Silhouette Romances destined to delight you. Look for one WRITTEN IN THE STARS title every month throughout 1991—only from Silhouette Romance.

STAR

Silhouette Books®

From *New York Times* Bestselling author
Penny Jordan, a compelling novel of ruthless passion
that will mesmerize readers everywhere!

Penny Jordan

Silver

Real power, true power came from
Rothwell. And Charles vowed to have it,
the earldom and all that went with it.

Silver vowed to destroy Charles, just as surely and
uncaringly as he had destroyed her father; just as he had
intended to destroy her. She needed him to want her . . .
to desire her . . . until he'd do anything to have her.

But first she needed a tutor: a man who wanted no one.
He would help her bait the trap.

**Played out on a glittering international stage,
Silver's story leads her from the luxurious comfort of
British aristocracy into the depths of adventure,
passion and danger.**

AVAILABLE NOW!

 HARLEQUIN